PENGUIN BOOKS

THE SPY WHO JUMPED OFF THE SCREEN

Thomas Caplan, a founder of the PEN/Faulkner Award for Fiction, is the author of three previous novels, *Line of Chance*, *Parallelogram*, and *Grace and Favor*. He lives in Maryland.

Praise for *The Spy Who Jumped Off the Screen*

"There is wisdom as well as considerable pleasure to be extracted from the stylish, involving, utterly contemporary puzzle that is this novel. . . . *The Spy Who Jumped Off the Screen* will keep you under its spell and stiffen your resolve to make the world a safer place for our children."
—President Bill Clinton, from the Introduction

"Thomas Caplan has crafted an absorbing thriller of intrigue and menace that draws you into a vortex you can't escape until the end. *The Spy Who Jumped Off the Screen* is the most ingenious thriller I've ever read."
—Clive Cussler, #1 *New York Times* bestselling author of *The Kingdom*

"A kick-ass premise . . . The novel boasts great, James Bond–style supporting characters. . . . And it has a story that, with its action and intrigue, is guaranteed to keep readers glued to their seats. . . . An excellent, don't-dare-miss-it kind of thriller."
—*Booklist* (starred review)

"Thomas Caplan channels Ian Fleming in this gracefully written, fast moving, all too pertinent thriller." —Robert Stone, author of *Dog Soldiers*

"With a dashing hero, an attractive jewelry designer, and a megalomaniac billionaire villain worthy of James Bond, Caplan brings to you a thriller for the modern day. You'll sail on a luxury yacht and get lost in foreign locales. Filled with passion and betrayal, technology and money-hungry men, this book will bring you up to a new level of storytelling, and keep you there for the entire ride. . . . Caplan gets into the minds of the main characters, showing faults, quirks, loves, and regrets, and how history affects the present. . . . Be ready for an adventure worthy of another classic battle between good and evil."
—*Suspense Magazine*

"A highly sophisticated and entertaining thriller! With enviable finesse and accelerating tension, Caplan introduces us to a world of high and low life, West Wing officials and computer paladins, Hollywood stars and global financial wizards. Don't pick up this book if you have made plans for the evening."

—Philip Bobbitt, author of *The Shield of Achilles* and *Terror and Consent*

"Caplan's business and international background, reflected in three earlier novels (e.g., *Grace and Favor*), give authenticity to this fantastic tale of intrigue." —*Library Journal*

"*The Spy Who Jumped Off the Screen* is a thrilling novel of espionage and derring-do, high jinks and high stakes, that unfolds rapidly against a canvas of seductive international glamour. But its grace note is the siren song of Hollywood that, out of nowhere, attracted then transformed its astonishing hero."

—Kevin Starr, author of *Golden Dreams: California in an Age of Abundance*

"An elegant thriller by an author with keen insight into the world of international intrigue, with finely crafted characters who will stay with you long after you have closed the book."

—Ted Bell, *New York Times* bestselling author of *Warlord*

"What an exuberant cast of characters—arms dealers, spies, movie stars, beautiful maidens, stolen nuclear warheads—and in Thomas Caplan, a gifted and sophisticated writer to direct the ensemble. *The Spy Who Jumped Off the Screen* is an entertaining romp." —David Ignatius, author of *Bloodmoney*

THE SPY WHO JUMPED OFF THE SCREEN

Thomas Caplan

Introduction by President Bill Clinton

PENGUIN BOOKS

PENGUIN BOOKS
Published by the Penguin Group
Penguin Group (USA) Inc., 375 Hudson Street, New York, New York 10014, U.S.A.
Penguin Group (Canada), 90 Eglinton Avenue East, Suite 700, Toronto,
Ontario, Canada M4P 2Y3 (a division of Pearson Penguin Canada Inc.)
Penguin Books Ltd, 80 Strand, London WC2R 0RL, England
Penguin Ireland, 25 St. Stephen's Green, Dublin 2, Ireland (a division of Penguin Books Ltd)
Penguin Group (Australia), 707 Collins Street, Melbourne,
Victoria 3008, Australia (a division of Pearson Australia Group Pty Ltd)
Penguin Books India Pvt Ltd, 11 Community Centre, Panchsheel Park, New Delhi – 110 017, India
Penguin Group (NZ), 67 Apollo Drive, Rosedale, Auckland 0632,
New Zealand (a division of Pearson New Zealand Ltd)
Penguin Books, Rosebank Office Park, 181 Jan Smuts Avenue,
Parktown North 2193, South Africa
Penguin China, B7 Jaiming Center, 27 East Third Ring North,
Chaoyang District, Beijing 100020, China

Penguin Books Ltd, Registered Offices:
80 Strand, London WC2R 0RL, England

First published in the United States of America by Viking Penguin,
a member of Penguin Group (USA) Inc. 2012
Published in Penguin Books 2012

1   3   5   7   9   10   8   6   4   2

Publisher's Note
This is a work of fiction. Names, characters, places, and incidents either are the product
of the author's imagination or are used fictitiously, and any resemblance to actual persons,
living or dead, business establishments, events, or locales is entirely coincidental.

THE LIBRARY OF CONGRESS HAS CATALOGED THE HARDCOVER EDITION AS FOLLOWS:
Caplan, Thomas.
The spy who jumped off the screen : a novel / Thomas Caplan; introduction by President Bill Clinton.
p. cm.
ISBN 978-0-670-02321-9 (hc.)
ISBN 978-0-14-312287-6 (pbk.)
1. Motion picture actors and actresses—Fiction.   2. Intelligence officers—Fiction.
3. Nuclear terrorism—Fiction.   I. Title.
PS3553.A584S69 2012
813'.54—dc23   2011032992

Printed in the United States of America
Designed by Alissa Amell   Set in Spectrum Mt Std

For Diana, Hugo, Isabella, Alex, George and Octavia
in limine

All the world's a stage,
And all the men and women merely players:
They have their exits and their entrances;
And one man in his time plays many parts . . .

William Shakespeare
As You Like It
Act II, Scene 7

INTRODUCTION BY PRESIDENT BILL CLINTON

I have been an ardent fan of thrillers for about forty years now. Good thrillers are a remarkably diverse lot. They may be long or short, set in the present, the future, the near or distant past, gritty crime stories, high-tech spy adventures, explorations of the means and motives of terrorists, or old-fashioned political tales of the soul-eating conflicts between power and principle. For all their differences, thrillers succeed when the action is gripping, the characters are compelling and the plot moves rhythmically, all within a story that both informs and entertains.

When reading really good ones we can hear the spoken words, see the scenery, know the characters and feel the blows, bullets and bombs. I've always wanted to write one, but so far my life has permitted me only the pleasure of reading as many as I can and, in the process, of coming to know a good one when I see it.

I think Thomas Caplan's *The Spy Who Jumped Off the Screen* is a very good one. It confronts what is arguably the greatest threat currently facing mankind—the proliferation of nuclear weapons and the possibility that they could fall into the hands of terrorists prepared to use them—and does so not with clichés but originality. And it has an original, appealing hero in Ty Hunter, a movie star and ex-military expert in Special Operations. Hunter could have stepped out of Alfred Hitchcock's imagination. Drawn into a crisis almost by accident, then pressed by the President to resolve it, Ty performs with the élan of a celebrated Hollywood actor and the skill and courage of a veteran of covert ops. As one character puts it, "It's as though Matt Damon really were Jason Bourne." For me, an even more apt analogy would be if Sean Connery, Roger Moore, Pierce Brosnan and Daniel Craig all joined James Bond in Her Majesty's Secret Service.

Where did Tommy Caplan come up with this idea: an undercover operative whose cloak is his own celebrity? It is a particularly compelling conceit in an age so obsessed with and easily distracted by such celebrity. With so many people grasping for fame, whether from talent, political success, physical attributes or outrageous conduct; with armies of photographers, tabloid journalists and political Web sites determined to eradicate the last vestiges of privacy by forcing even more fame on celebrities; and with millions of the rest of us savoring the rise and fall of celebrities that permeates all our media, the idea of celebrity as a cover for what is really going on is a guaranteed winner.

Of course, Hunter's exploits bear some resemblance to the real-life experiences of famous actors, including Leslie Howard and Sterling Hayden, as well as gifted writers Roald Dahl and Ian Fleming, and other artists whose double lives remain unknown. Yet Hunter is different because he is neither a well-intentioned amateur nor a full-time professional. Instead, he is a genuine patriot with great ability in two very different crafts because his life has been defined by two sudden strokes of fortune: the almost fatal injuries that ended his military career and the miraculous recovery that launched his life as a movie star. Predictably, his suffering of and recuperation from deep wounds and disfigurement have made him stronger, more interesting and more connected to the action in his films than most stars could ever be.

As it so often does to the heroes of Hitchcock films, danger finds Ty Hunter rather than the other way around. As he stumbles into, then struggles to prevent a transfer of nuclear warheads, we are introduced to a fascinating set of characters in a variety of circumstances, all presented with Caplan's critical eye and voracious appetite for details that provide both color and insight. We learn about the street plans of great cities, the layout of a fortress on Gibraltar, the history of ancient European buildings, the engineering of modern mega-yachts, the furnishing of elegant hotel suites, the consumption and pleasure of lavish meals and the making and marketing of fine jewelry. We also learn about where fissile materials and bombs might be stored and how they might be smuggled. And in some of the book's best written and most exciting scenes we follow a group of adventurous young high-tech wizards who employ cutting-edge technology to help Ty Hunter track and thwart the transfer of weapons and money.

Caplan's characters include two compelling villains, Ian Santal and Philip Frost, with outsized egos, complicated motives, interesting life stories and clever self-justifications; the love interest, Isabella Cavill, closely tied to both Santal and Frost yet saved from supporting their designs by her savvy, rebellious, incorruptible character and, inevitably, her attraction to Hunter; and a host of memorable lesser figures whose words, actions and motives give the story dimension and authenticity.

As *The Spy Who Jumped Off the Screen* unfolds, the reader visits, with a knowledgeable guide, places most of us will never go or fully understand even if we do, as well as fantastically rich and powerful figures who are part of the twenty-first century's global plutocracy, their lives conducted far from the experiences, concerns, and values of the vast majority of us. These particular plutocrats shield themselves and their dealings behind high walls of secrecy with tightly locked gates. Caplan pries them open, revealing a combustible mix of idle indulgence and moral arrogance, a callous disregard for the lives of lesser mortals and an unlimited capacity to be self-serving while pretending to be high-minded.

What we discover is ironic: a culture of privilege in which the biggest beneficiaries provide both fodder for what's wrong with our world and foot soldiers determined to destroy much of it, the good with the bad. No one gets out of *The Spy Who Jumped Off the Screen* completely unsullied, not even Ty Hunter. But this novel will make you glad all over again that there are people like him and his compatriots who risk their lives to defeat history's latest fling with the perversely imagined virtues of mass killing.

I first met the author when we were both incoming freshmen at the Georgetown University School of Foreign Service and had been assigned rooms a few doors from each other on the second floor of Loyola Hall. In my memoir, *My Life*, I recalled that the first time I met him he had a large rocking chair in his room and that "he told me he wanted to be a writer." We had both been enthusiastic supporters of the Kennedy presidency and, almost a year later, remained distraught by its tragic end. While John Kennedy's example had inspired me to enter politics and government service, his eloquence had inspired Tommy to put pen to paper. Our friendship was a natural fit: a would-be writer with an interest in politics and a would-be politician with an appreciation of literature. In the more than forty-seven years since, we've learned a lot from each other and shared some great times.

Our first campaign together took place a month or so later, when I ran for freshman class president. I can still remember the candidates' debate in Gaston

Hall and the prep before it. Tommy was there, giving me good lines and clever retorts, something he has done ever since, including in the preparations for my presidential inaugural addresses. It was a gratifying role reversal when he asked me to read and comment on an early draft of this novel. He knew I tended to read one thriller after another and probably thought that, in the process, I had become a pretty good judge of what makes a great one.

Tommy's language has always been more formal, less colloquial than mine, reflecting, in part, the different regions and cultures in which we grew up. Still, I have always appreciated the telling details, pitch-perfect conversations and beguiling casts of characters that marked his three previous novels, *Line of Chance*, *Parallelogram* and *Grace and Favor*, and are abundant in this one as well. The only problem I found in that early draft had to do with its pacing and tempo. Appropriate to the earlier novels, I thought it too languid for a thriller. With his permission, I recommended cuts of a few thousand words of dialogue and description in order to maintain the momentum of a terrific story. Tommy was gracious enough to say that he found these helpful.

Edits aside, the moment I encountered Ty Hunter, I knew the author had found someone who captured the zeitgeist. As the President who recruits Ty back to action tells him: "You're not what we call an 'invisible' exactly. Rather, you're invisible precisely because you are so damned visible. You've a reason to be anywhere, everywhere." His fame as an actor and global heartthrob gives Hunter access to places and people other covert operatives might not be able to reach while diverting suspicion from him—at least for a while. What sets him apart from conventional heroes of the genre is that where they would stand out, he fits in. This affords the reader a bird's-eye view of what characters are up to before they understand Ty's motives. Eventually, of course, some find those out. Then it's a good thing that, like all the best thriller heroes, Ty can take care of himself.

The thought and effort its author has put into *The Spy Who Jumped Off the Screen* are commensurate to the stakes involved, which warrant a reader's time. As I said above, no more important problem confronts us than nuclear proliferation, given the shadowy groups that have the inclination and ability to use them. The leaders of such groups can be difficult to identify, capture or kill. And because they are not part of a nation-state and hide in remote places or among civilian populations, the traditional deterrent of retaliation is meaningless.

This is a tale of the daunting challenge of separating the guilty from the innocent in a world where the two intermingle, and of thwarting the former's plans. From the moment we come upon each of the varied and colorful characters who populate this story we ask ourselves the same questions. Who are the real villains? What are their motives? How do they rationalize their actions—to others and themselves? Few of us will guess correctly in every instance. That's the fun of fiction, but the story also reminds us that in real life such mistakes have consequences. We must keep nuclear weapons from getting into hands that are prepared to use them. If we fail, our world will not be the same thereafter.

There is wisdom as well as considerable pleasure to be extracted from the stylish, involving, utterly contemporary puzzle that is this novel. From the lush suburbs of Kansas City to long abandoned missile silos beside the Strait of Kerch, from Hollywood to Prague, London to Morocco, along Spain's Costa del Sol and at every stop on its rapid-fire itinerary, *The Spy Who Jumped Off the Screen* will keep you under its spell and stiffen your resolve to make the world a safer place for our children.

Chapter One

Wilhelm Claussen had taken possession of his Bentley Continental Flying Spur six days before, but this afternoon was the first time it had left Mission Hills. Until now, when it wasn't garaged, it had graced only the well-tended driveways of his neighbors and, of course, the Kansas City Country Club. There the car jockey routinely awarded it pride of place, the first car anyone saw from the portico. Billy, as he was known to everyone (and, as CEO of one of the world's most important contractors, he *was* known to everyone who mattered) had almost bought the Mulsanne instead. The Mulsanne was bigger and more expensive; it, too, could be tuned in the aftermarket by a German specialist firm. Yet the Continental Flying Spur had youth on its side. And the insouciance of youth, Billy had come to fear, was the very currency with which he had paid for his success. He needed, somehow, to get it back.

"Have you read the papers?" the salesman had asked.

"That's been my habit. What in the papers?" Billy had replied.

"Well, it seems it's finally been proved that certain mechanical devices *are* effective at sexually stimulating women," the salesman had assured him dryly, then paused. "Chief among these is the Continental Flying Spur."

Billy Claussen had laughed. Even though he'd heard the joke before, invoking a different marque and model, he had to admit it made its point and very likely clinched the deal. Without it the stuffed shirt in him might have decided for the stodgier car or put off the purchase entirely. Times were not as good as they had once been, and no matter how well one's luck had held up, at least in comparison to others', it no longer felt quite so seemly to display the fact.

Still, a man only lived once, besides which, Billy had liked the salesman, appreciated his moxie and just how important the sale was to him. As he thought back to that day in the showroom, he smiled to himself. Jokes, unlike numbers, he could no longer remember. Too often he found himself lost or stumbling halfway through one. There had been a time when he'd been ready with punch lines—he, too, had been a hell of a salesman, after all—but those vivid days when he had gathered in rather than begun to dissipate his fortune felt long ago and irretrievable.

It was four days before Christmas, a time, if ever there was one, to put the stresses of life on hold. Waiting by the curb for his car to arrive, he could still hear the tinned Christmas carols of the shopping center's sound system. Considering the abnormally balmy weather this year, they sounded out of season, but the great spruce and the store windows were decorated and the Salvation Army soldiers—one man, one woman—were watching over their kettle, taking turns ringing their handbell. After withdrawing a five-dollar bill to give to the attendant, Billy Claussen noted that there were only twenties left in his old crocodile wallet—not counting, of course, the crisp hundred he habitually secreted there. He had already closed the billfold and begun to slide it back into his left hip pocket when he thought better. The speakers were issuing a bland choral rendition of "O Little Town of Bethlehem," of which, having been a choirboy at his first school, he knew all the verses by heart.

Where charity stands watching
 And faith holds wide the door,
The dark night wakes, the glory breaks,
 And Christmas comes once more.

What the hell, he thought. Whoever had taken it with him? Even nearby there were people on hard times. He removed a crisp twenty, creased it smartly in the middle and, with a smile that begged no recognition, deposited it in the Salvation Army kettle. At precisely which moment his precious Bentley arrived.

As he pulled away from the Oak Room and onto Ward Parkway the afternoon was escaping. He and Wendy had had a good lunch, two margaritas each, blackened salmon for him, sesame-grilled chicken for her. It was part of their routine when she was in town from New York: dinner somewhere very quiet, a night of lovemaking (and ferreting out each other's motives) in her hotel near the Plaza, then lunch out in the open for the world to see. Why not? They had met through business after all. Wendy had been his occasional mistress for not quite two years, since his vice president for strategic planning had hired the consulting firm she worked for to do a comprehensive review of Claussen Construction's operations. That review was long over. The contract for it had expired a few weeks before she'd first propositioned him. Now when she came to Kansas City, it was, nominally, to serve other clients.

Wendy was his son's age, but if that didn't bother her, it didn't bother him. She wasn't a kid. She had an M.B.A. from Wharton. He had been married three times, had left his first wife and been left by the two who'd followed her. Emotions perplexed him. He had walked out on the only woman he'd ever felt he couldn't live without, not because she'd changed but because he had. They had married at twenty-one, when he was already in a hurry and she was beginning to be satisfied. Their sex had been inexperienced but joyful. She had not known, wouldn't have thought to acquire, Wendy's tricks, nor had he required them in those days.

He guided the car into the traffic and accelerated as he waved good-bye. He didn't know when he would next see Wendy. He had no plans to go to New York before spring, but things came up suddenly or, if the urge struck, could be manufactured. Never mind all that now! He wanted to play with his car. A firm called Mansory, somewhere near Bayreuth, had fitted it out with an aerodynamic package, including a Pur-R-Rim integrated spoiler system, Hella daytime running lights, stainless-steel side and rear skirts and flank. The V-12 engine had been modified to provide 630 horsepower. It would accelerate from zero to sixty in 4.7 seconds, evolving in a tremendous peak torque of five hundred pounds even from low speeds. All this to be controlled from the luxury of a perfectly stitched Nappa leather and Alcantara interior with the latest genuine carbon-fiber fittings.

In the rearview mirror, as he headed southwest, he watched the silhouette of Country Club Plaza disappear and thought again of what a pleasant, desirable place this part of this city was. People he encountered elsewhere seldom appreciated the unexpectedly cosmopolitan nature of Kansas City, much less for how long it had prevailed. Take the Plaza, for example, which old man J. C. Nichols had developed in 1922 as America's very first suburban shopping center. Its Spanish architecture—towers, fountains, and sculpture—still cast an enchanted spell over the Brush Creek Valley. And the stores it housed were the equal, often the sisters, of those on Madison Avenue and Rodeo Drive. This was a confident but curious town, to which some came and from which others, such as Billy himself, traveled forth. And it was as nice a place as any he'd seen to call home: the United States still as it had been at its zenith.

As aware of his own moods as he was of the temperature, Billy wondered what had made him so suddenly wistful. He supposed there were any number of possible causes but gradually came to focus on two. The first was that he really did not like being recognized by complete strangers. Restaurant and hotel staff were one thing, but the general public was quite another. Ever since he'd agreed to appear in an advertisement meant to instill confidence in a large, abruptly faltering bank of which he was a major shareholder, he'd had the sense that his familiar, comfortable cloak of anonymity had been at least partially shed. A billboard version of that ad had forced this reservation to the front of his mind, and as he sped past it, he looked away.

The second reason, which had continued to unsettle him long after it should have, was a deal from which he had recently and precipitously pulled out, on the basis not of careful analysis but of instinct. For a time it had seemed to offer the promise of huge and quick rewards as well as a hard-to-come-by opening to an all-but-limitless new market. The man with whom he had struck his bargain was a friend, or rather they had for years shared what passed for friendship among people at their level. It was the others, the ever-changing operational people, the Russians themselves, who had eventually given him pause. The more he'd seen of them, the more suspicious he had become that, for them, lucre trumped judgment. And this had cut against his grain. The last of the developers he'd met had particularly irritated him: a patronizing, odious Cossack, whose skin all but swallowed his sweat. "How can we be sure you will deliver what you say you will?" the man had asked. What a question! Claussen Construction spanned the globe. It was number one because it was never late, never over budget, never anything but straightforward and professional. Surely, no one could say the same of any of the other partners in the deal. Nor could Billy even be sure what those men's true motives were, except that very likely there were more of them than they were letting on.

It was surprising how many suspicions could be pricked by a single, stupid question. Claussen Construction had been brought in to repurpose an about-to-be-abandoned Cold War military installation, perched along some godforsaken Russian seaside, as a five-star resort. Could the Russian syndicate already be angling to renegotiate Claussen's fees, or was something even more sinister afoot? Was it mere happenstance that the property being let go belonged to the army, or were they and the security services with which they worked somehow to remain involved as silent partners? Anything was possible. Billy had called the man who'd brought him into the deal in the first place. "I can't get a straight answer from any of them," he'd protested. "The same goon is never in the same place two days running. Hell, I'm used to playing on foreign fields, but not with a tribe as foreign as this one. They go way beyond anything I've seen. How can we be ready to do what they want us to do in the spring, which will be here before you know it, if we don't make a definite plan now? We can't. There's no way. We're late as it is. I shouldn't have to step in. My job is to deal with principals, not line men. And I don't know a genuine oligarch from a fake, or their military from their mob. What I do know is that there is all the difference in the world between extensive resources, which, thankfully, we have, and infinite ones, which we most assuredly do not. So, as alluring as this project once seemed and the whole Russian market may be, I can't let us become subject to the kinds of delays we've been experiencing and that now look to be downright inevitable. I can't sacrifice cranes and ships and men that are committed elsewhere—China, for example—to it, not when the boys in charge are going about things in their half-assed way, everyone shifting responsibility onto the next son of a bitch, but with his hand out."

"Let me try to sort it out for you," his friend had suggested, calm certitude in his voice.

"Too late for that," Billy had replied.

"As I recall, your contract commits you—"

"Through the end of this year," Billy had interrupted. "The first day of January, we're done."

"Have it your way," his friend had told him, "but until then don't do anything rash."

"I never do anything rash," Billy had said, wondering if the advice he'd been given was a friendly admonition or a threat.

You're judged by the company you keep—how often had his father drummed that lesson into him? Often and forcefully enough that until he'd allowed himself to be seduced into the Russian deal, he had never made a serious mistake, at least in his business relationships.

Oh, well, let it go, he thought as he caressed the steering wheel. He had cut his company loose from the operation at the first instant he could, the end of Stage One as defined in their agreement. It would only be days now before he would see the backs of these characters, wish them luck to be on the safe side, and preserve his self-serving friendship with the ordinarily useful fellow who had brokered the arrangement. Then he would smile, but he wouldn't give a rat's ass what hand fate dealt the others or their improbable, grandiose project. By his age, Billy thought, life had left him with a pretty good danger detector. When it went off, it was only prudent to step back.

He had just turned off State Line Road and was nearly home when something ominous appeared in his mirror and altered his mood: the flashing blue lights of a Kansas Highway Patrol car.

"Shit!" He should have expected it. The state police liked to take up positions near the Missouri line. He slowed down and, as soon as he was able to, pulled onto the shoulder of the leafy suburban road. When by reflex he reached toward the glove compartment for his registration, he suddenly tasted a crystal of salt on his lips and recollected the margaritas he and Wendy had savored before lunch, less than two hours ago. Immediately he tried to do the calculus, but he could not recall the rate at which alcohol departed the bloodstream. Hadn't he known it by heart at Stanford? He was positive he had, but that was thirty-five years ago. Whatever, there was one thing he did know: He would be damned if he'd lose his license so soon after taking possession of this car.

In the old days, troopers had been figures to contend with. Tall, square-jawed enforcers, their faces disguised by helmets and dark aviator glasses, they'd held the saddles of their souped-up motorcycles around the steepest bends, coming at you like hornets and always by surprise. Now they were pussies, bureaucrats barricaded in their sedans. Sure, they kept their lights flashing as they called or typed in your tag number, checking to be sure you weren't certifiably dangerous before they dared to approach. It was all by the book. Like so many touches of the modern world, it was one Billy Claussen found pathetic, although fortunately in a way he could contrive to his own advantage.

He took a deep breath, snapped shut the glove compartment he had already opened, released his seat belt, slid his left hand to the recessed carbon-fiber door handle, and squeezed it gently. That almost inaudible click—how he relished it! Billy grinned to himself, then wiped any residue of a smirk from his face. He hadn't much time. There was still a folded copy of that morning's *Wall Street Journal* in the center of the passenger seat. He sent it flying into the rear, using a low toss that would not be apparent from outside. In a second's glance into his rearview mirror, he observed the cop still writing, perhaps even still on his radio. So Billy decided to take the chance. His cover story, if he needed one, would be that he'd been looking for his documents. He doubted it would be believed. As if a child again, in a near somersault, he bolted over and between the front seats into the rear.

That was fun, he thought as he regained his composure, smoothed his shirt and tie, and arranged the trousers and jacket of the smart suit he had bought from the hotel tailor in Hong Kong. Though his adrenaline was racing, he unfolded the newspaper and willed himself calm. He memorized the headlines above one or two columns. Then he opened to page three and settled on a story about oil ministers meeting in conclave at that seven-star hotel in Dubai. What was it called? He'd been there. He should know. The Burj Al Arab! Well, that hadn't taken him too long to summon up. Perhaps he was in better condition than he thought. The hotel flew over the Arabian Gulf like a huge sail of glass and steel, and he remembered with pleasure the underwater seafood restaurant that could be accessed only by a simulated submarine.

To his left a shadow was approaching. The windows were tinted—not quite Mafia black from the outside, but darkened to a shade that made it difficult for passersby to peer through. Finally the trooper appeared at the driver's window. He waited for a second, then rapped the glass with his knuckles.

"Yes," Billy said.

When the driver's window failed to retract, the officer eased open the door, stepping back behind it as it swung out. This must have been standard operating procedure, Billy decided; nevertheless, it looked pretty silly. Hadn't the cop noticed that the door was already unlatched?

"Where's the driver of this car?" the trooper demanded, firmly but without belligerence. As Billy expected, he was a young man. It was probably the first Bentley he'd ever seen, much less pulled over. So he had to be credited with a certain degree of nerve. Still, in his soft features Billy saw not just the short horizons of the trooper's life but their consequences.

He put down the paper, looked up, and smiled. "How the hell should I know? You pulled us over. He panicked and ran off. This was only his second day on the job."

The cop looked at him sharply but without the incredulity Billy had feared. Billy returned his gaze—old man to young, rich man to wage earner. One of the factors that had decided him upon the Continental Flying Spur was that both driving and being driven in it felt appropriate. He hadn't expected to test that proposition so soon. "Sir," the cop said, "in that case you are going to have to drive this car home."

"I'm sorry, Officer, but that's just not possible," Billy explained, seeming to take the patrolman into his confidence. It wasn't a fact that Billy had ever spoken out loud, but he prided himself on his disingenuousness, his talent for disguising his true feelings. He could put an arm around another's shoulder, draw him—or her—into his most intimate confidence, establish the deepest bond on the spur of a moment, while behind this endearing mask he himself felt only contempt. It was part of who he was; he understood that, just as he understood how to tune it out when necessary. "You see," he added with a wink, "I've just come from lunch, where I had one or two adult beverages, shall we say, with a friend of the opposite gender. I don't know what the limit is, only that it's lower than it was when I was your age, a hundred years ago, and that I'm probably over it. It's one reason I employ a driver."

The cop hesitated. "What's your name?" he asked at last.

"Claussen. Wilhelm Claussen."

"Say that again."

Billy did.

"You're *the* Wilhelm Claussen, as in Claussen Field House?" So the boy had been at State.

"Don't look so surprised. What was your sport?"

"Football, sir."

"My favorite. Always wished I'd been better at it."

"I don't know," the cop said, as much to himself as to Billy. "Just a minute—please." He did a hesitant pivot, returned to his car. Billy sat still, making his patience obvious. He suspected it wouldn't be too long before a second patrol car dropped off another trooper and the two of them together would be back alongside the Bentley. That's what he would have done in the rookie's position.

Soon enough they were there. "This is Trooper Larrabee," the first cop explained, introducing a tall recruit close to his own age. "With your permission he will take the wheel and drive you home. How far would that be?"

"Not far at all."

"I didn't think it would be—very far, that is. This is certainly the neighbor-hood."

"Are you sure?" Billy asked. "It's most kind of you, but I don't want to get you into any trouble."

"Your driver, though. How long has he been with you?"

Billy smiled. "Two days, as I said. Johnny was brand new on the job."

"Johnny?"

"My chauffeur—that's 'chauffeur' with a very small *c*, I'm afraid. Anyway, I doubt he'll show his face around here for some time, if ever."

"And yet you trusted him to drive a car like this?"

"He had good reflexes."

"He must have," the trooper said. "But, if he should turn up—"

"I'll call you, of course. Right after I fire him."

"You beat me to it."

"I can't tell you how much I appreciate your help, Officer—"

"Darnall." the trooper replied. He pointed to the neat metal nameplate pinned above his shirt pocket.

It was too far away for Billy to read. "Officer Darnall," he repeated slowly, in order to give the impression that he was storing the name in his memory. "I'm most grateful to you."

Even through the blur of alcohol, Billy could see that the policeman's eyes were wide. The driveway that sloped and curved upward toward his house was paved with brick squares, each bordered by Bermuda grass. After spring, roses grew along the outside wall. At one point, just before the Tudor mansion came into view, a canopy awaiting them arched over the road on a high trellis. Billy's father had bought the house for him when Billy had just turned twenty-one and become engaged—to Maggie, the first of his three expensive, now-withering wives. That had been a clever piece of generosity: the old man's means of keeping the young buck close to home. If Billy had been smarter about things, he might have done something of the sort for his own son, Luke. But Luke showed no sign of settling down or assuming responsibility. How had he put it the last time they'd spoken by phone? He'd "always *love* but didn't really *like*" Kansas City. Something like that!

Reputation had two sides. The advantageous one had just been demon-strated by the ease with which Wilhelm Claussen had had his story accepted and so wiggled out of a charge of driving while intoxicated. The disadvantageous side was that it made you an easy mark. Luke, who had good looks and a mind that was far better than average, if undisciplined and frequently too curious, had not seen through most of the friends, especially the girlfriends, he'd attracted. Their alloyed motives would have been plain as day to Billy, and cer-tainly to his own father, but they remained invisible to the innocent Luke. There was no use denying it. Luke was not going to cut it in this world—not in any way that Billy understood or valued. Luke was a wanderer. He would become a hundred different people in his life, but none fully. Right now he was probably still in Palm Beach, playing with other trust-fund boys from the Mid-west, striving without any prayer of success to emulate the easy, guiltlessly dis-solute style of Eurotrash. There was nothing Billy could do. Luke was his mother's son. She had always forgiven his bad habits and, by forgiving, encour-aged them. She was not much better herself. She would have taken Billy's house, the house his father gave him, but for slipping up with his friend Jack Andrews and getting caught in the act. What the hell, she'd been a prize in the sack in her day. Billy never looked back for very long, always forward. And she had bequeathed Luke those high cheekbones of hers. They might help him in some unpredictable way one of these days.

Billy looked at the two young police officers one last time, even considered asking them inside before quickly deciding against doing so. He had made his sale. It was time to walk away. *Officers Darnall and Larrabee,* he thought, *if only you knew how fervently I wish my son had something of you in him.* Then he waved them good-bye, found his key, and turned it in the front door's lock.

Chapter Two

"Riley," he called, then quickly remembered that he had given his houseman the day off.

He hurried toward the staircase, whose banisters, like the lintels above every door, had been festooned with swags of fragrant pine and holly, then through the shadowy reception hall, in which could be heard only the measured swing of his grandfather clock's pendulum, and finally down the corridor to his library. There was mail on his desk, but he ignored it on his way to the bathroom tucked beyond the final of three alcoves of yew bookcases. As he relieved himself, his eye examined the photographs that lined the walls. It was a tiny cube of a room, but there must have been two dozen: Uncle Jimmy with Jubelea in the winner's circle at Churchill Downs; the house he'd grown up in, not half a mile from here, dripping with afternoon sunlight in the spring before it burned down—his mother's azaleas were in bloom; his frat brothers posed impishly on the eve of graduation—and Vietnam; most amusing of all, a black-and-white glossy of his father and several of his father's friends at a finca in Cuba taken sometime in the fifties. Twelve gentlemen, members of an exclusive fishing club on their annual expedition to tropical seas, stood in white dinner jackets and black tie on an esplanade. These men, who had once looked old to his eyes, now looked half a generation younger than him. The finca's "staff," all of them stunning girls in their early twenties, stood behind and to each side of the fishermen. Their smiles were open to interpretation.

One thing was for sure, he thought: It had been a better world, easier, more fun. Maybe Luke was right after all, to go where impulse and testosterone led him.

Billy looked in the mirror as he washed his hands. By God, he was showing his age! His hair, which had begun to gray at thirty-nine, he and his barber had at once done something about. His skin was another matter. There were crow's-feet at the corners of his eyes. His brow had creased and the folds above his lip sunk, extending toward his chin. The skin itself appeared older, thinner, here and there traced with blue, almost translucent. The sharpness of his features, which had made him such a confident young man, had been all but erased beneath the deposit of years. So what? He detested complainers and had no intention of turning into one.

Drying his hands, he glanced again at the finca—in particular into his father's eyes. Billy missed his father. Even as he prized the freedom he had inherited along with his father's shares and other worldly goods, he wished the old man had stayed around longer. The company he'd founded had grown thirty-fold over his son's tenure as chief executive. The perks of such a position had also become more polished. If not the Continental Flying Spur, which Adolph Claussen would have found too flashy, Billy would like to have shown his father the fleet of company jets in their own hangar at KCI. The hangar was meticulously kept, and the planes saved thousands of hours of employee time traveling to and from Claussen sites across the world.

Before sitting down to his desk, he looked out from the window behind it at the long, formal garden Maggie had planted. Terraced into the hillside, it was fallow now, but he had no difficulty imagining it in bloom. It was from just above the far tree line—although, seen from the other direction, the house he'd been born in—that a tornado had swept in when he was nine years old. He had never been more frightened; his heart had never beaten more rapidly. But even as he'd sprinted all those yards for shelter, a part of him had savored the idea of havoc, as if whatever was destroyed might be put back together again, improved.

On shelves on the opposite wall, his parents' collection of Hehe Boys, Chinese figurines, were arranged exactly as they had been in the gallery of the old house. He was not fond of them as works of art, never had been. Yet as evocations of another time—an era with its comfortable certitudes in place—they possessed for Billy a value beyond price. For a delicious moment, he looked around his library, a room none of his wives, no one but he, had ever touched. It was perfect, a chrysalis of his past.

There was not much in the day's mail to warrant his attention: a monthly newsletter from his New York club, a statement from one of the three personal checking accounts with which he paid for periodic indiscretions and which for that reason he always balanced himself. In the last month, sadly, there had been no such indiscretions, so he placed the red-and-white envelope in a drawer.

As he closed the drawer, the carillon of the hall clock chimed the quarter hour, eight smoothly ascending and then descending notes to which he'd been so accustomed since childhood that they now hardly registered. But it was the sound that came next and was at once followed by an absence of sound that alarmed him: a sharp creaking of the floor above, then quick skidding that ceased as abruptly as it had begun. Billy drew his breath and stood, attuned to the silence of his house. Moving toward the library door, he kept his steps light until he had positioned his right hand over the alarm button disguised in the intricate Greek-key molding.

"Hello," he called out, then waited in vain for an answer. "Hello," he called again. "Who's there?"

No answer came back.

"Riley!" he shouted again, wondering if he might have mistaken his employee's day off. He let go of the library-door alarm, fixing his sights on the wainscoting just inside the front door. On the left, beneath its uppermost molding, there was another button, and Billy moved toward it rapidly, as though it were the next base in a dangerous game of tag. At the foot of the staircase, he managed to flick both light switches with a single stroke, at once illuminating not only the clear-and-russet crystal chandelier that hung suspended on a velvet-wrapped chain in the oval stairwell but the second-floor gallery. Yet the light revealed nothing out of the ordinary, no clue as to what he'd heard, and so, as it continued, the stillness grew ever more unsettling. Again he drew a long breath but this time held it, counting as he struggled to hear inside the silence. *Eight, nine, ten,* he told himself. *Eleven*—oh, what the hell, it was no use. As he exhaled, a high-pitched wail issued from over his shoulder. He spun immediately and saw his five-year-old grandson, Stuart, mounting the mahogany banister at its summit, laughing, ready to slide.

"Don't do that," Billy told him. "You'll wreck the garland."

"I'll put it back," Stuart pleaded.

"No you won't. It's not that easy. It took them hours to install, to get it just right."

Stuart hesitated.

"Come down here," Billy said. "Let me have a look at you, young man. You've grown again, haven't you?"

"Yes," Stuart said as he jumped from the railing, then raced noisily down the uncarpeted stairs.

Billy hugged him, kept his hands on the boy's shoulders as they separated as if to study him anew. It had never occurred to him that he would have a black grandchild—but then why shouldn't it have? he mused. In her choice of a husband, as in just about every aspect of her life, his daughter, Cynthia, had broken with convention. "Where are your mother and sister?" Billy inquired. "I didn't know you were here."

"We came early," Stuart said.

"And you didn't hear me come in?"

"No way! We were watching a video."

"What were you watching?"

"I don't know. One Emily wanted."

"I see," Billy said.

"She has a crush on the guy who's in it."

"How do you know?"

"She told her friends. I heard her. Do you know Ty Hunter?"

"Not personally. I know who you mean, though."

"He's the one."

"He's a bit old for her, don't you think?"

"He's very old," Stuart agreed.

"I mean, he must be thirty, or even in his early thirties by now," Billy said, intending his sarcasm for his own ears only.

"Yeah, probably," Stuart said. "Anyway, Emily used to have his picture on her wall."

"Did she? When he was just starting out?"

"I guess."

"Now that you mention it, I think I do remember that." Actors as a rule were a group of which he took little notice. But only a few years earlier, the bank on whose board he sat and for which he'd reluctantly agreed to do that ad had considered using Ty Hunter in a campaign for its Captiva credit card. While the board had dithered, Hunter's career had taken off, and the new movie star's agent and manager had nixed any projects other than feature films. Which was a shame, Billy had always felt, because no matter how much they reminded him of carnival people, matinee idols were one step ahead of card issuers, having captured the hearts and loyalties of their customers well before they were of age to spend money or borrow with discretion. Since he'd been on the bank's board, Captiva had sent out millions of "preapproved" letters to college freshmen and the first-time employed. If such communications had come from a familiar performer rather than an impersonal financial institution, he suspected they might have yielded dramatically higher success rates.

Still, now that he recalled it, he remembered that something about that poster had stopped him in his tracks, as if the young movie star, with his fetching smile, his hair the color of butter and eyes the blue of Windex, might be more than an innocent object of affection—indeed, might be likely to infect his granddaughter with unrealistic dreams.

"Look, Stuart, do me a favor, will you?" Billy asked. "Tell Cynthia and Emily I'm home."

"Sure," Stuart said, and scrambled enthusiastically for the stairs.

"Where are we going?" Emily inquired a few minutes later, examining her fingernails as she hugged her grandfather. She had painted them chartreuse two days before, and the enamel was beginning to crack.

"The club," Billy said.

"Can't we go to Paolo's instead?"

"I thought you liked the club."

"I do, but Paolo's has the best music—and the cutest waiters."

"Only in the summer," Billy said. "Their patio's closed this time of year. You know that. And right now the guys who work out there are either in school or in Florida perfecting their tans." *And getting laid,* he thought, although he did not say so.

"Never mind," Cynthia said. "I've had a wicked week. For that matter, I'm sure your grandfather has as well. We'd like to have a drink and some decent food and conversation, in peace and quiet."

"I'll take your word for it," Emily said.

"Enough," Billy said, but quickly thought better of it and decided to relax. He did not want their holiday to dissolve into argument or sullenness. "Let me ask you a question, Emily," he continued. "Suppose we go to Paolo's another night."

"*Not* on Christmas."

"Of course not on Christmas. On Christmas we'll be here. When does your father get in, by the way?"

"Christmas Eve, I think," Emily replied, searching her mother's face for affirmation.

Cynthia nodded.

"How about the day after Christmas?" Billy suggested, smiling reluctantly. Only yesterday she had been a little girl, uncritical, adoring. How could he help resenting the displacement of her affection to someone else, someone younger, an object of fantasies that were not platonic? Time was passing more quickly than he'd expected, that was all. And Emily, as had her mother so many years before, was simply going through another stage. There was nothing anyone could do but grin and see her through it, as they'd seen her through her recent difficulties at school, in French and science classes. A girl's sexual awakening was no easier to manage than a boy's, he supposed, especially one as pretty as Emily promised to become.

"Yes, yes, yes," she said.

"Then that's settled," Billy proclaimed, wondering, as he invariably did—as he couldn't help but do—how genes could contrive to make siblings so different: one male, a future fullback and black, the other female, with a dancer's delicate bones and the pinkest cheeks he'd ever seen.

At seven o'clock, after baths, they gathered in the living room before a fire.

"Would you like a drink?" Billy asked.

"In fact, I think I would," Cynthia said. "The usual."

He went to the bar built into a nook opposite the large bay windows, and made two Rob Roys, mixing the Johnnie Walker Black, red Lillet, and Angostura bitters with an apothecary's precision. When he had finished and poured the liquor and crushed ice into sterling-silver Jefferson cups, he felt Cynthia beside him, her cheek fleetingly against his shoulder. Was this an apology for her mood or an expression of her exhaustion? As usual, Billy could not be sure.

"Have you done much hunting this year, darling?" he asked finally.

"I always do, don't I?" Cynthia replied, taking the cocktail from him. A taste for Rob Roys was something she had inherited from him. "Tuesdays and Thursdays, all season, whenever I can. What's the point of living where I do and not?"

Billy nodded. Horses—the entire equestrian life—bored him, but fox-hunting filled him with fear. He knew better than to say it out loud in his daughter's presence, but he was pleased that Stuart showed signs of sharing his disinterest and hoped that Emily, suddenly faced with the distractions of adolescence, might herself be growing less keen. There was a reason they called it "breakneck" speed, and he could think of no other sport in which experience so increased the risk of injury, even paralysis. Years in the hunting field seemed to embolden people, causing them to forget that it was not only their skill at play but also the simpleton brain of a fast and heavy animal in whose custody they had placed their lives. "None, I expect," he told her, not quite mastering a laugh and raising his glass slightly before sipping from it.

"Always have and always will." She took his hand, squeezed it, then let it go. Billy was still imagining his daughter on horseback. He couldn't help it. Fear had seized him, as occasionally it was apt to. What would he do if she fell? How would her high-powered lawyer husband manage the children without her? If she were to die, would his next wife, who would no doubt be younger, like them or even want them around? Why, for heaven's sake, didn't Cynthia sense the risk as acutely as he did? Why didn't she concentrate her energy on one of her other loves, such as gardening or yoga or paddle tennis?

"Well, knock on wood," he said, striking the chair arm three times.

"It's just my nature, Daddy," Cynthia said "that's all." Then, as she turned her face to the children, she gently patted the back of his hand.

Studying the fiery, opinionated creature to whom he'd given life without planning to, he could still not specify with which of her qualities her husband—any man, for that matter—might have fallen in love. Youth, he supposed, but that had vanished long ago, and anyway, youth was a mask. While it survived, a man could cling to the illusion that his lover's temperament might change, but once it fled, he was left with what had been there all along. Perhaps what Michael had responded to was the challenge of taming her, or—despite the electric tension that ran through her—he had blithely calculated that she seemed the right sort of woman to be his wife and the mother of his children. She was who she was, after all. She liked sex and would be unlikely to stray. It was too much to figure out at the moment.

Just then the doorbell rang.

"Who on earth could that be?" Billy asked.

"Your guess is as good as mine," Cynthia said.

"Could be carolers," Emily ventured.

"Could be," Billy agreed, yet at the door he found not a party of holiday singers but a lone, gaunt figure in a clerical collar. "Good evening," he said. "May I help you, Father?"

"Would Mr. Claussen be at home?" inquired the priest, without giving his name.

"You'll forgive my surprise. I wasn't actually expecting—"

"No, of course you weren't. I am sorry. Is this your wife?" the stranger asked, glancing at Cynthia, who had come up behind her father.

"My daughter, Cynthia," Billy said by reflex. It was more, he immediately thought, than he had intended to say.

"How do you do?" the priest responded. "I'd be most grateful if I might have a word with you, sir." The man appeared to be in his late thirties, Cynthia's age, and Billy wondered what he'd seen in his vocation that had brought such desperation to his eyes. A second later he gestured for the priest to follow him.

When they reached his study, Billy stopped abruptly. Behind him was the six-by-twelve-foot oil painting *The Cavalry Campfire* by Frederic Remington, which his father had given him after his mother's death and the older man's move to an apartment that was too small to accommodate it. "Are you from the local parish?"

"Not really."

"We're not Catholics. We're Episcopalians, which may not have anything to do with why you're here. What can I do for you, Father?"

The priest hesitated. Then, after gesturing for permission, he closed the single door to the front hall. "Oh, I'm afraid it's too late for anything of that sort."

"Sorry?"

"You've done just about everything you could do."

"Forgive me, but I really must ask . . . What I'm trying to say, as courteously as possible, is that we have dinner reservations—a family evening, you understand—and I really must watch the clock."

"Yes, of course, the clock," the priest replied, then sat down.

"Why are you here, Father?"

"Not for the reason you think."

"Are you sure? I may be a bit ahead of you on this one. What sort of donation did you have in mind?"

"One that's bound to surprise you," the priest answered, removing, from a side holster, the brand-new Walther P99 Compact he'd been given for this job.

"To which cause, may I ask?" Billy inquired, without at first noticing the priest reach inside his suit jacket. "You say you're not local and we're not among your flock—" His first sight of the pistol stopped him short. In the pit of his groin, he felt an immediate convulsion. Its supplier had fitted the weapon with a modified laser sight, whose orange-red pinpoint bounced along the surface of Billy's blue blazer, tracing his left rib cage and lung.

"The cause of justice?" the priest whispered. Billy thought he heard a question mark in this reply and wondered what, if anything, it might mean.

His visitor, moving behind him, motioned for Billy to step forward. Once Billy had complied, the priest slithered alongside him, carefully remaining just beyond reach.

"Justice?"

"Usury is still a crime, Mr. Claussen. You may have made it lawful; you and your like may have managed to pull that one off. I'll be the first to grant you that. But it's still a crime—in the eyes of God! Let me assure you of that."

"I don't know what you're talking about."

"*Thirty* percent interest? Then you change the terms of your own free will: double the minimum payment just like that when a man falls sick or his kid does and he's an hour late—or a minute, mind you, on the due date. That's all it takes."

"I see what you're driving at, but, really, Father—hear me out—you've got it wrong."

"No, no, no, no, no. You're the one's got it wrong. 'And Jesus went into the temple of God . . . and overthrew the tables of the moneychangers.' Matthew 21:12. It's the only time in the whole Bible when our Lord used force, which never crossed your mind, did it? It crossed Ezekiel's mind—he prophesied it. Listen to me. I had a job in an assembly plant coming to me. But then the job goes overseas. Better for everyone, the big boys say. Only that's in the long run, and we're a long ways from there right now. Our lives will be done before we get there, before we ever see any benefit, which I doubt there'll be. Anyway, the plant shuts down, and where do I end up? In a scrap-metal shop, working like a beast, and for what? I'll tell you what: no future, nothing, and no place nice, a certain number of calories each week, most of them from canned goods, and no health insurance. Where are you without health insurance? You're nowhere. But it goes up each year, cuts into what little else you have. And one day it's so expensive the man that owns the company tells you he can't afford to give it to you anymore. Who knows? Maybe he's telling the truth. Maybe he can't. So all of a sudden you're living at your own risk, and so are the people you love and can't do a damned thing for. Then your wife gets sick, and she's out of work for a while. And your boy gets sick, too. The big C, and he doesn't do so well. You apply where you can for help. You take him where they'll see him. You're the last people they call from the waiting room, where you can't even afford to buy him a drink from the vending machines now that the big corporations have taken them over. So while he's dying, you write yourself one of those checks the credit-card people used to send you with your bill. One hundred, then five hundred, it adds up. But you don't let it bother you in the beginning, because your luck is bound to turn. You hear stories about better jobs someplace else, or someone strikes it rich, wins a few grand in the scratch-off lottery."

Billy recognized the temper that so often lurked beneath the surface composure of losers, who lacked confidence, lived on a diet of Chinese whispers, traded in the inflated, counterfeit currency of half-truth and exaggeration. He studied the man in the clerical collar, looking for the right way to block or tackle, to disarm him without having the gun go off in the process. But the man was too far away. Billy said, "How did you find this house?"

"You made it so easy. *Architectural Digest,* simple as that," the priest announced, removing a few quarter-folded tear sheets from his jacket pocket. "'W. V. Claussen, Bragged Himself to Death.' How's that for an obituary?"

"You think I'm another one of those country-club guys, don't you?" Billy asked.

"Whatever, I couldn't say. I think you're lucky and careless with the people who aren't. That's all that matters."

"Lucky, sure, I don't deny that. But is that my fault? I'm not careless, Father. We've done a lot of good. We've brought liquidity to—I mean, we've put funds in the hands of—millions of people who would not have had them otherwise. And most of them have been responsible with their privileges, and their lives have been better, less rocky, and more comfortable because we've been there."

"And the rest you addict? We're the same people we always were, sir, but so are you. Don't you think we know that? You're the company store. Only now you've got the whole country, practically, under your thumb."

"That's unfair."

"We're not irresponsible, Mr. Claussen. Mark my words, you son of a bitch, we're nothing like irresponsible. Whatever we are, it's only what you've made us by insisting on your pound of flesh."

Billy looked through the windows at the dark sky of the solstice. "What do you want? Please understand. I am very sorry your son has died."

"I didn't say he was dead—not yet."

"Again, I'm sorry," Billy said. "If you need help—"

"I can assure you I don't. I've already found that."

"Good, I'm glad."

"From someone who understands the situation—what 'being fair' means— much better than you ever could."

"We're not as different as you think," Billy told him. "You don't know me well enough—"

"I know what I've been shown in *Forbes* magazine and the *Wall Street Journal* and *Architectural Digest*." The priest fisted the tear sheets.

Billy examined him, searching for any insight he might be able to put to use.

"Grandpa," Emily called. "Come on, or we'll be late."

Billy hesitated. He regarded the priest, especially the Walther upon which he kept an unshakable grip. It would not, he realized, be visible from Emily's vantage point even were she to open the door. That was helpful, for she was still too young to conceal her panic. "I'll just be a minute," he called back.

"Or else I'm coming in to get you."

"No," Billy admonished her.

"I am. You can't stop me."

"Emily," he said sternly. "Don't!" To the priest, he added, "Never mind my granddaughter. We can work this out. Whoever's helping you, I'm pretty sure I can better their offer."

The priest hesitated, then gave a thin, dismissive smile and shook his head. As Billy appraised him, he was clearly a man willing to chance his soul: a desperate, ineffectual, but dangerous man who would have to be outmaneuvered physically rather than with words. Even flattery was bound to fail at this point, Billy decided, which was unfortunate, because he was an expert at flanneling those from whom he wanted something. Here, however, his instincts told him that the wrong words might as easily provoke as placate his assailant. He would have to do that, of course, but at an instant of his choosing.

Something else bothered him. The disconnect between the man's weapon and clothing, between his diction and disguise, between the misery he had described and the vocation to which, if only in dress, he pretended, suggested that there must be more to the story. Could the man with the gun be aiming it on behalf of someone else? And if so, who was it who might want Billy dead, and why? He supposed, like most successful men, he had accumulated detractors. Yet from childhood he'd been among the anointed ones, a hail-fellow-well-met, courteous, if sometimes insincerely, to just about everyone. His success was to have been expected, not resented.

The priest asked, "How would you better the offer?"

"Well, first I'd have to know what the offer was, wouldn't I?" Billy asked. "I take it there was an offer. I mean, someone sent you here?"

"I don't believe that's any of your business. And I wouldn't describe it as an offer, more a meeting of the minds."

"Now we're beginning to get somewhere," Billy said, and turned to look at this room he loved.

"Keep facing the outside," the priest said sharply.

"I'm sorry. I don't want any trouble."

"Like I said, you should have thought of that a long time ago, before you decided to become a predator."

Now it came to Billy. Instantaneously, a blizzard of detail cohered into the only plausible explanation of what was happening to him. If he was right, he had no choice but to fight for his life, and the sooner the better. If he was right, the man beside him had come not out of vengeance, nor for retribution, but to silence him. Or perhaps the man himself had been tricked into coming, turned into a contract killer for the same people who had unnerved Billy and caused him to abandon the deal of a lifetime.

No doubt there would be many removes between the priest's anger and the real motive for this assault, but, deciding he had no choice other than to make one last attempt to cut through them, Billy said, "Hear me out, Father, please. I know this sounds mad, but you are being used, and not for the purpose you think."

"Used? That's for sure—by you. I've been used *by you.* Let's be honest!"

"Not by me, by whoever sent you here. There's more going on here than you can possibly know, Father, but then you're not really a priest, are you?"

"Give the man a prize."

"Grandpa," Emily called again. "Stuart won't get off of his computer."

"Get off, Stuart," Cynthia demanded from somewhere inside the house. Billy could not discern where, but her voice was shrill and carried.

"In five minutes," Stuart pleaded.

"Now," Cynthia said. "How many times—"

"Three minutes," Stuart bargained, in a whine.

"Grandpa," Emily insisted.

"Get off the computer, Stuart!" Billy shouted. "I'll be right there." But he kept his eyes on the priest. "It won't stop with me," he said in a lower voice. "Once you've done what they want you to, you'll be next. After that, the killing will just go on and on, but you won't be here to worry about it, will you?"

"Nice try," the man said, "a real nice try. So I guess you're a very imaginative guy. That's a shame."

The move Billy was contemplating was called an arm drag. It was one at which he had excelled in high school and particularly at Stanford. But this library was not a ring. Right now he had to lure his assailant closer. There was still too much distance separating them for him to make the move work, even in the modified form he was planning. Had Stuart been older or Emily stronger or less emotional, he might have called to them to join him. Cynthia could have been more useful, but after a drink and without any warning that she would be entering a trap, he wasn't sure. Even with pistol in hand, this man would not be able to overcome them all, but it wouldn't require much effort for him to pick them off one by one as they arrived or to take a child hostage. No, it was safer to face him down alone.

Billy took a cautious step back; by reflex the man extended his left arm, looking along the length of it, past the Walther's barrel, directly at him. "Calm down, will you?" Billy said. "I can't go anywhere."

The false priest, too, drifted back. "Damn right you can't."

"You'd better think about what I said."

"I have. It's a crock."

Billy moved with baby steps. He wanted to reverse their positions without the priest's realizing what he'd done. That way when his right hand flew up out of nowhere and suddenly struck the pistol, it would deflect any shot fired away from the house. He kept talking.

"I don't know what you think you're doing, going around in circles," commented the priest. "All you've managed to do is get yourself a lot farther away from your only possible escape route than you were before, which is why I let you do it. Didn't notice that, I'll bet, how much farther you are from the door."

Billy wished the priest had not been left-handed. It meant he would have to go for the man's triceps with his own left hand, after using his right in a hard swat to dislodge the man's grip on the Walther, or at least to deflect his aim, before Billy could spin him and take him from the back. With the weapon neutralized, there would be no contest. He sighed, as if to credit the priest for having gotten the better of him. He needed to stall, for just a few more seconds, to be certain he had not merely reversed their positions but was close enough. He would have to spring at the priest from this point, but it was as close as he was likely to get, and he decided he could do it.

He looked again at the sky above Mission Hills, hoping the priest's gaze would travel the same direction, if only for the necessary instant. When it did, Billy leaped. He let out a fierce, animal cry of attack as the outside of his right hand slammed into the priest's left thumb, flattening the pistol against his chest. With his left hand, Billy grabbed for the priest's triceps. Once he had gained a purchase on these muscles at the back of the upper arm, he would have the torque to turn the man around. Controlling him from behind, he would then have little trouble wrestling him to the floor.

They were staring face-to-face, the priest's forefinger still on the Walther's trigger, but its barrel, from which in their struggle the silencer had slipped, was now pointed to the window. Billy had the priest's upper arm, but only from the inside, not yet the back. He squeezed it, stepping forward into their match. Two or three more inches were all he required. Already he could see the fear, the resignation to loss on the priest's brow and in his eyes. Even so, the man managed to get off a stray shot.

"Daddy!" Cynthia called.

He could not reply as the priest struggled to release himself.

"Daddy!" Cynthia cried out once more.

"Grandpa," Emily called. "What's the matter?"

"Grandpa!" Stuart screamed.

"Stay back," Billy said as they opened the door.

"I've pushed the alarm," Cynthia said, restraining the children. "The police will be here any minute."

The priest kept silent. Billy still could not reach fully behind his arm. The two men watched each other. Each time the priest jolted toward freedom, Billy pressed in upon him.

"You won't get away once the police arrive," Cynthia said.

Emily gave her mother a reproving look.

Another shot fired.

Cynthia drew the children back.

With a sudden, forceful shudder and a knee kick to the inside of Billy's left thigh, striking the nerves at his groin, the priest managed to loosen Billy's hold on his shooting arm. He took advantage of the breathing room. A second, lower, street-fighting kick, quick and sharp at Billy's ankle, released that hold completely.

Billy said, "Don't!"

The priest took aim at Billy's lips. He fired three shots. "The blood of a blood-sucker," he declared as a dark puddle spread and stained the floorboards and coagulated in Billy's hair.

"Run!" Cynthia cried to her children, her voice, in shock, deeper, no longer brittle.

Stuart and Emily stood paralyzed by what they had witnessed. As if in disbelief at the speed and completeness with which death came, even their tears would not fall. Neither fear nor the instinct to self-preservation would connect their brains to their bodies, propel their fast legs as the priest moved toward them. The Walther's magazine held fifteen rounds. So he had, he calculated, ten left.

"No," Cynthia said.

"You should have kept the children out of here where they belonged. You should have kept them alive. I wouldn't have come after you."

"But we'd seen you."

The priest hesitated. "I guess you're right."

He shot Emily first, then Stuart, as the boy, in an attempt at manliness that was both premature and final, lurched bravely toward him. It was not until Cynthia had bent over the corpses of her children, her palms in pools of their young blood, that she was shot from behind.

Chapter Three

The young man in the Lincoln Navigator watched the priest come out of the driveway onto the winding, tree-lined street at exactly the point upon which they had agreed. The image in his new ATN Viper Night Vision Scope was sharper than he had expected it to be, and even from the safe distance of five hundred meters, he could make out the frenzied desperation of an amateur. He had heard the gunfire—too much—from the direction of the house and could only assume that Wilhelm Claussen had put up more of a fight than had been anticipated. Perhaps the man he had outfitted as a lowly parish priest had permitted himself to be engaged in conversation. That was always a risk when you involved someone with a motive, especially one at variance with your own. Such people liked to give voice to their grievances before they did their work— a mark of stupidity! And what had happened to the silencer? Now that the murderer was in view, searching the traffic for the vehicle he expected to rescue him, it probably did not matter, but it might have done.

Sirens welled in the distance, a music he found reassuring. Patrol cars, their overhead lights alternating rapidly, converged on the Claussen house from both directions, blockading its entrance, illuminating it with search beams. In total it took less than ten minutes for the officers to make their discoveries and for support and reinforcements to arrive, which, the observer thought, was efficient by any standard and all the more so for a department no doubt unused to such things.

The young man hid patiently until he was sure no ambulance had been summoned. His sole remaining concern was for the wretched fellow he had stalked in a chat room for debtors, then contrived to meet in a clinic for the chronically indebted that convened in a moldy walk-up office above a packaged goods and check cashing store in South KC. He had chosen carefully. The man had been the sixth or seventh he'd approached on the Net and the second with whom he'd made physical contact. The first of those had struck him as too weak, too tentative. To that one he had revealed nothing of his plan, extending only empathy.

But the more the next man learned about Claussen, the more enraged he had become. The young man in the Navigator had parceled out information, usually clippings from newspapers and society magazines, over several meetings, gradually bringing the dots closer until the distraught man could connect them on his own, all at once recognizing that his despair was but a part of the price paid for his better's sunny circumstances. It had always amazed the young man how incompletely most people understood the world in which they lived, how innocent they remained of the forces that determined their fate. In the end he had not been coy. Over an early supper in a roadside diner, he'd made his pitch. Wilhelm Claussen had hurt him, too, he explained. Never mind how, or the fact that he hadn't the nerve or skill to do the job himself. Take out Claussen and the distraught man's debts would be seen to. There would also be money for his boy's medical expenses and more than enough extra for him to start over somewhere else. The getaway would be arranged, in a cul-de-sac half a mile from the Claussen house. As a down payment, in a black nylon shaving kit were one hundred one-hundred-dollar bills, already circulated and unmarked. The balance would be paid once Claussen was dead.

The prospective assassin had listened carefully, all the while eating as though famished. No doubt the charbroiled prime rib in front of him was the best meal he'd downed in a long while, though not ever, for a lingering gentility suggested he'd known better days. Waiting for his reply, the younger man knew he had made the correct decision to corrupt a broken man rather than hire a professional. It was a plan without loose ends.

He had arrived in the United States as Jonathan Cazeneuve, holder of a Kenyan passport, six weeks before. On that visit he had registered at the Marriott Marquis in Times Square, bought tickets to two Broadway shows, and paid restaurant checks with a credit card in the same name. As Caswell Rubin, however, he had flown on to Chicago, and then, as Peter Steele, onward to Kansas City, where he'd had his first encounter with the man he hoped to employ.

At the debt clinic and in a nearby bar afterward, they had spoken three times: about the miseries of debt, the guile of creditors, the pressures and impossibility of life. The young man had grown stubble for the occasion, dabbed it with peroxide, and worn a theatrical wig. Lifeless chestnut flecked with gray, this had added at least a decade of defeat to his appearance. He'd tested it thoroughly, judging it sufficient to fool any surveillance camera beneath which he might inadvertently pass. As far as the candidate was concerned, Peter—no surnames having been exchanged between them—vanished into the city's underside between their meetings. Who didn't?

After two weeks Peter disappeared from Kansas City, as did Caswell Rubin from Chicago. As Jonathan Cazeneuve, he departed from New York, via London, for Nairobi. The next week, as Franz Schenkel, the crisp, dark-haired bearer of a German passport, he arrived in Washington from Frankfurt, took the shuttle into the city, and established himself at the hotel on Massachusetts Avenue that he'd listed on his landing card. After two days of regular comings and goings, as the dingy Peter Steele he had boarded a flight for St. Louis and there, once more as Caswell Rubin, rented the Navigator he'd driven across state. He had already manufactured an impressive inventory of identities. Caswell Rubin, in fact, had been fabricated several years before. A magazine subscription had been taken out in the name of a fictitious student on one midwestern campus. When, using that subscription list, a large bank had subsequently sent an offer of credit, their card had been accepted. Bills had been charged and paid regularly ever since. So the fictitious Mr. Rubin, alive in the consciousness of the financial world, would subsidize his part in the death of Billy Claussen with some of the same plastic that Claussen's bank had grown fat promoting. The sweetness of that irony was not lost on the young man.

As he observed the situation from the Navigator, he felt a surprising zest, which disturbed him, for he did not think of himself as evil. About violence—means in general—he was agnostic.

When no ambulances approached and enough time had elapsed for him to conclude that none had been called, he backed out of the shallow slag driveway and made his way toward a ridgeline, maintaining a steady speed of thirty-five miles per hour, braking for all stop signs. Once on this higher ground, with the Claussen property perhaps five hundred yards below and behind him, he removed a miniature radio transmitter from the console compartment. No sooner did he press it than a small firecracker exploded in the distance, only a few feet from the dark, vacant mock-Victorian cottage beneath whose eaves he had last spotted his dupe. As intended, the firecracker broke enough glass to set off the house's alarm; a highly pitched, undulating wail shattered the cool evening. Floodlights, sudden and bright, blazed from the cottage on every side, forcing the make-believe priest from cover and drawing the attention of the nearby police. All at once the stillness that shock had imposed upon the crime scene fractured, the routines of investigators giving way to the fury of a chase.

The young man continued for a short distance, then stopped the Navigator at the vantage point he had selected on his first reconnaissance of this operation. Farther along an unobstructed route to town and practically unnoticeable, it was close enough to the drama that after powering up his infrared scope he could monitor the priest's increasingly erratic flight. The man scurried north, then west, then north again, searching for the red Hummer Peter had promised would be at this cul-de-sac to evacuate him, the Hummer where he would find not only safety but all the money he would need to save his son and recover the lost ends of his own fraying life.

It took the police one and a half minutes longer than the young man had predicted to spot and gain on their quarry. Within another minute they had surrounded him, flushed him from a pathetic stand of forsythia that had gone brown and rigid with the season, trained their own lamps on him. Their K-9s barked. The murderer stood in the middle of the circular road, his dark shoes and trouser cuffs caked with mud, his clerical collar awry but still in place.

"Stop! He's a priest!" one officer cried out.

"We can't be sure," said another.

"Put down the gun, Father."

"Do what he says: Put down the gun, please!"

The priest remained still, his eyes looking past the police—surely for the Hummer, for Peter, for the freedom and anonymity that, if nothing else, had been his up until he'd shot the big tycoon, his daughter and grandchildren. Had he made a mistake? Maybe so, but it was too late now to rectify it. In life there was no going back. That much he understood.

So gradually he began to turn, as if the means of escape lay in the opposite direction. The police took aim. "Put your gun down, sir."

The image the young man watched in his night scope, although too pronounced in its greens and reds, was of a weak, impressionable face upon which reality was dawning slowly but with finality.

When the confronted priest raised the Walther, inserted its barrel deeply into his mouth, and, without hesitating, squeezed the trigger, the wretch collapsed just as the young man had envisioned he would.

Without regret, satisfied with the efficacy of both his perception and his methods, he started the Navigator's engine.

Manning a hastily established checkpoint at the foot of Billy Claussen's driveway, Trooper Darnall regarded Trooper Larrabee across the darkened landscape, his voice and expression still incredulous. "I can't believe it," he said.

"I know. I mean, he seemed like such a nice guy," Larrabee agreed. "Didn't you think so? Imagine leaving all *this* behind you! Holy crap!"

"Believe me, it's just the beginning," Darnall replied sagely as the flashing lights of their vehicles intermittently illuminated their faces.

"You know something about him?"

"Just what everyone does."

"Which is?"

"Come on, you're kidding me? The biggest man in the state. Did you hear anything up at the house?"

Larrabee shook his head. "Nothing official. I was there only a minute or two."

"Anything *un*official?"

"There were four of them: Claussen and, the sergeant thinks, his daughter and two young grandchildren."

"Shit!" Darnall told him.

"The perp shot himself."

"Who'd do something like this?"

"*Why*'s the real question."

"Money or love or hate," Darnall told him. "It's always one of the three. First thing they teach you in criminology."

"Okay, but who benefits if they're all dead?"

"They're not *all* dead. The old man has a son named Luke, one of those spoiled-shit playboy types. Been in the news."

"For what?" Larrabee asked.

"Being an asshole."

"It's like it goes with the job description. You have a father who's one way, a kid who's the exact opposite. Can I tell you something? If I'd been born rich like Luke Claussen, I wouldn't be an asshole."

"You wouldn't be you either," his friend told him.

"Bullshit!"

"Forget it. My guess is this asshole's a whole lot richer tonight than he was this afternoon."

Chapter Four

Very little about him was immediately apparent. Beyond the simple statistics that appeared on most of his driver's licenses and at least one of his passports, listing him as six feet one inch tall, weighing eighty-one kilograms or 178 pounds, having blue eyes and light brown hair, Philip Frost's exact nationality, background and profession ordinarily eluded those observing him, which was as he preferred it. Whether he was about to enter Europe or the United States, for example, he was seldom offered an immigration form by flight attendants. Isabella Cavill, whom he had been seeing for almost a year, knew, in addition to his moods, that he was a Sagittarius, but even she had not been able to disentangle the multiple strains of DNA that made him such a fierce but cool lover, so generous yet distant, so incisive yet detached. In his erect carriage and the forward thrust of his walk there was something Prussian, yet when he let himself go he could bellow with the unforced, ingratiating laugh of an American schoolboy, tease with the subtlety of a cultivated Englishman—and take a joke, too, but only one that went so far and no further.

He had been born in New York to a Swiss-German father and a half-Danish, half-American mother but as a child had not been educated there. Instead, for reasons put down to his father's job in the UN Secretariat and the constant and far-flung travel it necessitated, Philip had been sent to a minor English prep school then, at thirteen, to an elite institution just outside Geneva where he had numbered among his classmates one African and two Arab princes as well as the scions of at least a dozen well-known, worldwide industrial fortunes.

His four years at MIT had given him his first taste of life in the country of his birth. Why, after graduating, he had chosen the City of London rather than Wall Street in which to begin his quest had had more to do with fate than planning.

At a seminar during his senior year, he'd paid rapt attention to a guest speaker who had latterly turned from the analysis of particles to that of markets: a quirky, donnish man with the arms of a stevedore. Ian Santal had come out of nowhere to Cambridge University a generation before and there made a name for himself as a man of science. "A man of the Left, then of the Right and, both those passions having flagged, now of the moment" was how he had described himself to the students, and it was the fact that such range was possible that had intrigued Philip. He had pursued Santal and Santal had hired him. It was—or at least at the time it had seemed—as simple as that. The firm's trading rooms were in London, so that was where he'd gone, not because it was an agreeable city but because from it he could discern the clearest path to the future he coveted.

Could all of that—the firm's rise, then decline following Santal's departure, his own abandonment of finance for diplomacy, strangely at Ian's instigation—really have been as long ago as it was? All but a decade now? On the ides of March (aware he was the only one among present company who would recognize the date), Philip asked himself that question as he looked westward upon the Sea of Azov, with the Crimea in the distance. It was the shallowest sea in the world, forty-six feet at its deepest point, a northern recess of the Black Sea near Europe's winding border with Asia, accessible only through the narrow, gatelike Strait of Kerch that lay before him. It was not the season to be here, he thought, not the time of year when any but the most intrepid tourists would book into the new resort that in due course would replace the nuclear-missile installation that had once threatened Turkey and much of Western Europe. No, the tourists would come after the thaw and before the first frost, when the east wind no longer stung and the flat farmland was no longer winter white but a patchwork of mown green and yellow rectangles. They would pay top ruble, dollar, euro—whatever—in order to pass time at a seaside so pristine, in a venue haunted by the alternate history it had by a hairsbreadth escaped.

None of that was his business. As leader of the American team assigned to assist the Russian military in the decommissioning of its surplus nuclear weapons, he was here to make this particular dream possible, not to realize it. His own dream was elsewhere, allied to that of the developers only tangentially. For the time being, it was his job to erase the past, safely and to the satisfaction of everyone, even as it was his intention to shift a piece of it, assets that were literally priceless, onto his own account. No scion of industry possessed such assets; nor did any African or Arab prince, though several were said to have sought them. No academic had ever controlled nor trader dealt in such commodities. He had to smile, even allow himself a laugh. As with all the most brilliant plans, the genius of Ian's lay in its simplicity and patience. He had seduced the necessary parties long ago, had recruited Philip when Philip thought the reverse was taking place. Most of all he had guessed right: that in the aftermath of the Soviet Union's demise, Russia would require both practical help and geopolitical cover as it dismantled weapons systems that had become burdensome and superfluous. The task force at the top of which a man of Philip's personal and academic pedigree fit so naturally had been named after the American senators Sam Nunn and Richard Lugar, who had sponsored the legislation authorizing it. To Philip's surprise it had survived myriad recurring strains in relations between Moscow and Washington to continue its work without major impediment. And now, as it oversaw the dismantling of this remote and redundant warehouse and launching site, the last piece of Ian's puzzle appeared about to be set into place. What a puzzle it was! He had to hand Ian infinite credit even if it was he, Philip, who had refined it to his own advantage, given it a final twist, disguised it so cleverly that it could now be hidden, without fear of detection, in plain sight.

Andrej, who was his counter, exhaled deliberately, as though performing an actor's trick he had long practiced. After a pause he sighed and said, "I miss smoking."

Philip nodded.

"Did you ever smoke?" Andrej asked him idly.

Philip remained expressionless, hesitated, then said, "At school, for effect."

Andrej laughed.

But rather than join in, Philip froze.

"You cannot be serious," Andrej replied, notes of fear and pleading in his gruff voice. "It was an innocuous question. That's all."

"Be that as it may," Philip said.

"The man said *no* questions, and he meant *no* questions," Andrej muttered, not quite under his breath.

"I am glad we understand each other."

"Oh, we do indeed," Andrej answered. "After all, you are my retirement, my very comfortable, very early retirement. That, as I am sure you realize, is what this whole thing means to me. The South of France, or maybe Majorca! Only a fool would question a prospect so sweet."

"Where are we, then, Andrej? Beyond the point of no return?"

"For this stage the answer is yes."

"Excellent."

"You have a way with words."

"Not at all," Philip told him. "So twenty-one minus three still equals twenty-one?"

Andrej smiled. "And with numbers, too," he said.

"And three times thirty equals . . . what?"

"That, one supposes, would depend on the currency."

Philip smiled. "What those figures do add up to is a lot to move. Of course, one is only speaking hypothetically."

"Hypothetically, it should be well nigh impossible."

"But not *impossible*," Philip pressed.

"Timing is everything."

"Do you know what astonishes me?" Philip asked.

"I could guess, but no, I don't."

"In that case, Andrej, I'll tell you: The world's simply not paying attention. It's asleep."

"It does that from time to time. It all comes down to the economy, if you want my opinion. When things are going along pretty well, people don't want to worry. When things are going poorly, they're caught up in their own difficulties. They're not inclined to look about for more."

"Still, it's more luck than we deserve. We have to be careful not to take it for granted."

In the distance one squad of a larger team was in motion. As he turned to remind himself of its presence, what Philip saw were no more than stick figures, determined but undifferentiated, hard at work for their generous hazardous-duty pay, aware of what they were doing on only the most obvious of levels, like most of humanity if unlike him or Andrej and the few others Andrej had had no difficulty compromising. Lacking the instinct to connect the dots of life's affairs, they went about their business in workmanlike fashion, focusing only as much concentration as was required upon their jobs and reserving all the rest for the mix of joy and disappointment, anxiety and satisfaction they called their personal lives. For this, Philip was grateful. It made his task easier.

The few buildings nearby were low, roofed with shallow inverted saucers painted in splotches of green, brown and yellow in the traditional pattern of overland camouflage. Only the largest, a depot through which a graded roadbed dipped then rose, stood a single story high. And even it appeared less a structure entire unto itself than the partial eruption of an underground complex.

Across this barren landscape, the wind gusted, combing back the indolent grass, strewing twigs from distant forests. It was desolate, yet it was this very desolation, Philip knew, that would have given away the place's purpose to a practiced eye. Early in the Cold War, just after the Americans had deployed Polaris across their fleet of nuclear submarines, these silos had been buried underground, withdrawn from sight if not from readiness. Designed to house only intermediate-range missiles aimed at neutralizing their American opposite numbers in Turkey and the Shah's imposing military in Iran, they had been considered too close to the nation's natural border to be a fit site for intercontinental missiles. Such sites, like the weapons labs that produced the warheads, were typically far inland, such as Arzamas in the Nizhny Novgorod region and Snezhinsk in the Urals. Yet in the years of frenzy and jockeying that had preceded the old order's demise, and especially in the aftermath of that convulsion when Ukraine had broken away, the installation they were now decertifying had unexpectedly come to house warheads meant to sit atop intercontinental missiles, weapons that contained as many as thirty independently targeted reentry vehicles each. Many of these had been withdrawn from the Ukraine before its independence; fewer had arrived in port from nuclear attack subs in the Black Sea Fleet. Those had been days of escalating tension and little clarity in the evolving relationship between Russia and Ukraine. The Autonomous Republic of Crimea, home to the fleet's principal ports, had quickly become the target of pro-Russian separatists, many of them seamen. Ukraine's new government had rushed to establish its own nonnuclear navy from remnants of the old fleet. Across the region, flux had prevailed. Weapons and decoys were moved as if props in a shell game, under diminished scrutiny and sometimes haphazardly, a turn of events that had captured Ian Santal's interest.

As they proceeded toward their work, Andrej said, "I take nothing for granted. With our past we'd be fools to do so."

"Agreed," Philip said.

"When I was a boy, certain things seemed immutable. The Union of Soviet Socialist Republics was one of them. Now look what's happened. Probably there are soldiers on this base who were born after Russia and our near abroad went their separate ways. Czechs and Poles and Hungarians are Westerners today, practically, but where you feel it is when you're this close to Ukraine, because they are not only Slavs, they are our brothers and sisters. That is why we trusted them with so many of our weapons, not just because of their fortunate geographical position."

"There are no differences so profound as those between very similar peoples," Philip said. "Who is more like an Englishman than an Irishman or more like a Jew than an Arab?"

Andrej laughed, but only for an instant.

Ten minutes later, in the tiled depot, Philip kept careful watch as Andrej, witnessed by two others—one young and gaunt, high-cheeked, an officer in the Russian army, the other less erect, approaching middle age in an at-ease slouch that suggested bureaucratic rather than military training—certified the conveyance of each warhead as it rose from the cool, cavernous, stainless-steel armory one level below. Attuned to the moment he had been planning for, Philip remained silent, his emotions both hyper and subdued as the Russian and American representatives from the Nunn-Lugar task force and Nuclear Threat Initiative proceeded with their work.

Andrej stood next to him, his high Slavic forehead spotlighted by the soft blue-white glow of his laptop's screen. The computer was brand-new, ultrathin, as close to futureproof as any he'd ever held. He caressed it with protective pride even as it rested on the drop-down easel of his workstation. The protocol now under way was meant to be double-blind. As each crate was conveyed to him, he would check its details with the attentiveness of a librarian to its original label, then to the yellowing loose-leaf pages on which the same information had long ago been recorded by hand in fine strokes of blue-black ink. The holes of the narrowly ruled pages had been reinforced and each warhead indexed with a brightly colored transparent tab so that the inventory resembled a schoolchild's notebook. Only once these records had been matched and rematched did he scan in the bar codes affixed to the seals applied during the recent digitization of such information. Of these there were three: for the cross-barred pinewood crate that could have contained a grand piano but was in this case merely an attention-deflecting outer shell; for the lead liner just within; and, most crucially, for the warhead that had been inserted inside the liner. Having completed this task without error (and he knew that even a single misplaced character would start the process over from the beginning), Andrej would enter the codes' corresponding numbers by hand into his secure computer, following which, if the entries matched the computer's database, he would be presented with yet another series of figures, an eleven-digit composite of numerals, letters and symbols, one for each independently targeted reentry vehicle. Highlighting each of these in turn, he would enter first the installation code for their point of departure, second the code for the convoy in which they were to be transported, and finally the code for the destination facility at which the weapons were to be deactivated, disassembled and destroyed.

Twenty meters down the line, the exact process was repeated by his Russian army counterpart under the gaze of the American disarmament expert. After this each case was loaded aboard one of two trucks that—following a three-quarter-hour drive with land, air and sea escorts—would arrive at an otherwise disused rail station. There the transfer would be swift and, even as a wintry daylight lingered, floodlit. The final leg of the journey, entirely covert, would be across limitless fields still tended with scythes.

In all, twenty-one warheads were to be transported. And when the loading and recording had been completed at every stage, twenty-one crates of exactly similar weight and dimensions shone on every copy of the manifest. Therein was the elegance of Ian's conceit. In the confusion, madcap turmoil and despair that had attended the dissolution of the Soviet Union, Ian, by then trafficking far more profitably in contraband than in shares, currencies, or ideas, had approached his sometime client, sometime purveyor Colonel Zhugov, a man of humble appearance and expensive tastes, with a proposition. The good soldier had only to falsify certain records in certain places, had only to secrete and maintain within his impregnable base three warheads until the day came when either he would have to suddenly "rediscover" them to save his skin or, as Ian thought much more likely, it would become feasible to remove them. In the maelstrom of revolution, Ian believed, millions of accounts of all sorts would be fudged rather than justified. That was a lesson of history, he had told Philip.

Recalling this, Philip wished he himself possessed more of his mentor's patience and trust, more of Ian's confidence that no matter how far off, a path to the main chance would sooner or later reveal itself.

Back in the utilitarian office of the installation's present commanding officer, Andrej said, "It's a good thing a place can't think, can't know what's become of it, can't feel regret."

"Your sentimental nature never ceases to surprise me," Philip told him. "It's at odds with your uniform."

"All I meant is that one minute you are—what is the word?—the *cynosure* of the world's attention . . . well, at least that of other armed forces, your possible and probable enemies."

"'Cynosure,'" Philip repeated. "What dictionary have you been reading this time?"

"The *Oxford English,* of course," Andrej replied. "The word means 'center of attraction or admiration.' But from now on, no one will give a damn about this place."

"You're wrong."

"I wasn't thinking of tourists."

"You'll be surprised how many will come."

"No. They come already. The new ones will just be of a different type, a better class, the sort who would now fly off to Antalya. Anapa is just down the road. It has always had its share of tourists, more than ever since the old Soviet Union collapsed and taking one's holiday in Sevastopol and the like meant crossing the border into Crimea. I suppose what the builders have in mind is more on the order of Sochi's resorts."

"The artist's renderings," Philip said, "would suggest something more bucolic than grand. But you are correct; it's to be Russian in character."

"Of necessity," Andrej replied. "No one else can get there without the most enormous hassle."

Philip allowed himself a smile.

Andrej said, "I am sure it will be lovely, first class in every way, but even so, to be admired for one's natural beauty is not the same as to be respected for one's power."

"No, it isn't, nor is that an argument I was making."

"Real admiration is based in fear," Andrej declared coolly.

"What about attraction?"

"At the beginning not always, but eventually fear plays its part. No one will fear this place ever again, which is good, but sad, too, in its way. That's all I was trying to explain, Mr. Frost."

"What remains?" Philip asked.

"To sign off that the weapons are gone," Andrej told him. "That's it."

"All four principals must sign and witness that decertification order, if I remember correctly. Once that's done——"

"The guards can go home and the soldiers can go elsewhere. There'll be nothing left to secure. Then just you watch: The construction crews won't waste a day before they move in. I'm telling you, we'll hardly recognize this place in a month."

"Well, it's the new Russia." Philip sighed. "What can I say?"

"And where there's money at stake . . ." Andrej's voice trailed off. "Where is the seal, by the way? Do you have it?"

Philip shrugged off Andrej's impertinence. "Of course I have it. It's in my left coat pocket. I've been fidgeting with it all afternoon."

"Let's wrap things up, then. It's already dark, and I'd like to get back to my room, run a hot bath, change my clothes and pour myself a drink."

"You're entitled to do that," Philip said. "You've worked hard, done a fine job, too. But tell me, what will you do tomorrow, and the day after?"

Andrej hesitated, then shot Philip a sly smile. "Forget," he said with all the reassurance he could summon. "And you?"

"I'll anticipate," Philip told him. "That's the business I'm in."

Chapter Five

Gripping the lime green two-by-four rail that ran, hip-high, along the precipice, Ty Hunter stared south across the Mediterranean. It was late morning and the May sun was almost overhead. The sky was absent of clouds. Was it any wonder that this place had been named the Côte d'Azur?

"Like a shot rubber band," he explained into the mouthpiece of his phone's headset. "That's how I feel, to tell you the truth."

"Is it any wonder?" Greg Logan, on the other end of the connection, agreed.

"Not really," Ty said, "after four pictures in three years, two of them, as you know, very long shoots." To his right lay the Golfe-Juan, and beyond the far promontory that defined it, sat Cannes. It was the Film Festival he had come for—not because he had another blockbuster in competition or about to open, but because of the cameo role he'd taken, for scale, in *Something to Look Forward To*, which promised to be Greg Logan's comeback picture. It was Greg who had discovered him in the rehab center at Walter Reed seven years before. Newly photogenic after the sequence of surgeries that had followed the fiery crash of the armored personnel carrier in which, as the intelligence officer of a tactical infantry unit of the Third Army, he'd been traveling on maneuvers, Ty was then only weeks away from discharge from the hospital. Greg, who was still doing commercial films, had trained his camera on Ty's smile and, even before the half-hour promotional piece had wrapped, given the young soldier his card.

Now, as Ty watched motor yachts exit and enter the harbors on either side of the lush Hôtel du Cap, he thought that he could hardly have wished for better luck. With no specific job to go to once he left the army, he had decided to take a flier, called Greg, then bought the cheapest flight he could find to Los Angeles. He'd given himself three months to find his footing, but it hadn't taken that long, and he'd still had a reasonable portion of his savings in the bank when his first paycheck arrived. In a manner of speaking, he'd caught a wave, he realized, having appeared in Hollywood just as Greg had begun casting his first feature, a road movie called *The Boy Who Understood Women*. Although Ty had no idea from what reservoir of experience or imagination he'd summoned his portrayal of a young drifter who trades his life for his lover's, he had won an Oscar nomination for it, then, quickly in its aftermath, the roles that had made him the number-one box-office star in the world. Greg's own fortunes had fared less well over the same period, his projects becoming smaller, more personal and subtle in a marketplace that craved just the opposite. Everyone, however, had agreed that the script for *Something to Look Forward To* was brilliant and, if only there were stars attached, exactly right for a director of Greg Logan's sensibility. So Ty had repaid his mentor's faith, taken on the cameo role of a playboy Robin Hood, and, drawn by his presence, other stars had followed.

"Have you seen the trades?" Greg inquired.

"I haven't been awake that long," Ty replied.

"What time did she leave?"

"It must have been early."

"You're a lucky man."

"Not true. I spent the night alone, as I often do lately. Don't tell anyone?"

"If that's true, it was by choice," Greg said.

"You'd think so, but you'd be wrong."

"There were a lot of beautiful women at the *Vanity Fair* party. And the waters parted when you arrived. Need I say more?"

"Maybe I'm looking for something that's harder to find," Ty said.

"People do that," Greg told him. "It's usually a mistake."

"When I'm ready to give up, I'll give up. I'm not ready yet."

"Yeah, well, never mind. The buzz on the picture's fantastic. *Variety* loved it; so did the *Reporter.* They loved *you.* They loved everyone. I can't explain it. Sometimes people get it. Anyway, this time the ball landed on the right number. You know what you are, Ty? You're charmed."

"Wouldn't it be nice to believe that?" Ty said.

"You're a goddamned booster rocket, that's what you are."

"You made the film. The bows belong to you."

"So tonight should be pretty swell."

"By the sound of it," Ty agreed. "I've just been watching boats come and go, wondering which one it might be."

"'None' is the answer. *Surpass* is still in Monte Carlo. They'll come this way after lunch."

"Who did you say it belonged to?"

"Ian Santal."

"I've heard that name. I can't remember where."

"Man of mystery! Started out as an academic of some sort, then became, like, the world's biggest broker or something. I don't know of what. The important thing is that he's an old friend of Sid Thrall's. You know Sid."

"Who doesn't?" Ty asked. "He owns the studio. Of course I do—not well, but I know him."

"Actually, he used to own it. Now he owns a lot of shares in the company that bought it, but you're right, he still has his job. Sid's the reason we've been asked. He likes to shine in reflected glory. He'll want to show you off to his glamorous friend. Santal's goddaughter, who's English, is a jewelry designer in Rome and pretty good, I hear. The party's for her, to celebrate her new collection. So we can have a look at that and a longer one around the boat, which should be more interesting. I've never been on a three-hundred-sixty-foot yacht before, have you?"

"Can't say that I have."

"Anyway, I've got to get going. I have two interviews, a lunch, and meetings at two and four. I'll show up at your hotel at six, and we'll go on to the launch together."

"Sounds like a plan," Ty said. "Where are you now?"

"At the Carlton," Greg answered. "Half an hour, three-quarters at most, away."

"Call me if you need me."

"Be careful! It's always possible I will."

For a moment after he hung up, Ty continued to stare at the sea. He'd first seen the Med as a soldier. Even by stealth, in the twilight-to-dawn regimen of a commando, it had kidnapped his imagination. He'd always been attentive to history, and the lure of a sea that washed upon so many storied shores had immediately intoxicated him.

Ty's accommodation, befitting his visibility, was a seaside hut of a villa off a private path just east of the grande allée that ascended to the magnificent

Napoleon III hotel at the summit of the hill. Polynesian in inspiration, compact yet luxurious, the incongruous villa was a monument to 1950s chic. Returning to it, Ty thought it seemed the sort of place Sean Connery or Cary Grant might have put up. He drew a deep breath of coastal air that was also fragrant with the surrounding pine and roses. For the moment he slipped his BlackBerry into the side pocket of his Vilbrequin swim trunks that featured an almost comical pattern of banana bunches against a powder and steel blue background. The last woman he'd ever loved had bought them for him on Nantucket. In his bathroom he found the waterproof sunscreen he'd come for and, after applying it, placed his wallet, signet ring and the BlackBerry beside his other valuables in the portable safe at the back of the closet. For the safe's combination, he had, as usual, chosen the unforgettable last four digits of his U.S. Army serial number.

Returning smiles without breaking stride, he made his way across the terrace of chaise longues that were populated this week by movie-industry executives and ingenues, to the Eden Roc pavilion. Just before the changing rooms and lunch café, he turned left and, stepping up his pace, descended the steep staircase that had been cut into the rock. Beside him, the infinity pool beckoned, and he noticed that the name of the magazine that had sponsored last night's party had already been erased from its floor. When he reached its level, however, Ty chose instead the high diving board that rose over the Med just to his right. He waited behind a trio of ten-year-olds intent on outdoing one another's cannonballs, then, after a perfect half gainer and another minute or so of the Australian crawl, reached a pontoon from which he could regard the hotel and Cap d'Antibes in the distance, far enough away not to be recognized without binoculars. He wished he could see his own life and future as lucidly. The business had changed. What business hadn't? He was grateful to have cleared its hurdles when he had, even as he recognized that success was never a passive state for long. One rose or fell. Stars formed or died. Never mind, he told himself; there would be time enough for careful thought once he had a chance to rest. He was sure he'd made the correct decision not to read any of the scripts his agent had been sending on to him, for he was not ready to commit to a new role now. Going into character required reserves of energy and emotion that, after successive films, he had depleted. Although he had no doubt of his ability to replenish both, in the meantime the only part he wished to play was that of Ty Hunter getting on with real life.

Triangulating from landmarks on shore, he drew in his mind a straight line from the bobbing pontoon to the immaculate white house that stood, beyond a tended slope of grass, in isolation on the far point. Slowly, he began to swim this line, to and fro in more-or-less Olympic laps, changing his style with each turn. With his last stroke, which was as forceful as his first, his fingers found the brass hold on the side of the pontoon, and he released himself to its protection, buoyed on a soothing cushion of waves as he regathered his strength. Then he heard voices—two at least, perhaps more. They were feminine voices whose rhythm was familiar but whose language foreign. Listening intently, he decided it must be Russian, which was not a tongue he spoke or understood. Keeping his head just above the surface of the sea, he eventually caught sight of three young women in similarly slinky one-piece bathing suits. All were blond, long-legged, with high, full chests. At first he wondered if they were sisters but then, detecting a lack of sufficient intimacy in their manner, guessed not. Two of the women appeared to be engaged in a sharp exchange. When the third spoke, it was in English, with a pronounced accent but an intonation that suggested she had learned the language from an American. Her voice was higher than the others', nasal and shrill as if something ugly had been trapped inside a beautiful shell from which it was determined to force its way out. She said, "I can't wait to see it. I'm told he has the longest one in the world."

"Once upon a time perhaps," replied the woman farthest from her, "but no longer. Actually, it's not even in the top ten anymore. Believe me, I've seen them all."

"We believe you," replied the woman in the middle. "How long would you say it was, then?"

"Not even four hundred feet. The number three hundred sixty sticks in my mind for some reason, but I'm not sure why."

"Perhaps from geometry," said the woman who had switched the conversation into English. "Anyway, what does it matter? The longer the boat, the shorter the owner's equipment. That's what they say, isn't it?"

"As a general rule, it's true," one of the women replied.

"Do you know him?"

"Santal? Our paths have crossed, not professionally. Why do you ask?"

"I hear he is very generous."

"With things, perhaps, but not with his emotions."

"There's a girl in Saint-Tropez he gave a pair of earrings from Guardi in Rome. Rubies and marquise-cut diamonds. I happen to know that she had them appraised in Monaco at twenty thousand euros. Not bad! Of course, he paid her fee as well."

"Word is he wasn't always so generous. But who's to say? The man's a sphinx, simple as that. There has to be more there than meets the eye. Why else would he be thick as thieves with Philip Frost?"

"I know who you mean," put in the girl who appeared to be the youngest. "He's very dishy."

"Tell me that after you've fucked him."

"I wouldn't have thought he had to pay for it."

"Men pay for different things. Surely you've learned that by now. Some— old-timers like Ian Santal, for example—pay for intimacy, to stay in the game. With Philip's type it's just the opposite. What they want is distance and power. Oh, they'll pay a premium price, that's true, but they'll make you grovel for your money. Your very 'dishy' Mr. Frost, for example, throws out his wad of notes and makes his girls get down on all fours, like cats or dogs, just to collect them. I'll grant you he has a pleasant exterior, all very correct. He's a handsome man, no doubt very professional in bed. But he has ice in his veins, darling, not blood. And Santal dotes on him. Draw your own conclusions."

Ty smiled to himself. He had no experience of whores and had never over-heard their chatter. Amusing and instructive as it was, however, he decided that it would be imprudent—indeed, very likely injurious to his carefully wrought image—to linger. And so he submerged his face and dove away from the pon-toon, swimming far enough underwater that by the time he surfaced he and its present inhabitants could not be captured in the same camera shot.

Cliffside at the eastern end of the hotel's waterfront, an outdoor gym of a sort had been established; a rope ladder descended toward the sea, a trapeze and circus hoops swung above it. Ty made his way to the bottom rung of the ladder, then ascended quickly and jogged overland toward his villa. The hotel phone was ringing when he unlocked the door.

"Hello," he answered.

"It's me again," Greg Logan said. "Where were you? I tried your cell twice and got the same recording."

"In the sea," Ty said, "swimming. What's up?"

"Slight change of plan: Apparently traffic is at a standstill. I'm in the lobby of the Carlton. It's all anyone's been talking about for the last half hour."

"Is there an accident?"

"Don't really know. It may be there are just too many people. Anyway, *pas de problème,* really, as Sid Thrall has engaged a tender. So can we meet on Santal's boat instead?"

"We can, providing someone tells me how to get there."

"*Surpass*'s tender will be shuttling guests from Antibes. That much I do know. I'll find out more and text you the exact time and directions to the pickup point."

"I'm sure the concierge will know the latter."

"Why would he?"

"There are other people going from this hotel."

"Well, why not?" Greg Logan said. "But how do you know? I thought you'd been keeping to yourself."

"I have," Ty said.

"Did a little bird tell you?"

"A couple of them," Ty told him.

Chapter Six

At a quarter past six, on the advice of the hotel's enthusiastic young concierge, Ty took a car not directly to the southernmost quay, from which *Surpass*'s tender was to depart thirty minutes later but into the village of Antibes itself, where he strolled the narrow, cobbled main street as many of its shops were closing. With his baseball cap and Ray-Ban Wayfarers on and his pace quick, he was not recognized. He reached a café just short of the harborside parking area. There he took one of the bent-wire chairs at a round table for two near the front. The café's blue shutters had been folded back, and the salt air and the scent of ripe cheese from the *fromagerie* across the street were delicious. Lingering over a *citron pressé,* Ty watched the curious parade of locals and tourists, of French and North Africans, Americans, Russians and more exotic foreign nationals that passed before him. Because no one expected to see him, no one appeared to, which was by now a familiar dynamic as well as one for which he was thankful. Of all the things that had marked his life before he'd become famous, he missed anonymity the most. Not always, but often, certainly now. He missed youth, too, but no man could hold on to that very long. Anonymity was different. You had to give it away, and once you had, the deal could not be undone until time had faded the public's memory of you or you were no longer, in the flesh, the man the camera had once captured.

He kept an eye on his watch and with ten minutes to spare paid the bill and made his way toward the tender, past the berths of a dozen mega-yachts, each with security men stationed at its stern. Several had welcome mats bearing their ship's name spread out at the edge of the dock, but there was more suspicion than welcome in these sentries' gazes as he passed. To Ty's right, beyond the old stone harbor fortification, the sea was flecked with gold dust as the sun declined toward the Atlantic. At anchor in the distance lay *Surpass,* its cobalt hull and white bulwarks commanding deference.

To Ty's surprise there was no one else waiting on the pebbled concrete landing, nor was any tender in sight at a quarter to seven, the time he'd been assured by Greg's text message that it would depart. He had, he realized, half-expected the prostitutes from the pontoon, with a paunchy, hirsute, balding producer or two in their wake. At the *Vanity Fair* party, even on lounges beside the pool a few hours earlier, there had been any number of stars and moguls, not to mention eager starlets, who might conceivably reappear, champagne in hand, at a party aboard one of the world's most formidable motor yachts. But where were they? They couldn't all be coming directly from Cannes. Beyond the seawall only a few boats were in motion, all too large to function as tenders. Ty studied each one in the distance. Only the longest of them, a streamlined cigarette, appeared headed toward the quay, but it was far way. It was moving fast, though, and he trained his eye on it as it sped across the harbor like a sword upon the water at an incautious, no doubt unlawful rate of speed.

A few minutes later, its captain shut down its engines, and thereafter it seemed to glide alongside the stepped-down landing as if propelled by wind and current alone. The boat was at least fifty feet in length, with a sleek, low cabin beneath its bulletlike bow and a large aft deck. Its captain managed it with single-handed artfulness, looping but one stern line over a weathered cleat to hold it momentarily in place.

"Mr. Hunter?" the captain inquired in a voice—soft, feminine and English— Ty had not anticipated. "Of course you are. Will you come aboard, please?"

No sooner had Ty found his footing in the cockpit than the captain pulled in the line she had so deftly thrown, restarted the high-performance engines, and headed, at a less furious clip, for open water.

"I'm confused," Ty told her a few seconds later, as he approached the helm. For a craft of its size and power, this one was unnaturally quiet.

The captain turned toward him, a glint in her wide but wily green eyes. "By this boat," she asked, "by me, or by the fact that there aren't any other people?"

"All three, but I suppose it might be simplest to start with the last."

"Everyone else was asked for seven-thirty. Once we're aboard *Surpass,* one of the crew will take this boat back to the landing and collect them."

"One of the crew?" Ty inquired. "The way you say that—"

"Rather than me, though I could be one of them. I've certainly had enough experience."

"If you're not one of the crew, who are you?"

"Isabella Cavill," she said as she extended her hand. "In theory, the party you're on your way to is being given for me." She removed the captain's cap she'd been wearing, letting her long, auburn hair fall from it.

"In theory?" Ty repeated, memorizing the scene.

"It's hardly a secret that my godfather is a man of many simultaneous motives."

"Your godfather is Ian Santal?"

"He is," she said. The edges of her hair were now wet with sea spray, and she shook her head, lifting her face to the light.

"You're the jewelry designer," Ty inquired, "for Guardi, in Rome?"

"You've heard of it."

"Who hasn't?"

"You'd be surprised. Never mind, Mr. Hunter, you seem very well informed."

"I'm the curious type." Ty smiled. "Anyway, Miss Cavill, I look forward to seeing your collection."

"I look forward to showing it to you."

"Is that why I've been invited ahead of the others? So that you can give me an advance preview?"

"Hardly! You're the first because I'm a fan and I wanted to meet you. If I'd waited, there was always a chance I wouldn't. You know how people are at parties, especially when there's a film star and the festival is on."

"To tell you the truth, I'm still getting used to it."

"Good for you," Isabella said. "Now, tell me something else I've been wondering about. In *The Boy Who Understood Women*—"

"Did I actually lay down my life or was I simply in the wrong place at the wrong time?"

"You've been asked the question before?"

"Variations of it," Ty said. "The director wanted people to decide for themselves."

"I don't think you were in the wrong place at the wrong time. Something tells me you wouldn't be capable of that."

"You'd be mistaken. I've been there more than once."

"When you gave your life for that girl's, half the world fell in love with you. You must know that."

"From the cinema to the parking lot," Ty said. "A very short-lived, one-sided affair."

"Why are you alone?"

Her question startled him. He could not decide if it was innocent or blunt. He said, "My mother would say I'm particular."

"You're Ty Hunter. Surely a man like you can afford to be *very* particular."

Ty hesitated. "Can I?"

"I'm sorry," Isabella said. "I'm out of order."

"Don't let it worry you."

"I won't, if you say not to."

"I wasn't always alone."

"No surprise there, surely, but the way you say that . . ."

"She died," Ty said, before he realized he had. His voice choked.

Isabella turned from the wheel, her eyes suddenly sympathetic. "Recently?" she asked.

"Neither yesterday nor all that long ago."

"I'm sorry."

"She was a journalist—a photojournalist, actually, and a very fine one, too. In fact, she was just remarkable, so amazingly gifted . . . observant and brave. She'd won all kinds of awards for her pictures."

"What was her name?"

"Carolyn."

"That was my grandmother's name."

Ty smiled. "You would have loved her. And she would have admired your style, the way you pilot this boat. I mean, she had less fear and more spirit than anyone I've ever known. She died in the war in Afghanistan."

Ty's hand rested on the dashboard, and for an instant, by instinct and at a loss for other words, Isabella covered it with her palm.

"We're almost there," she told him at last, deliberately buoying her tone. "Watch carefully. You're going to enjoy this."

Surpass's bow was pointed into the wind. A smooth, elongated plane that rose, curling into a snarl, it appeared as menacing as a warship's. Isabella gave it a wide berth, as she had the stabilizer put out to the ship's starboard and now the one to port. Slowing her speed until the tender's wake ceased to disturb the sea, she circled in on the stern, where the ship's name rose in bold steel letters from an angled escutcheon. Two seamen in dark commando dress stood at attention on the low deck. As soon as Isabella had made the final turn of her approach, with no exchange of signal the seamen stepped away from the center, toward opposite gunwales as the gates of the deck drifted open and the stern itself began to lift.

Isabella steered the tender toward the shadowy bay, which immediately brightened as they entered it. As the stern closed again behind them and Isabella killed the engines, Ty was struck by the absolute silence that all at once enveloped them. When, in search of an exit, he stirred, Isabella gestured for him to remain still. The tender was at least four feet below the deck above, with no ladder in sight.

"Don't worry," she said. "It's all been thought out. That's how it is with Ian."

"Ian?" Ty asked.

Isabella smiled. "Very early on, he made it clear he preferred I call him by his Christian name."

"So he's *that* kind of man?"

"Men are one way or the other in my experience. Anyhow, who knew then that he'd become so much more than a godfather? He and my father were fast friends in their days together as young Cambridge dons, and after my dad's death he stepped in. Unlike my father, for whom the English language always remained a source of wonder and who was most at home in libraries and tutorials, Ian eventually strayed from academia."

"That's what the evidence would suggest." Ty smiled.

"He was too picaresque for it. I suppose he actually pioneered the idea of cramming successive careers into the same life: scholar, merchant banker, deal maker. Exactly how it's all added up to quite so splendid a life as the one he now lives remains something of a puzzle to me."

"Even to you?"

"Ian never talks about money. He's old-fashioned that way. He thinks it bad manners." Observing Ty's reaction, she added, "Oh, I've heard the stories, most of them anyway, about what a fierce, intimidating, enigmatic figure he is to so many. Knowing him, however, I discount them. The people who tell them are hardly friends or intimates. In most cases they've probably never so much as met him. Perhaps they've caught a glimpse, but, trust me, that would be all. What they are is either mischievous or jealous, or else they're simply people who like to hear themselves sounding knowledgeable about someone so famous and famously inaccessible. Where I am—and have been—concerned, he has always shown the gentlest of souls."

Ty smiled. He had no reason or inclination to dispute the opinion of such an attractive woman.

The tender was rising, although it was difficult for Ty to tell exactly why, impossible for anyone to hear seawater flowing into the bay, as though it were the lock of a canal. When the boat had lifted so that deck and dock were level, Isabella took the lead, and they stepped easily onto a narrow treadway floored with tightly woven steel mesh that both facilitated drainage and impeded slipping. The wall before them, in whose sheer metallic surface they could make out reflections of themselves, opened as they approached it, and they entered a compact octagonal lift that moved with the same eerie absence of noise as everything else aboard *Surpass*. Ty was certain that the yacht's machinery must have been installed with the double-resilient mounting he had encountered previously only on naval vessels, but he decided not to mention the fact for fear it could direct their conversation toward areas he had sworn never to discuss.

According to the lift's control panel, they were ascending from Level One. Apparently this particular carriage terminated at Level Two, but there was also a heat-sensitive square labeled LEVEL ONE—SUB.

"Sub?" Ty inquired. "Any lower and we'd be in the sea."

"It stands for 'submarine,'" Isabella explained.

"How dull of me not to have guessed," Ty told her.

"Go ahead, push the button. It won't work. It will only work for Ian. It has his iris stored in its memory, no one else's."

"I'll take your word for it," Ty said. "Have you been in the submarine?"

Isabella shook her head. "No one has," she replied. "It's there for escape in an emergency, not pleasure. For that, Ian has the tender we came in and another a bit smaller that's better for skiing, as well as a small sloop, several Windsurfers, and lots of Jet Skis."

"A girl could have fun."

Isabella smiled. "It's the name of the game, isn't it?"

"For some people," Ty said.

Now they were in a narrow passage whose walls were covered in soft, tufted suede trimmed with a bronze handrail and whose floors were teak-and-wenge parquet. It was subtly but amply lit. They followed it forward, several times making sharp right-angle turns before arriving at another, more commodious lift that took them to Level Seven, which was known as the owner's deck. It was smaller, more intimate than the decks below, sections of which Ty could survey from the guardrail.

"Ian?" Isabella called out.

"Only be a second, darling," came her godfather's reply from the recesses of his cabin.

When he appeared, he was wearing carefully cut linen trousers, a French dress shirt with its top two horn buttons left undone, a light silk jacket of robin's-egg blue and new espadrilles. An imposing man, he had a body that was thickly set and callused, as though from years of heavy labor, but he moved with an agility and a grace that belied appearances, and the lines of his face were as lean and chiseled as his well-known arguments. "There!" he exclaimed, as though relieved to be done with whatever preparations he had undertaken. "You are obviously Mr. Hunter, about whom Isabella has told me so much."

Ty shook Ian Santal's extended hand and, as he did so, stole a glance at Isabella, who seemed unembarrassed. He supposed she was used to her godfather's candor.

"Or about whom she knows less than she thinks," Ty said.

"Are you a keeper of secrects, then, Mr. Hunter?" asked Ian Santal. His tone was genial, teasing.

"On the contrary, my life's an open book."

"Called *People* magazine," Isabella appended.

"Watch her." Ian smiled. "She'll have you wangled into one of her adverts before you know it."

The thought had not occurred to Ty, and he studied Isabella, evaluating her flirtatiousness in a new light. Since fame had become a salient fact of his life, he'd met most types of starstruck young women: true fans as well as those merely infatuated by image, silly ingenues, blatant starfuckers, even desirable young women intent, owing to some unobvious insecurity, on proving their desirability at ever more rarefied levels. He'd thought that Isabella might be among the last group, or simply a rich girl at play in a world of men. He had guessed that she was available, if not exactly easy to acquire or hold on to. Now he wasn't so sure. Clearly she was setting him up—but for what?

"Are you interested in masks?" Santal asked.

The question took Ty aback—until he followed the older man's line of sight. Flanking the entrance to what appeared to be Santal's quarters were two vivid theatrical masks, the one on the right primarily magenta with chalk-white lips and brows, that on the left primarily turquoise with identical features.

"They are Venetian, fifteenth century," Ian Santal explained.

"They're lovely," Ty replied.

"What do you collect, Mr. Hunter? May I ask?"

"So far mostly memories," Ty answered.

Isabella smiled.

"I've just bought my first house," he continued, "but I haven't thought much about how to fill it."

"And why is that?"

"Time," Ty told him.

"Always the problem," Santal agreed. "Truth be told, I didn't take you for a collector—or, should I say, someone especially intent on seeing and appraising the collections of others."

"Why is that?"

"In my experience most such young men are either poofters or thieves. You do not strike me as the former, and clearly you've no need to be the latter."

Ty forced a smile, then hesitated. "I take it you collect masks."

"He collects everything," Isabella interjected.

"It's a disease, I fear," Santal elaborated. "One that afflicts those of us whose talents fall short of our aspirations. I suppose one might say we are aesthetes rather than artists. What we cannot create, we purchase. Sometimes, however, if we manage to do it well, we bring things together in a way that produces something if not entirely then at least in some part original."

Ty shook his head, as if to dismiss Santal's self-deprecation, but he took the older man's point. The movie business was filled with people who, having tried and failed on the creative side, had hung in—as executives or agents or even grips—simply to be near it. "Everything?" he repeated, glancing first at Isabella, then at her godfather.

"Yes, or almost," Santal conceded, "although of course in different places. Aboard *Surpass* I have only works of art from civilizations that border the Mediterranean: Venetian, Roman, Neapolitan, Greek, Turkish, North African, French, Spanish, you name it. Here they are together, as though the Pillars of Hercules were still one mountain, as though time and nature had not separated peoples—indeed, as if they had not separated themselves."

"Tell Mr. Hunter your theory," Isabella said. "You might as well. You're this far along."

Ian looked puzzled.

"About the film you plan to make one day," she prodded.

"'Once hoped to make' might be more accurate. No doubt now it will never happen."

"Oh, really," Isabella said. "When is the last time something you wanted to happen didn't happen?"

Santal demurred. "What Isabella is talking about is a story I wrote for her when she was still a young girl, just coming into her own," he explained. "It took place among a group of cavorting, hedonistic characters in ancient Alexandria, am I right?"

Isabella nodded. "The Society of Inimitable Livers, they were called. Antony and Cleopatra were members. They were a club dedicated to debauchery and excess."

"You came to understand that later. Back then I intentionally kept those facts hidden. Anyway, they were having a high old time when out of nowhere—literally—someone arrived from somewhere else. Not just one someone either, but an entire colony of them from another planet or universe, who knows? So this elite society and the people it disdained had to make common cause all of a sudden, because they had no other choice. People in that part of the world weren't very good at doing such a thing. They weren't then. They aren't now. The idea's mad, of course, but I love it—for that reason. I won't live to see it; I'm sad about that. But if you asked me whether there's one more thing I'd like to see before I croak, that would be it: aliens here or on the way. Entirely benign ones, mind you! Because I would like to see my fellow human beings get their act together and do it quickly. I would like to see a world in which it was not so plainly necessary for people to hold each other off."

Isabella fixed her eyes on Ty's. "There! What do you think of that?" she asked.

"It's quite a pitch, a lot to digest."

Santal glanced at the De Bethune DB15 Complication watch on his wrist. "Give Mr. Hunter the tour, will you, before our guests swarm in and you can't? I'll join you in a bit."

"We'll see you later, then. Oh, and please call me Ty."

Santal nodded. "It's Ian," he said.

Isabella led Ty away from the owner's quarters, beyond a whirlpool, to a teak staircase that led to the bridge deck directly below. From there, past a canopied outdoor dining area whose elliptical table was set for twenty-two, they entered a Georgian dining room whose long, polished-mahogany table was set with white place mats and sterling flatware for a similar number. The center of the table was dressed with elaborate candelabra flanking a spectacular silver epergne. On the far wall were mounted a magnificent pair of George II rococo girandoles.

"It's beautiful, but it doesn't seem, if you'll pardon me, particularly Mediterranean," Ty said.

Isabella laughed. "This room's the exception that proves the rule. I think it reminds Ian of England, particularly Cambridge. But the prints on the walls are Italian. Look: Tintoretto, Burrini, Rosa, Leonardo."

Farther forward was a Moorish saloon whose walls were covered with Islamic art and upon whose floors lay Persian carpets. Its ceiling, leafed with gold, rose in the shallowest of Byzantine domes.

"Sometimes," Isabella said, "when one's been aboard for a while, it's difficult to know what port you're in, to remember where you've been or where you're going."

"Right now we're on the Riviera," Ty said. "At least I think that's where we are."

"Ah, the Riviera," Isabella repeated. "Once upon a time, we wouldn't have been here in May."

"Wouldn't we? Why?"

"It wasn't always a summer resort, you know. People used to come in winter."

"What changed that? The weather?"

"Don't be silly. It was the fashion that changed, not the climate. Picasso came here, as did Matisse and Léger. There was an American couple called the Murphys who ran a sort of salon in their house, the Villa America, which is just over the hill in the distance. F. Scott Fitzgerald and Ernest Hemingway came to it, and they all played together. You know how it is: Where certain people go, other people follow. Eventually Grace Kelly made a film with Alfred Hitchcock here and soon thereafter married Prince Rainier of Monaco. But you're right. We *are* on the Riviera!"

Music eddied from the long deck just below. As voices quickly followed, Isabella grew quiet. "It looks as if we'll have to cut your tour short," she said. "I'm sorry."

"Another day," Ty told her.

"Another day," Isabella agreed wistfully, then settled her arm gently around him, capturing his neck in the crook of her bare elbow, drawing his face toward hers. Her kiss was immediate, deep, and long.

And then it was over. Her hand was back at her side, barely touching his.

"I apologize," she said. "It won't happen again."

"But what if I'd like it to?" Ty asked.

"It can't," Isabella said.

Ty glanced at her left hand, as he had a few moments after she'd collected him from the quay and as he always did upon meeting beautiful women. There was no ring. "Then why did it happen now? Will you at least tell me that?" At once he regretted the almost adolescent plaintiveness of his tone, but, catching him unawares, Isabella had stirred something inside him, catalyzed an emotional, even physical reaction that no one else, he realized, had done since his lover's murder in that absurd theater of war that was now the Hindu Kush.

Isabella cast her glance down, then up at him once more. "Two reasons, if you must know. Because I've never kissed a movie star before. And because, as you said yourself, you collect memories."

"And so do you?"

"And so do I," Isabella said, then vanished among her guests.

Chapter Seven

At the foot of the stairs, focused on Eduardo Arrigimento, the Rome-based producer who'd backed Greg Logan's film, stood the three whores Ty had avoided on the pontoon that afternoon. In the soft light of evening and their expensive clothes, they looked so innocent that, when introduced, Ty elected to treat them as he would have Eduardo's nieces.

"Do you live in Beverly Hills?" the loveliest of them asked.

"No, but nearby," Ty replied.

"I want to go to Beverly Hills," the same girl said. Her diction was guttural.

"So do I," said the tallest of her friends.

"I've been there," said the last. "It's nothing much."

"There's Tiffany," proclaimed the first. "So how can it be nothing much?"

Ty grinned and set off through the expanding crowd, pausing only to hug Greg and greet Sid Thrall, to a less congested spot a short distance forward on the port deck. He had never been political or socially eager. By nature he was not a party person, except when a party consisted of friends, or at least people he already knew. One of the things about fame he'd lately come to enjoy was that it relieved him of having to make an effort he'd often felt unnatural. Every actor had an inventory of smiles, and as Ty Hunter, America's leading man, he had discovered that once he'd matched one of these to an occasion, he had only to select a spot where he felt comfortable and the party would come to him.

The port-side railing, with its view of an impending sunset, had seemed as good a place as any, and he spoke a few words to all who found their way there: colleagues of Isabella's from Guardi; film financiers from Dubai and Hong Kong; dowagers from villas on the Caps or in the hills above them, usually with their mute and handsome walkers half a step behind; established and would-be producers; artistic and business-minded directors; actors and actresses both ascendant and near death, famous and merely hopeful. The pressure of others waiting for his time kept any single conversation from becoming too involved, permitting him to dispense charm in small doses and reserve his affection for the few people who really mattered to him.

He was in the middle of an interesting conversation with one of France's most famous celebrity chefs, a severe, unabashedly ambitious character of about fifty with graying temples but playful eyes, when he thought he heard a dull thunderclap, then another, louder, and one immediately after that. Above the horizon, just over the culinary entrepreneur's left shoulder, Ty quickly made out the approaching helicopter, an EC130 B4, whose rotors, though quieter than most, had forced a pause in their conversation. The chef turned, too, and with most of the other guests focused on the aircraft swooping toward them. It was an elegant piece of machinery, painted in the same deep cobalt as *Surpass*'s hull.

"Sheer exhibitionism!" the chef exclaimed.

"Why don't we wait to see who gets out before we jump to conclusions?" Ty suggested.

The chef moistened his index finger, raised it to eye level, then brought it down in a single, rapid stroke in front of him, as if to say, *Score one!*

When the bird had alighted on the crossbar of the encircled H that marked the helipad on *Surpass*'s aftmost deck, its rotors dipped like gulls' wings and wound down to a still hush. Then, as the party's roar began to rise gradually from the interruption, a solitary passenger emerged from the starboard door. Tall and slender, in a gray English suit, the young man did not look up to return the crowd's gaze but moved toward the shallow overhang that marked the entrance to one of the ship's many passages.

Ty wondered who the new arrival was and where he'd gone. When, after a few minutes, the newcomer had still failed to materialize at the party, Ty concluded that he must be staying aboard *Surpass,* a notion confirmed when the same man eventually reappeared wearing a tropical blazer. Even in casual clothing, however, this object of Ty's curiosity maintained a courtly bearing, just shy of military.

As discreetly as he could, Ty kept his eye on the man. Instinct told him he should. He wasn't quite sure why. Or was he? Following two brief social interactions, from both of which he nimbly extricated himself, the stylish figure ultimately made his way to where Ty's subconscious must, he thought now, have known from the beginning that it would. Isabella, in midsentence, smiled, then slowly drew him to her. Turning from the revelers, she slipped both arms around the man's neck, leaned up, and kissed him with a passion oblivious to its surroundings.

Ty moved off in the opposite direction. He was not sure what game she was playing.

A few minutes later, where the deck ended at the open doors to the ship's library, he heard her call his name and stopped.

Isabella rushed toward him, the new arrival just behind her. "Mr. Hunter, there's someone I want you to meet."

"Of course, Miss Cavill," Ty replied.

"Don't be silly. Call me Isabella. This is Philip Frost."

"Hello," Ty said, extending his hand. He couldn't help it: The whore's insight filled his memory and disgusted him. This was the man who forced women to grovel.

"How do you do?" Philip said.

"Philip," Isabella said, "where do I begin? Philip is . . . everything to me. He's Ian's protégé and my—"

"Muse," Philip interrupted. "I'm her muse. At least that's what Isabella tells me."

Ty smiled. "I'd believe her if I were you."

"I do," Philip said, with a chill in his voice.

"Have you seen my new pieces?" Isabella asked them both. "They're on exhibit in the library. Come on, I'll show you."

"Lead the way," Ty said.

Philip nodded. "I can see where this is going," he said. "In no time you'll be the new male face of Guardi."

"I'm afraid not," Ty said.

"And why is that?"

"I don't do ads."

"What a luxurious position to find oneself in," Philip said.

"Except in Asia," Ty said.

"I'm sure the market there is different," Philip said.

"They take a more positive view of actors advertising," Ty said.

Isabella paused. "You mean they don't fear that commerce corrupts art?" she asked.

"No," Ty said. "I suppose they don't."

"Tell me," Philip inquired. "How long are you in Europe?"

"I leave the day after tomorrow. I'm here to help a friend's film, in which I had a very unimportant part, at the festival."

"That's too bad," Philip continued.

"It really is," Isabella added. "Otherwise you could have joined us for a cruise."

"Thank you," Ty said, "but I have a house waiting."

"The one you just bought?" Isabella asked. Then, directing her smile to Philip, she added, "I brought Mr. Hunter out on the tender."

"Did you? That was thoughtful."

"No it wasn't. You know I'm a fan."

"Just teasing," Philip said, and laughed quickly. "I know you are."

Ty examined Isabella's eyes. Why had she kissed him, led him on, then dropped him? Was it freedom she wanted or merely proof that she could have it? Was she trying to make Philip jealous or playing to the crowd she must have known would be watching? He said, "It's an old wreck, really, that I've bought. A great eclectic mansion in the most beautiful canyon, but it needs an awful lot of work, and now's the time."

"Are you working on another film?" Philip asked, almost idly, but piquing Isabella's attention.

"Not at the moment," Ty replied. "I've just finished four in a row. To be honest, I need a break before I decide what I want to do next."

"Who you want to be, you mean," Philip added.

"Yes, in a way," Ty said, "exactly."

"It makes perfect sense," Philip said.

"Can't your house wait a week or two?" Isabella asked, with more politesse than expectation in her voice.

"I wish it could, but I have whole teams lined up: architects and builders, not to mention a decorator and landscapers. You know the drill. One thing can't be done without the other, and if you don't get the first things started . . ."

"I can only imagine," Isabella agreed.

"Plus, I have to make a stop on the way." No sooner had the phrase escaped his mouth than Ty caught himself. For it was an engagement he'd been asked, indeed cautioned, not to discuss. The invitation had arrived, as if out of nowhere, during his first afternoon at the Hôtel du Cap. His agent, Netty Fleiderfleiss, had called from Los Angeles in a state of high excitement.

"'On the way,'" Isabella repeated. "That's a curious way of putting it."

"In New York," Ty dissembled, "which means I can't fly over the pole, so the whole trip is that much longer. But it's business. If it weren't, I wouldn't do it, not in a million years."

"Well, it all sounds very glamorous, doesn't it, Philip?"

"*Very* glamorous," Philip told her.

"What do you do, Mr. Frost?" Ty asked.

Philip hesitated. "A little of this, a little of that," he ventured. "Dreary stuff in comparison to your world."

"Philip's a diplomat," Isabella said, "a banker-turned-diplomat, who may be about to turn banker again."

"A strange destiny for a man who trained as a physicist, wouldn't you say?"

"I don't know," Ty said. "Life's full of tricks."

Chapter Eight

Outside the owner's cabin five minutes later, Philip took a seat on a curved banquette open to the sky. The human music of the party floated upward, but he did his best to put it out of his mind, to hear only the soft lap of the sea against *Surpass*'s hull and stabilizers. He had always preferred to concentrate in silence or, at minimum, in the absence of others' words. He liked the Med, relished its soft, sweet, careless ways. Indeed, there had been times when he wished he had been born along its shore, heir to its beneficent maternal vision of a God who provided her children with the most temperate of climates as well as uncomplicated laughter and the ready availability of carnal love. Alas, he hadn't! The genes he'd been selected to bear were those of hunters of wild beasts in dark forests, evaders of stags and lightning. Their God had forever dwelt in the sky, beyond ever re-forming clouds, producing thunder at twilight to rouse them from any episodes of disobedience or laxity. No man, not even one possessed of Philip's fortitude, could by any act of will convert himself into the product of a separate, equally ancient history or set of expectations.

When Ian finally appeared from his cabin, he said, "I am sorry to have kept you."

Philip stood. "Actually, it's quite the reverse."

Ian nodded his acceptance of Philip's apology and beckoned the younger man to follow, past the mounted Venetian masks into a study lined with floor-to-ceiling bookshelves, its walls covered with green mohair velvet and its floor by a Turkish rug. Once inside, Ian closed the door, then took a seat at his enormous Chippendale desk. "Can I tempt you?" he inquired.

Philip demurred as Ian chose a cigar, a Cohiba Robusto.

"You don't mind?" Ian asked.

"You know I don't," Philip replied.

When the cigar had been lit, Ian said, "Our friends in Naples, how are they?"

"Much of a muchness," Philip told him. "One can never be sure if they are genuinely curious or if they've simply come to take for granted that feigning curiosity raises their price."

"Go on."

"Not that I'm complaining, mind you. It's a lovely port to work in, deliciously corrupt."

"And that corruption can cost precious time," Ian said, "which I'm sure is what delayed you."

Philip sighed in agreement.

Ian said, "I have to admit it can be amusing. The last time I was there, an American woman, who was obviously a major heiress, was staying at the same hotel. She had her very large family with her. On their way to the airport, a scooter pulled up next to the passenger side of her limousine and its driver threw a rock through the car's window and snatched the handbag from her lap before speeding off. As it happens, she had all their passports and air tickets in that bag, which left her with no choice but to order that the car immediately turn around. By the time they'd got back to the hotel, her handbag was already in the possession of the hall porter, who discreetly asked if he might have a word with her. The money was gone, naturally, he explained, but the remaining contents, including of course those passports and tickets, could be reclaimed for a small ransom. As you say, there's something delicious about such seamless corruption."

"One has to remain on guard, but it has its uses, certainly," Philip assented. "Our cargo made its way there, disguised on the first leg as building supplies, then as level-three turbines bound in due course for the Southern Hemisphere, some for Africa, more for Latin America—in other words, machinery that's a bit stale for Europe, past its sell-by date, not worth paying too much attention to."

"But you are telling me—suggesting, rather—that someone did pay attention?"

"We'll never know for sure. Whatever leaves Russia arouses interest. Not to worry. The fact that it bore the Claussen imprimatur or at least the imprimatur of the Claussen subsidiary that's partnered with the Russian outfit went a long way toward allaying suspicion. You were right about that."

"Poor Billy," Ian said.

"I still can't believe it," Philip said.

"*There* was a man who appreciated life, a man who was never afraid. He would go where angels feared to tread. As long as I'd known him, that was the case. Rather a lot of people would have instantly backed off anything having to do with Russia. Not Billy. He saw the potential in developing there from the get-go. It excited him. You could see that in his eyes. I don't know who said or did what that caused him to change his mind so abruptly. I asked him, naturally, but he was vague about it. Sometimes cultural divides are too wide to be bridged, I suppose. Or perhaps that was simply the excuse he manufactured and his real reasons had more to do with the state of his own business than with us or any of our people."

"You don't think he had become suspicious?"

"Not for a moment. If he had, he would have alerted the authorities."

"He was playing one game. We were playing another. You don't believe that a man as clever as Billy would have figured that out?"

"Trust me, Philip. The way Billy would have seen it, this was just another in a long succession of profitable deals between us. I put him next to a juicy project, he paid me a handsome fee: business as usual. If he'd grown nervous, it was over something else."

"I defer to you. I never met the man."

"You would have enjoyed him. Anyway, it's a pity he couldn't have had a longer, better final act."

"If Claussen had lived and actually had parted ways with us—" Philip ventured.

But Ian stopped him. "We would have found other cover without too much difficulty. There is, after all, an enticing profit to be made on that peninsula."

"What other cover could have been as immaculate as Claussen's?"

Ian regarded Philip with sudden circumspection. "We might have been forced to accept a somewhat higher level of risk. So what?"

"Very bad timing for Billy, to say the least," Philip said, "but it did play into our hands. That's all I was suggesting."

"The world's gone mad," Ian said. "At least too many of the people in it have."

Philip nodded then resumed, "Of course, the fact that our cargo is bound where it is bound rather than, say, to Tunis or Algiers was also useful. And there *were* building supplies and there *were* turbines, lots of both scattered throughout, in case anyone looked, which they didn't. Why would they when it could only complicate matters and they're being paid to keep out of the picture?"

"I'm still not sure I understand the reason for the delay."

"There were a few more—unanticipated—palms to grease, a few more minds to set at rest, that's all."

"Where? In the Bosporus?"

"Inevitably in the Bosporus, and also at Gallipoli and Çanakkale. All very matter-of-fact."

"Why do you imagine *they* might have been suspicious?"

"These are people who do not think conceptually. They think practically. Contraband is their stock in trade. They wouldn't understand any other kind of shipment, but there is contraband fashion, which is a specialty of the Camorra. Then, in addition to drugs, of course, there are contraband videos, software, arms, meaning guns or perhaps grenades; really, contraband everything. All appear on their schedule of tariffs. Their concern is that higher-tariff merchandise not move under the guise of anything less."

Ian drew a long puff on his Robusto, exhaled it carefully. "Therefore you paid the going price for guns?"

"Not quite. To do so, especially too readily, might have gotten them thinking: What could be more valuable than Russian guns?"

"Very cunning."

"One is careful, nothing more. They wouldn't have leaped to the right conclusion. It's too far above their pay grade. But any conclusion might have gotten them interested in opening a crate or two, and if they happened to open the wrong one, then I would have had to depend on their not recognizing what they saw. Not a bad bet, even then. We had layers of disguise to rely on. By the time they'd left the train, our three pieces of cargo looked, as you know, like used generators. And they were so marked. As such, they were not things anyone had any use for any longer. Not at all good enough for the new Russia. Somewhere before they entered the Bosporus, they had become, to the eye if not a more practical test, run-of-the-mill turbines in need of reconditioning."

"How did you doctor the manifests?"

"That wasn't necessary," Philip explained. "Secondhand engines, generators, and turbines fall into the same category. They're designated by the same code."

"That's fortuitous."

"Nothing's fortuitous."

Ian laughed briefly, perched his elbow on the edge of his desk. "Do we have an estimated time of arrival?"

"Surely that's the last thing we want until our friends on the other end of this transaction are ready."

Ian nodded. "I was simply testing you. There is no margin for error in a deal of this nature."

"Has there ever been a deal of this nature?"

"An interesting question, to which my answer must be an emphatic no. Neither the opportunity nor the appetite to seize it and, by doing so, shoulder such astounding risk has ever previously presented itself."

"Nor has anyone brought your imagination to bear on such a set of events," Philip offered flatteringly. "In effect, you created your own opportunity."

"One mostly does," Ian reflected. "When a moment in history arrived on one's doorstep, I extrapolated well from it. That's as far as I am willing to go—and that was the easy part. The hard part will be seeing it through without drawing the attention of those who might seek to take our bounty off our hands. One false step now and we will find ourselves in the crosshairs of every security service in the world, not to mention other outfits that abide by even less forgiving rules. We are no match for any of them. So the trick must lie in remaining invisible. Even if they should draw conclusions that seem to implicate us, on inspection we will be as we always are: enjoying our good fortune and lavishing it on others in plain sight. Who but we could maintain that façade and at the same time, in an almost supernatural act of legerdemain, broker the greatest deal in history? By all means, Philip, maintain your paranoia. It's your strong suit. Just don't show it."

"I try to think not of the ultimate reward but of the job immediately to hand," Philip said.

"Right. This is your main chance, just as it is, if not my last hurrah, then at least my crowning achievement."

"In the meantime we have a plan to stick to. Where are our counterparties, I wonder?"

"The last I heard, they were still in Geneva."

"They can drink there. They enjoy that," Philip said.

"Don't be so sarcastic," Ian admonished him, "and don't underestimate the value of hypocrisy."

"I was at school in Geneva. I know the lay of that land. Anyway, they'll want more than three warheads before they part with their cash."

"They will. And they're entitled to it."

"Did Zhugov have the codes? That seems reckless."

"Only elements of them," Ian said. "You are being unusually direct."

"Until now I've had—and felt—no need to know."

"What's changed?"

"Nothing," Philip said, smiling. "I am simply interested in how the final pieces of the puzzle are to be fitted together. Having done my part, I think I should be allowed that much curiosity."

"Calm down," Ian insisted. "I was just having a bit of fun with you. You deserve to be put in the picture, and for more reasons than you think. First, as you say, you've done your part. Second, someone, other than an aging trader who's smoked and drunk too much in his time, must be trusted with the information. What's mine will be Isabella's one day, and I very much want that to be as much as possible. I've had many joys in this life, but no children. She's the closest thing I have, and she couldn't be closer if she were my own flesh and blood. Whatever happens, I'm trusting in you to look after her."

Philip stared directly into Ian's eyes. "I hope it goes without saying."

"I'm afraid it has to, my boy. I have no one else I can turn to."

"May I give you some advice?" Philip asked. "Stop trying to convince yourself you're older than you are. You are neither an old man nor one on the verge of old age. You're in your prime, with decades to go. You're seasoned. You're there—"

"Wherever 'there' is?" Ian interjected.

"Aboard *Surpass,* to start with," Philip said. "You can have anything you want. Half the young women in the world would think they'd died and gone to heaven after one look from you."

"That's very gracious, if not entirely true."

"You know what I mean."

"Only too well," Ian told him. "Now, about the codes: The elements Zhugov lacked were, alas, to be found in Moscow, where I've also done business."

"How long have you had them?'

"Is that any of your business?"

"No, but I'm glad to see you've taken my advice to heart. You're already beginning to think like a younger man."

There was bliss in Ian's smile. His ego was his soft spot. He said, "In fact, they were the first part of the equation. You do play backgammon, don't you?"

"Naturally."

"Have you had a look at the set on the gaming table?"

"I haven't," Philip said, but did so then.

"Have you ever seen a nuclear code?"

"I've seen the discs, of course. As I understand it, the codes themselves are algorithms."

"In a manner of speaking," Ian told him.

"Are you asking if I normally visualize shapes or velocities from mathematical symbols? The answer is sometimes, but only with effort and not day in and day out. There are people who do. There were a number with me at MIT, but I was never one of them. That's a gift you're given. You cannot learn it. It's like perfect pitch. Or any other gift that counts."

"The term 'algorithm' conjures two contrasting images, wouldn't you agree? The first is of a device, which in fact need be no more than a scrambled SATCOM phone. The second is a series of symbols, perhaps equations or formulae, perhaps not, that can be recognized by the weapon itself and allow it to activate; an infinitely elaborated version of your basic remote control.

"We are not talking about identifying who may or may not be in authority on any given system at any given point in time. We're a step beyond that: where a nation's command center is when it gives the instruction to launch."

"So the codes you were supplied were the ones effective at the moment Zhugov sequestered the warheads."

"Precisely," Ian said. "Think of it as a dialogue. Each party talks and responds to the other. But there's no going forward unless and until you have and have made sense of both parts."

Philip arrowed in. "So since everything's a game, you've hidden the codes in your backgammon set."

"Amongst other places," Ian suggested.

"May I ask where?"

"In a microchip just beneath the inlay on red's thirteen point."

"And it's SATCOM ready?"

"My customers would not be satisfied in any other way."

"What makes you so sure they won't use the warheads once they have them?"

"They would need a more effective delivery system than the one they now possess."

"In time they might acquire one."

"That would be possible only from Iran today, and there's too much bad blood on both sides for that. Tomorrow, who knows? North Korea and Ukraine have sold ballistic missiles, though, so far, smaller ones. Pakistan may go into the market. So might others, in due course. Somehow I don't believe that it will matter. True enough, the world—certainly this corner of it—is unusually combustible these days, but whether they style themselves monarchs or revolutionaries, we are dealing—as I've only ever dealt—with men who love power, not death. Everyone has his principles, and that is and always has been mine."

"I fully understand. I wouldn't be involved in this otherwise. But suppose they do sell them?"

"No doubt it will be to like-minded people for a very large profit. Who am I to try to squeeze the last drop of juice from an orange?"

"Who is anyone, really? Only a fool fails to understand that once a thing's gone, it's gone. In a way that's the first rule of business. The sorts of things we are concerned with, mind you, mustn't be allowed to go into the wrong hands, ever. But I take you at your word that these won't. Actually, I'll even go a bit further. The conventional wisdom may be that proliferation is entirely a bad thing. The more players with arms, the greater the chance one will go off, even trigger another, which will trigger a third. That's the accepted logic. Yet it contains a perfectly obvious flaw. Could not one equally argue that the wider the distribution of nuclear arms, the more certain it becomes that the result will be a standoff?"

"One could do so very plausibly," Ian said, exhaling the pungent smoke of his cigar, "and I have many times, as you know. You're preaching to the preacher."

Philip's emerging smile struck Ian, not for the first time, as that of a corrupted angel. "And if that is true, then we are not only making an indecent day's profit. We're also providing a service to humanity."

Ian's blue eyes glimmered. Such was the nature of the human condition, locked in its morphing death dance of evil and good, he thought, that no individual could be expected to fix it with clarity. "History," he said, "has arrived at stranger conclusions."

Chapter Nine

Early in the morning, after Greg Logan's film had been screened, Ty took a NetJet flight from Nice to Washington. At Dulles Airport he quickly cleared both immigration and customs and collected the rental car he had prearranged, a deliberately inconspicuous Taurus. As instructed, he followed the access road to I-495, the Washington Beltway, and the heavily trafficked inner loop of that to I-270. Within an hour he was exiting onto Maryland Route 15, at the Victorian spa town of Thurmont. Past the town he ascended toward higher elevation. A blacktop running a ridgeline of the Catoctins led him at last to a campsite marked only by number and approached by an unremarkable road through high forest. Some way down this road, out of sight of ordinary traffic, stood the gate to an unspecified military installation.

The Naval Support Facility Thurmont, colloquially known as Camp David, was both larger and busier than Ty had imagined: an unexpected, landlocked outpost of the U.S. Navy incorporating a village of cabins for the use of the President and his guests as well as barracks and facilities for several hundred staff. He parked, as directed, in front of a low gray-clapboard building that held a theater and a bowling alley. The camp's commander welcomed him there and promptly ferried them, via golf cart, along gravel paths that descended to his cabin. This bungalow sat on a slight hill rise a short distance from the President's. Beyond a shallow vestibule its floor plan centered on a comfortable sitting room of the sort that might be found in any good American hotel. Directly off it, at right angles to each other, lay two more or less identical bedrooms, each with its own bath. A sailor placed Ty's bag on a stand in the one directly opposite the front door.

The camp commander, who also bore the rank of naval commander, said, "Dinner will be at seven o'clock in Laurel, which is at the other end of this road on the left and by far the largest of the lodges. You can't miss it. Remember, out this door, left, and left again."

"Sounds easy enough," Ty replied.

"In the meantime have a nap or a walk or both. If there's anything we can do for you, someone's always at the other end of the telephone."

"Thank you," Ty said, then after the captain had departed, settled into a corner of the striped-chintz sofa. On the glass coffee table before him rested a bowl of fresh fruit. He picked up a small bunch of seeded red grapes. As he devoured these, he paged through the leather-bound guest book that rested on the same table. In neat type it listed all the previous occupants of Dogwood as well as the dates of their visits. Among the long record of officials and presidential friends were many names he recollected from the newscasts and newspapers of his childhood.

A few minutes later, Ty had ambled only as far as the bungalow known as Holly, on the front porch of which a man sat on a rocker, a book open in his lap, his face raised to the breeze, when he heard a golf cart coming toward him from behind. He and the man on the porch nodded to each other, after which Ty kept walking until the golf cart pulled to a sharp stop beside him.

"Mr. Hunter?" inquired the young officer at its wheel.

"Yes?"

"The President would like to see you, sir."

Ty's expression showed his surprise. "Now?" he asked.

"At Aspen Lodge, sir," the officer said, gesturing toward the passenger seat.

The large living room of the President's lodge was L-shaped, with a cathedral ceiling. It was paneled in yellow pine. On the far wall, panoramic plate-glass windows that could not be opened looked across the valley to mountain foliage in the distance. Nearer, an old plantation of tall evergreens stood just below a ridge on the horizon. Off to the left, a single fairway and putting green had been built into the hillside that fell away from the house. And to the right of this, a kidney-shaped swimming pool, bordered by flagstone, had been terraced into the land.

Ty was still taking in the view when Garland White appeared from a hallway at the front of the lodge.

"Good afternoon, Mr. Hunter. Thank you for coming," the President said, with more intimacy than Ty would have expected considering that they had met only once before. Politicians could be funny that way, Ty thought, having met a number of them by now. Either they drew you in or pushed you away; sometimes both.

"Mr. President," Ty replied, instinctively straightening himself. Garland White struck him as the kind of man who habitually appraised the weight and fitness of those he encountered. As with most politicians, there was an aspect of the peacock about him. Middle-aged, with dark hair grayed at the temples but dyed above, he was a couple of inches shorter than Ty. Although he did not possess the kind of looks that would have won him approval from casting agents in search of a leading man, his features were arranged with camera-friendly symmetry.

"What an absolutely glorious day Daphne has for her sixteenth birthday," the President mused. "She'll be thrilled you're here. Thank you for coming."

"It's my honor," Ty replied. "Thank you for having me."

"I hope you don't mind, but I was eager to have a word with you, in confidence, before you're surrounded by adoring teenage girls."

Ty smiled. "Just so you know," he said, "they're a little younger than my usual demographic."

"Women become more sophisticated every year," Garland White reflected, "which is a real shame. These days the only people who don't want to be grown up are grown-ups, am I right?"

"I suppose it's the old 'the grass is always greener' phenomenon," Ty said.

From the dim dining alcove where a swinging door opened onto the kitchen, a Filipino steward wheeled in a trolley bearing a selection of tea and coffee, bottled drinks, a brimming silver-plated ice bucket and glasses.

"Tea or coffee? Or something stronger?" the President asked.

"Tea, please," Ty told him.

"China or India?" the steward inquired.

For an instant the question threw Ty. "China, please," he replied at last. "Is that Lapsang souchong I see? That would be perfect, with no milk or sugar but a slice of lemon if you have it."

"Have a seat, please, wherever you like," the President told him. "If you don't mind, I've asked George Kenneth, my national security advisor, to join us."

Ty offered a faint nod but remained silent.

"Here he is now," the President said, shifting his focus to the front door, where a man of willowy frame paused uneasily as he balanced a stack of variously colored folios cradled in the crook of his left arm. Something about him was familiar to Ty, who could not for the moment place him.

"Sorry," Kenneth apologized, abstractedly and without appearing to mean it. His diction was cultivated, his manner, although he looked to be only a few years older than Ty, world-weary.

Initially, their conversation felt idle. Then, when the steward had completed his service and retreated, Garland White began, "I'm sure it's needless for me to say this, but I will anyway. This conversation could not be more sensitive."

"Understood," Ty said, although he did not yet.

"You have never been to Camp David before, and you were here today solely for Daphne White's birthday," George Kenneth added, settling into his seat.

"That's how I remember it," Ty agreed.

"Anyway, Ty," the President went on. "May I call you Ty?"

"Everyone else does."

"Your security clearances have naturally lapsed."

"It's been a while." Ty felt suddenly anxious, in the grip of forces beyond his control.

"After you left the service, why would you need them? Last evening, as certain facts began to emerge, I took the liberty of having them reinstated. You are now, once again, 'Yankee White.' Not that you will be speaking—or must ever speak—of these matters to anyone not in this room at present. The precaution is more for my benefit than yours."

"Classified information is classified *for* the President," George Kenneth explained. "Legally, he is free to disclose it to whomever he wishes. Politically, it could create a firestorm if he were ever to do so."

"No one 'not in this room,'" Ty repeated slowly and softly, as if conjuring all possible ramifications of that condition.

"Unless such a person has been authorized by one of us," the President said. "For all intents and purposes, that means no one else in the administration, no one on the Hill—"

"They're all footnotes straining to jump into the main text," Kenneth added dismissively. "It also means no one in the press, obviously, and no one in your family or in your bed."

"Does the name Ian Santal mean anything to you?" the President asked.

"I was at a party on his yacht only the night before last."

"We know that."

"Am I being watched?" Ty asked with mounting, barely concealable irritation.

"By the paparazzi, not by us," the President assured him. "Your photograph was on the wire."

"How much do you know about him?"

"Only that he can be charming. That he is a collector, of lots of things. That he believes and hopes there's life in outer space. And that he has a beautiful god-daughter."

"Santal's been on our radar for quite some time now," Garland White continued. "Originally as a trafficker in ideas, wistful ones for the most part, and for many years now, although our people were never able to pin it on him, we're pretty sure in weapons."

"Ever more nasty ones," George Kenneth said, stirring cream and sugar into a cup of steaming black coffee. "High-end stuff by now, even perhaps of the ultimately catastrophic sort."

"You won't be surprised to learn he didn't mention that," Ty said.

"I'll come right to the point," Garland White said. "Over the years Professor Santal maintained many friendships in Russia. No doubt these were born during his days on the Left, but when circumstances made it desirable to do so, he adjusted to market forces just as they did. The most intense of these friendships was with a Colonel Zhugov, who had responsibility for some of the Soviet Union's most advanced nuclear weapons. We have picked up chatter suggesting that recently an unspecified number of those may have gone astray and may now be on their way to market."

"What kind of chatter?" Ty asked.

"Neither reliable nor unreliable," George Kenneth answered. "It might be a rumor pure and simple. Or it could be a rumor based in fact. We have very little to go on, but what we do have suggests that some sort of deal's afoot. Buzz among the competition, you might call it—questions without answers, jealousy and curiosity, the usual vain search for an angle in."

"None of it from Zhugov, I assume."

"Not from his grave," George Kenneth replied.

"Forgive me. You hadn't mentioned that. When did he die?"

"What is today—Friday?" the President asked. "He would have died on Sunday, isn't that correct, George?"

"Of natural causes?" Ty inquired.

"Ostensibly," said Garland White. "He was sixty-three years old, retired. It's said he suffered an acute myocardial infarction, which he may well have done. Equally, he may not. Our Colonel Zhugov, it turns out, was a bit of a hypochondriac. For any number of years now, he's had all of his medical checkups done in Germany. None, other than simple chronological age, ever turned up any risk factor for heart disease, not elevated cholesterol or triglycerides or blood pressure, nada. Of course, anything's possible."

"And he did die."

"Thirty-four years before the age at which his father did," George Kenneth clarified. "Thirty-six years before his mother's age at the time of her demise. He hailed from hearty stock."

"I don't mind telling you I'm a bit confused," Ty said.

"When the Soviet Union fell, chaos, if it did not exactly reign, was more prevalent than many reports would have suggested."

Ty hesitated. "Are you suggesting there were loose nukes after all?"

"No. I am suggesting that we don't know, with one hundred percent certainty, that there were not. Very likely we will never know—unless one goes off."

"If the chatter isn't baseless, you suspect that Ian Santal may be implicated. And given that he lives on a ship and is very selective about whom he invites aboard, you think I might be your way in. Obviously you have no one inside, and as improbable as it might strike some people, you've concluded that I'm your best candidate."

"Ah, the fog lifts," George Kenneth exclaimed, not unpleasantly.

Now Ty remembered where and when he had previously encountered Dr. Kenneth. It had been a few years before. They'd been guests in separate segments on *Charlie Rose.* George Kenneth had been in Washington that day, Ty in New York, promoting his latest film on the eve of its opening weekend. They hadn't actually met, but Ty recalled that the onetime Harvard professor had been hawking his book, *Cooperation and Cooption.* Somehow the dryly academic title had stuck in Ty's mind, and he had judged it a distant long shot for the bestseller lists. Yet, to his astonishment, it had grown, gradually by word of mouth, into a cult favorite. A banner on the cover of the last edition Ty had seen in an airport bookshop had boasted, "Over One Million Copies in Print."

Garland White gave his aide a taming glance, then turned back to Ty. "Will you do it?" he asked.

"It would be difficult, sir."

"Is that because of your other commitments?"

"It's because there aren't any, actually," Ty replied. "A little more than forty-eight hours ago, as you know, I was aboard *Surpass*. I was asked there because my friend Greg Logan had been invited by Sidney Thrall, who heads the studio that released *Something to Look Forward To.* Sid knows everyone everywhere. I suppose it's his business to. Anyway, the party had nothing to do with any movie—or with the festival, officially. It's just that there were a lot of us in town, and apparently Santal thought we'd be a good audience for his goddaughter's jewelry. She's a designer."

"Yes," George Kenneth said, "we know."

"Then you also know that she is ravishing and saucy as hell and, well . . . I would have taken a real interest if her boyfriend hadn't turned up."

"That would be Philip Frost?" George Kenneth pressed.

"It would," Ty said.

"Frost is a good man," Kenneth continued.

"What makes you say that?"

"I was at MIT with him. Actually, I was a few years ahead. I didn't know him all that well, but I always admired the way he comported himself, and it was obvious he didn't miss much."

"Philip Frost, whom I've never met," said Garland White, "would seem to be one of us. He's been fully vetted and worked as a diplomat, on our side. It was Mr. Frost, in fact, who led the team that decertified the last installation that was under Zhugov's command."

"And apart from that being a very convenient coincidence?"

"He is dead certain there was nothing out of order there, which was in the Strait of Kerch, near the Sea of Azov, between Ukraine and Turkey."

"But?" Ty continued.

"Naturally, he can't vouch for sites where he was not present."

"And there are a number of those?"

"By definition."

"You'll forgive me," Ty asked, "but if Philip Frost is as unimpeachable as you suggest and if Santal is as dubious, why are the two in bed together? And if they aren't, why is he not your best route in?"

"The answer to your question is complicated," George Kenneth said.

"Perhaps it needn't be," Ty said.

"Do I detect jealousy?"

"Isabella Cavill is a lovely woman, if that's what you're referring to, but right now it couldn't be clearer that she's Philip Frost's lovely woman. The lady's made her mind up. Call it jealousy if you insist, but I'd have to put aside my instinct and experience to accept your positive views of Mr. Frost. There was a lot of innuendo circulating."

"What kind of innuendo?" the President inquired.

"Personal."

"How would you rate the source?"

Ty laughed, conjuring the Russian whores whose conversation he had overheard. "Impeccable," he replied, "although unlikely to be credited by any agency."

"I see," said Garland White.

Returning to his previous line of argument, George Kenneth said, "Philip Frost went to work for Santal after college, when Santal was running a financial house in London. That operation was scrutinized by everyone and his cousin and at the end of the day was found to be in perfect order. It certainly was when Frost left. After a few years there, he'd come to feel he lacked a sense of purpose, or that's the word. He'd made some dough, enough to free him, and decided he was better suited to diplomacy. He applied, was accepted . . ."

"But by then he'd also met Isabella?" Ty prodded.

"I suppose he must have," Kenneth said.

"And you believe that Isabella is the tie that binds?"

"We can only operate on that assumption."

"But you haven't quite convinced yourselves, have you? Or why would I be here?"

"If we're wrong about Mr. Frost," the President said, "and we'd put all our eggs in that basket . . ."

"I'll tell you what the problem is," Ty said. "I made a huge point of the fact that I couldn't wait to get home and take a break at last because I'd been working flat out for a couple of years. I told them about my house and all the work *it* needs and the plans I have for it and how much effort and how many people all that will require. I didn't realize it at the time, but I probably did so as much to convince myself as them. I liked Isabella, right away. I admit that. And I thought she'd come on to me. Then, when Philip appeared and she kissed him the way she did, I suddenly realized that she hadn't. She was just another flirt playing her game from the moment she picked me up in that harbor. Hell, I wasn't a movie star anymore, just a teenager who'd had his feelings hurt. So I decided it would be better to spurn the Riviera than have it spurn me. That's the truth, and I'm afraid it means there's no way I could go back there anytime soon. I'd have no credibility. They'd smell a rat."

"Suppose your house were to burn down," George Kenneth said.

"That's not funny," Ty snapped.

"Nor did I mean it to be. Nor do I suggest a fire. I meant it only hypothetically, as a possible cover story."

"We're straying from the point," the President said. "Let's come back to it. Why don't you let *us* worry about surmounting such obstacles? If there are missing weapons and there is a connection between them and Ian Santal, we need to know what that is and soon. And no one but you is in a position to help us do so. That's the essential thing to keep in mind."

"Me? I'm an actor."

"Don't be disingenuous," Kenneth said. "You're much more than an actor, and you know it."

"When you were a mere second lieutenant in the army and attached to Task Force 508," the President asked, "what were you then? You were a commando in an oiled-cotton sweater who possessed every martial-arts skill known to man."

"Not *every*," Ty said.

"You spoke Mandarin and Arabic and Spanish with a fluency that made you indistinguishable from any native."

"My father's doing," Ty said. "When I was seven and a half, we went to live in Venezuela. Then, from the time I was ten until I was almost thirteen, we lived in Kuwait and for a short time in Saudi Arabia. My father's company had contracts with oil companies in those days. He designed and managed their security systems."

"Be that as it may, you were assigned to a team composed of Army Delta Force,

Marine Special Ops, Navy SEALs, and British SBS, a team so secret it didn't have a name, only a number that would disappear the moment it was disbanded. And what was your role? Long before you found your way to Hollywood, it was to play a part, wasn't it? On that initial foray into Central America, you were not an American officer but a Canadian entrepreneur with a grievance sufficient to justify murder. Obviously you played it to the hilt and were scary enough that the *narcotraficante,* who was a Chinese Trinidadian, if I have my facts right, and spoke or would speak only Mandarin, talked at once, and so the contraband weapons, which were much less dangerous in that circumstance, were intercepted."

Ty remained silent as the President spoke. On the screen of his imagination he saw the deck of the ship they had boarded, the faces of men he had killed.

"And in the South China Sea," Garland White continued.

"Never mind," Ty said. "You've made your point."

"You're the man on the ground, Ty, the person we all agree we've been lacking. You're not what we call an 'invisible' exactly. Rather, you're invisible precisely because you are so damned visible. You've a reason to be anywhere, everywhere."

Ty could no longer contain his own laughter.

"What's so funny?" George Kenneth asked.

Ty inhaled a deep breath. "In my line of work, you get used to being pitched," he said, "but not by the President of the United States."

"There's a first time for everything," Garland White replied. "Do you know what your last commanding officer wrote about you? He said Hunter will do 'fifty percent more to make a thing five percent better.' That's it in a nutshell. You are a proven performer. And you're right: We have nowhere else to turn. If we're wrong, then it was all in a good cause. But if our suspicions prove not to be unfounded and the wild animals should get free of the zoo, if something does happen, what then, Ty? We would have no notion of what or where or when or who was behind it. Then again, at T plus one second will anyone be counting?"

"Granted, there's always the danger you'll turn out to be the cat we can't walk back," George Kenneth added after a few seconds, letting his eyes drift upward as though he'd discovered his halo was askew, "but what other option do we have?"

Ty contained his smile. The metaphor was spook language for an action that, once committed to, could pose consequences that were not easily undone. Ty had first heard the phrase from his father's lips so long ago he couldn't recall the circumstances.

"You'll have to keep your eyes open," the President said.

"When I was a kid, my father and I used to write detective stories," Ty told him. "Well, he wrote them, of course, but we'd sit side by side at the table in our club basement and every few sentences he'd ask if I had any ideas, which usually I did. Sometimes, later on, long before I ever went into the army, much less acting, we'd talk about those days. They were my childhood. I loved them. But by then I knew what he was trying to do. He was trying to interest me in his business. 'You don't know it yet,' he'd say, as if the eventual discovery would be one I'd cherish, 'but you were born to do this kind of work.' I suppose that after my accident and so many lucky breaks I thought I'd finally escaped this sort of thing. I was wrong, wasn't I?"

President White nodded. "We can't escape the times we live in," he said. "None of us can." Then he began to stand, and Ty stood, too, and they shook hands.

Chapter Ten

The old house, in which he had grown up and in which his father, without Ty's realizing what he was doing, had taught him the rudiments of tradecraft, looked better than ever. Far back on a wooded esplanade high above the Potomac, it had been recently repainted. A new shake roof had been put on the year before and new windows, where needed, installed the previous autumn. There was a new kitchen with wide pine floors, black granite countertops, and a Sub-Zero refrigerator. But they had not cost the house any of its mid-twentieth-century character. His mother had seen to that. To Dorothy it was not simply a house, but a place in which her dreams had finally come true, then vanished. It was the repository of the emotional relics of her life: her son's child-hood and rehabilitation, her husband's love and death. Ty could never approach it without experiencing both joy and melancholy, never drive—much less walk—toward the eastern end of Rialto Way without seeing his father, a large, vital man unknowingly in the final moments of his life. There had been thunderstorms that August, lightning riving the sky. A fierce, slanting rain had descended with more insistent pressure than Ty had ever felt in any downpour before or since. An old oak no one had thought frail had been struck, its roots upended in a front yard several houses down the block. The top of the tree had smashed into the hood of a silver-blue Toyota Cressida. On the sidewalk, limbs of the same tree pinioned a small girl to the ground. She lay hurt yet still conscious when help had arrived. Will Hunter had fetched his gas-powered McCulloch chain saw, confident that he could manage to extricate her. "Thank God it wasn't the trunk that fell on you," he'd told her. "You're going to be just fine—just fine—and in hardly any time. Hold on, now, dear." He had been careful, as he always was, severing the limb far away from the girl. His work done, he'd handed the tool to his son, taken a step forward, then seemed to jump slightly before going quiet and falling backward. He had not seen the downed power line.

At seventeen Ty could grasp neither the magnitude nor the permanence of what had happened. He tried in vain to resuscitate Will, thrusting all his weight onto his father's chest, heaving, crying out as he did. Again and again he exhaled his own breath into his dad's unresponsive lungs, as if the hinge of fate could somehow be manipulated back. It would be more than six months before the finality of that afternoon became real to him, displacing dreams in which Will Hunter still spoke and moved as he had for all of Ty's life.

"Let's go over the whole thing one more time," Ty's mother told him as they ate lunch at her kitchen table. The window beside it looked out on sloping woodland that from spring through fall could pass for country. Dorothy had fixed him his favorite, Maryland crab cakes, which she bound with a paste of egg whites and panko. "The girls will ask me about it, you know?"

"The girls?" Ty inquired. "Which girls are those?"

"At the hairdresser's."

"Oh."

"And at bridge."

"Of course."

"At the gym, in my aerobics group, *and* at yoga. They always ask about you. Sometimes they seem to know more about what you're doing and . . . well, especially who you're dating than I do."

"Or than *I* do, probably," Ty said. "You have a full life, don't you, Mom?"

"I fill it," Dorothy Hunter said, then paused.

"Could you fit in a week in California? Actually, as long as you like."

"When you have something to show me," Dorothy said, "sure."

Ty looked at her with complete understanding. What she was doing was giving him time, breathing space, as she always had, in childhood when he'd nearly broken under the weight of his father's expectations and his schools' curricula and even more so since his accident. "A man on the move needs a place where he can stop," Dorothy said, "and just be who he is for a little while."

Ty's thoughts hung suspended in the shaft of spring sunlight that lit his mother's kitchen.

"Ty, can I give you some advice?" she asked.

He nodded.

"Find someone to hold on to," she said. Then, when enough time had passed and he'd responded only with a familiar expression that suggested he was far away and lost in contemplation, she adopted a lighter tone and added, "So you still haven't told me anything about Camp David. Was the President nice?"

"Very nice," Ty told her, snapping back.

"And Daphne?"

"Sweet, and not in any way affected. Neither were her friends."

"How many were there?"

"I didn't count. Half a dozen, maybe."

"And that was all?"

"That was all," Ty confirmed. "It's actually a very simple place—nice cabins, fantastic trails, a refuge. We had dinner. They screened Greg's film. Everyone seemed to like it. We bowled a few games. Then the kids went their way. The President and Mrs. White went theirs. And I went mine. What's the matter?"

"To be honest, I was hoping for more . . . glamour."

Ty wondered if his mother sensed his evasions. "Sorry," he said, "but that was the extent of it."

"Well, never mind. Did you happen to notice those beautiful plates you sent me from Florence last year?" she went on, glancing toward the glass doors of her Early American hutch. "I think they look just so nice in there, don't you?"

On his flight to L.A. that evening, after two extra-dry martinis, Ty struggled to put the weekend into perspective. Adjusting the angle of his seat and footrest, he watched the G550's lengthened shadow skirt the cloudscape. It was hypnotic, especially as viewed through the plane's huge windows, and in no time, as he invariably did aloft, he began to see his life, both his past and recent events, with distance.

He had not thought as an intelligence officer for a long time, he realized, and yet he'd become an intelligence officer precisely because the way of thinking it required came naturally to him.

At Fort Huachuca—or Thunder Mountain, as he'd learned to call it during those months in Arizona—he had trained in detection and interrogation rather than code breaking. He had requested a branch transfer after four months of advanced infantry training at Fort Benning, Georgia, and been granted it, he believed, on the basis of his unusually precise and capacious memory (the same knack that helped him learn lines so easily), his instinctive ability to ingratiate himself and, most of all, his father—particularly his father's insistence that he be tutored in foreign languages, beginning with Mandarin as a child. The college-bound son of the local laundry owner had taught him for the first six years of his life. In adolescence Ty had let the language lapse, but in college, when he'd needed to raise his grade-point average, it had come back to him with surprising ease. The laundryman's son, it turned out, had given him perfect vowel sounds, a second tongue. The President was correct. Ty had soon discovered that on the telephone he could pass himself off as Chinese.

Through middle school he had taken lessons in tae kwon do, then judo and jujitsu. His father had called these sports "the final means of communication." At the time Ty had resented Will Hunter's iron insistence upon their worth. Now, though, he had black belts in three martial arts as well as an inculcated fearlessness in the face of danger.

Suddenly he wondered if he might have use for those skills and that fearlessness again. In his army days, he had played his cards as they lay, done the best he could at each job, hoping that somehow effort and excellence would yield success and satisfaction. He did not have any specific future in mind, but the nearness of death had concentrated his energies and given him a determination to fulfill his dreams long before they'd become explicit.

After his armored personnel carrier had flipped over and caught fire, he'd come to feel that he had survived by chance and was alive on borrowed time, without any real right to be.

It had happened at night somewhere out in the middle of Texas, not too far from Fort Hood, where they were based. He'd been along for the ride. At the University of Virginia, he'd been a ROTC cadet, and that had been the deal for which he'd signed up: four years of his life for four years of college and a bachelor of science, which still didn't strike him as half bad when he thought about it. If people wanted to know more—because there was no one to whom he could even allude to the truth and because he'd been ordered to flush certain memories from his mind—he would ramble. "Say the word 'infantry' and you think of boots on the ground," he would tell them, "men marching and all that. But these days it's all mechanized. Oh, we marched, but not nearly as much as we drove around in APCs. Just to give you some idea, the Third Army now has a hundred and fifty *more* tanks than did the old First Armored."

His whole time in the hospital and rehab, almost eighteen months when he added it up, he'd kept telling himself, *You're being tested, Ty.* The notion had taken root and fortified his spirit through some pretty dark days. Prior to that he'd been just another guy, not a cover boy. He'd been looking for the right woman, not a thousand of the wrong ones. He might have become any one of a hundred travel-ing salesmen or lawyers or midlevel executives flying in an economy section rather than privately. Or was his memory fooling him? He'd gotten knocked around plenty. He'd fallen for girls and been pushed away more often than he cared to remember. "Oh, I'm so flattered, *but . . .*" they'd say. Yet he was far from the only one. The same thing had happened to 99 percent of the guys he'd hung out with. What choice had they had but to make a habit of unrequited love?

After the crash, of course, things changed. Right away it had been apparent that a lot of reconstruction would have to be done if he were ever going to do anything as basic as chew or smile. So, naturally, when the option had presented itself, he'd thought why not let them improve a few things, correct nature's flaws while they were at it?

As he sipped his gin and the juniper berry freed him from his inhibitions, he wondered once more what it was that, despite his astounding good fortune, still unnerved him. Ever since his recovery, he'd worn his face as a mask. He couldn't help it. It was this new face that had brought him into focus for Greg Logan and that had eventually brought him fame, then fortune. But was his public in love with someone who only appeared to be Ty Hunter? Would anyone—or could he even enable anyone to—see past the cut-out-and-keep boy from his original Abercrombie & Fitch ad, see beyond the man the world had come to know to the one only he did?

In a sense it no longer mattered. His life had taken yet another unexpected turn. Who knew where it would lead? He inhaled a deep breath, endeavoring to still the sudden conflict between his old training and fresh emotions. He was neither paranoid nor lacking a skeptical turn of mind. The imagination, which could be so useful to an actor finding his way into a character, could never be controlled completely, and as he contemplated the assignment the President had asked him to complete, he began to embroider one scenario after another, each more alarming than the one it replaced. The more he thought about it, the more inevitable it seemed. How could it ever have been otherwise? Despite the inordinate randomness and improbability of his own life, human nature remained what it was and always had been. This world remained this world. Simply because Ty Hunter had stepped aside from it for a delightful, carefree moment did not mean that the age-old tournament of good versus evil had ceased. For seconds, as he drifted off, stanzas of his father's favorite hymn moved yet again upon his lips:

> *Once to every man and nation*
> *Comes the moment to decide,*
> *In the strife of truth with falsehood,*
> *For the good or evil side.*

A man's past is part and parcel of his future, he reminded himself as he reawakened. The context of his or any life was inescapable.

It was dark by the time his plane put down at LAX. The driver from the car service, yet another once-hopeful actor fending off middle age, was waiting for him at baggage claim. They chatted until their abrupt amiability came to feel forced, then grew quiet again.

It was Saturday. The young were out in the warm and fragrant night. The soft tops of their convertibles had been retracted; their music pulsed and receded along the freeway, inducing Ty to put down his own window so that he could savor it more fully. The air, in which scents of the warming Pacific and lushly overgrown foothills collided, was ripe with the possibility of utter if temporary happiness that for a century had been the city's siren song.

They took the Sunset Boulevard exit from the 405, banked and wound round its curves for several miles until they turned left into a canyon past Bel Air, ascended Pinnacle Drive, and entered the gates of La Casa Encantada, which was now, improbably, Ty's home. La Encantada, as he had quickly come to call it, had been built in the twenties by one of the great stars of the silent screen who had failed in his attempt to transition to talkies. Far from the forbidding mansion Ty had expected when he'd first heard it was for sale, it was a cheerful, sprawling place, lamplit now but filled with sunlight from dawn through dusk. Its rooms were decorated without regard to its Spanish-Moorish exterior in a jolly pastiche of English and French styles of the last three centuries. He had bought the house with its furnishings, which had included low coffee tables and swiveling ottomans, three-legged chairs, lacquered Chinese commodes and other eccentric but socially practical pieces that had been designed by the well-known actor-decorator Billy Haines in the thirties and now gave the place a distinctly Old Hollywood air, the illusory depth of a high gloss.

He tipped the driver, turned off the alarms, left his cases in the front hall to be dealt with the next morning, and made his way immediately through the sitting room on the west side of the house and onto a terrace of hand-glazed tiles.

A step down beyond a hedgerow, pandered to by royal palms, a swimming pool of pink alabaster had been built into a ledge of the lush hillside, its privacy ensured by stands of spruce and eucalyptus.

Ty shed his clothes and dove naked into the cool, dark water. After ten laps he paused and looked up at the partially illuminated mansion, its intricate silhouette eerie against the night sky. He knew that, like much of the town and many of its inhabitants, his house was an illusion, a magnificent façade upon which years of superficial surgery had forestalled any intimation of the decades of structural decay beneath.

Irritated, even if intrigued that his long-anticipated chance to concentrate on renovating his home was to be disrupted by the President's unexpected request, he put his face back into the water and began the first of another round of ninety freestyle laps, turning at each end with the urgency and concentration of a natural competitor, propelling himself with a commando's power.

After drying off, Ty went immediately to his bedroom. His housekeeper had prepared it that afternoon, and he felt comfortable, if momentarily lonely, in the enormous bed. He fell asleep quickly, without setting an alarm for the first time in months.

At 7:43 A.M., however, the insistent ringtone of his BlackBerry startled him from a dream in which both he and the world had been much younger. Fragments of it lingered in his consciousness as he groped for the device on his nightstand. He had been a frat boy in Charlottesville, en route somewhere with his friends, but where exactly? All save the setting of his dream dissolved the instant he palmed his phone. The message he received was from NetJets, confirming his booking of an overnight flight from L.A. to London in three days. As he read it, his temper rose. He had made no such reservation, but had no difficulty imagining who had. He saved the message, then turned back onto his side in a vain attempt to recapture sleep.

Chapter Eleven

From the terrace of his hotel suite, Philip Frost studied the medieval façades and rooflines of Prague. He had arrived at the Four Seasons after midnight, so this was his first glimpse of the city in daylight, and almost immediately his gaze was caught by a small wooden skiff bearing an oarsman and his girl along the Vltava. High on the opposite riverbank, the morning sun dappled the crenellations of Prague Castle.

At twenty minutes to eight, dressed for the business day, he proceeded to breakfast in the Allegro Restaurant, just off the lobby. He was the third customer. The maître d'hôtel led him across the polished marble floor to a table for two, where he assumed the seat facing the door.

"Will anyone be joining you?" the maître d' inquired.

"Yes, one gentleman for certain," Philip replied. "And perhaps there might be another coming along a bit later."

The maître d' nodded. "Coffee?" he asked, handing Philip a menu.

"Please, black," Philip said. "Then I will wait for my first guest before deciding."

The wait was short. No sooner had the maître d' departed than Sven Lorentz appeared. Tall and balding, he had the aspect of an aging footballer.

Lorentz took his seat and appeared immediately comfortable in it. "My, my." He sighed but smiled at Philip. "So it's come to this, has it? I have to admit it's sooner than I would have predicted."

"Really?" Philip asked. "I would have said just the opposite. Three years, after all, is a long time for a man to be doing the kind of work I've been doing."

"It's very important work," Sven replied, perusing the menu.

"None more," Philip said, "but arduous, and even the best intentions have half-lives."

"Are you getting stale?"

"Tired maybe, but not stale. Of course, the thoroughness involved *is* exhausting in its way. But that is not my dilemma. Think back a few years, Sven. There comes a time, doesn't there?"

"Could it be that all you need is to refresh your perspective?"

"I'm listening."

"There is more involved in deterring nuclear threats than disarming and decommissioning weapons, as crucial as those protocols are. For instance, one might concentrate on the emerging science of nuclear forensics. You have the necessary background, and you could do a world of good there."

"I don't see myself in a laboratory somehow."

"Logic suggests that the only sure way to dissuade a nation with nukes from selling them, or even giving them away to a sympathetic proxy, is to leave no doubt in its leaders' minds that whatever mask or masks they've contrived will be pierced, expeditiously, even from debris, and that once their identities are known, they will be subject to what President Kennedy, at the height of the Cuban Missile Crisis, so colorfully termed 'a full retaliatory response.'"

Philip nodded. "We both know there are better candidates for that sort of work than me. And besides, it doesn't pay well."

"It pays enough."

"I'm not a rich man, Sven. I might have been by now had I stayed on in the City. Mind you, money hasn't been my priority up to this point, but a man's life changes. How can I settle down and take on responsibilities without enough of it?"

"What's her name?"

"Isabella," Philip answered.

"Still?" Sven did his best to sound surprised. "The same woman for quite some time now. It's almost out of character."

"You've met her."

"Only in passing."

"Nevertheless, you're not blind."

"No, but love is. Is that what you expect me to say?"

"I'd expect you to say that in this case it obviously isn't. Let me be candid. I have enjoyed working with you and our group immensely. It has been the greatest privilege of my life, as well, at times, as one of the great pleasures. In all modesty I think I've excelled at the work, too. To use a cliché, I do feel I've 'made a difference,' which is satisfying."

"You have. You're my top performer, numero uno, but you already know that. To say I'm reluctant to lose you is to understate things woefully, but I do understand."

"And I am reluctant to go, but at the end of the day a married man, perhaps a family man one day, has to think of more than himself."

Sven shook his head. "As usual you win the argument," he said. "I concede. Anyway, congratulations are in order. When did you decide?"

"I've been in the process for quite some time."

"What I meant was, when did you make it official?" Sven said, tucking into the first of his eggs.

Philip smiled ruefully. "We haven't yet," he admitted.

"But she has accepted your offer?"

"She will."

"You seem very confident, even for you, Philip."

"It's my nature," Philip said.

Sven swallowed. "Well, I suppose you've every right to be," he continued. "It *is* the age of preconsummated marriage, after all."

"Exactly," Philip told him.

"Your replacement— No, I don't like that word; it doesn't fit. Your *successor* will be Rhys Llewellyn."

"So I've been told."

"He wanted to join us, but his flight from Brussels arrives a few minutes after my train back to Vienna departs."

Philip nodded. "I'm grateful to you for taking the time to let me tell you in person what I couldn't put in my letter."

"You're welcome," Sven Lorentz assured him.

"I will bring Llewellyn entirely up to speed," Philip said. "I won't leave you in the lurch. Don't worry about that."

"No," Sven told him, "I won't. Where will you base yourselves?"

"Probably in Rome to start with," Philip said, "even if it necessitates a bit of a commute for me. Isabella has a job there that she loves. I'll find something."

"You'll miss the buzz," Sven said, "the high of saving the world from itself, all that."

"Maybe," Philip replied, "or maybe not."

Chapter Twelve

When the landline at La Encantada finally jingled Ty stared at the old avocado telephone and let it ring three times before lifting the receiver. There was a point to be made. Even though he knew better than to ask what precisely was to be expected of him, much less when or where, he was still the number-one box-office star in the world, a man ready to be helpful but not toyed with.

"Yes?" he said.

"Ty, it's Zara, darling," announced the exuberant, unexpected voice on the other end.

Ty smiled to himself. "Where are you?"

"At your gate," Zara Chapin said. "You've changed the fucking security code without telling me."

"They just did it. I only found out myself yesterday. I was going to call you later."

"Nice recovery, but never mind."

"It's the truth," Ty replied.

"What's the code?" Zara asked.

"I'll let you in from here."

"What's the code?" she repeated.

"Be a good girl," Ty said, "and I'll tell you," then pressed the remote that retracted La Encantada's gates.

To Ty, Zara appeared to float, appropriately goddesslike, along the columned portico that led to his front door. Without breaking stride she crossed his threshold, clasping her arms about his neck, drawing him to her, kissing him fully on his lips, deliberately but with a passion more recollected than felt. He inhaled the trace scent of her usual perfume, tasted the sweet beeswax of her lip balm. She felt comfortable, comprehending, most of all trustworthy. They had ascended to fame within months of each other, costarred in a picture, become involved on location, then gone their separate ways, not because the attraction between them had waned but because their trajectories were too distinct and powerful to remain for very long entwined.

"So," Zara exclaimed softly, "you're really back!"

"Touch me!"

"Oh, I have, darling, and I intend to."

Ty laughed.

Zara said, "You know you've caused me to lose a bet with myself?"

"Which was?"

"That you wouldn't actually make the break, that you'd find another project, attach yourself to it, keep right on going with the throttle open."

"You're right," Ty said. "Your bet's lost. What about you? Are you working?"

"Not really. I have a few days of looping lines, that's all. My next picture doesn't start until September."

"Sweet," Ty said.

"Isn't it?" Zara replied emphatically, and let her hand drift lower to settle beside his.

Ty squeezed it. "Did anyone spot you on your way over here?" he asked.

"Unlikely. I came in my trainer's car."

"And how did your trainer get home, or wherever she had to go next? In your Porsche?"

"Bingo! I even gave her one of my scarves to confuse any paparazzo."

Ty looked at Zara and smiled. "Did your mother ever tell you that you were dangerous?" he asked.

"All the time," Zara said.

"I've missed you," Ty told her.

"I can't imagine why, with all the starlets in Cannes."

"Starlets." Ty sighed. "The stuff of schoolboy dreams!"

"I wouldn't believe a word of it," Zara told him, "except that there weren't any pictures of you in the press, and I'm sure they tried. I beg your pardon, there *was* one picture—that one with Greg Logan."

"By design," Ty said. "Otherwise I hid."

"Alone?"

"A gentleman doesn't talk," Ty teased. "Yes, alone."

"I guess I'm not surprised."

"What does that mean?"

"Only that you can be picky, darling," Zara said.

"What makes you think I'm picky?"

"You should be able to answer that question yourself. You're Ty Hunter. You were in Cannes. And you met *no one* who elicited an erection?"

"Right," Ty lied.

"Well, that's a damned shame, isn't it?"

"Not with a gorgeous woman like you in my life."

"Don't be disingenuous. We have each other, but don't. We understand that."

"We do."

"What does Nikki Finke call us in her blog?"

"'Friends with benefits.'"

"How original!"

Once they entered the cavernous bedroom, Ty hesitated, then, leaning Zara against a blank space of wall, kissed her more deeply than before. He had made love and even begun to relinquish his emotions to other women in his long search for love or solace, yet, from the first, with Zara his instincts had told him to proceed not toward commitment but in a two-step of abandon and caution.

Naked, it was Zara who kissed her way down his body. Ty placed his palms on the sides of her temples, ran his long fingers through her hair, losing himself in the moment. Finally, before it was too late, he drew her upward until her forehead nestled at his chin. Sliding his right hand gradually down her back, he cradled her and carried her to bed.

Atop her he smiled, slid inside her, moving in a slow rhythm that she caught. Zara leaned back onto the down pillows, and soon Ty settled another beneath her. He traced his fingertips across her nipples, raised her, went deeper, accelerating.

Afterward he leaned over her. That it was a classic film moment was not lost on him: her hair amiss, her breasts exposed, the expensive bed linen ruffled just enough. He ought to have lit a cigarette, handed it to her, then lit another. But neither of them smoked.

"What do you feel like doing?" he whispered.

"This," she purred. That was all. Before he knew it, Zara had reversed their positions, was draped over him, nibbling his lip. Her hair fell across her breasts, but Ty pushed it back. When he was hard, she squeezed him tightly, then lifted herself before at last inserting him and riding.

Ty found it almost unreasonably fortunate to have such beauty, so much glamour, and so few demands available in the same person. If a part of him craved more, wanted not to give up on the simple promise of love, another part was content with a reality that left him, at least for the time being, both satisfied and independent.

Afterward once more, as if to taunt him, his imagination returned to Isabella Cavill. He had not mentioned her to Zara. Now he wondered why. There had been nothing between them, nothing to hide beyond his incipient, soon-thwarted lust. Yet long before the President's charge, something about the young Englishwoman had frightened him, as though she might have power to summon feelings that could cost him control of his life.

"I suppose we should have lunch," Zara said.

"That's a great idea," Ty agreed.

"Do you have anything here?"

"All kinds of welcome-home presents."

"Sounds delicious! Let's have a look, shall we?"

They settled on cold chicken and salad and ate it at a round table near the tennis court, because the sun was directly overhead.

"Are you going to the Thralls' party on Wednesday?" Zara asked idly.

"I don't know anything about it," Ty replied. "I saw Sid in Cannes."

"Have you gone through your mail?"

"Not yet."

"I'm sure you were asked. Mitzi practically asked me if you were coming when I ran into her the other day. We could go together if you like."

Ty hesitated. "I'm not sure about Wednesday," he said.

"Why? What's Wednesday? Never mind, it's none of my business."

"Nothing important, it's just that I may have to be away for a few days."

"You're chasing a script. I can tell."

"I'm not," Ty assured her.

"I'm not that easily fooled, darling. So please don't try."

"I am not chasing any script or any project. I promise."

"Of course you aren't," Zara mocked. "Look, Ty, you may have fallen into the business by accident, but come on, you've been an actor all your life, haven't you? We all have."

"Until I was twelve, I wanted to be a spy," Ty protested. "'Agent 008,' that's what I called myself as a kid."

"Two sides of a coin."

"Not really."

"Have it your way, but you have to admit that both spend most of their time pretending."

"Actors lie to tell the truth," Ty said.

"Do they," Zara asked, "always?"

It was evening by the time Ty, alone once more, found the invitation to the Thralls' party. Nominally in honor of Mitzi's birthday, it was also a benefit in support of her favorite charity, the Motion Picture & Television Fund. It was bound to be an enormous affair, at which he would be but one star among a galaxy. If he could be there, he would. Otherwise he would send his regrets. As he tore open envelopes, separating bills from personal letters that had been collected by his housekeeper at the post-office box he kept under another name, he still had no idea what the White House had in store for him, much less whether Ian Santal was actually implicated in the theft of nuclear weapons or Isabella Cavill somehow involved. Were those weapons even missing? It was possible he might be going off on a wild-goose chase, not to save the world from nuclear terror but to correct an accounting error made by accident in a time of revolution.

He had connected his iPod to the speakers in his study and, as he worked, listened idly to Leonard Cohen. The tracks had been scrambled, and he was waiting for "Hallelujah," one of his favorite songs since high school. Right now the singer was doing a live performance of "Bird on the Wire," another track that suited Ty's ambivalent mood, and for a moment he found himself mouthing the familiar lyrics.

By the time "Hallelujah" finally began, the shadows outside had deepened, and Ty concentrated upon the garden as though he were once more a child, fearful that the world itself would vanish with the day. Even in his brief, episodic stewardship of La Encantada, he had absorbed a sense of its landscape, especially of the patterns laid down by the still or swaying limbs of its trees in different winds. He had always been attentive to his surroundings, but the unusual blend of his training at Thunder Mountain and eventual experience as a special operative had imparted professional techniques that intensified his powers of observation. They had taught him to evaluate every element of every scene as a potential clue, to register subtle as well as salient details, and to be alert to change, particularly when it could not be readily explained. To a young officer embarked on a hazardous mission, spotting the slightest variation in a current or wind, in vegetation or the placement of an apparently innocuous object often meant the difference between living and dying.

As he studied the garden in the waning twilight, his eye was caught by a sleek, moving figure far too dark and fast to be the branch of any tree. One minute it appeared to fall through the open air; the next, with the tenacity of a wildcat, it pressed itself against the steep hillside until to all but the most attentive observer it had rendered itself invisible.

At once Ty felt his old instincts, the product of the same intensive training, respond as he smoothly shifted gears from fear to action. Careful that his own movements not betray him, he retrieved his Glock 23 .40-caliber semiautomatic from the holster he'd designed and had installed in the well of his mahogany sea captain's desk, secreted the weapon in the waistband of his trousers, and let his polo shirt fall over it. Then, with calculated nonchalance, he moved across the study toward its exterior door. There was no time to call the security patrol, and, this being Sunday, his housekeeper was off. He opened the door, stepped away from its sill. It was a risk he knew he had to take, and he struggled both to keep his stride casual and to listen for any sound, to be alert to any sign of approach. There was none, and after two seconds he pivoted and took direct aim at the motionless figure dressed in black and clinging to the canyon ledge. Judging by the position and length of his lifeline, the intruder had been rappelling from the summit of the ridge.

"Drop your firearm. Then come down slowly," Ty commanded. "Keep your hands where I can see them."

The figure did not respond.

Ty said, "When you reach the ground, place your hands in the air."

Still the intruder did not reply.

"I meant what I said," Ty continued, his temper spiking. "I am going to count to three. I don't want to shoot you, but I damn well will. All right, one . . . two . . ."

Now, suddenly, the figure flew toward him, then back to the rock and did not rise again.

"Stand up," Ty said.

But the only response was an outdoor silence in which, Ty knew, stealth could easily be masked as nature.

Ty drew a long breath. "Stand up," he commanded again.

"Behind you," a soft yet threatening voice announced, followed by a tae kwon do knife-hand strike to Ty's wrist powerful enough to dislodge his pistol.

Chapter Thirteen

Philip had encountered Rhys Llewellyn once or twice before but had not recollected how stolid he was. The earnest Welshman arrived just before lunch, which, on the advice of their office's Czech liaison, they took far from the center of things, at the Huang Hue in Vršovice. This was a corner restaurant, in style as simple as its neighborhood, but the food, fusion with an emphasis on the Asian, was superb. Philip ordered Szechuan fish, Rhys garlic chicken, and they shared several other dishes between them as Philip briefed his successor on both Nunn-Lugar's and the Nuclear Threat Initiative's projects-in-progress. That Llewellyn had been chosen to follow him both pleased and irritated Philip. It pleased him because his vanity could not suffer the indignity of being supplanted by an equal and irritated him because he had valued his former position more highly than he ever could Rhys's talents.

They drank water instead of wine, took random trains on the metro, spoke only banalities in the taxi they shared back to the Jewish Cemetery, where more than twelve thousand worn or crumbling stones were crammed into a pitiful hollow at the center of the Old Ghetto, and which, from the Middle Ages to the Enlightenment, had been the only burial ground permitted to Jews. Generations of bodies, perhaps one hundred thousand of them, lay layers deep, the last interred in 1787 according to one semiofficial guidebook.

Philip bought their tickets even after the docent had advised that it would soon be closing time. The few other tourists in the disturbingly bucolic glen were plainly oblivious to them, drifting trancelike from the Old-New Synagogue or past the walls of the Pinkas Synagogue, which were inlaid with memorials to the dead of the Holocaust.

Rhys looked up from the Pinkas Memorial, his questions many but slow, his voice mellifluous and soft, as if the stygian gloom could somehow be dispelled by conversation.

By the time the new man had set off for his inaugural round of talks with defense and security officials from the Czech Republic, Philip felt satisfied he had provided Rhys as comprehensive and confidential a debriefing as possible and was thereby concluding his short diplomatic career as he had begun it, with a flourish that put him beyond reproach or comparison.

He was pleased with the way things had fallen into place. He had wanted to speak in person to Sven in order to assure himself that Sven harbored no suspicions and was withholding nothing from him. Sven had just happened to be in Prague on business of his own. And Prague, because it was neutral territory and in high season a destination that could be open to an almost infinite number of explanations, had seemed an advantageous place to conduct the other, more important business before him. When the fates aligned, Philip mused, success came almost too easily, but when they didn't, even the most heroic efforts could not always prevent calamity. For this reason he had always gone to great lengths to deny fate room to maneuver.

By example Ian had taught Philip his technique of conducting the most sensitive conversations in public, on the move, and in venues that no one who might have an interest in overhearing them could predict. If at first Philip had found the notion counterintuitive, by now he had long since come to see the wisdom in it. Not only did it handicap potential surveillance, it allayed suspicion.

Later, as the sun slipped below a deepening cover of cloud and Philip stood fast against a cloister wall of the Clementinum waiting for Andrej, he thought back to his handover meeting with Rhys Llewellyn and savored the delicious irony that he had taught the government the very tradecraft he'd learned from Ian.

Andrej, who as usual had preferred to spend his idle time in proximity to books, emerged from the former Jesuit monastery, now the National Library, wearing a guarded smile. With no more than a nod of recognition, Philip, staying just to his collaborator's right, assumed the Russian's pace. In the street the percussion of their soles against the paving stones echoed through the shallow urban canyons.

They walked with apparent aimlessness until at the end of Liliova Street they found themselves gathered into the crowd of tourists by the Old Town Bridge Tower. Borne left into Karlova Street, with the sanctuaries of the Clementinum to their right and the Palace of the Lords of Kunstat to their left, they continued toward the eastern gate of the Charles Bridge.

"For almost four hundred years, this was the only crossing of the Vltava," Andrej remarked as they came through the tower arch. "Charles IV commissioned it in 1357. Peter Parler, one of the most famous Czechs ever, built it. And do you know why it's so strong? Because they mixed the mortar with eggs."

"I thought this was your first time in Prague."

"First time in a long time," Andrej corrected, "but I have been here before." Then for a few seconds he went silent. He had been, he thought, to most capitals and also many tucked-away places in the near abroad. Once upon a time, his work at the GRU, the main intelligence directorate of the Russian armed forces, had required it. "Anyway," he continued, "there's great history to the statues. For the first couple of centuries, the crucifix, third up on the right, stood all alone. Then I think the one of St. John Nepomuk was the next after that. He was a great hero to the Jesuits, vicar-general of the archdiocese, but he'd angered King Wenceslas IV over some point of church politics, and so they tortured him and threw his body off the bridge. There was a lot of that sort of thing."

"Everywhere," Philip added.

"Sadly," Andrej concurred. "One supposes it is simply a virus that must run its course."

"Through different civilizations at different times," Philip added.

"Precisely," Andrej agreed. "Do you see those gilded words on the crucifix? They say 'Holy, Holy, Holy Lord.' But the church didn't pay for them, and neither did the king. They made one of the Jews do it to punish him for blasphemy."

"Alas," Philip said with a laugh, "we've been consulting the same travel guide."

On the distant hill, Prague Castle and Hradčany glistened, backlit by the declining sun. They walked toward it, losing themselves in the tide of students and tourists. Several young men they passed wore billboards advertising concerts in the Old Town. By the statue of St. Augustine, a young woman sold cut daffodils. Farther along another offered silk scarves, stylishly displayed through small holes in a white-enameled easel that rested atop a weathered pantechnicon. A gentleman in a frayed coat and a wool tie hawked postcards, film, assorted sundries.

Now, at last, they walked deliberately, still away from the Old Town, all the way to the steps to Saská Street by the Judith Bridge Tower and from there to the Malá Strana, the Little Quarter that sloped beneath the castle.

Finally Philip said, "This seems as good a place as any to do business."

"It does," Andrej agreed.

"Your message was cryptic."

"Of necessity," Andrej replied in a carefully modulated voice. "As I suggested, one has the feeling there are questions being asked."

"What sorts of questions?" Philip replied.

"Banal on the surface, but they are questions with implications. In my experience those are the most dangerous kind."

When Philip made no response, Andrej continued. "How could Zhugov have afforded such a large suite at the Palace Hotel in St. Moritz, for a month no less? Or to take that villa every summer in the hills above Monte Carlo? How could he have afforded the casino, to play at the tables and for the stakes and with the women he did? He must have known that an eye is kept on such things. So perhaps there is an innocent explanation after all. But the difficulty with explanations is that they prompt further questions, don't they? Was he in bed with an oligarch? If so, since when, and which oligarch, and on what deals? Let's face it: Everyone knew he traded a bit on the side. It was a perk of office. But to live so well, he would have to have traded more than seems seemly."

"Can you pinpoint the source of these questions?" Philip asked.

"No," Andrej said, "but they have been raised and repeated within the walls of Main Directorate Number Four. That much I do know. Could be it's jealousy and no more than that."

"Could be," Philip repeated, "although it's rare to be jealous of the dead."

"From what I hear, the supposition is that he may have profited from his friendship with your friend Santal."

"He wouldn't have been the first to have done so."

"No, I'm sure."

"Do the questions stop there?"

"Yes, so far."

"How can this be?"

"Are you asking if your name has surfaced? The answer is no, not yet—and, honestly, I doubt it will."

"Why shouldn't it? I am known to be close to Ian Santal."

"So are many others who remain above suspicion. But come on, you are on a different plane. As the people who evaluate such things would view it, you are there to legitimize him. He has sought you out for that reason, all the more credit to you! Nor do you concern yourself with the kind of boring, questionable but profitable material in which he might sometimes trade. You are ridding the world of danger. Eliminating, not adding to, its perils. The fact is that by its very conceit our operation lies beyond the imagination of the bureaucrats. The numbers are all in perfect order, and as long as that's the case, they cannot conceive of theft on the scale we've achieved. After all, nothing's missing!"

Philip mulled Andrej's reasoning. "I hope you're right," he said.

"I am right," Andrej said, "but I thought you should know."

"Thank you. It was the correct decision."

"It's the fear of guilt by association that protects you," Andrej added obliquely. "Having lived with it so long that it has become part of our nature, we Russians are wary of invoking it. If it were once more to become our standard, everyone would be in the gulag. So in a strange way it is your shield rather than your vulnerability."

By this time they had crossed the Čertovka, the Devil's Stream. On the northern side of Grand Priory Square, undisturbed since the eighteenth century, stood the former palace of the grand prior of the Knights of Malta. Across from it the baroque masterpiece Buquoy Palace was now the French embassy. In this tranquil square, Philip stopped abruptly and surprised Andrej, who had not realized that their conversation was over, by offering his hand. "It's a comforting thought," Philip declared, almost in a whisper, before he hailed a taxi that had just discharged its passengers. He waited until the old Audi had progressed to the far end of the square before announcing his destination as the Powder Tower by Prague Castle.

"Closed at this hour," the driver said.

"Never mind, I'm to meet someone nearby."

When the taxi reached the vicinity, Philip kept his eye out for tourist restaurants, then, settling on a pleasant, crowded one at random, instructed the driver to stop. As if in search of the party with whom he was to rendezvous, he shot his glances left, right and behind, making certain he had not been followed. Finally, with an air of exasperation, he advanced past the packed outdoor tables into a quieter, half-full interior of dark pine. Opera posters, many of them old but still colorful, had been placed into identical baroque frames and were spotlighted at intervals along three walls. In the distance, beyond the service bar, he spied the public telephone for which he'd been searching. There he carefully tapped in the number of a small hotel in Naples.

"*Estensione tre-due-sette,*" Philip told the operator without mentioning a name. When that extension was answered, he switched into matter-of-fact English. "We spoke sometime ago," he said. "Do you remember?"

"Yes."

"Good, because there has been a slight change of plan, nothing serious. For the time being, we've decided to go with the second option."

"The *second* option?"

"Exactly."

"You may consider it done."

"*Grazie,*" Philip said.

Chapter Fourteen

When Philip returned to the street, he walked east for several minutes until, satisfied that he was alone at the edge of the Ledebour Garden, he hailed another taxi.

"The Still Life restaurant in Liliova Street," he told the new driver, who found their way to the restaurant through a dimly lit maze of brightly repainted façades.

Aromatic with thyme and paprika, alive with conversation and laughter, the Still Life was a sequence of simply furnished rooms whose ecru walls were hung with oils and watercolors by local artists. Now, in the middle of dinner, it exuded that buzz that Philip had always preferred in restaurants. His table was waiting in a cheerfully lit corner

"I'm expecting a guest," he told the waiter.

"She has just arrived," the waiter said, gesturing toward the corridor that led to the ladies' room. When she emerged, Philip's eyes came alight.

Ordinarily, in Rome or London, anywhere he shared territory with Isabella or might have been recognized, Philip would not have dined with a prostitute in public, but Prague felt more hospitable to such a risk, as if its ancient shadows and centuries-old layers of intrigue supplied a perfect disguise. He could almost hear a haunting zither as he stood, with a kind of mock graciousness, to pull back his guest's chair. She was just right, as they all had been since he'd struck up his arrangement with Dieter Albanese, the fashion photographer who found them for him. Were he to be discovered with her, he would have only to introduce her as a colleague from this or that government or organization. He had no doubt she would pass.

He'd had his first whore at seventeen, having tagged along to Paris to stay with a school friend during the Christmas holidays, as his own father had been occupied elsewhere. The brothel to which his friend had introduced him, allegedly descended from the fabled Madame Claude's of a couple of generations before, had been located in a slim house in the seizième, not too far from the Champs-Élysées. The Corsican who'd admitted them had exuded a phony bonhomie, and the parlor had smelled of fresh paint. Finally a party of dewy ingenues had descended from the stairwell to join them. They might have been the boys' slightly older sisters, from similar backgrounds, bound for similar futures. Their deceptiveness had enhanced their allure. Philip had gone off with the redhead, the memory and even the taste of whom flashed back to him now, because until Dieter that Parisian adventure had set the standard.

"Paulina," the new girl whispered, putting forth her hand with assurance. "Dieter said he thought I'd meet your expectations."

"Ah, yes, Dieter," he repeated, "indispensable Dieter!"

"To so many of us, in so many ways," observed Paulina.

"He's very thorough."

"He is in love with beauty, that's all. What's wrong with that?"

"Nothing in the least, but it is not only beauty he loves."

"Everyone needs money—everyone who doesn't have it. To Dieter, people are works of art. Well, certain people, the ones whose genes have managed to express themselves in a way that's pleasing to the eye. And there is no more shame in trafficking in their beauty, before it perishes, than there would be in buying or selling photographs of them."

"Interesting," Philip said, "although I wouldn't beat the idea to death. You're Czech?"

"Isn't it obvious?"

Philip gave a grudging nod. "And how old?" he asked. "Don't lie."

"Twenty-two."

"And still a student?"

"Part-time," Paulina said. "I also work in a government office."

"Doing what?"

"Not much. I file a lot of paperwork for people trying to get back property that was appropriated by the Communists, sometimes by the Nazis. I distribute forms."

"And how did you find your way to Dieter?"

"He found me."

"I'm not surprised."

"Thank you."

"I'm sure Dieter told you the rules."

"Has he ever failed to?"

"Never," Philip said.

"He told me you would establish them."

"That is correct. You must accept it. Do you?"

"Yes, in your case."

"Because?"

"Like you, I suspect, I enjoy testing my limits."

"Is Paulina your true name? Never mind, what does it matter?"

"It doesn't."

"We dine as though we are two professionals, acquainted but not intimate. I don't enjoy eating alone."

"Who does?"

"Afterwards we shall return separately to my hotel. You will have a key card and precede me to the suite. Everything you will require will be there. From that moment forward, you will do as I ask, submit to my will in every respect, then leave before dawn, making no disturbance when you do. You will not ask any questions whatsoever. Should you be asked with whom you dined this evening, you will say that I was a man with Czech roots who wondered if he might be able to lay claim to something or other. Make up a name, the less precise the better. Out of loneliness or brazenness—who are you to say?—I asked you to dinner, after which you've never seen me again."

"What if we actually should see each other?" Paulina ventured.

"We behave as we would with any stranger, but the chances of such an encounter are low."

"I've heard of men who will only fuck a girl once."

"It would be wrong to take it personally," Philip said.

They chose the same dinner from the menu. With it they drank a bottle of Ryzlink rýnský 2000. It was a sweeter wine than Philip might have chosen elsewhere, but he was determined to taste whatever was authentically Czech.

"I *am* impressed with how the great families have managed to reassemble their fortunes," he said idly, "especially the princely ones, the Lobkowiczes, for instance, with their wonderful palaces here and in the country."

"It *is* impressive," Paulina agreed.

"And also ironic," Philip said, "since it is possible only because you Czechs were never strong enough to defend yourselves from your neighbors. Too weak to make a stand, you had no choice but to surrender and bide your time."

Outside, in the distance, a solitary French horn blew the two-four rhythm of Ravel's *Boléro* into the night. Halting after the first bars, the horn repeated itself.

"It must be difficult to imagine." Paulina sighed. "Isn't it?"

"What's that?"

"Being rescued from Hitler by Stalin!"

Chapter Fifteen

Early the next morning, Philip awoke to find Paulina gone as instructed, her lingering scent the only trace of her presence. After breakfast on his balcony, he exited the hotel, turned the corner into Křižovnická Street, and walked briskly toward the Old Town. Beyond the boulevard, large old buildings, some of whose exteriors were still stained with the soot of the twentieth century, shared blocks with others that had been recently sandblasted and immaculately restored.

Intending to exercise his mind as well as his limbs, he gradually picked up speed, and by the time he reached Staroměstské náměstí, the Old Town Square, could feel that admixture of relief and prospect that had always ignited his imagination. Along the square's south façade, he recognized, from ancient pictographs, "At the Golden Unicorn," which occupied the same building in which Franz Kafka had once attended a literary salon. That was the first landmark he'd been given, and, registering it in his memory, he began to move away from the colorful row of Gothic and Romanesque houses and head at first east, then gradually north, distancing himself from the medieval Town Hall Clock, upon whose intricate blue, orange and gold astronomical dial the earth remained fixed at the universe's center.

From there he continued along Maiselova until Kaprova forked to the right, then followed that until the first corner, where he had no choice but to stop for the traffic signal at Žatecká. This was his second landmark, and by the time he reached the amber light at Valentinská his destination was in full view.

He had slowed to an amble long before he reached it and entered the shop as if on impulse, almost reticently stepping down its three wide and graceful marble steps into a mahogany repository of music boxes the likes of which he had never seen. Oddly, except for the bell he'd triggered by opening the front door, the deep, vaulted room was enveloped in museum-like silence. Arrayed in its high display windows and upon the rows of shelves that covered its walls were hundreds of players of various descriptions, sounds and worth. One by one he tested those that bore signs inviting such tests.

"Are you the gentleman who called earlier?" the shop assistant inquired.

"Yes, about the music-box jewel case advertised in this morning's *Post.*"

"It's just over here," she told him, directing his attention to a small, elaborately inlaid rectangular prism of exotic woods he found it difficult to recognize.

Smiling broadly, Philip measured the music box against the length of his hand. He was in luck. It was not only exquisite but of a size and weight he could easily manage to carry back with him. "It must play Dvořák," he said.

"Forty-nine percent of the music boxes in Prague play Dvořák," the shop assistant replied. "Another forty-nine percent play Mozart. The remaining two percent cover the rest of the catalog. Why must it play Dvořák?"

"Because it's meant to be a souvenir from Prague."

"Well, it's a very nice one, isn't it? And at one hundred twenty euros, excellent value."

"Can you wrap it," Philip asked, "but leave one side open so that I can place a card inside?"

"You can do that now if you like."

"No, I can't. I haven't yet thought of what to say."

"Never mind, it will come to you, I'm sure."

When the transaction was complete, Philip thanked her and, once outside, began to retrace his steps toward the Old Town Square. As soon as he was out of sight, however, instead of completing that route, he turned, by habit, into a side street and walked a square block out of his way to avoid being followed before it came to him that, at least in this instance, he had nothing to hide.

Before he'd stumbled upon the fast lane to material riches, when ideas still mattered more than practicalities, Ian never flew. It had been a matter of principle. Having been schooled in England and settled there as a young don, his horizon had not stretched beyond Europe. He'd captured the sweet innocence of that period of his life, especially its summer holidays, in his first book, a slim memoir entitled *Train Travel,* for which he had not expected even to find a publisher but which was still in print in paperback. The book's original jacket passed across his mind as he listened to Philip on the telephone.

"The children are going to stay with their minder a little longer," Philip said.

"Are you sure that's wise?"

"It's only for a short time."

"The essential thing, at moments such as these, is to retain a Zen-like calm, to keep one's balance and distance from events."

"Quite," Philip agreed.

"It's all part of being careful. Where are you now?"

Philip looked out the window of the sedan he'd arranged through the hotel. "I don't know," he answered. The driver was following back roads, along which traffic flowed fitfully.

Soon, though, they were in the clear, and he could see that they were about to arrive at the Hlavní Nádraží with ten minutes to spare before his train. "The station," he told Ian at last.

"I am surprised you're not flying."

"My meetings in Geneva aren't until tomorrow. Besides, the idea of a train seemed restful."

"Bound to be, and educational. I've done some of my best thinking on trains, as you know."

"Only too well," Philip assured him.

"Mind you, it's always useful to bore our watchers, and few things succeed at that like a long, drawn-out journey by rail. I'm sorry I won't be able to meet you and Isabella in Rome on Thursday evening," Ian continued, "but I shall much look forward to having you both here at the weekend."

"Ian?" Philip said.

"Yes."

"No one's watching."

Ian stifled a laugh. "Isabella's father," he told Philip, "was positively brilliant at magic—as an amateur, of course. Had he not chosen to devote himself to the Romantic poets, he could have managed a very successful career on the stage. A thousand eyes could be fastened upon him and not a single one spot his sleight of hand."

Philip hesitated. "I take your point," he admitted.

No sooner had they hung up than Philip's driver pulled alongside the station's entrance off the Wilsonova.

Philip flagged a porter, and the two, ferrying his Valextra cases, made their way beneath the carved female statues that marked Prague as the Mother of Cities, then under the art nouveau station's high glazed and stained-glass dome. In the morning light, the large, clean, crowded terminal had the air and bustle of a market. A bouquet of baking bread, brewing coffee, bacon and cinnamon still drifted from the surrounding food stalls.

At the barrier to the platform from which the Geneva train was due to depart, Philip hesitated. The porter regarded him warily until Philip shrugged. Without speaking, as though the innocent mistake had been entirely his, he withdrew the ticket from his inside jacket pocket, glanced at it, then redirected the porter with his trolley to a platform two away, from which a train to Vienna was scheduled to depart seven minutes later.

Chapter Sixteen

Even sotto voce, Oliver's accent sounded, Ty thought, as though his old friend had ten thousand plums in his mouth.

They were on the tennis court at La Encantada, in the third game of their set, when the FedEx truck arrived just before ten-thirty on Tuesday morning. At the sight of Ty's housekeeper hurrying along the flagstone path with the overnight letter, they suspended play.

Oliver took the letter from her.

"What the hell are you doing?" Ty asked. "I'm sure it's addressed to me."

"Do you know what it is," Oliver asked, "or where it came from?"

"Not yet, obviously."

"I do."

Ty gave Oliver a sharp look. "You're playing a dangerous game," he said.

"We're on the same team," Oliver replied.

"We almost weren't," Ty said. "I almost put fourteen rounds into you the other night when you made that drama-queen entrance of yours."

"You have that backwards, don't you?"

"No, I don't think I do. You wouldn't have killed me. You knew who I was. I had no idea who you were. Added to which, *you* were trespassing on *my* property, not vice versa. You SBS guys are all the same: too daring by half."

"Never mind," Oliver said, "it's served you well in the past."

Ty's mind flashed back to the black-ops mission they'd undertaken together in the South China Sea. He caught his old friend's eye and smiled. Oliver smiled in return, that nomad's smile Ty remembered only too well.

"What's in the envelope?" Ty inquired.

Oliver withdrew an unmarked manila envelope and then, from within it, a smaller white one that bore a stiff white card of invitation. In black letters appeared the words:

The Master of the Household
Having Been Commanded by Her Majesty the Queen
Requests the Pleasure of the Company of
John Tyler Hunter
at
A Performance of *Something to Look Forward To*
The Odeon Leicester Square
London W1

"You need an excuse to be back in Europe. As excuses go, this one does nicely."

"How did you pull it off? Or did the President?"

"Cheek cut by charm," Oliver said.

"Seldom known to fail," Ty agreed.

"Plus, both the young princes are in the military. Let's leave it at that, shall we?"

At twelve forty-five, wearing loafers, gray slacks, an open-neck checked chukka shirt and a lightweight navy blazer, Ty approached the table for two in the front garden of the Ivy on Robertson that had been set aside for Netty Fleiderfleiss.

A waiter was pouring bottled water when Netty alighted from his Porsche and began to table-hop his way toward Ty.

"You scrub up nicely," Netty teased upon final approach.

"Thanks," Ty said, without returning the compliment.

Netty nodded, tightened his bow tie, then quickly smoothed the jacket of his bespoke suit. Ever since he'd arrived in Hollywood, half a generation ahead of Ty, Nethercott Fleiderfleiss had cultivated the style of a fogy with edge. Originally contrived to suggest a bridge between art and commerce, it had long ago become second nature to him, a half-truth he'd conveyed so often he now believed it himself. Understanding this, Ty had always found the shtick amusing, for he knew that it was founded on an encyclopedic knowledge of the history of American film as well as of the standard motion-picture agreement and its mutations. More important, Netty saw to the heart of things with unusual speed and resistance to distraction.

He offered his hand. "Ty," he said as he lowered himself into his chair. "It's nice to see you home."

"It's nice to be home," Ty replied.

"Well, anyway," Netty continued.

"Anyway," Ty said.

"You're in a nice place, a nice time of life."

Ty laughed. "It'll do."

"But it won't last, you know that? You'll have to make the most of it."

"What do you want me to say? You're right."

"I need you to tell me I'm right?" Netty asked. "Wait till I'm wrong, please! My only point is, you've got a lot on your plate: a future to think about, a house to spruce up, a personal life that . . . well, ain't what it should be."

Ty sighed. "All work and no play."

"All work and plenty of play," Netty replied.

"Have it your way."

"It's not play that's missing from your life, kid. It's commitment. A wife and kids!"

"Ease up, will you? All in due course, I've told you that before. At the moment what I need is simply to rest, to take a few deep breaths and assess things, make sure I'm still the commanding officer of my own life."

"So who's stopping you?"

"Things come up. You know how it is."

Netty nodded. "I know that in your career you're batting a thousand."

"Therefore I can afford a little downtime—"

"Take as much as you need."

"—without committing myself to any project?"

"Absolutely, without even picking up a script until you're ready and hungry to work again, but what you don't want to do—and this is my whole point, kiddo—is wake up and find that your personal life just flew by while you were looking out the window."

"Trust me," Ty said, "I know what I'm looking for."

"Maybe you're looking for something that doesn't exist," Netty suggested.

"I found it once. I will again."

"Not Zara?"

"Not Zara," Ty said. "With Zara it's fine but—"

"Such a shame," Netty said. "It would be so good for both of you."

"We'd kill each other."

"You'd make news, like Brad and Angie, Tom and Katie. You'd understand each other."

"A necessary but not sufficient condition for any marriage," Ty smiled, "no matter how brief."

"You don't want people to start wondering," Netty said.

"They can wonder all they like," Ty said. "When I'm ready, not before, I'll surprise them."

"Well, I'm glad to hear that at least," Netty said. "By the way, are you going to Sid and Mitzi's thing tomorrow night?"

"Zara asked me the same question."

"And what was your answer?"

Ty hesitated. "No can do," he said.

"You should," Netty told him. "You really should."

"I know, but I just can't."

"Why is that? Don't make me pull it out of you."

"I've had a better invitation," Ty explained. He hoped that Netty did not see he was playing a part. The point of this lunch was to initiate a drumbeat across the business, both announcing his departure, so soon after his return, and making clear the reason for it.

Incredulous, Netty shook his head. "Better than the Thralls?" he asked.

Ty removed the royal invitation from his jacket pocket and handed it to Netty, who raised the blue pince-nez reading glasses that hung around his neck. The magnets of their separate halves clicked into place over the bridge of his nose. "First the President of the United States, now the Queen of England!" he exclaimed after a moment. "What's next? Onto the throne?"

"I'm open to the possibility," Ty told him.

"I don't get it. It was practically a cameo role."

"What's there to get? People liked Greg's film. They liked everything about it, not just me. Fact is, I was lucky to be in it. I'll tell you what you always tell me: Never question success."

Netty shot Ty a severe look. "You live a charmed life. That's all I can say. When do you leave?"

"This evening," Ty replied.

He had one more stop to make before his departure, and knew he had to make it alone.

The Malibu Beach Colony was in high season but midweek doldrums when Ty arrived at Zara Chapin's house, driving, instead of his F430 Spider, the hybrid Greg Logan had given him for his role in *Something to Look Forward To.*

More contemporary than any of its neighbors—"Bauhaus by way of China," she called it—Zara's house was long and relatively narrow, a sequence of single-story, double-height pavilions drifting toward the Pacific. Overwhelmingly glass but framed in bronze, jungle wood and Venetian plaster, these pavilions were set back from a garden by deep overhangs that served to protect the house from both downpours and the sun.

Zara was lying on a chaise beneath a trellis on the lanai. As Ty approached through the living room, his sense of smell became confounded.

"It's not exactly honeysuckle," he said.

"No, but you're right. Honeysuckle is part of it."

"Part of what?" Ty asked.

"Today's aromatherapy," Zara explained, as though there should not be a need for her to do so. "Let's see, you also inhaled lotus and orange and lime blossom, vanilla, anise, white jasmine and . . . I don't know, darling, I can't remember what the last ingredient is."

"Ginger," Ty replied matter-of-factly. "I definitely smelled ginger. Practically tasted it, in fact."

Zara clasped the top of her bikini in place and sat up. "Why are you here?" she asked. "It's too late for lunch and too early for a *cinq-à-sept*. We've already said hello. So this must be good-bye. Is it?"

Ty hesitated. "Not if you'll come with me."

"With you where?"

Ty produced the royal invitation.

When Zara had read the card, she looked at him as though she had confused him with someone else. "Jesus Christ!" she exclaimed.

"Come on, it will be fun."

"Fun? I guess it will be, but I can't. I just can't. Think about it. How much notice are you giving me?"

"Well over an hour," Ty said, hiding his relief at her unavailability. He and Oliver had agreed that this simple, last-minute invitation to Zara would be the most efficient way to send word of his unexpected return to Europe through the community of actors and artisans who made up the creative side of the motion-picture business and the journalists and bloggers who chronicled them.

"It's impossible, and you know it."

"I know no such thing. Spontaneity's always been your middle name."

"My middle name is Gertrude, which is why I never use it."

"What do you have on your calendar that's better?"

"Sid and Mitzi's—you know about that. Also, my yoga instructor is due here tomorrow morning. She was having hot flashes last week, so we've got lost ground to make up. And just at the moment you will be bowing your scrumptious torso to Her Majesty, I will be working with my regression analyst—who I don't mind telling you is *very* hard to book, much less *re*book."

Ty looked puzzled. "What in hell is a regression analyst?"

"Someone who can tell you who you were in your past lives," Zara explained, as if Ty were a schoolboy who ought long ago to have mastered such facts. "It takes a great deal of experience."

"I'm certain it would."

"Don't laugh! We have exteriors, darling, but we also have interiors. And it's absolutely vital we take care of both. Just the same, I'll give you a reason you won't think frivolous," Zara said. "The day after that, I am guest-starring in an episode of *Entourage.*"

"*You* are?"

"Didn't I tell you? I'm playing one of those rare actresses whose career defies the currently diminishing trajectory of stardom. In other words, myself."

Ty laughed.

Zara reached up and kissed him, dispassionately, on the lips. "Fingers crossed," she said, "knees bent. See you when I see you."

Chapter Seventeen

To Campo de' Fiori, just across the Tiber and southeast of the Vatican, dawn brought a transitory quiet. With the young at last asleep in the wake of their revelries, for a moment the Renaissance returned to the quarter. Proud façades and vacant streets stood in stillness as, beyond the Capitoline, the Quirinal and the Esquiline, the sun, as yet without warmth, ascended. Along the Via Capo di Ferro, while the first stalls of the nearby piazza market were being prepared for the day's sales, Isabella Cavill slowed from her long jog. She knew the area intimately, even the textures and irregularities of its pavements, but now, deep in thought, she was almost oblivious to her surroundings.

She loved Italy, especially Rome, and had done well by herself here, but tonight would be the night that counted. Her collection, to be unveiled at a party at Guardi's retail palace on the Via dei Condotti, was to be her first since assuming charge of the venerable firm's design team.

On impulse she decided to enter the Santissima Trinità dei Pellegrini. The figures in Guido Reni's altarpiece, *Holy Trinity,* especially the crucified Christ against the clouded cerulean sky, seemed to transcend gravity, to rise as one observed them. Isabella had long thought this one of the most beautiful and haunting paintings she had seen. For a moment she entered a pew and knelt. She was not a Catholic, nor even particularly religious. She had been baptized and, while at school, confirmed in the Church of England. But rather than denominational, she had always considered herself spiritual, a believer that God not only had been but remained in the world and could be glimpsed there at odd moments, just as He could be in great works of art.

A few minutes later, she was back in daylight, running again, relishing the sight of Rome coming to life for another day: the jacketed businessmen on their way to their offices, the young mothers tending their children toward school.

By the time she reached her apartment, she had run over five miles, feeling simultaneously exhilarated and exhausted. She slowly drank most of a bottle of Acqua Panna as she browsed a few of that morning's English newspapers as well as her favorite fashion Web sites on her laptop, pleased that the London edition of DailyCandy.com had selected her collection's unveiling as the event of the day.

Eventually she drew a bath, pouring a spoonful of floral bath oil under the fast tap. Above the ceramic tiles beside the tub, an enormous mirror fogged at its corners, but enough of it remained clear for her to observe herself stepping into the steaming water. She was twenty-seven and, although she had often been told she was beautiful, she knew her imperfections. What was beauty anyway, but a moment in time? She wondered for how much longer it would linger. Actually, she was further along in her career than she'd expected to be at this age, and she had settled into a relationship that seemed to have the potential to ripen rather than dissolve or explode, as past loves had done. So what was it she found so disturbing and unnerving in such quiet moments? Time, Isabella supposed. In her mother's generation, a woman of her age would not have been thought young. She closed her eyes as she played with such thoughts. She was certain that Philip would call soon, yet wondered when.

After she had toweled off, she stretched herself across the large, high bed, naked beneath a light blanket.

A moment later she found the remote and turned on the television, surfing channels in search of one in English. She had already raced past Sky when she realized that the face on the screen was familiar and returned to it. The interviewer, with elegant Caribbean diction, was finishing her question, but the camera had already zoomed by her to focus on the actor whose new film was under discussion. The sight of Ty's debilitating smile reminded her of their impulsive kiss less than a week ago.

"In those days," Ty was saying, "I couldn't get recognized standing on Sunset Boulevard beneath a billboard for my new film, with a triple-life-size picture of me on it."

"I find that difficult to believe," the interviewer prodded.

"As did I," Ty told her.

Isabella laughed.

"So much of everything is luck," he continued. "All you can do is to follow what you love and hope you're good at it and pray it comes out well in the end."

When the interview was done, Isabella cast off the cover, threw her legs over the bedside, and walked to the armoire, where, with her usual mixture of calculation and impulse, she retrieved the elements of her day's costume, the first of which, she decided, would be a large square scarf in vibrant green and golden hues. One shade of its many greens matched her eyes, and the silk fluttered in the draft.

When her mobile rang, Isabella took several deep breaths and settled back onto her bed before answering it. When she did, she heard Philip's voice, astonishingly clear above the noise of the metropolis.

"Where are you?"

"Just finishing up in Geneva," Philip lied. "My plane arrives at Fiumicino at two-seventeen. I've arranged a car. Where shall I have it take me?"

"Here, of course," Isabella said.

"Shall I grab lunch on the way or—"

"Probably so," Isabella answered. "I'll be in the shop all day, seeing to things, frantic, but back as soon as I can be. Right now I don't have any notion when that will be. Call me on my mobile after you've arrived. By then I should have a better idea."

"Certainly, darling. Now as to this evening, what exactly is the plan?"

Isabella smiled to herself. It was so like him. People were planners or they weren't, and Philip, much like her godfather, had never demonstrated either a taste or an aptitude for spontaneity. "The reception is from six to eight," she replied. "You'll be front row center when the curtain goes up. Safe to say we'll be out of there by nine. Then we're going to dinner at Due Ladroni."

"Delightful, we're in sync," Philip said. "That's all I need to know. Can I bring you anything?"

"Just yourself," Isabella told him, "rested and ready."

"I've got to tell you," Philip said, "things look very promising here."

To Isabella's ear it sounded as if he had rehearsed the line. "That's brilliant. I'm so glad."

"Although I'll have to put a Geneva address on my business card, because that's where the firm is headquartered, I'll have a lot of free rein. These days one can work from anywhere. . . ."

As he spoke, a thin FedEx envelope was slid under Isabella's door. She walked toward it, pressing the phone to her right ear.

"Rome or Spain or anywhere," Philip was saying. "We'll have more time together. Plus, I'll be making money, not disarming weapons. Altogether more agreeable, wouldn't you say?"

"I would," Isabella replied while with her free hand she scooped up the overnight letter and pulled the tab that ripped it open at its top. Inside she found a heavy white envelope addressed to her and inside that an invitation.

"Well, isn't that thoughtful!" She sighed.

"What? What are you talking about?" Philip asked.

She let the phone drop for a second onto the seat of a chair. By the time she picked it up, she'd collected her thoughts. "Sorry," she said. "It was nothing at all, really, just an old friend writing to wish me luck."

"That's nice," Philip said abstractedly.

"It is," Isabella agreed. "I mean, it's sweet."

As soon as she hung up, Isabella studied the card with the intricate lion-and-unicorn seal engraved in red at the top. She wondered if Ty understood that for an English girl it amounted to a summons. It was kind of him, she thought, but brazen, too, for he knew she was involved with Philip. The invitation was addressed to her alone, not to her and Philip, nor to her and a guest—and, even more disturbing, it was on the shortest possible notice. The royal premiere was scheduled for the very next night. She assumed that the event must have come together with unusual speed, for Ty had not mentioned it aboard *Surpass*. Indeed, as she recollected, he had longed for nothing so much as his return home to his new house to rest. Isabella knew that she was expected to remain in Rome for at least the next several days. There would be customers, many in town for the opening, who would wish to consult her about setting certain gems in her new designs. Her employers at Guardi, who ordinarily gave her wide latitude, would take a dim view of her abandoning the firm at the very moment it was poised to profit from her work. And she already had an appointment the following afternoon with Sheik al-Awad, a relatively new client from Abu Dhabi who had attended Ian's party for her aboard *Surpass* and expressed unusual enthusiasm for her work, hinting that he thought several of her designs worth setting with important stones. To leave a man of his wealth and inclination stranded at the Hotel de Russie, even for the Queen of England, would almost certainly cost Isabella her job.

She placed the invitation on a table and returned to her bedroom to dress. By the time she was ready to set off, a solution had come to her. Work had to come first. Nor could she risk irritating Philip by abandoning him so soon after his arrival. He would instinctively feel that it was Ty Hunter, not the sovereign, to whom she was granting precedence. She would reply to the invitation the next morning, with demonstrable regret. By then it would be too late for her to travel to London in time for the performance. She would claim to have found the invitation only late in the evening, after her return from work and the debut of her new collection and a dinner that followed, when all the palace offices would have been shut tight. She would have loved nothing more, she would say, then beg forgiveness and be granted it, for neither Ty nor the palace could expect her to turn her life around in a matter of hours. And for the time being, until it was in the past and she could use the episode to prove her devotion to him rather than risk arousing his jealousy, she would not breathe a word of it to Philip.

Chapter Eighteen

There was, Isabella understood, more than one Rome. There was the ancient city of seven hills founded along the Tiber River by Romulus after he had slain his twin, Remus, more than two thousand seven hundred years ago. Then there was Ancient Rome, a republic that became an empire, the site of the Aqueduct, the Colosseum, the Baths of Caracalla and the Forum. Later still there was the Rome of the early Christians and the rising Church, medieval Rome in its deceptive sleep, after which had come the Rome of the Renaissance—Michelangelo's, Bernini's, Raphael's, Bramante's and Cellini's Rome—the city whose streets were glorified by a reawakening of classical ideas transmitted through the genius of such artists and financed by wealth from every point in Christendom as its owners sought proximity to and the favor of the Holy See.

Guardi's flagship was of the latter period, a marble-and-stucco palazzo that had been refurbished several times over the centuries, including twice in the fifty-five years since Guardi had taken possession of it. The latest streamlining, only a few years old, had left the building with a pointedly unembellished, almost monastic air, despite its high frescoed ceilings and ornately plastered walls.

Isabella entered by a side door that led to a sleek vestibule decorated in quilted lilac suede, from which an elevator rose on the right. To the left lay the sales floor, which wrapped around a geranium-filled courtyard garden on three sides. Beyond them Isabella could see that the staff had nearly completed its morning ritual of removing the leather-and-felt trays of jewelry from the underground vault and arranging their contents in their assigned showcases and vitrines.

Her *ufficio* was located at the far end of the design studio on the fourth floor. As she made her way toward it, she stopped at several desks to view the sketch pads and computer screens of the staff of six over which she had recently come to preside. The artists, three men and three women, were all young and thinking ahead, by at least a season, trying to intuit what balance of opulence and restraint would come into fashion and sell. For the moment Isabella found herself unable to focus on anything but the evening ahead, the reviews that would or perhaps wouldn't appear in the next day's papers, sales that might or might not be made. Imagining the trajectory of her career paralyzed her, and she had long ago learned that the only thing that could dispel anxiety was work.

She took a cappuccino from her assistant, Balthasar, seated herself at her desk, scanned the e-mails in her business account, flipped through her actual post, listened to her voice mail, and was yet again reviewing the catalog for that evening's debut when she decided to pay an unscheduled visit to the workshop on the floor below.

It was a large, bright room that, as always, both elated and humbled her. Twenty-six men and seven women were employed there, not one of whom stirred, much less looked up, when Isabella arrived. Though they were subject to constant video surveillance, Isabella understood that it was not fear but pride that kept them so obsessively focused on their work.

The polishing department was at the forefront of the shop, presided over by a jowly Sicilian with long, straight black hair, black eyes and a whiskey-reddened face. He and two younger men worked at wheels fitted with buffs of chamois, muslin, felt and satin, holding each just-fabricated or repaired piece of jewelry at the right angle to the right buff for the right amount of time to remove any lingering imperfections and bring up the natural luster of the metal. On a smooth white cloth beside a shallow vat of alcohol and the hot, soapy tubs in which just-polished pieces were given a final bath before being displayed or delivered, three rows of Isabella's glistening creations lay drying.

Beyond the polishing department, the room divided, with bench jewelers, including goldsmiths and stone setters, on the left and a state-of-the-art model-making shop and casting room on the right, each facing inward so that natural light fell from the high, arched windows over the jewelers' shoulders and onto their benches. In the center of the room, partitioned off by a half wall and a step above the workshop's level, sat its foreman's office. The half wall had been painted in Guardi's trademark lilac and was topped by a white marble counter across which works-in-progress regularly flowed. Isabella nodded to the foreman as she passed, noticing that one of her bracelets and several pairs of her earrings were even then awaiting his fastidious inspection.

Although in many modern workshops the lines between jewelers of various skills had lately begun to blur, at Guardi the traditional divisions endured. Stone setters, ranked by experience, were at the top of the hierarchy and sat beside one another at the far end of the room. Goldsmiths were similarly grouped, with the brazing furnace nearby. Between the two sat a pair of enamelists, both young Italian women of Isabella's age. All wore matching slate blue aprons.

The model maker's lair, essentially an outpost of the design studio above it, was more pristine and quiet, for the sculpture there was done mostly in wax. Today its employees were working on special-order pieces unrelated to Isabella's collection.

Careful not to disturb him, Isabella approached one of the senior stone setters as he finished the diamond pavé on a pin for that evening's debut. "*Buongiorno,* Jacopo," she said.

"*Buongiorno,*" replied the jeweler, whose hands as they gripped the miniature trapeze in flight were unusually steady for someone of his age. "I love this piece," he said familiarly. "It makes me laugh."

"Then it's worth it," Isabella gushed.

"You have a good eye," Jacopo told her, "but more important you bring a sense of play to your work. That's what makes the difference."

Isabella smiled at him. Her maternal grandfather had been a master jeweler, had worked for decades in a famous trade shop in the shadow of the London Silver Vaults and then, for a few years before he'd succumbed to emphysema, had his own bench in a smaller operation in Golders Green, closer to his home. She thought of him as she watched Jacopo. He was a man of craft, not fashion, who had valued quality in workmanship above all else. What his hands had made was tangible and beautiful and easy to call his own. To see her celebrated for a few whimsical sketches, no matter how voguish, then marketed as a brand, would have perplexed him. He would have been happy for her, of course, but wouldn't he have wondered and worried, too? Why hadn't she bothered to get the basics down?

"*You're* what makes the difference," she told Jacopo, leaving him to move through the shop and thank the specialists who filed, soldered, hammered, twisted and straightened precious metals into treasures bearing Guardi's imprimatur and now her own.

No sooner had Isabella returned to her office than Balthasar interrupted her. "Lapo's secretary just rang. He's on his way," Balthasar said. "I thought you'd like to know."

Lapo was the middle and most elegant of the three Guardi brothers, who still owned a majority stake in the firm. A relentless perfectionist, he was also the most demanding.

"Could you gauge his mood from hers?"

"I long ago gave up on that," Balthasar replied. He was lanky, with a face from an ancient Roman coin and long and lovely hands that Isabella thought must have been formed already knowing how to draw.

"You're right," she said, then heard the door of the elevator open and close in the distance. "*Grazie*, B."

"Not to worry," Balthasar told her. "Truly, this collection cannot miss. Trust me: There's no one harder to please than me—you know that. So if *I* love it . . ."

"Ciao," Lapo said, entering Isabella's office as Balthasar nimbly withdrew.

"Ciao," Isabella replied.

"Relax," Lapo said. "I am the bearer of good news."

Isabella took a deep breath. "Stage fright." She let it out. "What sort of good news?"

"All in due course," Lapo told her. "Come with me, will you?"

The spine of the building was a circular staircase of travertine marble. Lapo ushered Isabella through the zigzag entry that led from the design studio to the frescoed gallery that surrounded the staircase on the fourth floor. Summer sunlight played on the stained-glass dome above. On the ground floor, the first shoppers of the day had begun to arrive. Lapo bounded down the stairs, indifferent to the workshop on the third floor, the executive offices on the second, the curtained salons that lined the first, and the retail activity at street level. At the base of the staircase, he hesitated as Isabella caught up with him, then, flashing his key card, beckoned her through the entry to the Guardi vault. In the anteroom two guards sat at opposing desks while, behind mirrored walls, others lingered in reserve. Isabella had heard the dueling rumors that Guardi's security force was drawn from the ranks of the Swiss Guard that protected the Pope and Vatican or else from the Mafia itself in a form of high-end protection, but, as such things were not her concern, had immediately dismissed them from her consideration. Enfolded within Italy was layer upon layer of mystery she, as an

Englishwoman, could appreciate yet never comprehend. She accepted that reality, believing that, while momentarily Roman, she should at least attempt to savor an elegant subterfuge that would have appalled her at home.

Lapo brought his right eye toward the retinal scanner and waited for the gates of the vault to retract. When they had, he gestured for Isabella to precede him, and they walked together to a far corner of the cool room. With two separate keys, Lapo opened a deposit box high in the wall before them. From this he removed a long black steel carton, its old borders etched in gold leaf, and, from that, two long rectangular leather trays with fitted lids. He beckoned Isabella to take a seat opposite him at a small desk that had been built into a nearby alcove. The top of the desk was covered in cappuccino suede, and he settled the leather trays gently upon it. "What do you think?" he asked as he lifted the lid of the first.

The gemstones inside were several times larger than Isabella had anticipated and, as Lapo held one after another up to the light, appeared saturated with Technicolor. An intense round fancy blue and an oval canary diamond must each have weighed more than ten or twelve carats. The matched pair of marquise-shaped red diamonds was a bit smaller, but by far the largest and deepest of that color she had ever seen, so vivid they reminded her of strawberries. Isabella studied each stone thoroughly through her loupe, holding it within the points of her tweezers, angling it gradually against the bright, even overhead light.

"This ruby's as big as a hen's egg," she said at one point.

"What an interesting way of putting it," Lapo told her.

"I can't take credit for it. It's a line I remember from a story."

"What story was that?"

"'The Diamond as Big as the Ritz,' by F. Scott Fitzgerald," Isabella said. Her eyes moistened as she spoke, for it had been her father who had introduced her to Fitzgerald and sparked her lifelong fascination with the sort of breezy, innocently sophisticated Americans who filled his fictions.

"I am afraid I don't know that story," Lapo said, then smiled. "I am not very literate, alas."

"Listen to you," Isabella replied, dismissing his modesty. "What are your plans for all these stones?"

"It's your plans that matter," Lapo told her.

Isabella put down the Burmese ruby she'd been examining. "You're kidding. You have to be."

"Not in the least."

"Then I'd like to know why not. These gems are entirely out of scale with the pieces in my collection. I'd have to make all new models."

"That thought had crossed my mind," Lapo said.

"And even if I did, the settings and stones would not be harmonious. My pieces are lighthearted, playful. These are serious gems."

"They are *very* serious gems indeed, but tastes do vary, and your settings may be more appealing than you think."

"To whom?"

"Sheik al-Awad, among others."

"I can't imagine why. If I were able to buy stones like these, I would set them very simply, in platinum surrounded by diamonds so that they could speak for themselves, not force-fit them into pieces whose real value is in their design. My collection is based on acrobats who might have come out of the Cirque du Soleil. A carat is an enormous stone in one of my pieces. It's a different thing entirely. You know that."

Lapo Guardi folded his arms and leaned back in his chair. "There's much in what you say, but at the end of the day we must be in the business of accommodating tastes, not dictating them."

In her imagination Isabella already saw herself in the workshop, making and supervising the making of new wax models. When those figures were complete and judged suitable for the remarkable gemstones before her, rubber molds containing the exact negatives of the models would have to be made and the centrifugal casting done from the kiln exactly as Cellini had done when he introduced the lost-wax method. Yet what was to be the result of all this work? No matter how exquisitely wrought, would the new pieces be as spirited as, would they exist in harmony with, the rest of her collection? The question was not hers to decide, and she modestly nodded her assent to Lapo.

"This is just the beginning," he said.

"It's mad. There must be thirty million euros represented in these two boxes."

"Closer to forty."

"Don't get me wrong. It's wonderful, but why?"

"Shall I tell you the truth?"

"You'd better."

"It's because certain people, whom we are fortunate to count among our clients, simply do not trust in the rule of law wherever it is they come from. And they no longer trust either the solvency of Western banks or the secrecy of Swiss banking laws. They worry about the former for obvious reasons: too much risk taken on by bankers better suited for baccarat. And about the latter they worry not only that the names of account holders and the amounts of their deposits might be divulged to authorities but that even the contents of vaults under the Banhofstrasse and in the mountains might eventually be scrutinized—in the name of transparency, mind you, as though that were a sacred and invariably good thing. Added to these concerns is, of course, portability. The amounts in which such people deal have become so large that it would require carloads of gold, even at today's high price, to move it. Jewelry, however, particularly from a collection like yours, with no mention of a center stone or two, still flies below the radar and remains easy enough to transfer from one generation's pocket to that of the next."

"Very interesting, I have to admit," Isabella said. "When we first talked about my coming to work for you and then about launching my collection, you said stones had become commodities and that in today's world the real profit was in design. Things seem to have changed."

"Actually, they haven't," Lapo assured her. "What I said then is still true, but these are special circumstances. With one-of-a-kind stones like these, one is less in the jewelry business than in the upper reaches of selling fine art."

"Or gilts," Isabella said, and smiled. "Tell me, do I sense the hand of my god-father anywhere in this process?"

Lapo laughed. "Not directly, not that I know of—and I would know. He's your biggest booster, of course. But people do not buy such treasures as these merely to support a friend's goddaughter."

"No," agreed Isabella, "I'm sure they don't."

Chapter Nineteen

Their dinner party was on the balmy and fragrant terrace at Due Ladroni in the Piazza Nicosia. They were twenty-four in all, at three tables of eight.

"Quite a name for a restaurant," one of Guardi's best clients, an elderly Roman count who had married an American heiress from Tulsa, remarked to Isabella over a first course of sliced raw sea bass.

"I know," Isabella said, and beamed an ingratiating smile. "It means 'Two Thieves,' doesn't it?"

"Literally," the count told her. "After the war, two brothers opened it as what they called simply Tavern. Very few people had money in those days, and the place caught on by offering exceptionally good homemade food for cheap prices. Working people came first, and soon a more fashionable crowd followed. When the brothers began to raise their prices in consequence, their customers gave the restaurant the name it bears to this day."

With the festivities still going strong nearing midnight, Isabella commenced a circuit of the tables and ultimately found herself seated next to Sheik al-Awad, an elegantly turned-out, not-quite-rotund man of shorter-than-average height, whose soft smile and honeyed voice seemed perfectly matched.

"I am honored," he told her.

"Queen for a day," Isabella said. "And I'm twice lucky, as I believe we are lunching together tomorrow."

"An event to which I very much look forward," Sheik al-Awad replied.

"Lapo showed me the *most* amazing stones this morning," she gushed.

"I trust him implicitly," Sheik al-Awad said.

"Your wife is a very fortunate woman."

"Remind her of that when you meet. I beg you."

"She's here with you tonight?"

The sheik shook his head. "She is at our home, with the children," he explained, his eyes then twinkling as he issued a gentle nod in the direction of a celebrated Italian cover girl at the next table.

"Well, at least someone's lucky," Isabella came back in a determinedly neutral yet sophisticated tone.

"Oh, no, no, no," the sheik interrupted. "These jewels are for *my* collection. Of course, one never knows when he'll meet a lady he enjoys and when that happens, it's nice to have something to offer her."

"Take the pigeon's-blood ruby," Isabella said. "I've never seen one like it."

To this Sheik al-Awad replied hesitantly, "You have a lovely way with words: 'pigeon's blood.'"

"I wish I could take the credit, but I didn't make up the phrase." Isabella started to say that "pigeon's blood" was a bog-standard professional phrase but quickly stopped herself, feeling suddenly uneasy. "It's difficult, isn't it," she continued, "when one sees so many brilliant stones all together, to remember that ruby and sapphire are practically one and the same?"

Sheik al-Awad nodded. "Yes, it is," he said.

"Both corundum," she said.

"Both corundum," he repeated.

"And yet, now that I think of it, I've never seen a red sapphire," she said, baiting her trap, for there was no such thing. A red sapphire *was* a ruby.

"Haven't you?"

"Never. Have you been collecting for a long time?"

"I have been around for a long time. So I suppose my answer to that question must be yes."

"What other gems have you collected?" Isabella inquired. "There must be so many lovely ones."

"Yes indeed," the sheik replied.

"That's wonderful," Isabella said, regarding him carefully. She had no idea what sort of game he was playing or who, if not Ian, had put him up to it—nor, so long as he could fund his purchases, had she any business trying to find out. She had seen enough of collectors over the years, however, to recognize that, unlike his intended acquisitions, Sheik al-Awad was not the genuine article.

It was not until a quarter past one that Isabella and Philip were alone in her flat in the Trastevere. "It went well, didn't it?"

"How could it have gone any better?" he asked as he squeezed her hand. "Another day, another triumph."

"Are you too tired?" she asked.

"No," Philip said.

She was wearing a dress of a young designer friend of Balthasar's, a light jade V-neck with draped shoulder details. Once she had loosened its obi-wrap belt, it was easy to step out of. "When I was at university," she said, "we used to pull all-nighters."

"As did we," Philip said, and then kissed her.

As he disrobed her, Isabella thought, not for the first time, that there was something boyish about him. His natural grace could not disguise impetuousness so fierce and selfish it was almost cruel. In bed he was like a dancer, in control of every muscle and movement of his body. So that when his left hand skimmed the flesh above her rib cage and from there across her breast, it was as soft as a current of air. She loved beauty and from the first had found Philip beautiful. Yet something about his beauty disturbed her, as if he had been sculpted rather than born. Oh, he was alive and knew how to please her, how to seduce and tease, enter and withdraw by surprise. But it was not his skill that had kept her interest, rather the part of him he withheld. She knew he was hiding something. And whatever it was had frightened her before and worried her now. She was not drawn to milquetoasts. A woman who wanted what she did from a man and from life would have to learn to look away from time to time. She understood that and, by now, how to manage the flow of potentially disturbing information from her brain to her emotions. How could she not, with Ian as her formative male role model? Men worth possessing could not be possessed, but acknowledging that truth made it no easier to resist them.

"You missed me?" she whispered with a sudden unease once he was spent.

Philip sighed. "I missed you."

"I missed you, too."

"It's going to be better from now on. We'll be together."

"You'll be in Geneva."

"I'll have a desk in Geneva. I told you: I'll be my own boss."

"That will be good. How *was* Geneva?"

Philip touched her shoulder. He had no wish to lie but, for her benefit as much as his, could not tell her that he had been in Vienna instead. Isabella would grasp the reason in time, accept that a man either took or missed his chances. "Geneva was the same as ever: slippery," he said.

"I know what you mean," she said softly, sitting up a little. She was too tired to stay awake for long, yet still too excited to sleep. "God, I'm glad you're here."

"You're not the only one," Philip said. He knew her well enough to know she was game, but before he began again he studied her. Unlike other women whose beds he had shared, Isabella could hold her own anywhere, in any company. She could make him proud. At school he'd had classmates whose mothers, still elegant and enthralling in middle age, were more or less matriarchs of dynasties. Isabella could be such a figure. He harbored no doubt about that and for a moment wondered why he needed anyone else, anything more. The answer, he suspected, was embedded too deeply in his being to be plumbed. He was who he was.

That was the nature of things. Gatherers of power led rapacious, messy lives, but lives that were remembered and important. The dual aspects of his character had long been clear to him, and when the thought suddenly struck him that he resembled that figure of adolescent fantasy, the vampire who yearned not to be undead, he laughed silently. In the beguiling young woman who seemed to love him, he discerned a perfection and normalcy he knew he could never attain on his own.

"*Buono?*" he asked, as he slipped inside her.

"*Sì,*" she said, doing her best to disguise the reluctance that had gradually overtaken her mood.

Philip tightened his grip. "*Buono,*" he repeated.

In the morning she cooked their breakfast in her tiny, ocher-tiled kitchen, placing strips of bacon in fastidious tic-tac-toe patterns in a large skillet and frying fresh eggs up on top of them.

When Philip came to the table, he brought a large box wrapped in lime green paper with a purple bow.

"What's this?" Isabella inquired.

"A souvenir," Philip said, "of Prague. I meant to give it to you before your party, but the day got away from us."

"We were casualties of our own hospitality, as Ian would say."

"Not quite casualties."

When Isabella had unwrapped the package and withdrawn the musical jewel box, she lifted the lid and the mechanism within began to play Dvořák's *Czech Suite,* op. *39.*

"It's divine," she said. "In fact, perfect."

"But not big enough for your collection?"

"Perhaps as it once was, not as it's becoming. That's another thing. Wait till I tell you what sorts of stones Lapo intends to set in some of my pieces."

"Large ones, I hope."

"So large I'll have to redo some models. They're lovely, of course, but I'm afraid they overwhelm my designs."

"What a nice problem to have," Philip said.

"Yes, I suppose it is," Isabella agreed as she lowered the top of the music box. "Anyway, thank you, thank you! I love it. You always know just the right thing. You're amazing."

"Actually, it's as much a precaution as a souvenir."

Isabella could tell he was teasing. "A precaution?" she repeated.

"It can be dangerous to leave a pretty girl alone in Rome."

"I wouldn't know. All I do is work."

"That would be sad if true. Fortunately, I don't believe you."

"The only other man in my life in Balthasar."

"Balthasar is not a man," Philip said.

"Now, now," Isabella said. "I suppose the problem is that everyone who might be inclined to give it a go knows I'm taken."

"That means nothing to Romans," Philip said. "You know that. For a girl this city must seem to offer an abundance of riches. But if you are a man, there's so much competition. Elsewhere it's different. Take New York. Especially if you're foreign, it's not difficult to win over girls there. Half the men are gay. The other half care only about money. There is no one left for them. But in Rome even teenage boys sneak their girlfriends into the Forum after dark. In Rome if you like a girl and she's attractive, you're up against professionals."

"There's no one more professional than you," Isabella said as the kettle whistled.

She was tending to it when the telephone rang. "You wouldn't get that, would you?" she asked Philip as she poured the bubbling water into a *cafetière*.

"Of course," Philip said, marveling at the habit English girls had of constructing requests in the negative. "*Pronto*," he said into the receiver.

"This is al-Awad."

Philip hesitated. "I'm sorry. You took me by surprise. How did you know I was here?"

"I didn't. Who is this?" asked the sheik.

"Philip Frost, of course."

"Oh, hello, Philip, and very sorry to disappoint you, but I was trying to reach Isabella Cavill."

"She's right here."

When her brief conversation confirmed the time and venue of their lunch, Isabella returned to press the filter of the *cafetière*.

Philip said, "I didn't know you knew al-Awad."

"Yes you did. He was there last night."

"Many people were there. Do you know them all?"

Isabella ignored the question. "He's a client of Lapo's," she said.

"I'm glad to hear it."

"Honestly, Philip! He came on with us to dinner."

"You could have fooled me, but then I don't know him by sight, only over the telephone."

"And how, pray tell, is that? Does he collect the nuclear arms you disarm?"

Philip shook his head at the absurdity of such a thought. "He's an investor in the fund I'm going to be running."

"Bully for him," Isabella replied.

Chapter Twenty

To Ty, in the fresh light of the English morning, there seemed something prematurely old about Oliver. Fatalism lurked at the corners of his eyes, the eyes of a man drawn to the edges of things, who had become addicted to shadows and danger. Such a man, Ty recognized, would not find it easy to return to London or Cambridge or Eton for very long.

At the Signature base at Heathrow, Oliver preceded his friend off the Boeing business jet that had brought them, over the North Pole, from Los Angeles. By the time Ty reached passport control, Oliver had already found his car and set off toward the M4 and London. Ty had only just identified his baggage when he was greeted by the driver from Claridge's Hotel and a pencil-thin young woman from the local public-relations office of the studio that was distributing *Something to Look Forward To.* He followed his minders to the waiting Mercedes S-Class.

"Mr. Thrall said to tell you he has forgiven you," the publicity girl told him, "but only because it's the Queen. He also said he was confused by the letters behind your name and that I should ask you about them."

"Did he?" Ty said. "I wrote his wife, Mitzi, a note, explaining what had happened. After my name, on impulse—really, I mean just as a joke—I put the letters CBE."

"But you aren't, are you?" inquired the young woman with an audible gasp. "Can an American be a Commander of the British Empire?"

"Your guess is as good as mine. It's an abbreviation I came across in a script once, and I thought it would throw Mitzi and Sid. They're such Anglophiles, as maybe you know."

"I didn't."

"Oh, yeah. English chintz, English furniture, other people's ancestors on their walls. It's their thing. Anyway, that's not what I meant the letters to stand for. I meant them to stand for *Can't Be Everywhere*."

The publicity girl laughed. "I'll be sure to tell him," she said, then handed Ty a copy of his itinerary.

An hour later Ty had finished unpacking his suitcase and was standing beneath an enormous round showerhead as torrents of hot water washed the residue of his long journey from his skin.

When the telephone rang, it startled him, but he took the call on the wall unit just outside the shower door.

"On the way up," Oliver said.

"Give me five."

"Four fifty-nine . . ."

Ty was in one of the hotel's bathrobes when he answered the door of his suite. "You're like a bad penny the way you turn up," he told Oliver.

"Bad news," Oliver said.

"It's a long way to have come for that. Shoot!"

"She can't make it."

"The Queen?"

"Hardly. Isabella Cavill. She just called in her refusal. Apparently the invitation didn't reach her until this morning. That's her excuse, in any event. We know it was delivered yesterday."

"Signed for?"

"Don't you think that would have been a bit over the top? Let's look on the bright side. She knows you're back in Europe and have the best reason in the world to be here. She knows you were interested enough to invite her. We also know that her collection debuted last evening in Rome, so it's not entirely unlikely she's tied up there."

"Perhaps we should have invited her boyfriend as well," Ty suggested.

"It would have been out of character."

"For me?"

"For Ty Hunter."

"Where does this leave us?"

"With Plan B. Actually, still Plan A. It was always a long shot she'd appear.

You go to the premiere. You have fun. We'll play tomorrow when it comes. Let me pose a question. If you had received the invitation without any involvement from me or anyone else, would you have asked her?"

"Yes, I think so."

"And would you be tempted to pick up the phone and ring her now?"

Ty looked at his old friend with disbelief. "Not after she'd turned me down."

"I was sure you'd say that," Oliver said, "but I'm glad you did. As far as you are concerned, I've been seconded by the palace to see you through the hoops."

"Fine."

"We'd never met until today."

"Should we be talking so openly?"

"The suite was swept for bugs five minutes before you entered it. It will be swept again every time you leave and just before you return."

"Any other security precautions I should know about?" Ty asked.

"The couple in the suite next door—they're ours. They don't know anything about anything except that you are a guest of Her Majesty and famous in your own right. So it's only natural you might need a bit of interference run."

"Where will you be?"

"From here I go to the palace to review plans with the household staff, make sure there are no last-minute changes. From there I'll go to my flat, then be back here to collect you at half five sharp."

"Then it's showtime."

"'The roar of the greasepaint, the smell of the crowd,'" Oliver told him, "or have I got it backwards? If you want to go out for anything, do. One of the studio's blokes can go along with you—or not, whichever you choose. The essential thing is to behave as you would if you had nothing else in the back of your mind."

"Beyond sleeping with Isabella Cavill, you mean?"

"A fine and completely understandable desire," Oliver replied. "In the meantime, if you're feeling frustrated, there's a very spiffy gym on the top floor."

"I know."

"Of course you do. For a moment I forgot. You've stayed here before."

"A couple of pictures ago, while we were shooting at Pinewood, Claridge's was my home away from home, except that I didn't actually have a real home then."

"Maybe people like us shouldn't."

In the car, on the drive to the Odeon Leicester Square, Oliver said, "It's all very simple. You bow, not deeply. A graceful nod will do. On first meeting the Queen, it is 'Your Majesty,' after that 'ma'am.' The rest of them are 'Your Royal Highness.' The younger they are, the more relaxed about this sort of thing. Remember, they'll be as dazzled to meet you as you are to meet them."

"I'm full of respect but never dazzled," Ty said. "And when the film is over?"

"There's an after party in aid of the Great Ormond Street Hospital that we've rather tagged onto at the last minute."

"In that case I should probably stay on for a reasonable amount of time."

"It would be a pity not to. It's at Winfield House in Regent's Park, the home of the American ambassador," Oliver explained. "Very swell."

"What about after the after party?"

"I'd forgot what a night owl you are."

"I'll be on my second wind by then. We *are* starting early, remember."

A minute or two away from the red carpet, they were now in the Haymarket. "The Queen will probably not go to Winfield House," Oliver said. "Prince William and the Duchess of Cambridge very likely will. Harry's a dead cert. Later they may go on to Boujis or Mahiki, or, who knows, now that they're all adults, to Annabel's."

"Are we adults?" Ty asked with a wink.

"In the minds of others," Oliver replied.

"As I recall, you're not supposed to go to certain places if you're a man over thirty or a woman over twenty-five."

Oliver nodded. "Film stars excepted."

"Would you have it any other way?"

"When was it ever?"

"And it's not only film stars," Ty continued. "Billionaires also get a free ride."

"Another perk of the undeserving, but then you can't fight nature. Women are affected by the physical attributes of men, Ty. There's no getting around that fact. From fourteen to eighteen, it's the face that counts with them. From eighteen to twenty-five, maybe thirty, it's the body. After then, except for a precious few, it's the wallet."

Ty was surprised by how relaxed royal formality was. He was the first through the receiving line, followed by Greg Logan and his awestruck eleven-year-old daughter, Lily. He managed gracefully deferential yet far from obsequious bows and blushed with pleasure when the Queen told him she had seen and enjoyed both *The Boy Who Understood Women* and his second film, *Fortune's Wind*. Oliver had been right about the princes and the elegant new duchess, whose welcoming smiles and enthusiastic questions about how certain scenes had been filmed Ty found flattering even though they seemed to cast the few years' difference in their ages as larger than it was.

When the Queen told him she found it "astonishing, almost magical, really, how quickly and completely certain actors, such as you, Mr. Hunter, are able to assume not only the role but the entire identity of a character, to make people believe you are someone you aren't," she stared directly into his eyes, holding them for an extra second. This caused Ty to wonder whether—and, if so, in how much detail—she had been briefed about the operation that was under way.

"It's very kind of you to say so, ma'am," he replied.

"Or aren't someone you are," Her Majesty added. "It's a gift, of course."

Later, as they arrived at Winfield House, Ty pressed Oliver on the question.

"That's difficult to say," Oliver answered. "One can never be sure, although one suspects there's far less she doesn't know than that she does."

"That's the feeling I had. But I could hardly ask."

"Indeed," Oliver agreed. "Anyway, you know what they say. There are no such things as secrets, only people who find things out a little later."

The reception hall of the American ambassador's residence, a large bright, square room, immediately reminded Ty of La Encantada. In the center of it stood an imposing and eccentric table, a gilt-bronze-mounted burr elm with a porphyry top that Ty was almost sure had come from the same hand as one in his own house. This impression intensified when he and a few other VIPs, including the royals, were ushered into the Green Room for a pre-reception reception with the ambassador and his wife. There the avocado-and-coral palette, the Chinese wallpaper, the woven carpet with its subtle dragon design, the waxed-pine pelmet boards that contained the curtains within the windows, even the Jiaqing vases that had been adapted as lamps evinced unmistakably the Hollywood glamour of Billy Haines. Ty smiled to himself at the thought that this should be the face America had chosen to present to the mother country and, as he did so, felt a little homesick.

The ambassador, when Ty inquired, confirmed that the media tycoon Walter Annenberg and his wife, when he'd been ambassador to the Court of St. James under President Nixon, had indeed hired William Haines. "You're very knowledgeable, Mr. Hunter," the ambassador said with a smile.

"Only accidentally in this case," Ty told him.

As the room filled, Ty studied the faces and expressions, the stance and dress of those who surrounded him, careful to betray no more than an actor's natural curiosity in new surroundings. He wondered who if anyone knew of his assignment or even of his connection to Oliver; who might possess even one fact that, in the wrong hands, could thwart his mission. It was unlikely that the ambassador, a sixty-eight-year-old businessman bundler of campaign funds from the Upper East Side of New York, with no previous experience in foreign affairs, would have any knowledge of Oliver Molyneux's background in the Special Boat Service or MI6. The CIA station chief was another matter, of course, but which one was he? Ty searched among the guests, eliminating those connected to the film or the film business as well as those whose features, Savile Row suits, or chancy frocks gave them away as English. Then, in a far corner of the room, he noticed a man with receding, silvering hair whose tortoiseshell reading glasses dangled from a black cord around his neck. The man was of average height, with just the beginning of a paunch. Innocuous but intellectual, he seemed stranded in middle age, somewhere between forty-five and sixty. Ty recognized the man as having been cut from the same cloth as many of his father's friends, an almost perfect specimen of a type he had been familiar with since childhood. He did not wish to encounter the man more directly because he did not want to provide the probable spy an opportunity, in turn, to appraise him. The fewer people who knew or even suspected his role, the safer he and Oliver would travel, the more likely they'd be to succeed in uncovering and, if need be, foiling a transfer of missing nuclear warheads.

Outside the sprawling Georgian house, on the wide garden lawn, two geodesic domes had been inflated and were now illuminated by soft lights.

Ty left the private reception with the ambassador, his wife and Greg Logan and made his way toward the bar in the smaller tent. It was always the same, he thought, as a few fans approached and others receded, some eager to express their approval, others equally determined to respect his privacy. When someone said "Fantastic" or "Loved it" or "You were *never better,*" he smiled and thanked the person, offered his hand, and immediately deflected the compliment to his director. He was signing an autograph when a waiter passed, offering flutes of champagne from a silver tray. He took one and the instant he did so became aware of an immovable figure just over his right shoulder. He shifted slightly, curious why it did not shift with him, if only to avoid collision, then saw that it belonged to a woman, not too tall but lithe, in a pale blue dress whose jagged hemline might have been cut for Peter Pan. Her face was a few inches from his, almost too close for him to register its subtle beauty, but she was laughing as she gazed down. When Ty's eyes followed, he saw that the toe of his slipper was pressing down on one of the points of her dress.

Embarrassed as he withdrew it, Ty said, "Sorry, I seem to have you kidnapped."

The young woman nodded. "What do they call it when you begin to fall in love with your kidnapper? Stockholm syndrome?" Her English was almost too exquisite, her accent well traveled, if not foreign.

"Would you like a glass of champagne?" Ty asked.

"Why ever not?"

"I'm Ty Hunter."

"I know."

"And——"

"Who am I? Maria-Antonia," she said. "Maria-Antonia Salazar."

"Well, Maria-Antonia Salazar, here's a health unto you," Ty said, raising his glass.

"That sounds like a line."

"You're correct. It's from my last film."

"Did you get the girl in that one?"

"Naturally. That's why they pay me the big bucks."

"So I take it you're a man who plays the odds."

"What else can a fellow do when he doesn't have a script to go by?"

"Wing it, I suppose."

"Very dangerous," Ty said.

"Let's dance," Maria-Antonia said.

"Only if I lead," Ty told her.

"Why do you say that? It suggests you might be a disappointing lover."

"My reviews suggest the opposite."

"But you're too much of a gent to cite them?"

"You'd think less of me if I did."

"Who's to say?" Maria-Antonia replied. "It's the kind of thing I decide for myself."

"You're very confident."

"I was born that way."

"Which is fortunate," Ty said.

"Usually," Maria-Antonia agreed.

"I still want to lead."

"Because it's been such a long time since you've done anything else?"

"Partly that," Ty said, "but there are also other reasons."

"If you insist," she said. "I mean, I'm not your shrink."

"I don't have a shrink."

"Everyone should."

"I disagree."

"You disagree a lot."

"Only when you force the question," Ty said. "Now, if you don't mind, I'd like to kiss you."

"Then please do. I'd like you to."

"You're not afraid you'll become tabloid fodder?"

"I'm not afraid of much."

Before their dance they finished their champagne in silence, then made their way to the larger dome. Beneath the summer sky, they moved arm in arm across the soft, sweet-smelling lawn, their fixation with each other captured by the digital cameras of other partygoers as well as the benefit's official photographer. As they approached the dome, they were drawn to the interplay of light and shadows upon the higher reaches of its convex surface. Inside, the music was throbbing and fast, and they headed toward the dance floor, which was tiled in Brazilian ebony. Between its squares, lights twinkled in random sequence, and they could feel its vibrations through the soles of their shoes. It was above them, however, that the mood of a moment was set, then altered and altered again. For the inside of the dome was a concave movie screen of 360 degrees. No sooner did they step onto the floor than they were riding twenty-foot waves, ascending, then balancing themselves at the crest of each, then high in the saddles of camels, galloping toward sunset, then skiing pristine glaciers by moonlight and descending vertiginous waterfalls with reckless glee. When the tempo finally let up, Ty drew Maria-Antonia closer to him and kissed her again, more passionately than before.

"Do you sail?" Maria-Antonia asked softly, slowly opening her eyes once he'd stepped back.

"I can handle myself on a boat," Ty replied.

"We leave tomorrow."

"We do?"

"From Stansted Airport," Maria-Antonia said. "My boat is already on its way from Sardinia. It will be in Marbella by the time we get there. You can sail for as long as you like."

"It's an enticing invitation."

"Then accept it."

"I'll have to check a few things."

"Naturally. Where are you staying?"

"Claridge's."

"Alone?"

"That remains to be seen."

"I love Claridge's, but I don't go to hotels with men I've just met," Maria-Antonia said. "Even movie stars."

"But you do ask them to go off sailing in strange seas on a moment's notice?"

"No woman can follow and lead at the same time."

"I know. We've been through that. Ten minutes ago I would never have expected to say this, but I want to make love to you."

Maria-Antonia smiled. "I know you do," she said.

In his suite Ty said, "Why is it always the same way? Hard as you try, you can never catch fate. Then, just when you give up trying, it catches you."

"The gods are amusing themselves," Oliver replied. "It's the way of the world."

"What am I doing talking to you, sipping single-malt scotch in a five-thousand-dollar-a-night hotel suite at this hour when I should be ravishing the very delicious Maria-Antonia Salazar? If I'm really Ty Hunter, there's something wrong with this picture."

"Not every woman is Zara Chapin, available upon demand without demanding anything in return."

"Thank you for the valuable nursery lesson," Ty said, "but I'm afraid I've been learning it by experience lately—tonight with Maria-Antonia and last week when Isabella Cavill opened the door then, half an hour later, slammed it in my face."

"Shame about that," Oliver said.

"What the hell, she's young and beautiful and rich as Croesus and likes to play games. How smart she is remains to be seen. I'll tell you one thing, though. I don't care how clean Philip Frost is in George Kenneth's eyes or anyone else's. I don't trust him."

"Why would you? You're jealous."

"It's more than that. I heard some whores talking about him on a pontoon at the Hôtel du Cap. He makes them grovel for their money."

"If that's true, Isabella will see it eventually."

"I don't know. Women don't always."

"She's the one on whom you should be concentrating."

"Why do you say that? Maria-Antonia hasn't shut any door yet. Well, except for tonight," Ty said.

Oliver poured two more fingers of Laphroaig into both their glasses, sipped his slowly, then hesitated. "She *will* shut it," he said.

"You don't know that," Ty replied, before the implications of Oliver's remark had fully registered.

Oliver remained silent but kept his eyes on Ty.

"Or *do* you, you son of a bitch?" Ty pressed.

"She's ours," Oliver said.

"Yours?"

"Ours, yours—in this case there's no difference. We're a unit."

"Well, she's the damnedest agent I've ever seen, as well as the most convincing liar. Why wasn't I told?"

"That's my fault. I knew you'd go for her. I thought it would be more credible and, believe it or not, easier on you if you didn't know you were performing."

"Easier on me?"

"I thought you'd want to get your rocks off, not fall in love," Oliver said sharply.

"I'm not in love."

"Apologies in that case."

"So I'm flying another thousand miles in order to go sailing with a prick teaser I have no chance of screwing, all for England and St. George?"

"Not *only* for England."

"You know what I mean, you duplicitous little shit."

"And *you* know what *I* mean."

"Right now I wish I didn't. Right now there's a big part of me that would like to wring Maria-Antonia's ever-so-elegant neck."

"That's exactly how I hoped you'd feel. Hold on to those feelings, Ty. You're going to need them soon enough."

Chapter Twenty-one

Photographs of Ty and Maria-Antonia Salazar appeared in three newspapers the following morning. The most intriguing picture, of the couple embracing on the dance floor, teased readers from page one of the *Daily Mail*. Inside, another picture showed them holding hands as they maneuvered their way across the lamplit garden at Winfield House. The *Daily Telegraph* featured portraits of them on page three and asked, IS TY HUNTER THE SORCERER WHO HAS AWAKENED A FAMOUSLY RECLUSIVE HEIRESS FROM HER LONG SPELL? The *Times* cautioned, FANS FEAR TY HUNTER HAS GIVEN HIS HEART—AGAIN. Below the headline was a photograph in which his adoring expression and her compelling profile said more than any exposé could.

Oliver had collected the newspapers from the cloth bag hung on the outside door of Ty's suite and handed them to Ty, without speaking, when he arrived before breakfast.

"I volunteered for service, not humiliation," Ty remonstrated. "Don't play with me like that again."

"I haven't any plan to."

"Keep it that way."

"We're due at Stansted at eleven."

"Two questions: First, is Maria-Antonia Salazar her real name?"

"No, it's a legend."

"Is she married?"

"Yes and no."

"What the hell does that mean?"

"They're having difficulties."

"People in her line of work often do."

"It's his line of work as well."

"'Double the pleasure, double the fun,'" Ty said, "an old saying of my mother's."

"Not invariably the case," Oliver replied.

"No."

After they had phoned in their order to room service, Oliver took a deep breath. "I have the next pages of the script," he announced. "Is this the time, or would you prefer to wait?"

"I didn't know there *was* a script."

"It's partial, of course. Once you've made contact with last week's love, you'll be flying on your own. For the meantime you can't take your mind off Maria-Antonia. That's what the notes say."

"Which service devised this soap opera?"

"It's a collaborative effort, really."

"That's what it sounds like. So I'm besotted?"

"You're keen. It's unbecoming for a star to be besotted."

"When does that change?"

"It doesn't. It goes the other way. The lady will give you the cue."

"You're not going to tell me her real name."

"For your own safety. You might slip and use it."

"I've never flubbed a line on set in my life. It can be ten grand a take."

"The stakes here are much higher."

"Yeah, well," Ty said.

"Maybe someday," Oliver told him. "Right now, remember, you don't know anything about her except that she races your motor. What you hear, you store but immediately discount, because in your line of work you've heard a lot about people that didn't prove true. The more rumors that surface about her, and particularly her fortune, the harder they'll be for anyone to pin down. You get the idea."

"All too clearly," Ty said.

The yacht chartered was a Swan 100 with a racing-green hull, teak decks and a semi-raised saloon. It had been organized in London and paid for by a wire transfer drawn on a private bank in Bermuda. The Bermuda account, which was overseen by a firm of investment counselors secretly connected to the Central Intelligence Agency in the United States, had over the years borne any number of names but according to the most recently adjusted records had belonged to Maria-Antonia Salazar since shortly after the untimely death of her entirely imaginary first husband, a Latin American merchant banker and one-time sugar broker, six years previously.

On the flight out, Maria, ebullient and entranced, kept up her act from the evening before. Ty understood that this was for the benefit of anyone who might be observing them, especially the flight crew, who, like the crew attached to the yacht itself, were young and no doubt lacking in means and could be presumed to be willing to compromise the privacy of their clients in return for sufficient compensation from the press. When she squeezed Ty's hand, he squeezed back a little too strongly. He had faked romance before on-screen but had never enjoyed it. Even less did he enjoy feigning it now, knowing there was no romance where he had so recently felt its spark.

Onboard the yacht, which had been christened *Vendavel* after a regional wind, they took the forward cabin. They sailed until just before sunset, then dropped anchor in a cove beyond the harbor, where they dined as the sun disappeared behind a distant ridge and the western sky turned the color of burnt orange. Across a folding table on the aft deck, they locked eyes, saying little, communicating by tiny yet important alterations of expression. Quickly, Ty put himself into character, playing to Maria-Antonia's moods and lines but now and then upping her ante and taking control.

They went to bed early, and when Maria-Antonia abruptly drifted off, Ty was suddenly glad for a long break between scenes and the low waves that gently rocked *Vendavel*.

Dawn came with surprising suddenness. No sooner had the horizon fallen away to the east than sunlight flooded their cabin. After her shower Maria-Antonia appeared tense. Not knowing what had catalyzed the sudden deterioration of her mood, Ty nonetheless decided to play to it. He would appear as decent as she was spoiled, as placating as she was implacable.

By the time they finally emerged on deck, *Vendavel* was already under way. The Norwegian first mate, a compelling young Viking not yet twenty, held the wheel while his Aussie captain examined waypoints for the day's journey. The captain's girlfriend of the season was a quiet Scottish girl, who, having finished a Cordon Bleu course in Paris, served as cook. The scents of frying bacon and steaming coffee drifted upward from the galley.

"Good morning, ma'am," offered the enthusiastic first mate.

Maria-Antonia ignored him initially, then, thinking better of her decision, said, "For some, possibly."

"Yes, ma'am," he replied, although he looked away rapidly to hide his contempt.

In a voice long used to having even its most impulsive whims gratified, Maria-Antonia said, "Captain, before you have us all off on a long tack to nowhere, I would like to have a stretch."

"The sea is lovely," the captain told her, "warm at the surface and clear as far down as the eye can see. I was in myself less than thirty minutes ago. Very refreshing!"

"On *land*," Maria-Antonia said.

"Well, that's another matter, then, isn't it?" the captain said, at which his mate sighed, then busied himself coiling lines.

"Moreover, we've barely set foot in Puerto Banús, certainly not in daylight. It would be a pity not to give Mr. Hunter a proper picture of it. Surely you agree."

The captain gave her a full-on but disdainful smile. "It's my job to agree."

"So it is, I suppose," Maria-Antonia said.

A moment later, when Ty appeared, he was grinning. "Something smells good," he declared.

"You bet your life it does," the captain replied.

Ty seated himself on the boat's port side, across the table from Maria-Antonia, to whom he offered an exaggerated, mocking, evanescent smile. He wondered how Greg or any of his other directors would have judged the performance he and Maria-Antonia were putting on. Would they have seen through it? He doubted it. Improvisation was dangerous, but when it went right, it verged closer than any script to the truth. He had to take his hat off to his co-conspirator, even as he knew he was being played by her. "What's your pleasure, madam?" he asked, almost insolently and with a wink to the captain.

"We're going ashore," Maria-Antonia replied matter-of-factly.

"As I'd surmised," Ty said.

"When we changed course?"

"It was a sign, coming about that abruptly."

"You don't mind?"

"What choice do I have?"

"If you have an opinion, voice it."

"My opinion is that going ashore in a fantastic boat like this one seems preferable to walking a gangplank."

"You have a way of putting things," Maria-Antonia told him.

"Thank you."

"That wasn't meant as a compliment."

"So it was more of a warning?"

"Have it your way."

"What's really a pity," Ty said, "is that we can't *both* do that."

The early light was unkind to Puerto Banús, which stretched out before them like an abandoned stage. The specialty shops that lined the *muelle* were still shuttered, and only a few stray figures wandered in the distance. It was just too deluxe, Ty thought, as he followed Maria-Antonia along a harborside where haute couture, haute bling and haute handbags were on display in the windows of outposts of just about every major international designer.

"I know it's over the top, but I *love* it," Maria-Antonia said without slowing the rapid pace she'd set.

"Good for you," Ty replied.

"You don't?"

"I'm a Jams and frayed-chinos kind of guy."

"Now you tell me."

"When I come into a new port, the first thing I look for is the chandlery; after that, maybe, a dive that offers false courage to sailors."

"In which case your luck's run out," Maria-Antonia said. "Even so, it might interest you to know that everything you see is not only named after but was conceived *and* built by Franco's favorite developer."

"How surprising!"

"Laugh if you will, but there are berths for almost a thousand boats," she continued. "That one over there, moored by the old tower, belongs to the king of Saudi Arabia."

"I suppose if I were King of Saudi Arabia, I'd want a boat just like that."

"Perhaps you'd prefer the desert."

"I wouldn't."

"What you fail to understand is that understatement never flourishes for very long where overstatement is possible."

Ty laughed. "I had no idea you were so philosophical."

"Why would you?"

"Beats me," Ty said. "What's that?"

They had arrived at the center of the harbor, and ahead stood an enormous, at first perplexing statue.

"A surrealist rhinoceros by Salvador Dalí," Maria-Antonia explained. "It weighs three tons, or so I'm told."

"Of course it is. How foolish of me!"

Two streets back from the harbor, on a corner and with tables set out on the pavement, they found the coffeehouse for which Maria-Antonia had been searching. It was crowded with fashionable patrons, abuzz with their morning chatter, and pungent with the aroma of espresso beans being ground and brewed. They ordered two lattes and took two English-language newspapers from the spindle rack on which they were held. They found a table, sipped their coffee and read in silence, Ty the sports page of the *International Herald Tribune*, Maria-Antonia the *Daily Mail*. As the sun rose, Ty opened the striped umbrella in the center of their table. Maria-Antonia suddenly laughed.

"What's funny?" Ty asked.

"I doubt you'd understand."

"Try me," he suggested.

"No," she said. "We don't have the same sense of humor, you and I. If nothing else, *that's* become clear enough by now."

"*Do* you have a sense of humor?" Ty snapped.

"There! You see what I mean."

"I didn't come out here to be needled and provoked."

"Why *did* you come?" Maria-Antonia demanded.

"It's an excellent question," Ty said. "I must have lost my head."

"Apparently," she agreed. "Boys will be toys, of course, but you actors, you're a breed all your own. You think you're so special because the spotlight falls on you and the footlights brighten your makeup, but really you're all the same! And what sort of person wants to spend his life becoming other people, and never for too long, rather than the one he is?"

"It's a job," Ty said, "like any other."

"Bullshit! You don't believe that for a minute."

They had begun to draw the attention of those surrounding them, particularly of a young couple who had seemed otherwise engaged only in sending and receiving text messages.

"What I don't believe is that there is any role I or anyone else could play that could ever satisfy such a professionally dissatisfied person as you."

Maria-Antonia hesitated. "You're over your head, Ty," she told him, as if in confidence yet loud enough to be overheard. "You're in danger of drowning. Why not head back to shore before it's too late?"

Ty rolled his fingers on the edge of the table. "You're a beautiful woman," he told her, making no effort to mask the sarcasm in his voice.

"Thank you. You're a beautiful man."

"But that's all?"

"I'm afraid it is."

"You're wrong."

"I'm not. Shall I put it to you bluntly? What you are and what you have are simply not enough."

Ty shivered, pretending to be simultaneously stung and released from inhibition by her sharp words. "Shall I tell you what *you* are?" he pressed, angrily.

"Besides beautiful," Maria-Antonia snickered.

"Yes. You're spoiled. You're a bitch. And, even worse, you're a lousy lay. Trust me," he added. "I'm an expert in these things."

It was then that Maria-Antonia's right hand, in which she held a tumbler of water, drifted gradually back, then sprung all at once forward, splashing Ty's hair and face. Water ran down the open collar of his polo shirt in icy dribbles. She kicked back her chair and stood abruptly. "The captain will leave your things on the dock," she said coolly. "I wouldn't waste too much time collecting them."

"No, I won't," Ty said, his instinctive temper flaring anew, "not in *this* den of thieves."

Chapter Twenty-two

Balthasar Fratangelo was beside himself. Although he had trained and begun to make a name as a designer rather than a gemologist, he was giddy in the presence of important gems. In his custody now—or rather in the locked attaché case of the strapping courier who, to Balthasar's delight, had accompanied him to Spain—were several of the most spectacular stones he had ever seen: pink and blue diamonds, Colombian emeralds, Burmese rubies and Kashmiri sapphires magnificent enough to justify the private Citation CJ3 in which they had been transported from Rome to the Costa del Sol—or, as Isabella jokingly referred to it, the Costa del Crime, that swath of resorts that stretched south from Málaga to Gibraltar.

Standing before her desk in the atrium that served as her studio when she was staying with Ian, Isabella carefully removed each stone from the paper in which it had been enfolded and placed it on a felt tray next to a sketch pad bearing her latest designs.

"It seems that things have gone upmarket in a hurry," Balthasar told her.

"There's no accounting for taste," Isabella said.

"You're telling me," he replied. "I thought the idea was that your line would bring young people to Guardi. I hadn't realized it was aimed at the *big* budgets."

"Nor had I. People with a lot of money sometimes have peculiar ideas."

Balthasar shrugged. "You would know more about that than I would."

"From proximity, not experience," Isabella said, casting her gaze about the sleek glass prism in which they found themselves. It was one of several that stood against the Andalusian hills near Casares, connected by fantastic corridors that tunneled through the landscape and that, in total, formed Pond House. The idea had been Ian's: transparent structures that, at the right angle, became all but invisible and at one with the lush and private arcadia in which they'd been established beside a man-made pond. Of varying sizes, the cubes had been built at diagonals contrived so that no interior could be glimpsed from any other.

"A distinction without a difference," Balthasar suggested, without elaborating. After all, it was common knowledge, at least among those in the know at Guardi, that Ian Santal had no natural heirs and no one as close to him as Isabella. And Santal was a European, not an American philanthropist. Where else would his fortune go?

"Shall I tell you what worries me?" Balthasar went on, still transfixed by, but now also apprehensive about, the loose gems on the table. "When people see pictures of your fabulous designs with these fabulous gems, they may be disappointed once the gems are taken out of the equation."

"Who said anything about pictures?" Isabella asked.

"I just assumed—"

"That these pieces would serve as a kind of haute couture and the basic line as prêt-à-porter?"

"More or less."

"No, no, not at all," Isabella said. "This is a strictly private sale, B, a one-off."

"Who am I to take exception to that? Although you have to admit it's curious. I'm supposed to see them into the safe," Balthasar said. "Where is it?"

Isabella laughed. "I could tell you, but I'd have to kill you."

"Buried deep in the hillside, I'm sure. Still, those are our instructions, aren't they, Arturo?"

The courier nodded.

"Ian will sign for them," Isabella said. "I've already cleared it with Lapo. Call him if you like."

"They must be worth tens of millions of euros."

"Call him."

"I believe you," Balthasar said. "Even so, I think Arturo should, simply as a matter of protocol."

"I agree," Isabella said. "I'll ring Lapo and put you on."

Arturo nodded. "Balthasar said you were a great diplomat," he told her. "Thank you."

Isabella caught the lilt in Arturo's voice and smiled. He was a strong young man with a swimmer's body and an innocent face, B's type exactly. "Where will you be staying?" she inquired.

"At the inn you suggested," Balthasar replied.

"It's sweet," Isabella said.

"I've never been to this part of Spain," he continued, "only to Barcelona. Arturo's never been."

"It's beautiful," Arturo said.

"We thought we'd make a weekend of it," Balthasar explained. "I can help you if you need help. Otherwise we thought we might rent a couple of Vespas and, you know, tool around."

Isabella said, "I'd ask you to stay here, but . . ."

"Mr. Santal's in residence and might not understand."

"Oh, no, wrong! He'd be the first to understand. He's the original connoisseur of blurred lines. Philip, on the other hand, will be coming down, and he—"

"Likes his privacy," Balthasar said, suddenly reaching into his valise. "Well, who can blame him? Not to worry. I almost forgot. We brought you the newspapers from Rome."

"That's very kind. Thank you."

"Quite a scene nearby," he said, "wasn't it?"

"What sort of scene?" Isabella inquired. "I've no idea what you're talking about."

"I can't believe that. Between Ty Hunter and some rich bitch called Maria-Antonia Salazar, or something like that. It's absolutely page-one stuff. Didn't you tell me you'd met him?"

"I did, very recently, at Cannes."

"The man gets around. It's all on YouTube, by the way."

As Isabella scanned *Il Messaggero,* she said, "I'll look out for it."

"Actually, you don't have to. I have it on my iPad. I thought you might be amused."

The YouTube clip, which picked up when Maria-Antonia told Ty that "boys will be toys" and continued through her dousing him with ice water, riveted Isabella, who despite her involuntary laughter declared, "That poor man," when the last image dissolved. "I wonder where he went."

At that moment a mahogany bookcase swiveled silently forward from the corner of the rock wall the atrium shared with the hillside and Ian Santal strode into the room. In needlepoint slippers, he seemed both at home and intimidating.

"Ian, I think you know my colleague Balthasar Fratangelo," Isabella said. "And this is another colleague, Arturo. I'm sorry I never got your surname."

"Montanarelli," Arturo told her.

"Arturo Montanarelli, who also works at Guardi."

"How do you do?" Ian inquired, locking his eyes on each, shaking their hands as though the young men were his equals.

"*Look* what they've brought. I said you would sign for them. In fact, we were just about to ring Lapo."

"Yes, let's do that," Ian said. "Where's the dotted line?"

Chapter Twenty-three

Oliver Molyneux said, "I'm sorry."

"Am I supposed to say that's a good start?" Ty asked. "If so, all right, it is, sort of, but you're still screwed in my book."

"I'm sure," Oliver replied. "Just tell me another way we could have gone about it that would have worked."

Ty said, "You have me there. It did work, didn't it?"

"Because it was spontaneous, that's the only reason."

"Not the *only* reason."

"Okay, you have talent. M-A has talent. How many times do you need to hear it?"

"Credit where credit is due," Ty teased. "She trained as an actress, didn't she?"

"You could tell?"

"Oh, I could tell."

"It was her dream once upon a time."

"Yeah, well, not everything works out the way it should," Ty said. "Prizes don't always go to the best."

"Never mind that now. M-A's found her stage."

They were in the sitting room of Ty's suite at the Marbella Club. Oliver had arrived a few minutes before, wearing a wide-brimmed straw hat and sunglasses that gave him the air of a gentleman planter and made him difficult to recognize. He had not approached the door of the secluded, seaside hacienda until he was certain that no one was watching.

"So what do we do now? Wait?" Ty asked.

"And wait."

"It's too early to call L.A. I can't wake Netty at three o'clock in the morning. On the other hand, I don't dare let him happen upon the story before he's heard it from me first."

"Netty is not our primary concern."

"Depends upon your point of view," Ty said. "He sets his alarm for eight o'clock. I'll call him at eight-oh-one, maybe minus a few seconds. Do you think it will be in the trades?"

"That's hard to say. Given the time difference, there's a good chance. I know it's already hit TMZ."

"Even if it has, so what? Do you really think our target audience has her eyes glued to TMZ?"

"Stranger things have happened. Anyway, from there it will go viral before you can say, 'Tousled Ty Tussled and Tossed.'"

"You've been waiting all day to say that."

"Actually," Oliver said, "about an hour and a half."

"If it doesn't work, I hope you and your friends really do have a Plan B."

The telephone rang before Oliver could reply. Ty picked it up on the second ring. "Hello."

"*Hola,*" came a Spanish voice, "is Housekeeping. May we check the minibar?"

Ty took a deep breath. "Later, please," he said. "I haven't touched anything."

"Later, *gracias,*" the voice told him.

Ty glanced at Oliver, shook his head.

A minute later an envelope was slid under Ty's door. When he unsealed it, he found a message from the concierge: *"Isabella Cavill called you. Please return her call."* There was a mobile number based in Rome.

Ty passed the message to Oliver, then closed his eyes.

"What are you doing?" Oliver asked.

"Counting down slowly from sixty," Ty whispered. "It's a way of casting off impetuosity."

"Another actor's trick?"

"In a sense," Ty said. "Quiet!"

When Ty had finished, Oliver said, "I admire her serve."

"Confident girl," Ty agreed. "What do you say? Shall I give it a shot?"

"Not from that," Oliver replied, gesturing to the BlackBerry cradled in Ty's palm.

"Why not?"

"Hold off for a minute, will you?" Oliver said, removing an outwardly identical device from the pocket of his linen trousers.

"Now I get it. You're auditioning to play M in the next Bond flick."

"If you want to flatter yourself, go right ahead. In the meantime, shall I explain how this one works? First, it functions in two modes: basic 4G and encrypted. Press and hold the capital and E keys for three seconds and you're in the latter. Do it one more time and you're out. Press and hold the capital and S keys in the same manner and it becomes a satellite phone—or not. And yes, before you ask, it *can* function in both sat and encrypted modes simultaneously. As a satphone it's registered to the Spanish weather office, although that's neither here nor there. But wait, I've saved best for last."

"You sound like a TV pitchman," Ty told him.

"What the hell! It's a living. Anyway, you're not going to believe this. In encrypted mode the phone has the comical feature of disguising, to any interloper, the conversation being had or text being sent. Whatever number you ring will register as coming from your house, or studio, or agent, from each of which place lines have been diverted."

"With the appropriate permissions?"

"Without, I'm afraid. Even better, if you press and hold H whilst you're speaking, anyone listening in will hear a humorous—in fact occasionally ridiculous—conversation. D (which no doubt stands for 'dour') will tune the eavesdropper in to serious chat on a completely irrelevant subject. N will give them nonsense . . . well, not exactly nonsense, but a conversation whose transmission appears to go in and out, to the point that neither heads nor tails can be made of it."

"I've got a lot to learn," Ty said.

"You're a quick study."

"Who told you that?"

"A little bird called personal experience."

"Oh, that," Ty exclaimed. "What if they confiscate my phone?"

"It will appear completely normal, but they won't because you are who you are. What they *will* do is listen in."

"I take it you've been able to monitor *their* communications."

"Only up to a point," Oliver explained. "We've not been able to hear anything said in Santal's sanctum sanctorum. It's lead-lined, jammed."

"Where is it?"

"Aboard *Surpass*."

"Ask a foolish question . . ."

"Of course, there may well be another one at his house, but he receives relatively few people there."

"So I'm to penetrate what the NSA and GCHQ Cheltenham have thus far found it impossible to do?"

"Santal would expect radio waves and every kind of computer code. What he won't expect is you."

Ty's smile was sardonic. "Or that's your hope anyway."

Oliver nodded. "It's only your life," he said. "Since when were you so cautious with that?"

As the silence that followed grew strained, the telephone rang once more. Ty looked at Oliver, then lifted the receiver.

"Is that Ty?" Isabella asked in her cut-glass English accent.

"Isabella Cavill!"

"You remembered my voice."

"Doesn't everyone? How did you find me?"

"First, let me say how sorry I was not to have been able to join you in London for your premiere. Very swell, it sounded!"

"You were missed."

"I would have been missed at work—permanently, if I hadn't stayed in Rome to follow up on the debut of my first collection. Not to evade your question, I saw the papers, so I knew you were not a million miles away. Then I put myself in the mind of someone in your position. Where would *I* go? The Marbella Club, obviously."

"But I'm not registered under my own name. At least I don't think I am."

"You're not. But you *are* registered under the same pseudonym you used at the Hôtel du Cap. The captain of Ian's boat had a record of it from my party. I took a flier that you'd used it before and would again—and it appears I guessed right. Who is Orlando March anyway?"

"A character my father and I used to write stories about," Ty said.

"How long will you be staying?" Isabella inquired.

"I'm not sure."

"Then come to dinner tomorrow evening, eight for eight-thirty," Isabella suggested.

"Eight for eight-thirty," he repeated.

"You're a stranger in a strange land," Isabella told him. "You need friends."

Chapter Twenty-four

In the distance, through the transparent wall as he approached it, Ty made out Philip Frost. And when he entered the pavilion of Pond House in which dinner would be served, it was Philip who greeted him, with a strong grip and a warm manner.

"First things first: What can I get you to drink?" Philip asked.

"That's a good question," Ty said. "My usual's a martini, very dry with a twist."

"Same as mine," Philip said.

"But tonight I was thinking of something more summery and . . . well, more Spanish," Ty said.

"Such as what?"

"Perhaps a Mojito?"

"Have a martini. Crispin makes the best in the world," Philip said, gesturing toward a tall black man in a tartan kilt who was already busy serving drinks to Ian's guests. "He swirls an ice cold crystal glass with Lillet blanc, then mixes Plymouth gin with a glance in the direction of France and a lemon peel twisted as only he can twist it."

"You've convinced me," Ty said.

"Two martinis up, please, Crispin," Philip said.

Crispin Pleasant smiled. "They're on their way," he replied, his diction still that of Barbados, where Ian had found him.

"So," Philip said, "it seems you've returned sooner than you expected."

"Once upon a time, I controlled my own life," Ty said with a wry smile, but keeping his eye sharply on Philip, "no longer."

"It happens to the best of us," Philip said. "I myself have just taken a new job and so am in the process of getting used to new masters. So far, so good, but it's always tricky, isn't it?"

"Actually," exclaimed Isabella, making a sudden entrance, "there's nothing tricky about it! Philip positively adores being based in Geneva. He was there at school, and we all know how some boys can never bear to grow up." At this she smiled ruefully, leaned up and kissed him. "Hello, darling," she added.

"Darling," Philip echoed, then, to Ty, said, "The fact of the matter is that for the moment I've been seconded to my firm's Gibraltar office. My commute is only as far as the Rock."

"He does it on his motorbike," Isabella added.

"It's the fastest way, especially at the frontier."

"Cool and dangerous," Isabella said, then, turning to Ty, offered him successive cheeks. "Hello there. I'm so glad we could get you."

"Your competition was room service," Ty told her.

"I don't believe that for a minute. Anyway, your timing couldn't be better. Tonight we're a party of twelve, including one of Gibraltar's leading politicians and the British admiral who commands the NATO base there."

"It sounds interesting. I've never been to Gibraltar," Ty said.

"Really? Then you shouldn't miss it," Isabella told him. "It's a fascinating place."

"Much like Zurich, with better weather," Philip said.

"And apes," Isabella added with a laugh.

"You're kidding," Ty replied.

"They're all over the mountain. They'll steal your handbag or your camera. They're playful, but you have to be careful," Isabella said. "And that's just on the surface of the mountain. Inside it there are all sorts of labyrinthine tunnels left over from its days as a fort."

"*Are* they over?" Philip inquired. "I'm not so sure. Admiral Cotton, for example, commands his staff and forces from a very sleek headquarters that was once one of the largest tunnels. How they hollowed it out one can only imagine, but it surveys the straits between Gibraltar and Jebel Musa fourteen miles away."

"Jebel Musa?" Ty inquired.

"It and Gibraltar were once one mountain," Ian interrupted, advancing toward them, "until the tectonic plates shifted, dividing not only them but Europe from Africa. If you studied Greek mythology, you know them as the Pillars of Hercules. Plato believed that the lost continent of Atlantis lay beneath them and that they marked the end of Hercules' travels as he performed his Twelve Labors. The Romans believed he smashed through the mountain on his way to the western edge of the known world."

"How fascinating," Ty said. "When did the plates actually shift?"

"It's a constant process, as I am sure you know," Ian said, donning a professorial mask that was new to Ty, although he suspected the older man had a mask ready for every audience and situation, "one that plays out over hundreds of millions of years in what are called Wilson cycles, after the Canadian geologist who originally described them. Continents form, break up, disperse, then reassemble. Nothing is as permanent as it appears to a human within his life span. By about six million years ago, Spain and Africa had collided, enclosing the western edge of the Mediterranean. Four million or so years before that, other collisions had sealed off its eastern edge. Thus constricted, the inflows of its rivers proved insufficient to maintain its sea level, so the Mediterranean dried out. Those rivers, however, were relentless. They kept pushing forward, far beneath the level of the Atlantic Ocean. Eventually one managed to cut through sufficiently to allow the waters of the Atlantic to begin to flow back in. It is likely that this flow, not Hercules, cut the Strait of Gibraltar. Of course, whether those mountains mark the entrance to the Mediterranean or the exit from it to the larger world beyond depends upon one's perspective."

"Well, I've learned something," Ty said. "I can't wait to see it."

"I can't wait to show it to you," Ian said, "if only by way of thanking you for having added such a note of glamour to our little party."

Ty shrugged. "I think the last thing any party of yours requires is more glamour—not that I bring any."

"Oh, but you do," Ian insisted. "It's not every day we have a film star, especially one of your magnitude and who's come to us directly—well, almost—from Buck House."

"I've never been to Buckingham Palace, if that's what you mean. The premiere was in a theater."

"Just slang," Ian said. "It was Buckingham House before it was Buckingham Palace, you see."

Very deftly, Ian maneuvered Ty toward his guests, beginning with his elegant lawyer, Riccardo Haslett, and his wife, Olivia, who lived in nearby Sotogrande, as well as Olivia's sister, Elvira, a twice-divorced, immaculately turned-out equestrienne then, as often during the polo season, visiting from Gloucestershire. Beyond them were Sir Timothy Foo and Lady Foo Fan Dang, an almost legendary couple from Singapore whose daughter, Catherine, had both begun and concluded her merchant banking career on the trading floor of Ian's old firm.

Tim Foo began their conversation, pointing to Ian. "Do you have any idea how long I've known this man?" he asked Ty. "Since he was a don and I a fellow of his Cambridge college. Where *did* the time go?"

"They say every day passes more quickly than the one before because it represents a diminishing percentage of your life," Ty said, "but I'm not so sure."

"Aren't you? And why is that?"

"Because I've spent days on certain sets that felt like they would never end."

"How true," exclaimed Lady Foo.

"My wife Celia was an actress," Tim Foo explained as Ian departed.

Lady Foo smiled. "'That was long, long ago,'" she said, "'and in a universe far, far away.'"

"Am I missing something?" Tim Foo asked. "I didn't realize Ian was in the film business."

"Is he?" Ty asked.

"If not, I must tell you I'm surprised. Ian seldom has people to Pond House or aboard *Surpass* to whom he has merely a social connection, although I suppose, being who you are, you're the exception that proves the rule."

Ty shrugged. "I take it, then, that you and Ian are more than old friends."

"Indeed we are old friends, and yes, I've also invested in some of his projects, as has he in my funds."

In rapid Mandarin, in order to disguise her words from Ty, a frowning Celia Foo said, "The way you say that, you would think he hadn't gone on to bigger and better."

Ty immediately looked away, suggesting that her foreign words meant nothing to him.

"Now, don't be unkind," Tim Foo told his wife, nodding to Ty with an expression that both begged his indulgence and implied that the matter suddenly under discussion was of some urgency. "Family crisis," he whispered in English.

"Three times we've asked him to our parties—in Singapore, Shanghai and London—and three times he has had better things to do," Celia noted grudgingly, still in Mandarin.

"Obviously he's got a lot on his plate," her husband told her.

"There was a time when you would have known exactly what that was."

Tim hesitated. "Perhaps that's true," he said. "Anyway, we're here."

Celia nodded reluctantly. "And I can't help wondering why."

"Life is relationships," Tim said calmly. "We nurture them or we don't."

"Ah, but relationships with whom?" Celia inquired. "Who exactly are all the new people in our friend Ian's life, so many of whom, from what I gather, seem to be from the Middle East? What roles do they play in the grand mise-en-scène he takes such joy in creating around himself everywhere he goes? We'll never know is my guess, because the great man is so jealous of his little secrets." Abruptly resuming in English, she turned to Ty and said, "Sorry, very rude of me to slip into another tongue."

At dinner Ty was seated between Isabella and Eloise Cotton, the admiral's longtime, formidably constructed wife.

"When you go to Gibraltar," Eloise Cotton said, "you must be sure to see Ian's office. It's on the opposite side of the mountain from Giles's, looking landward over the airport and harbor."

"So I've heard. I would love to."

"I'm afraid that Giles's office is off-limits," Eloise continued, "even to me."

"Except on certain occasions," Giles Cotton interjected from across the polished round table. He was a big, genial man whom Ty had already overheard telling one rambling story after another without ever reaching a punch line.

"Oh, *that*," Eloise remarked disdainfully, turning to Ty. "They have a reception one day every year, for the local VIPs—VSIPs, I call them: very *self*-important people—and even then most parts of the place are cordoned off."

"Nothing so secret in my little shop," Ian said. "Acres of files and bills of lading, HM's customs forms, et cetera, everywhere one turns. Boring, boring, boring they are, too!"

"You're being modest," Isabella said. "It's like Aladdin's cave. It cries out mystery."

"To you," Ian said, "perhaps it does, because you are an artist at heart, my darling, and because you don't work there. If you did, I've no doubt you'd find the boredom suffocating."

"Mr. Hunter doesn't work there either, so he may well agree with me. Anyway, we're not going to settle this now."

"How long will you be with us?" Eloise Cotton asked Ty.

"That's a hard one to answer," he said. "Not long, in all likelihood. This whole trip pretty much came up out of the blue."

"The last time we met," Isabella said, "you were so eager to get back to your new house and all the work being done and contemplated there."

"What an impressive memory," Ty observed. "When I did get back to La Encantada, I quickly discovered that the house is undergoing the kind of renovation you can't live around for too long."

Isabella suppressed a smile. "Tomorrow we go to the bullfight," she said.

"Indeed we do," Ian said, then, after catching Isabella's eye, added, "You should come, Mr. Hunter. And anyone else who would like to is more than welcome."

"Enough of this 'Mr. Hunter,' please," Ty said. "I thought we'd straightened that out aboard your boat."

Ian nodded.

"Do come, Ty," Isabella said. "You'll enjoy it. Have you ever been to a bull-fight?"

"Never."

"All the more reason, then! At the very least, you'll add to your inventory of experience, which has to be a good thing for an actor."

"You can stay overnight in one of the guest rooms," Ian offered. "The Marbella Club is too far to drive anyway, especially after drink and with the Guardia Civil in the mood they're in lately. So it's settled?"

"I suppose it is," Ty agreed, after what he judged an appropriate pause.

"You and Philip are about the same size," Isabella said.

Philip, plastering a smile to his face, said, "I'm sure I can find something suitable for you to wear."

"Thank you very much," Ty told him.

"Pleasure," Philip replied.

After he turned out the light but before he went to sleep, Ty picked up the BlackBerry Oliver had given him. It was nearly midnight—considering the time difference, a credible time for him to call his house, his production company at the studio or his agent. He pressed the pad at its center, thought about holding down the *E* character until the light behind the numbers blinked, but decided that it would risk provoking suspicion to encrypt a conversation one end of which could easily be overheard by other means. Instead he pressed then held the capital N in order to make the conversation seem subject to interference and thus unintelligible to any intruder. From his list of contacts, he highlighted his agent, Netty Fleiderfleiss, then pressed the green call button. Seconds later he heard the single-spaced rings of an American telephone.

The intercepted call was answered before the third ring had been completed. "Hello," Oliver said.

"Hi, Netty," Ty replied. "Do you have a cold? It sure sounds like it."

"The usual summer drip," Oliver responded, playing along. Trusting as little as necessary to chance, they spoke in an impromptu code even beneath the protective layer of technology.

"You won't believe where I'm going tomorrow."

"Knowing you, I'm sure you're right, but try me."

"To a bullfight."

"A bullfight?"

"In Seville."

"According to the papers," Oliver said, "you were just in one at Puerto Banús."

"Oh, that," Ty said.

"You're not going to the bullfight with that bitch?" Oliver asked.

"Jesus, no," Ty said. "With friends. In fact, I'm staying with them now."

"Glad to hear it. Don't even think of becoming a matador. Your face is too valuable."

"So you've told me once or twice before."

"It's the box office talking, not me. The box office talks to the front office. That's why they talk to me. You know how it works. By the way, I had a chance to go by your palace, if that's the reason for your call."

"It was one of the reasons," Ty replied. "What's the story there?"

"'Creative destruction,' I think is what they call it. They're working, but they're a long ways from there yet. Incidentally, sorry about the bust-up of your pickup—forgive me, but I don't know what else to call it."

"Plenty more fish," Ty said.

"When are you coming home?" Oliver asked. "Do you know yet?"

"Netty, I have no idea. Maybe soon, maybe later. For the moment I'm here and have no reason to be there."

"Don't you want to hear about the Thralls' party?"

"Is there anything to hear?"

"Come to think of it, I don't suppose there is."

"Bye, then," Ty said.

"Yeah," replied Oliver, "bye-bye."

Chapter Twenty-five

"Tell me again what Andrej told you," Ian said. "And, Philip, don't leave anything out this time."

They were in Ian's study, yet another, smaller, soundproofed glass structure in the Pond House complex. In the dark of the Spanish summer night, the room glowed, its sleek furnishings and Arabian carpets unpredictably harmonious.

Philip replied, "He said questions had been asked, as high up as the Main Directorate Number Four, about Zhugov."

"I expected there would be."

"You hadn't mentioned it. Anyway, Zhugov, as you know, is dead."

"A fact that pains me," Ian said. "I had wanted him to prosper. He deserved to."

"I'm sure you're right and that he was a very nice man, but he cut an outrageous profile, which might have become more dangerous if he'd cut it for longer. His tastes were growing ever more expensive and flamboyant. What can I say?"

"That you had no hand in his death. You could say that."

"Of course I didn't," Philip said. "You know better than that. It's a very different thing to note that a man's death is convenient than to have had a hand in arranging it."

"That's true," Ian said. "I apologize if I sounded accusatory."

"Accepted," Philip told him. "Anyway, it was known that he and you had dealt hands to one another from time to time."

"Neither of us made much of a secret of that fact, but the devil lies in the details. How much was known about those 'hands,' as you put it?"

"Andrej couldn't say."

"So naturally you're wondering if you are tarnished by your association with me. That's another well-known fact, after all."

Philip paused. "It is," he replied, "but Andrej assures me that I'm not. So far I'm in the clear, and he expects it to remain that way."

Ian shook his head, not at the accuracy of Andrej's prediction but at the ease with which people were fooled by credentials—the right family, the right school, the right posting, such as Philip's to the Nunn-Lugar initiative. "Because of your good works, I take it?"

"Apparently so," Philip said.

"Nevertheless, on your own initiative you had our cargo re-rerouted?"

"Yes."

"Don't you think I should have been made aware of this before rather than after the fact?"

"We had a contingency plan in place for a reason. All I did was activate it."

"By doing so you also risked activating more interest in our turbines. Did that occur to you?"

"Naturally, but the risk seemed small in comparison with the risk of doing nothing."

"Think about whom you're dealing with."

"Our friends in the Camorra are as interested in handing off those turbines and being paid their last installment as we are in taking receipt of them."

"In all probability, but they're human. Don't forget that. They possess curiosity. What if, once aroused, they pursue it?"

"What if? Your question, in this context, is hypothetical. Anything is possible, sure, I'll grant you that, but the real what-if question here is this: What if, Ian, you *are* under closer scrutiny than you think? Not for cargoes that no one knows exist, that according to the best-kept records don't, but because some suspicious bureaucrat or eager politician playing cop has decided you might have had your hand in Zhugov's pocket or he in yours? What if, while they're building their petty case, a precious cargo lands right at your doorstep and they say, 'What's this—let's open it and have a more thorough look'?"

Ian swallowed hard. "Be that as it may," he said, "my earlier point still stands. I should have been made aware of your action *before you took it*, not simply before you'd left Prague for Geneva."

Philip studied his mentor. There were times, grave and pivotal moments of which this was one, when Ian's famously piercing eyes seemed only to refract the available light. "I agree," Philip said, "and I'm sorry. It won't happen again."

"No," Ian said. "Well, good night."

Chapter Twenty-six

The bullfight, one of the last of the season, was held in the Plaza de Toros de la Maestranza in Seville, a two-hour drive north by northeast from Pond House. They arrived at the ring with time to spare and so, before entering their box, toured the nearby Museo de la Real Maestranza de Sevilla, where Ian carefully explained the history of the bullfighting artifacts on display, including a cape that Picasso had painted. Of the guests at the party the evening before, only Ty and the Foos had joined the excursion, so once they made their way past the main structure's baroque façade to their assigned seats, Ty was surprised to find a number of vacant chairs, indicating that others were expected.

Ian beckoned Ty to the front-row seat beside his own, gesturing that he was to assume it only temporarily, until a guest of higher rank or more immediate importance arrived. "*Corrida*—that's the Spanish word for bullfighting . . ." Ian began. "You don't speak Spanish?"

"I took it in high school," Ty said.

"The corrida is older than you might think. It goes back to the ancient Greeks and Romans, so it's one of the very oldest traditions in the world."

"I read that on one of the plaques in the museum."

"You may also have read that for a long time it was reserved for royalty and done from horseback. Sometime after the fifteenth century that changed. The sport gradually became less formal, more impromptu."

"I see," Ty said, sensing that Ian had been waiting for Isabella and Philip to take their places higher in the box before turning to the subject on his mind.

When they had, he said, "You've got yourself into a bit of a situation, haven't you?"

"Go on," Ty said.

"One with three corners. Those are never good."

Ty raised his eyes, as if to look over his head and back at Isabella and Philip. "*I've* gotten myself into nothing," he said.

"That is beside the point."

"Your goddaughter called *me*."

"After you invited her to meet the Queen. Make no mistake. I have nothing against you, Mr. Hunter. In fact, I rather like you. Had I had a talent such as yours, a face such as yours, I should think that I, too, would have rolled the dice. Alas!"

"You've gone rather far on your own talents."

"Thank you. I've been fortunate. You must understand something about Isabella. She is beautiful. She is talented. She has a way with people, a certain style. Even when she was a young girl, her father used to say that she entered a room as though she were in a classic film. She has always been enamored of film and film stars. Need I say more?"

"I'm not trifling with her," Ty said, squirming slightly as he smoothed the lapels of Philip's splendid summer jacket, feeling suddenly uncomfortable in the other man's clothes.

"No, you wouldn't dare," Ian said. "Don't you understand? People such as my goddaughter, who dwell in the world of style, even when they make their names and fortunes there, are inevitably prone to place too much importance on unimportant things. It's a habit and a vulnerability of their nature and occupation. I don't want her hurt. If she enjoys your company, as I do, and you enjoy hers, that's fine. But I implore you, do not lead her on! Do not break her heart!"

"I wouldn't think of it."

"In my experience, which is not so limited as you might imagine, people of the stage often turn on a dime."

"That's not entirely fair," Ty protested.

"But it *is* my impression."

"I beg your pardon, but Isabella seems very happy and more than satisfied with Philip. I can't believe my appearance on the scene has affected that."

"Philip Frost has a lot to recommend him. Still, I can't help but wonder, is she truly in love? Or is he, for that matter? I can't see into their hearts."

"This is *your* country, *your* box. Last night it was *your* house and *your* party and, before that, *your* yacht. I would be ungracious if I didn't ask, what exactly would *you* like me to do from this point on?"

Ian smiled. "Treat her as you would wish to be treated," he said. "She is a grown woman with a great deal of experience, a kind heart and a fine mind. She no longer needs me for much, except now and then to protect her from herself. I'll tell you what I don't want to see. I don't want to see—and *will not* abide seeing—her sweet and lovely face in tears on the cover of some glossy fan magazine or cheap, vulgar tabloid." A vein rose in Ian's forehead as he spoke. "I will not see her life, her name, everything she's worked for tarnished because her heart got ahead of her brain."

Ty waited until he was certain Ian had calmed down. "None of that will happen, I promise you."

Ian put out his hand, and Ty shook it. "You're a gentleman," Ian said. "Now, how much do you know about this sport? Where should I start?"

"At the beginning—" Ty said, but Ian's attention was immediately distracted by the arrival of a pair of Arab businessmen. Of medium height and in their mid-forties, they had caught his eye from the entrance at the top of the box and were now descending toward the first row.

"Salaam," Ian said, offering a quarter bow, a single revolution of his hands as he made it, a gesture of respect. "Now that the Al-Dosari brothers are here, the corrida can begin. Sheik Wazir, Sheik Fateen," he continued, urging them forward, "may I present Mr. Ty Hunter?"

Both men smiled. It was clear to Ty that Ian enjoyed having surprised them.

They possessed such an intense resemblance to each other that Ty was sure they must be twins. As a boy, in Kuwait and then Saudi, he had heard of Crusader Arabs, modern-day men and women who bore the genes, especially the brilliant blue eyes, of Northern European invaders. But he had never seen one. Now, suddenly, here were two at once, their black hair tinged with russet.

As Ty stepped back, Philip approached. "Wazir, Fateen," he said, with an absence of reserve Ty had not previously seen him show to anyone.

"Philip," the nearest of the Arabs replied, with suspicion in his darting gaze.

"I trust your trip was not too taxing," Philip said.

"Not in the least," the other brother replied.

Ty studied the men. Quite apart from their unusual eyes, there was something both disturbing and familiar about them. He had come upon their type before, first in his previous incarnation as a soldier in special ops. Like the arms runners and *narcotraficantes* he'd dueled with then and a few "financiers" he'd encountered on the periphery of the movie business, these two Crusader Arabs were decidedly men of the world, dapper men whose fine, exactly right clothes and studiously cultivated manners could not quite hide the menace that lurked beneath their surfaces.

Philip gestured for them to take seats in the front row next to Ian, but they remained standing, poised as if to flee, while the latter spoke. "He belongs to you now," Ian said, lightheartedly, his eyes in motion to and from Philip.

"Ah, but we are expecting great things from him," said Wazir.

"We shall do great things *together*," clarified Fateen.

As if he had practiced the speech, Wazir said, "Surely. The de Novo Fund will bring together the capital and energy of parts of the world that have too long been at arm's length from one another. Who better to lead it than a man of Philip's education and experience and high purpose?"

So, Ty thought, the Arab twins were here because they were Philip's new employer, another twist of fate no doubt managed by Ian. That left Sir Timothy and Lady Foo. Where did they fit in? Ty wondered as Isabella approached to fetch him.

She was wearing a beige linen suit, the jacket of which came down over her slender hips. Her hat, a shade lighter, featured a wide brim. "Do sit with us," she beckoned. "You'll have more fun."

"Yes, ma'am," Ty replied. "I meant to tell you earlier: Your suit is beautiful."

"Thank you. I found it in a consignment shop in Paris. It was designed by Gustave Tassell. Real fifties movie star kit, don't you think?"

"I do, just like my house."

"Very Audrey Hepburn, that's the effect I'm going for," she added with a wink. "Shall I tell you about the main attraction?"

"Please," Ty said. "Your godfather was about to when—"

"Something came up. Been there, done that."

"I'll bet you have," Ty said. "I gather Philip's gone to work for the twins."

"Indirectly," Isabella said. "Philip is now chairman of de Novo, but it's largely their money . . . well, theirs and their friends'."

"De Novo?" Ty inquired. "That's paradoxical, isn't it? A Latin name for an Arab fund?"

"It's globalization. The name comes from the Latin for 'anew, a fresh start.' Their idea is to use their investments to help forge a new and better relationship between our civilizations. That's what attracted Philip. Whatever he does, even when it involves making money, has to be for a higher good or he simply is not interested."

"That's admirable," Ty said.

"*I* think so," Isabella told him. "Anyway, back to bullfighting. Ordinarily there are six bulls in each corrida, two for each event. You'll see, in the ceremony that's about to begin, the toreros will be introduced, immediately after which they'll request the keys to each bull pen."

Ty studied the unfolding scene. "What's the difference between a torero and a matador?" he inquired.

Isabella laughed. "The difference between an actor who has just got his first decent part and you," she said. "Once the bull is released—"

"The shit hits the fan," Ty interrupted. "Sorry, couldn't help it."

"In a manner of speaking," she replied. "The fight is divided into *tercios*. In the first *tercio,* the torero will employ a purple-and-yellow *capote*. During this part of the fight, the picadors, two men on horseback, will use a spear to weaken the bull, with the goal of forcing it to keep its head down. After that comes the second *tercio,* the *suerte de banderillas*—"

"Don't tell me too much too soon," Ty said. "You'll spoil the story."

"As you wish."

"Isabella," Celia Foo said then, speaking across her husband. "I wonder if there is an extra scarf anywhere about. This sun is very hot."

"Isn't it?" Isabella agreed as she began to search through the large pigskin tote bag she'd brought with her. "Here you are."

"Thank you," Celia said. "I am going to wrap my face in it like a mummy."

"Be careful," Tim Foo said.

"It preserved *them* well enough, didn't it?" Celia told him as a man whom none of them could identify made his way into their box.

"I am looking for Dr. Santal," the man said.

The use of the honorific "Dr." suggested to Isabella that the visitor might once have been Ian's student. It was difficult to place the man's age, for he appeared both young and worn. His chestnut hair was still as thick as it must have been in his university days and still unmarred by gray, but there were crow's-feet etched beside his eyes, which looked dry and distant. "And you are . . . ?" she asked.

"Luke Claussen," he said.

Isabella hesitated. It took a moment for his name to register.

"My father and Dr. Santal were friends."

"Of course, I know who you are. I was very sorry to hear about your father's—"

"Murder," Luke said, completing her sentence.

"Exactly, his very sad death," Isabella continued. "Ian will be so pleased to see you. Is he expecting you?"

"I'm afraid not," Luke Claussen said.

"Never mind," Isabella said.

Luke put his hand up. "I was going to call him later today or perhaps tomorrow, but I overheard someone in the bar say that he was here, and . . . well, I thought I might come by just to say hello."

"You are here with friends?"

"Yes."

"Good. Come on," Isabella said, encouraging him down the steps, through the prestigious *barreras,* toward ringside. "Ian," she said as soon as he had paused in his conversation with the Arab twins.

"Yes, my darling," he replied, leaning back over his shoulder.

"This is Luke Claussen," she told him. "He heard you were here tonight and stopped in to say hello."

Ian appraised the man. "Billy's son?" he asked.

Luke nodded.

"I *loved* your dad," Ian said. "I can't tell you how much his death distressed me."

Luke paused. "It had that effect on a lot of people," he said. "Thank you for your kind letter and your contribution, by the way."

"It was the least I could do. Come sit by me."

"I won't stay long. I'm not here on my own."

"Stay as long as you like," Ian said as Philip, Wazir and Fateen abruptly shuffled chairs to make room for Luke.

"Who was that?" Ty asked when Isabella returned to her seat.

"Luke Claussen. His father was a friend of Ian's, an American tycoon who met a very bad end. You may have read about it."

Ty shrugged, suggesting that he hadn't.

Isabella looked at him curiously. "It was in all the papers," she said, "even over here. It was a gruesome murder. Not only was his father killed, but his sister and her young son and daughter, who were staying with Mr. Claussen for Christmas."

"Now that you mention it, I think I do remember hearing about that. It was really awful," Ty said.

"The son's better known than he thinks he is," Isabella said.

"Is he?"

"He's sort of a player, or was—big talker, big boozer, big loser at the tables."

"Or that's the word."

"From many sources, but you're right, I've no firsthand experience. So I shouldn't judge."

Ty wanted desperately to include himself in the conversation then taking place, in full view in front of him, between Ian and Luke Claussen but realized that it was not feasible for him to do so without arousing suspicion. He wished his telephone had been equipped with some sort of surveillance capability, though in such a crowd any device would be almost impossible to aim unobtrusively. So he sat back and watched as the initial *tercio* began.

Between it and the second, the *suerte de banderillas,* in which three of the toreros would attempt to implant two flags each into a charging bull, Ty noticed Luke stand up and make his way toward the exit. When he reached the row in which Isabella and Ty were seated, he slowed to a stop, then leaned in to thank her. Offering only a perfunctory smile to the Foos, who were seated between the aisle and Isabella, he did a double take when he saw Ty.

"You had a moment of doubt," Ty said.

"I thought that was you. Then I said no, couldn't be. Luke Claussen," he said, extending his hand.

"Ty Hunter."

"I know. Everyone knows you. I'm sure you're used to that by now. Anyhow, it's nice of you to pretend you aren't."

"What do you mean by that?"

"You gave me your name. You didn't assume I knew it."

"My parents brought me up right."

"Listen, I know you're busy here, but after the first corrida would you come over and meet my friends? They'd get a real blast out of it if you did. We're just two entries down."

"Sure," Ty said before Isabella had a chance to give a different answer.

"*I'd* love to, but—" Isabella explained, remaining still, letting only her eyes wander toward the Foos and Ian's other guests.

"I understand," Luke said.

"But there's no reason Ty can't join you."

Luke hesitated. "You're not together. I'm sorry, I misunderstood."

Isabella blushed.

Ty said, "We're together, but we're not *together*, if you get my meaning."

"Well, that's too bad," Luke said. "Shall we say before the *suerte suprema*?"

"You bet," Ty said. "That's my favorite time to do just about anything."

Luke shook Ty's hand a second time, nodded to Isabella and the Foos, then departed quickly through the shunt that led back to the main concourse of the *plaza de toros.*

"What the hell is the *suerte suprema*?" Ty asked Isabella after Luke was out of sight.

"The third *tercio,* as I'm sure you've already guessed," she said. There was disbelief, if not outright irritation in her voice.

Ty ignored it. "Which, I'm assuming, is when the torero faces down the bull and flashes his famous red cape—"

"It's called a muleta."

"I'm glad to know that. And that's also when he kills the bull with his sword?"

"Yes," Isabella said, "as it charges him, and the quicker the kill, the better. That's what it means to be a matador. The crowd can offer the praise of the multitudes, or it can be very unforgiving."

"Tell me about it," Ty said.

Isabella smiled faintly. "Why do you say that? You've never faced an unforgiving crowd, have you?"

"Not since I got lucky."

"It was nice of you to say you'd join them for a few minutes. It surprised me, though. Why did you?"

"You told me the man's father and sister and his niece and nephew were murdered very recently. How could I say no?"

"Luke Claussen didn't seem to be in mourning."

"People deal with grief in different ways. You don't mind, do you? I don't have to go."

"Of course I don't mind," Isabella said. "In fact, I think it's noble of you."

"It's not," Ty said.

"It is, even if he turns out to be just another obsessive fan, because you don't know that yet, do you?"

"I know only what you told me."

"I didn't tell you that Luke Claussen is one of the richest men in the world."

"No, but it wouldn't have made any difference if you had. Money can't buy you back your father, as we both know."

"As we both know," Isabella repeated softly.

It was unclear whose box Ty was entering, but it was almost exactly like Ian's. It took him a moment to locate Luke. Once he had, the incredulous stares of those around him gave way to well-honed smiles as Luke introduced him to his coterie. Expensively dressed and apparently less than intent on the spectacle unfolding before them, most were drinking tostadas or rubias, the dark or pale lagers of a local artisanal brewery.

Ty took a tostada.

"What brings you to Spain?" Luke inquired.

"Luke doesn't read the gossip pages," said one of the young women, an American in her early thirties with lustrous golden-blond hair otherwise found only on small children.

"He's a smart man," Ty said. "The answer is, I played a hunch. They don't always pan out."

"No," Luke said, "they don't."

Having been introduced to the movie star and in several cases squeezed into a snapshot beside him, the others gradually began to drift out of his orbit, leaving Ty alone with Luke.

"And you? Is Seville one of your stomping grounds?"

"Not really. I was passing through, mostly for the polo at Soto, and you know, friends of friends . . . That's the way it goes, isn't it?"

Ty shrugged. "I've been working too hard to remember if it is or isn't."

"I know you've had a lot of pictures out," Luke said, "practically back-to-back, am I right?"

"You're right."

"I'm afraid it looks like my life is about to take an abrupt turn in that direction," Luke declared, a newly wistful note sounding in his deep bass voice as a trace of sadness crossed his face.

Ty knew enough to be careful. "What do you mean?"

"You may have heard that my father died and that there were other deaths in my family."

"I did," Ty admitted quietly. "I'm sorry. I wasn't sure what to say."

"There's nothing *to* say, but thank you anyway. I'm afraid the net result of it all is that—some people would say for the first time in my life—I'm going to have to take on some responsibility."

"That may come more easily than you think," Ty said.

Luke took a long pull of his lager. "I hope so. As the last of the Claussens, I'm suddenly the largest shareholder in a company I spent my whole fucking life running away from. I'd still be running away if there were anyone left between it and me, but there's not. There are good executives, thank God for that. But that's all they are: well-paid, well-meaning, capable executives, not more. My father was a motive force."

"I get the picture," Ty said. "He was a friend of Ian's, wasn't he?"

"Definitely," Luke said. "That's why I wanted to say hello to the old coot. I'm sure I've met him before, actually, but that would have been a long time ago, when I was seven or eight years old."

"People change," Ty said, "especially over that amount of time."

"Damn straight," Luke said. "Anyway, it's like I was saying, even the finest executives are only as useful as the charge you give them, right? *You* have to know what's going on. If you don't, they'll know you don't. I guess what I mean is that maybe business is my thing and maybe it isn't, but I damn sure don't want to be fooled out of a fortune. So I'm doing the rounds, learning what's in the pipeline and where, who I can trust and work with and who I can't. That's what I've been doing in Europe—mixed in with a little pleasure, of course."

Ty nodded.

"How well do you know Ian?" Luke asked.

"Not well. In fact, this is only the second time I've met him. The first time was just last month."

"That girl Isabella's something, isn't she?"

"Yes," Ty agreed, "really something."

"Who's she seeing? She must be seeing someone."

"You met him, I think. Philip Frost."

Luke started.

"Do you know him?"

"No one does. He was a year ahead of me at Rosey, but light-years ahead in other ways. We weren't really friends, nor were we enemies. Philip was far more serious about everything than I was, even if at the same time he could be reckless. We climbed the Giferhorn together once, I remember, if only because that mountain was the most dangerous around and absolutely off-limits. We were crazed. We did it at night. You may never have known exactly where you stood with Philip, but you could trust him with anything, which may sound paradoxical, but it was true."

"Maybe that's what Isabella sees in him."

"You should make your move," Luke suggested. "She'd go for you. Trust me. I have almost perfect instincts about these things."

Ty laughed. "You're not interested?"

"I wouldn't get anywhere."

"Why sell yourself short?"

"Listen, I'm nothing if not brutally honest with myself. That young woman is a perfectionist, and I am rather blatantly imperfect."

"Opposites attract," Ty told him.

"Seldom the case in my experience," Luke replied. "Anyway, back to Ian. He's a piece of work. My father was fascinated by him. Guys like them, they're genuinely intrigued by each other."

"Sounds reasonable," Ty said.

"Aren't you fascinated by other movie stars?"

"I wouldn't use that word exactly."

"But come on, you keep your eye on them. 'A man should both appreciate and fear his rivals.' That's what my father always told me. My point is Dad and Ian Santal dwelled in the same neighborhood on Olympus, if you catch my drift. Oh, they were probably very different in many ways and very much the same in others, but there's no mistaking it, they were—*are*—a species apart, more like gods than men. So I was glad to reconnect with the old guy, because I have a lot to talk to him about."

Ty let silence fill the pause, then, as if spontaneously, asked, "Did they do a lot of business together?"

"Once upon a time," Luke said, "not so much lately. At least I don't think so. Truth is, that was one of the things I was glad to have a chance to talk to Ian about. Somehow or other he'd gotten my father involved in the redevelopment of a Russian resort."

"Forgive me, but that sounds like an oxymoron," Ty said.

"Nope," Luke said. "I've seen the pictures. The place is as beautiful as anything you could possibly imagine. It's up at the top of the Black Sea, on the Strait of Kerch."

"Never heard of it," Ty said.

"By the Sea of Azov," Luke continued, "the shallowest sea in the world. You have to love those names, don't you? I mean, some of them sound like they come straight out of Grimms' fairy tales. They can scare the shit out of you."

"Now that you mention it."

Luke regarded Ty thoughtfully. "Well, maybe not you," he volunteered, "but my father must have felt that way, because he eventually pulled out of the deal. That's another thing I wanted to talk to Ian about, but he couldn't give me a reason for my father's pulling out. When I asked him whether it was really true that my father had decided to bail on the project, all he said was, 'To my astonishment, yes.' What does that mean?"

"Impossible to say," Ty concurred.

"Of course, he said that Dad must have had 'other priorities,' but as to what those were or might have been, he either didn't know or wouldn't say. So I asked him another question, to which I got a more satisfactory answer, although not an entirely satisfactory one. If Dad and the company did pull out, I asked, why hadn't every last bit of Claussen Inc.'s involvement ceased by this time? All he said in response was that the company had been engaged to clear the site, that there were these stages in the contract and they couldn't leave until they'd completed their obligations through this stage or that. 'One doesn't just turn off a switch,' he said. 'These things have to be wound down. There is a process.' Those were his exact words. It was more than a bit patronizing, but probably true."

"I'm sure," Ty said, doing his best to display enough interest to keep Luke talking, but no more.

"'Are you still invested in that deal?' I came right out and asked him," Luke said. "'No,' he told me, 'that's not my modus operandi. I put together deals. I take a piece. As soon as the time is right, I sell that piece and move on to take another piece of something else. I do not operate businesses.' Well, fair enough. Good luck to him!"

"Absolutely," Ty said.

By the time they left the *plaza de toros,* the long, sweet light around the summer solstice had faded, and they drove back in convoy, buzzed by alcohol and the adrenaline that had flowed since the last wounded bull had suddenly charged, then come within inches of killing the torero who faced him. An air of letdown lingered as they drove through the winding, narrow, steeply graded roads of Andalusia and moved steadily away from the evening's primordial excitement toward a calmer, more normal world. Ty was with Isabella and Philip in the second Mercedes, Tim and Celia Foo in the forward sedan with Ian, Fateen and Wazir having left them to head elsewhere. Halfway to Pond House, the telephone in the car carrying Ty beeped twice.

Isabella answered it. "Oh, hello, missing us already, are you?"

"Always, when you're not here," Ian said. "I've just had a word with the captain. Day after tomorrow, just after breakfast, does that still suit?"

"It suits me to a tee," Isabella replied. "Let me just check with Philip. . . . Day after tomorrow to sail, early start? That's still on with you, isn't it?" she asked.

"It's in my diary in big red letters."

"How can you be sure without looking?"

"I know because *you* wrote it in," Philip said.

"Ty," Isabella said. "You're footloose and fancy-free at the moment. Would you like to join us?"

"On *Surpass*?"

"You won't believe it. It's *so* cool it will take your breath away."

"I've been aboard, remember?"

"For a party," Isabella said, "which is an entirely different thing from a cruise."

Ty studied Philip, who was doing his best to mask his disgust at Isabella's impulsive invitation. "I don't want to be in the way," Ty said.

"There will be people coming and going—not just businesspeople, glamorous people, too, and some not so glamorous whom Ian finds interesting. The last thing you'll be is 'in the way.' "

"That's true," Philip said. "It's not hard to get lost in the crowd if one finds oneself bored to tears."

"Then I'd love to come," Ty said, "but please run it by your godfather before I accept."

"I'll do that right now," Isabella said, picking up the phone. "Ian, you're big on having movie stars aboard—"

"I've never seen myself in quite those terms," Ian interrupted, "but yes, by all means, Ty would be most welcome if he can spare the time."

Isabella nodded.

"How long a cruise?" Ty whispered.

"A week, plus or minus," Philip whispered back.

Isabella covered the mouthpiece momentarily with her palm. "You can go ashore at almost any time, anywhere."

Ty raised his thumb and forefinger in a circular shape.

"I have a feeling he can spare the week," Isabella told Ian.

Chapter Twenty-seven

Oliver stood in the windowless reception room of NATO HQ in Gibraltar. Recessed in the gunmetal wall behind protective glass were dioramas portraying important moments in the history of British Gibraltar. Each featured elaborate ships' models and multitudes of miniature sailors and soldiers. Oliver was studying one entitled *The Relief of Gibraltar by Admiral Lord Howe, 11th–18th October 1782* when the receptionist, a sturdy female lieutenant in dress uniform, said, "Commander Molyneux."

"Yes."

The receptionist looked toward a door on her left, one that would have appeared more at home in a Georgian house than an aboveground seaside cave.

Seconds later the door opened outward and laughter could be heard as Admiral Giles Cotton escorted his guest, an adviser to the island's chief minister, to the exit. "Tell me that one again," the Gibraltarian said. "I want to be sure I've got it right. 'What's the difference between a vitamin and a hormone?' That's it, isn't it?"

Giles Cotton nodded. "You can't *hear* a vitamin," he whispered, making a display of his discretion in front of the receptionist.

No sooner had the visitor withdrawn than the receptionist, interrupting her commanding officer's stride, said, "Admiral, Commander Molyneux is here to see you."

"Oh, yes indeed. I nearly forgot," replied Giles Cotton, who approached Oliver, offered his hand, and said, "Come this way, won't you, Commander?"

Oliver followed him as the heavy paneled door closed with quiet precision.

"It's counterbalanced," Admiral Cotton explained, having noted Oliver's reaction. "It has to be, since beneath the shiny veneer it's armor plate."

The left wall of the corridor was transparent yet soundproof, affording a comprehensive view of a high-tech office wherein dark composite desks and state-of-the-art terminals arranged in pods stretched as far as Oliver could see. The absence of the normal hum of a work environment made the large room seem farther away than it was and eerie, as though it were being spied upon, its occupants' privacy violated. The wall on their right was cave rock, formed of long, uneven ledges in which openings that had once been gun emplacements were now sealed with thick glass. Pausing before one of these, Oliver took in a sweeping panorama of the straits, with Arabia in the distance, then noticed that in a few of the lower emplacements video cameras had been set up, pointed at the sea.

On a wall of Admiral Cotton's office the input from these and other cameras was displayed in a chessboard of monitors. Opposite, behind his desk, hung an enormous oil painting in an elaborate gilt frame. Oliver recognized it as *The Defeat of the Floating Batteries at Gibraltar, 1782* by John Copley. "That can't be the original," he said, "can it?"

"I fear not, but it's a very fine copy," Admiral Cotton replied. "The original hangs in the Guildhall in London. Have a seat, Commander."

"Thank you."

"You've come all this way from Legoland," Admiral Cotton said, referring to the headquarters of the Secret Intelligence Service, on the Albert Embankment of the Thames. "I am sure there must be a good reason."

"Unfortunately, there is," Oliver responded.

"I am more familiar with your organization than you may suppose," Admiral Cotton said. "The grandfather of a great school friend of mine helped to found it."

"Who was that?"

"As he never himself acknowledged his role, I shouldn't say. Like much of the modern world, it sprang to life in embryonic form after the Second World War when the Soviet Union and a newly communist China had suddenly become our enemies. In those days it was called Office for the Exacerbation of Sino-Soviet Relations! How's that for dry British humor?"

"Classic," Oliver said, and laughed. "I hadn't heard that before. I wonder what the service would be called if it were being named today. Who would our masters designate as our primary enemies? Our world's too complicated to say with any certainty, isn't it?"

"It's very complicated."

"Let me be direct," Oliver said. "An extremely dangerous cargo may soon pass through or by Gibraltar. Or it may not."

"If it did, where would it be bound?"

"That's impossible to say, but Gibraltar, because of its geography, could be the gateway to many destinations."

"Do you suspect a direct connection to anyone here?"

"No," Oliver dissembled, "unless you can give me a reason to think otherwise?"

"Who am I to think anything of the sort?" Giles Cotton said. "My job is to run a naval station and protect an important British and NATO asset. To that end I've worked very hard to maintain cordial relationships with prominent members of the small community here. As you might imagine, everyone knows everyone."

"In its way it's also a rogues' gallery, isn't it?"

"You wouldn't be the first to draw that conclusion," Giles Cotton replied, stroking his formidable chin. "Of course, there are many sun-seeking retirees with nothing more on their minds than today's golf game and tomorrow night's dinner, and many locals who, like people everywhere, simply do the best they can within the confines of their own world. But I take your point. We also have perhaps more than our share of shifty ones."

"There are a lot of Russians about these days, aren't there?" Oliver inquired, wishing to sidestep the name of Ian Santal.

"Not so much on Gib as along the coast, and fewer than there were before a number of the more visible and overleveraged ones went bust. Among those who remain, of course, are the leggy, beautiful creatures who work in restaurants and bars and hotels."

"Of course." Oliver smiled.

"They are the most numerous by far, but I doubt they are trafficking in anything more dangerous than love and whatever baubles they wangle from their lovers. Some may use drugs. The other group is one I call the mini-oligarchs. They're not the ones whose names keep turning up in newspapers and magazines, but they made their way out of Russia with a certain amount of loot, and they've found their way here to enjoy it."

"It's one flight pattern," Oliver continued. "At this point it's not a person or any group of people we are looking for, but a cargo."

"What sort of cargo? For you to be involved, I assume it must involve weaponry of some sort."

"Or material for weapons, possibly," Oliver said, again intentionally to distract. "Gibraltar is far from the only place of concern to us at the moment. My colleagues in those other places are doing exactly what I'm doing, although it's more complicated where there's no British sovereignty."

"How can I be of service?"

"You do have radiation sensors in place?"

The admiral looked at Oliver with new intensity. "I'm certain you already know that we do."

Oliver nodded.

"Who else knows?"

"No one here, and for the time being no one should."

"That's to state the obvious."

"Allow me to be a bit more specific. The substance of this conversation must not go down or even up the chain of command."

"A bit irregular, is it not?"

"If it weren't, it would be done by someone else," Oliver said. "The PM and the First Lord have been briefed. You will receive orders through the usual chain of command that will seem unrelated to the possibility I've mentioned but that will provide you the flexibility you'll need should your help be required."

"Which no doubt would be on a split-second basis?"

"If that need arises, we could require rather a lot of help on very short order indeed," Oliver said. "So let's hope it doesn't. In the meantime I'll keep in close touch. Please do the same."

"Quite a place," Oliver said. "Part fortress, part palace. You could shoot a film in there, except that permission would never be granted. You enter and exit by what looks like the opening to a cave, in darkness for twenty meters or so until you turn to your right and ahead there's a shadowy lobby, walled off by tinted glass. Once inside, it's brighter. There are military police, a discreet but deterring barrier, and beyond that a lift that ascends to where the action is. Oh, and did I mention there's a sentry box outside the original entrance? So there's no real attempt to hide what's there, simply to make it mysterious, I think."

They were seated in the living room of a rambling hacienda situated in a hollow on the way from Pond House to Marbella. The old structure stood beside an abandoned mill, and the gurgle of a natural stream could be heard through its opened doors. The room's furniture was comfortable and worn and covered with the hair of a German shepherd and a Pekingese that belonged to a local potter, a widow whose husband had been killed in the al-Qaeda bombing at the Atocha Station in Madrid in March of 2004. In the years since, she had occasionally offered her home as a safe house to American and British intelligence services.

"Did he know anything?" Ty inquired.

"I don't think so," Oliver said. "It's not the kind of secret one would be likely to share, especially with him."

"But he's a friend of Santal's."

"All part of his job, as he sees it. Sidney Thrall is a friend of Santal's, too, and you've made films at his studio. In fact, to an outside observer *you* are a friend of Santal's. You attended the same party the Cottons did. Not very long ago, you even graced his yacht. This is not our grandfathers' world, where the righteous and the evil retreated to their separate base camps. We live side by side in a world of very few uniforms now."

"Hear that bell? Class is over," Ty said.

"Hold on a minute. I wasn't winding you up for the hell of it. I was attempting to make a damned important point, which is that whether it's just Santal and Frost or whether there are others involved, they are not going to give themselves away. We have to find the weak link in their plan, stress it and crack the whole bloody thing open from there. Only then will Admiral Cotton and his forces be of any use."

"It's nice to feel needed," Ty said.

"I'm glad you're happy, because this is a puzzle SIGINT can't solve, only HUMINT," Oliver continued, employing the professional slang for signals and human intelligence.

"Speaking of HUMINT, I had a valuable talk in Seville with Luke Claussen, who turned up out of the blue."

"So your e-mail suggested."

"The guy's very concerned that his company has kept up its involvement in a Russian deal that Santal put his father into a whole lot longer than it should have. You know the one, that resort that's going in near Kerch."

Oliver nodded. "We both know it's a stretch, but the powers-that-be in Washington still stand by their team's decertification of that site."

"Even though the decertification team was headed by Philip Frost?"

"*Because* it was headed by Philip, I think. You heard George Kenneth yourself. He has a sweet spot for the fellow. Who knows, maybe they were fuck buddies back when Philip swung both ways."

"You're kidding?"

"I am, as far as I know. I have nothing to base that theory on, but how else to account for Kenneth's incautious loyalty?"

"They belong to the same old boys' club," Ty said, "that's how, and maybe it's enough. It blinds them to each other's faults."

"Whatever. It is what it is," Oliver said. "As to Claussen's vessel, no cargo, nada, was unloaded from it in Istanbul."

"That's a relief," Ty said.

"Possibly so," Oliver replied. "During its one-day layover in the Bosporus, the ship did take on some computer components, mostly small, lightweight stuff from India and China, also the usual teas and quite a lot of textiles. It's still the Silk Road, after all."

"Let me guess," Ty said. "The teas and textiles were unloaded in Naples."

"Along with several crates of computer components, but none of the generators or turbines or other material from Kerch," Oliver said.

"Why are we so certain of that?"

"The cargoes were sequestered."

Ty rolled his eyes. "How thoroughly were the crates that *left* the ship searched?"

"My understanding is that that was done by the Italian authorities."

"Answer my question."

"I thought I just did. According to their head man, they do have neutron detectors set up, but no spectroscopic gamma-ray equipment. How thick their wall of radiation-portal monitors is isn't entirely clear either. Of course, presuming there were warheads aboard, we've no idea how or how well they might be shielded."

"It's a good bet that if they got as far as Naples under the Claussen imprimatur, they'd make their switch there. No one in their business flies under the same flag for too long."

"Yet they might well in this case," Oliver said, "when the flags they're flying can be presumed to deflect suspicion as completely as Claussen's and the Stars and Stripes. That's why we had the Italians checking the Claussen ship's cargo crate by crate."

"With what results, may I ask?"

"All the crates marked as containing turbines contain turbines."

Ty studied Oliver. "And you're satisfied that the Italians were thorough?"

"As best one can be," Oliver replied.

"Which could mean any one of the following: that this particular ship is uninvolved in any conspiracy, that there is no conspiracy, or that three surplus turbines came aboard in Istanbul to take the place of three of the original pieces of cargo from Kerch that were then unloaded in Naples. If the last were the case, those would have been the loose warheads."

"It's a theory, but then why didn't the sensors pick them up?"

"I'm guessing they would have been well shielded, but even so. Sensors depend on one thing even more important than that."

"Go on."

"Someone has to turn them on in the first place and be paying attention to them," Ty said. "Do you know if they were functioning properly when those computer components and teas and textiles were offloaded?"

"I can't give you a concrete answer to that one. Our people have raised the very same question any number of times, but they haven't yet received a definitive response one way or the other."

"Which in itself is a bad sign," Ty said. "I'm pretty sure I know the answer, but the cargo that went ashore was meant to stay ashore, and it was fungible, wasn't it? I mean, it's hard to follow a trail of tea leaves."

"Almost impossible," Oliver concurred. "Of course, the left hand in all likelihood wouldn't know what the right was doing. Anyone who happened to look the other way would more likely be responding to a bribe than functioning as a cog in a larger conspiracy. It *is* Naples, when all is said and done. They not only practice corruption there, they savor it. Have you been to Pompeii?"

"Never," Ty replied.

"It's bang next door, you know. Even that long ago, corruption thrived there. The sailors who arrived in port spoke different languages, of course, so the city employed a kind of sign language not all that different from international road signs today. For example, the route to a brothel and the brothel itself were marked by an erect penis raised from the stone."

Ty laughed. "We're getting off the point, aren't we?"

"Not so far as you may think," Oliver said. "The point is that even if there are warheads on the loose, there's no way in hell we're going to track them from their source, especially now that they may have passed through the maze that is the Neapolitan waterfront. There are just too many places to look, and we don't have enough people. Nor can we track down and follow every ship, railcar and lorry we know to have been there when the warheads might have been, much less those that were there but we didn't and still don't know about. The conclusion is pretty obvious, isn't it?"

"It has been all along," Ty agreed.

"We'll have to trace them back from their intended destination. There's really no other choice."

"Which is where I come in," Ty said.

"Which is where you come in," Oliver said. "The search for clues starts there."

After Ty briefed him on the dinner party and the bullfight that had filled his two previous evenings, Oliver said, "You're on your way back to the Marbella Club to collect your things. Do that! Check out and pay with a personal credit card, one you would ordinarily use. Then go directly back to Santal's. The car you used to come here, you rented it, am I correct?"

"Yes. The hotel got it for me."

"How do you know it hasn't been equipped with a transponder since its arrival at Pond House?"

"Shouldn't you have made this point before now?"

"Not really," Oliver said, "if only because I have such faith in you. Tell me, what did you do?"

"Jammed it," Ty said. "When I'd gone far enough, I pulled to the side of the road, found the GPS where I would have least expected to—"

"Where was that?"

"Smack under the spare tire in the trunk. I wrapped it in a piece of tinfoil I'd found in the mini-kitchen off my bedroom. I'll unwrap it just before I return to the motorway."

"You took the scenic route."

"That will be my excuse if I need one, which I doubt I will. The device is a piece of junk. I'd bet it's only there for his guests' protection, in case they get lost. If they were genuinely suspicious, they'd use better equipment and make it harder to find."

"By the way," Oliver said, "on your new BlackBerry, there's a GMT function that can also be used to jam GPS, mobile phones and the like. And it's easy to remember—"

"Don't tell me," Ty said, "I hold down the G, M and T keys simultaneously."

"You're a quick study. It's been designed not to overtax an already overburdened mind."

"Custom built, in other words."

"You said it, not me. Now, as to your cruise, we don't know everywhere you're bound, but we do know that one port will be Tangier. Ian has made arrangements to meet people there, and the ship's captain has been in touch with the harbormaster."

"Don't lose track of me," Ty said.

"*Surpass* would be difficult to lose track of," Oliver replied.

"I didn't mean on *Surpass*. I meant in the casbah."

"You've seen too many old films."

Ty nodded. "Scary, isn't it?"

Chapter Twenty-eight

Ty's stateroom was located on *Surpass*'s guest deck, at the far end of a corridor from the one occupied by Isabella. He was led toward it by a steward, a taciturn young Algerian with a compact but toned physique.

"You're fortunate," the steward told him. "Vanilla is my favorite stateroom." Noticing Ty's curiosity, he added, "All the rooms are named after orchids, mostly exotic species. For example, Miss Cavill's stateroom is Epidendrum."

"I see. And Mr. Santal's, what's his called?"

"It's the only one that doesn't have a name."

"How about Mr. Frost's?"

"His is Vanda. We passed it on the way here."

"So it's near Isabella's?"

"That's one way of putting it," the steward said. "All the staterooms are suites; those two—Vanda and Epidendrum—are adjoining."

"How handy," Ty said. "What makes you so fond of Vanilla?"

"That's hard to say. I always have been. It's bright and large, and . . . well, the most famous people we get aboard *Surpass* usually stay there."

"I'm flattered," Ty said as a courier suddenly approached them.

"I'm looking for Epidendrum," the courier announced.

"Behind you," the steward told him. "Never mind, though, Miss Cavill is not in her room at present."

"Would you happen to know where she is?"

"Whatever you have for her you can leave with me. I'll see that she gets it."

"I'm afraid that's impossible in this case," the courier said.

The steward grimaced. "Because it requires *her* signature?"

"It does," the courier said.

"Well, I'll try to raise her, then," the steward said, removing the chrome intercom from his belt.

Before he had pressed her extension, Isabella appeared behind him, catching him off guard. "It's all right, Jean-François," she said, with a smile that dispelled his concern. "I've been expecting this gentleman."

"Very well then," Jean-François said. "I'll just see Mr. Hunter settled."

"Plenty of time for that," Isabella replied. "Hi, Ty," she said, offering him her right cheek. When he had kissed it, she turned her left toward him. "We're in Europe," she explained.

"Hi," Ty said.

"Jean-François," Isabella said, "see to it that Mr. Hunter's things are in his room, would you? Ty, please come with me. There's something I'm dying to show you."

The sitting-room walls of Epidendrum were covered in lemon yellow suede trimmed with white moldings and a bronze-and-teak handrail. Light from a sun still high in the eastern sky flooded through its oversize elliptical portholes. Once the courier had departed with his signed receipt, Isabella pried open the large box he had brought her. Inside was a thin black cowhide attaché case. From a trouser pocket, she removed a small key, then used it to unlock the case. "Close your eyes," she told Ty before lifting the lid. "Perhaps you'd better sit down."

"I have a strong constitution," Ty said.

Raising the top of the briefcase, Isabella began to laugh. *"Chacun à son goût,"* she said.

"I beg your pardon," Ty said.

"Sorry. You don't speak French?"

"I deliver my lines in English," Ty said.

"American English, as a matter of fact," Isabella added, but with no trace of condescension in her voice.

"I'm from Virginia," Ty said. "It's been a long time since we were a colony. Anyway, you know what they say about Americans and foreign languages."

"Pretty much the same thing they say about *us*," Isabella told him. "All right, go ahead! Feast your eyes!"

Beneath a soft black foam cover and velvet cloth, fitted neatly into recesses that had been expressly hollowed out for it, rested a spectacular parure, a necklace, bracelet and earrings set with matching blue diamonds, set off by smaller white, pink and canary ones.

"Wow!" Ty exclaimed. "They're something, but if I were giving a present like that to a woman like you, I would do it in person."

"That's always the problem. Jewels like these usually come with a curse."

"And what's that?"

"The men who give them."

Ty smiled. "Before I met you and Ian, before I'd come aboard *Surpass* and stayed at Pond House, I'd begun to think I was doing pretty well. But this is another world."

"Do I detect false modesty?"

"Awe, that's what you detect. Did Philip give them to you?"

"Philip?" Isabella laughed. "Now you *are* being absurd. He was a public servant until the day before yesterday. You know what sort of salary that brings."

"I don't know anything about Philip."

"A symphony of frost and flame, no pun intended. That's what he is."

"If not from Philip, I suppose they must be a present from Ian?" Ty prodded, trying to maintain the light tone of their banter.

"One can dream," Isabella said. "Silly man, they're not for me. I'm in the jewelry business, remember?"

"I remember very well, but the pieces I saw when we met after Cannes were—"

"Much smaller, I know."

"They were beautiful. I loved them, but they were more casual."

"It seems I've gone upmarket since then."

"All the way up. What caused the sudden change, if you don't mind my asking?"

"Surely you can guess the answer to that: a client or two. With great wealth goes great eccentricity. My new clients seem to like the idea of mixing style and substance."

"Sounds like a lucky break."

"The Guardi brothers are happy about it."

"What about you?"

"I'm happy enough. Personally, I think we're mixing apples and oranges, but it's not my money. And the people whose money it is see it differently. They want me to adapt *my* collection for *their* jewels. Who am I to complain?"

"Does this jewelry have a history?" Ty asked.

"Not much of one," Isabella said. "It was only assembled over the last decade by a tycoon from Malaysia or Indonesia, maybe Thailand. He commissioned it for his wife. She had it with her in Paris when she decided to leave him. He fought that at first, but this sort of jewelry is often the price men pay for their philandering."

"I don't want to be crass," Ty said, "but what are we talking about here?"

Isabella shrugged. "Lapo could tell you that better than I. For insurance purposes, I believe I heard someone say just upwards of fifty million."

"Dollars?"

"Euros. And this is just what came today. It's by no means all. There are lots of loose gems still in papers I brought with me from the house."

Ty's eyes widened. "It's a lot to take responsibility for."

"Actually, the jewelry's safer here than it would be in Rome. *Surpass* may look like a yacht, Ty, but just beneath the surface it's really a battleship, and its crew are warriors. Take Jean-François, for instance. He grew up in Marseilles, along the waterfront. Not too long ago, he was a mercenary in Iraq, then Afghanistan."

"On whose side?"

"Whose do you think? His own," Isabella said. "Isn't that what it means to be a mercenary?"

Dinner that night was served on bridge deck, at a long, candlelit table by the pool. To Ty's surprise, Wazir and Fateen Al-Dosari had returned and were seated at right angles to each other on the striped U-shaped sofa where the party had gathered for drinks. Also present were the Greek banker Harry Kosmopoulos and his much younger German wife, Anna. Harry, who still retained some of the swagger of the ocean-racing sailor he'd once been, was already engaged in conversation with Raisa Gilmour when Ty appeared. The subject under discussion was gems, for the now-elderly Raisa had inherited both her late husband's Zurich-based business and his knack for high-end collecting.

"Of course, the difficulty began when the various labs sought to grade precious stones," Raisa intoned. "Their intentions were the highest, but I am afraid that as they solved one problem, they inadvertently created another."

"What do you mean?" Isabella inquired.

"Works of art are not commodities," Raisa explained. "Great gems are like great pictures, each a thing unto itself, not necessarily better or worse, but different from all the others. There is a romance to them that even the finest laboratory's grade can never hope to distill. That's why I like so much what I've heard about your new designs, my dear, because they are not cookie-cutter, am I correct?"

"Well," Isabella said sheepishly, "the basic line is a line. We start with a model and cast many identical pieces from it. What I believe you're referring to are the pieces I'm making for some more important stones."

"Exactly those," Raisa confirmed.

"Those will be . . . variations on a theme, yet each one of a kind."

The older woman smiled, then looked at her glass.

"Have some more champagne," Ian said as Crispin Pleasant, in a freshly pressed tartan, topped up her flute of Krug 1996.

Harry said, "We opened a bottle of '85 the other day, and it was surprisingly delicious. I had bought a case, then forgot it was in my cellar and left it to lie down much too long, but it turned out to be lovely nonetheless, sweet if not so bubbly. Of course, the cork didn't pop."

Ian's eyes lit up. "Good bottle of wine like that, the cork oughtn't to have popped," he said, "but emitted the sigh of a contented virgin."

"You're incorrigible," Anna told him.

"So I've been told," Ian replied, raising his glass. "'Champagne to our real friends,'" he suddenly toasted, in a deliberately mysterious key, "'real pain to our sham friends.'"

Harry hesitated. "A most interesting toast," he observed.

"It's all in good fun," Ian assured him.

"Of course it is. Did you just make it up? You *are* clever."

"I wish I could claim authorship, but I fear it goes back at least two centuries—to America, I believe."

"Does it? I've never heard it before," Ty said, "but I'm going to try to remember it."

"That shouldn't be difficult for an actor," remarked Anna with a seductive smile.

"What an idyllic evening!" Harry exclaimed, as though he had just noticed.

Anna nodded her agreement. "Where are we?" she asked.

"The nearest lights are Melilla," Ian said.

"Melilla is Morocco?" Anna asked.

"It is. Yes."

"But we are not going ashore there?"

"I hadn't planned on it," Ian said. "If you'd like to, of course . . ."

Anna waved away the thought.

"There's more to see in Tangier," Fateen told her.

"Certainly more decadence," Wazir added. "Tangier is famous for it."

"Once upon a time," Raisa said preemptively. "Have you been to Tangier, Mr. Hunter?"

"I haven't," Ty said.

"Nor I," interjected Philip.

"Well, it's an old haunt of mine," Ian said. "It elicits a flood of memories every time I go there. I look forward to sharing some of those with whoever comes along."

"Sadly, *we* leave you tomorrow," Harry said. "I believe you are not due in Tangier until the day after, isn't that so?"

"You are correct," Ian said. "You'd be welcome to stay."

"That's kind, but I'm a slave to my diary."

"Not as long as you're aboard *Surpass*," Ian insisted, then looked ashore and mused. "Beyond each horizon one encounters an entirely different civilization. Where else is that as true as here? You know, I love the Arab as much as I love the European one, but what I truly love is this sea, the Med itself, with its ebbs and flows."

"Speaking for myself, I would be content never to leave this ship," Anna said.

"I know what you mean," Ian replied. "Here one is away from yet smack in the middle of everything."

"That could be a perilous place to be in a collision," Raisa suggested.

"The much-predicted clash of civilizations?" Ian asked. "Not to worry, civilizations don't collide. Ideas do."

"Armies have been known to collide," Philip said.

"Indeed," said Fateen cryptically. "Both the visible and the invisible ones."

"Yes, well, there's always that problem," Ian said.

After a starter of jamón serrano with chestnuts, then a beautifully cooked fish risotto and assorted cheeses and biscuits, Ian stood and was quickly followed by the other men present. Taking his cue, Ty began to follow them toward the stairway that led to the owner's deck above but stopped when Jean-François blocked him at the first step. "You'll excuse us for a few moments," Ian called over his shoulder, with pleasant firmness.

"Stay with us, Ty," Isabella added. "Keep us company."

"Of course," Ty said.

"Don't take it personally," she told him. "Life with Ian is always like this, a sort of kaleidoscope where one minute life is pure pleasure, the next deadly serious business, the one after that a blend of both. No two moments are ever quite the same. Would you like a cigar?"

"No, thank you."

"Or a glass of orujo?" she continued, with a fresh glint in her eye. "In which case I'll join you."

"Ouch," Ty said, "but sure."

The orujo, fermented from the skins of pressed grapes, was aged and amber in color. It was also 50 percent alcohol, and later, in his stateroom, Ty sensed it had put him at a sudden remove from the world. He felt insistent throbbing at his temples as he typed out an encrypted e-mail to Oliver. The room was sumptuous and bathed in the soft coral glow cast from its silk lampshades. Ty turned out the lights before texting, not knowing where cameras, as well as microphones, might be hiding. He depressed the *H*, wondering exactly how a humorously encrypted e-mail to Netty might appear, if intercepted.

"Glamorous, but so far only social, no substance, no idea who anyone is," he typed, after which he listed the names of those on board.

"If anyone is up to anything, no one talks about, or even around, it. After dinner, men retreated to owner's quarters. I was barred."

It was not long before the flashing red light on his BlackBerry alerted him to an incoming from Oliver.

"Use your high-tech charm," it read. *"It's all we've got."*

Lunch was the centerpiece of the next day. Held on the "beach club," a square of teak, chrome and fiberglass that unfolded from *Surpass*'s aft starboard hull to float as a pontoon, it featured a Romanian dancer-turned-businessman by the name of Aurelien Strigoi; a Pakistani mathematician, Rahim Kakar; a septuagenarian

Indian industrialist, Ajay Prajapti, and his handsome, suspiciously diligent son Akshar; and Ch'ing Shih, a Chinese property developer who had recently been on the cover of the Asian edition of *Fortune*.

When Philip arrived without Isabella, who was busy working on designs for Sheik al-Awad, Rahim Kakar said, "Well, I suppose this gives new meaning to the term 'business lunch.'"

"It's nothing of the sort," Ian said. "It's a gathering of old friends."

"Upon which I fear I'm intruding," Ty said.

"Quite the contrary," Ian said. "We all need someone to hear our stories for the first time."

"He's not kidding either," Ajay Prajapti said.

"Take Ian at his word," Aurelien Strigoi said. "One ordinarily doesn't wear a swimsuit to a business lunch, after all."

Ty laughed. "That's a very good point."

"The truth is that we are not conducting the least bit of business," said Ajay. "We have in the past and doubtless will in the future, but today we are here simply to enjoy Ian's incomparable hospitality. Actually, we're—"

"More like cardinals paying our respects to the Pope," Aurelien suggested. "Sorry, Ajay, I didn't mean to cut you off."

"One has to pay respect to a man with such a yacht," Ch'ing Shih said.

"What Aurelien says is true," the elder Prajapti told Ty. "Our respect for and devotion to Ian are the ties that bind us. Even I've learned from him, and I am old enough to be his father."

"Hardly," Ian said, then, turning to Ty, added, "They flatter me. Aurelien was my student, you see, a very long time ago. Brilliant, he was; left with a Double First. So brilliant, in fact, that from day one he never bought any of that nonsense about flattery getting you nowhere. That's true, is it not, Aurelien?"

The Romanian nodded reluctantly.

"Ajay was a client, and Rahim and Ch'ing were my partners when I still had my firm in London. They've both gone on to bigger things."

"Suddenly it's dawned on me," Ch'ing said.

"What has?" inquired Aurelien.

"Why Mr. Hunter is here with us, of course. You're going to play Ian in a film, aren't you? Ian in his salad days—now, that would be some film!"

"I'm sure it would. I'd love to see the script," Ty said.

"Problem is, only one man could write it," Rahim said, "and he won't. For the life of me, I don't know why. I've been trying for donkey's years to get him to write a memoir."

"Too many tales to tell," Ian said dismissively.

"Nonsense," Rahim said. "You are a subset of one. Very few great business-men are also thinkers. Just go back to the articles you published when you were at Cambridge or to those quarterly reports and bulletins your old firm used to issue. They were masterpieces, chock-full of your theories. Even in the prefaces to the catalogues raisonnés of your various collections, you usually found a way to expound one thesis or another. So why not put your memories down on paper, too, preserve them for posterity?"

"They're too personal," Ian said. "I have always enjoyed writing about big subjects, not myself. And I haven't done that in quite a while. The last such piece I published was one the *Economist* invited me to write in their little book that previews the year ahead."

"I remember it caused quite a stir," Aurelien said.

"The truth, any challenge to orthodoxy, often does," Philip said.

"I admit I enjoy cutting against the grain from time to time and turning conventional wisdom on its head, not so much now as when I was younger."

"What was the subject of your piece?" Ty asked benignly.

"Weapons of mass destruction," Ian replied. "All sane people seem to agree that the fewer there are, preferably in the fewest possible hands, the safer the world is."

"And you disagree?"

"Not entirely. I simply chose to argue the contrary point. Given that inequi-ties among people and nations and groups are inevitable, might not the best way to stop bullies be to empower their potential victims with the tools necessary to protect themselves?"

"At first you read me the riot act, didn't you, Philip? But eventually you came round."

"I came to appreciate the argument," Philip explained, "as an exercise in logic, not necessarily as a prescription for the world's troubles."

"The problem, obviously, is that to prove any such thing would require that an experiment be conducted in the real world, something that's most unlikely to happen."

"Mercifully," Philip told him.

Later that evening, after Ian had retreated to his private quarters, he received a call from Aurelien Strigoi.

"Do you have a moment, Ian?"

"Haven't I always for you?"

"You have. I'd prefer to speak in person, if you don't mind."

"Come up to my deck in five minutes. I'll tell Jean-François to expect you."

"I don't want to disturb you if you were doing something important," Aurelien protested.

"Reading Thucydides *is* important, but, like almost all the most important things in life, it can be postponed."

"Thank you."

Once inside, having accepted both an Armagnac and a small cigar, Aurelien Strigoi said, "Something's been bothering me. I'm sure it's nothing, but I wanted your assurance that that's the case."

"Go on, please."

"The other day I was in Vienna. I have interests in several businesses there, as you know. It was toward the end of the day. I was in the Kärntner Ring. I was getting into my car when I saw, or thought I saw, Philip Frost preparing to enter the building next door to the one I had just come out of."

"What sort of building?"

"An office block," Aurelian replied, "mostly financial offices. It's that sort of area. I'd just been to see my bankers, in fact."

"You didn't speak to him then?"

"No. Well, yes and no. I mean, I called out to him, but he didn't reply. He did turn when I said 'Philip,' the way one does when one hears one's own name, but then his face went absolutely blank. I don't know how to say this, and thus I will do so gingerly. He had the look of a man who has been caught by a close friend prowling a red-light district."

"Could be you were mistaken."

"Possibly, or, more plausibly, he truly didn't see me. I made a joke of it on the way up from lunch."

Ian took a sip of his Armagnac. "What was his reaction?"

"It was the first time I'd seen his composure crumble. He did his best to hide it, naturally. The man has commendable deportment. But a shock of such magnitude cannot be entirely internalized. I'll tell you what I said. I told him the damnedest thing happened to me in Vienna. I'd seen his twin brother. Did he have a twin? I asked him. He smiled, shook his head. He stalled while he calculated. I let the matter go. I had no business questioning his movements and wouldn't have thought twice about it if he'd admitted he'd been there but had not seen me when he'd spun around as he did. Even so, I was nearly certain he was lying. Then it caught me, the detail that made me positive he was: his signet ring. He has it on today. When he'd turned around and looked about in Vienna, he'd shaded his eyes with his left hand. That ring on his pinky caught the sun and reflected a bright beam."

"You were that close?"

"Yes."

"Why are you bringing this to my attention?"

"Because many people who engage in financial shenanigans these days find themselves some sort of base in Vienna from which to do so. A man I heard of not long ago employed a secret Viennese account, a secret intermediary in Singapore, and an equally secret trust in Vanuatu. The whole thing came to a bad end for those credulous souls who couldn't resist involving themselves."

"How regrettable," Ian observed.

"My point is," Aurelien continued, "I don't invest with you because of whatever your next project consists of or doesn't. I do so because it's you. You know that, surely. My trust is in you, not the details, beyond the fact that they are backed by your integrity. What are we up to together at the moment? 'Beats me,' as the Americans say."

Ian smiled naughtily. "Really," he said, "I hope not."

"What I do know is that you and Philip have had a business as well as a social relationship, that the young man's an acolyte of yours and now working for your friends Wazir and Fateen Al-Dosari."

"All true," Ian said.

"I rest my case."

"Signet rings are not at all uncommon. As for any other elements of confusion, it's frequently hard to tell purebred dogs apart."

Aurelien hesitated before saying, "I thought you should know."

"And now I do. Thank you, my friend."

Chapter Twenty-nine

Shaded by an awning of wisteria and palm fronds, Luke Claussen sat on the terrace of the Rock Hotel in Gibraltar, sipping his glass of manzanilla and wondering why Admiral Cotton had booked lunch for three rather than two. The old art deco hotel, which dominated a panoramic view of the Bay of Gibraltar, the Spanish mainland and the Rif Mountains of Morocco in the distance, had a distinctly colonial air. Its white wrought-iron furniture, starched pink tablecloths and tended gardens reminded Luke of Kansas City, especially Mission Hills, where he had grown up.

"Sorry to keep you," Giles Cotton said upon arrival.

Luke stood, and they shook hands quickly. "Such a delightful place to wait," Luke replied.

Cotton ordered a manzanilla for himself. It was not his habit to drink during the day, but he was determined to keep his guest company. Luke Claussen was just the sort of man in whose corporation a retired naval officer with a distinguished record might find a suitably rewarding position. "That stuff is hard to resist," he said, glancing at Luke's pale sherry. "Something about its salty side, I suppose. Thank you for coming to see me, especially on such short notice."

"I was honored when you called. In fact, I've been hoping for the chance to talk to you, or at least to someone who might be able to give me an idea of what the hell's been going on."

"I'm afraid I don't understand."

"I've had reports that the authorities are scrutinizing our ships as though they suspect something foul," Luke said. "If there is a problem, I'd like to know about it more than they would."

"Which authorities?"

"The Italians, for a start, but ever since my father got us involved with a project in Russia—something he immediately regretted, by the way, and withdrew from as soon as he was able to—there seems to have been a change in how we at Claussen are perceived. I can't say by which department or service or even country. It's more of a general thing, but I've had many reports that my people feel there are eyes on them that there didn't used to be."

"Is that what's brought you to this part of the world?"

"I'm embarrassed to say that it isn't. A leopard can't change his spots overnight. I came for the fun of it."

"Please forgive me for asking, but as no one around here was quite sure, is your connection to Claussen Inc. a formal one?"

Luke laughed. "An interesting choice of words," he said. "I'm not our company's CEO or even chairman of its board, although I suppose if I suddenly went mad, I could be. It's still a private company, as perhaps you know."

Giles Cotton nodded.

"Very few in the world are as large. When it came to business, my father was an absolute genius. As the bearer of his genes if not abilities, I now find myself the company's principal shareholder. Because of that, people tell me things." As Luke finished, he was aware that something over his shoulder had caught the admiral's attention. Then he sensed the approach of another person, a shadow at first, then the sound of footsteps.

"Afternoon," Oliver Molyneux said breezily, withdrawing the chair at the place setting beside Luke.

"Afternoon," Giles Cotton said, without standing. "Luke Claussen, Oliver Molyneux. Oliver Molyneux, Luke Claussen."

The two men regarded each other and shook hands, whereupon Oliver sat.

Admiral Cotton tapped the face of his watch.

"Sorry," Oliver said. "Couldn't be helped, I'm afraid. There was a delay at the frontier. I see you've already got a head start on me."

"Order whatever you like," Giles Cotton said. "I must say you look very refreshed for a man who's been stuck in traffic."

"I was up in Valderrama playing golf," Oliver explained matter-of-factly.

"Really," Luke said. "I was there yesterday."

Oliver smiled. "Actually, I was just having the admiral on. I wasn't really in Valderrama, much as I would like to have been. I settled for a run through lovely La Línea instead."

"Anything to get the old heart rate up," Luke mused. "Are you a golfer?"

"Guilty," Oliver replied.

"I am, too. I don't know why. I'll never be any better than average."

"One plays against oneself," Admiral Cotton said, "or one is doomed to disappointment."

"My grandfather disapproved of the game entirely," Oliver said. "He felt that it was for people whose estates weren't large enough to walk around."

Luke laughed. "But you disagreed?"

"Yes, perhaps because the estate went to my father's elder brother."

"What line of work are you in, Mr. Molyneux?" Luke asked.

"I'm a civil servant," Oliver said.

"Here or in Britain?"

"Wherever."

"And what brings you to Gibraltar, if I may ask?"

Admiral Cotton studied both men and kept his silence.

"Actually," Oliver said, "I am here, amongst other reasons, because I rather desperately need your help."

Luke looked perplexed. After a moment he said, "And how can I be helpful?"

"First by allowing me to ruin your holiday," Oliver told him. "Then by making a damned unpleasant spectacle of yourself."

"Why would I do either?"

"It's a long story."

"It's a long afternoon."

"Not only is the story long, it's complicated and incomplete. And I'm not even at liberty to tell you everything I know."

"I only met you a moment ago. Why should I believe a word of what you're telling me?"

Oliver glanced in the direction of Admiral Cotton.

"Well, I grant you that you come with good references," Luke said. "Do I have a choice in this matter?"

"Of course you do," Admiral Cotton said.

"Up to a point," Oliver added.

"One question before you tell me anything else," Luke demanded. "Is whatever it is you're doing being done in the interest of America or just Britain? I am an American, after all."

"Both," Oliver replied. "We're very much a joint task force."

Luke hesitated, trying to take the measure of both men. "This is crazy," he said. "I'm the last man you should want on your side. Ask anyone. They'll tell you. I haven't amounted to much. I'm a wastrel, a playboy, the latest incarnation of the prodigal son. All I can say is that my father cast a long shadow and there were times I had to run pretty far to escape it. I've spent quite a lot of my life searching for adventure. That part's true. Yet the only kind of adventure I ever seem to find is the artificial stuff, which never does the trick. So here I am up to my ass in the usual nonsense, with a little work thrown in, and adventure with a capital *A* finds me. Some joke, wouldn't you say?"

Chapter Thirty

Two hours before sunset, *Surpass* dropped anchor at the western end of the Bay of Tangier, just within the breakwater. From the avenue d'Espagne along the crescent of waterfront, its dark hull and white decks transfixed passersby, ever more so as the descending sun inflamed the sky, framing the ship against a briefly swirling palette of gold, coral and summer blue. In the northern distance lay Tarifa, the ancient Spanish gateway to Europe, the port of entry from which the word "tariff" derived, and those aboard *Surpass* could spot the red-and-white *FRS Iberia* hovercraft as they plowed the open Med on their opposing transits between Tarifa and Tangier.

From the main deck, Ty surveyed the horizons as the yacht rose and fell in rhythm with the sea. It was a rhythm he knew well from other voyages, first as a child on the Chesapeake, later as a soldier on special ops, and he knew that his body had to get used to it anew each time he set sail. He had adjusted well to this cruise but felt far less sanguine about the success of his mission. He had uncovered no evidence implicating Ian or Philip in any plot to acquire or sell nuclear warheads. Indeed, their behavior was suspicious only if one were predisposed to see it as such. It was true that Ian surrounded himself with a questionable if colorful assortment of business and social acquaintances, but so did many men of great wealth. It proved absolutely nothing. In fact, a compelling argument could be made that no man undertaking the kind of theft and sale the President and his advisers feared that Ian might be involved in would dare squander his concentration on such frivolities at a critical moment.

Philip was another matter. Ty did not like him yet had to ask himself why. The obvious answer was that without Philip Ty would be able to pursue Isabella. Beyond that was the Russian whores' gossip he'd overheard on the pontoon at the Hôtel du Cap. But what if those women had been making up or embellishing stories? He had to allow for that possibility.

Among the exotic cast of characters he had encountered at Pond House and aboard *Surpass*, he found it difficult to distinguish likely suspects from innocent bystanders. Having overheard Celia Foo's complaint about her and her husband's recent exclusion from Ian's inner circle, he felt confident they were uninvolved. He felt just as sure that the Al-Dosari twins were trouble and that if a conspiracy was under way they were bound to be part of it. Their recent hiring of Philip to run one of their funds fit neatly into this theory, but it was still a theory based on instinct and conjecture rather than fact. Of the others he'd met, who could say?

Still, he had a disquieting feeling. In a milieu where practically every event, motive and personality was subject to alternative explanations, something seemed out of order. He sensed this in the same way he could tell at a glance that a scene in a film was or wasn't right. To figure out exactly what was wrong, however, would take much longer. As he reconsidered the events of the last few days, he kept coming back to Raisa Gilmour's conversation before dinner, then to the extraordinary gems that had arrived for Isabella. Ty appreciated Isabella's playful designs, but even she had seemed astonished at being asked to adapt them for such magnificent stones. Could the improbability of that commission be related to the sale of weapons of mass destruction? For the life of him, Ty did not see how and thought it more likely that it was simply another instance of Ian's working in the background to promote his beloved goddaughter. Even so, it bothered him.

If there was any opening to any secret world aboard *Surpass*, he suspected it would be found in Ian's quarters, but he had been expressly excluded from them. Why, on the other hand, should he have been included in a discussion of business in which he had no part? At least on the surface, Ian's behavior seemed perfectly explicable.

His mind was still churning when he was surprised by Ian's voice behind him.

"¿En qué piensas?" Ian asked.

Ty was careful not to react to the Spanish. "Sorry," he said.

"What are you thinking?" Ian translated.

"What else *could* anyone think? What a beautiful evening this is."

"God's paint on God's canvas!" Ian exclaimed. "That's what I call sunsets like this one. Have you been enjoying yourself?"

"Very much so," Ty replied.

"I'm glad, although I fear I've failed you as a host."

"Failed me?" Ty asked. "Quite the opposite, I'd say."

"I would like to have spent more time with you than I've been able to so far. Everyone in the world wants to know Ty Hunter. I have the chance and don't take sufficient advantage of it. Never mind, we'll make up for it in the days to come. In fact, why don't you come up to my deck and we can have a drink now? Unless, of course, you have other plans."

Ty shook his head. "Not one," he said. "I'm yours."

Once inside his study, Ian pointed to a leather Queen Anne chair. "What will you have?" he asked.

"It's too early for a martini. Perhaps a glass of champagne?"

"That *would* do nicely, wouldn't it?" Ian pressed a button.

Crispin's Caribbean voice came over an invisible speaker. *"Yes, Mr. Santal."*

"Two glasses of champagne, please," Ian told him.

"I hope you don't mind, I Googled you," Ian said. "Not to pry, but because I was so intrigued to have you aboard. I must tell you that I've never seen so many pages devoted to one person in my life."

Ty felt a sudden tightness in his chest, a deep internal chill. He said, "They're not all gospel."

"I'm sure they aren't, but if even half of what they say is true, it's been quite a ride, has it not?"

"For which I'm very grateful," Ty parried.

"I hadn't realized you'd been discovered whilst you were still in the army."

"That part's true." The question at once convinced Ty that he would have no choice but to act his way out of Ian's trap—if it *was* a trap rather than an expression of genuine curiosity. As they spoke, Ty kept his eyes fastened on Ian's, endeavoring to determine the probability that he had found Ty out.

"What did you do in the army?"

"Hurried up and waited, isn't that how the old saying goes?"

"What branch were you in?"

Ian Santal was far too sophisticated to raise this question idly. "Intelligence," Ty replied, making the word seem as banal as he could. He ought to have anticipated this, he thought. The President and George Kenneth and Oliver Molyneux ought to have anticipated it. After all, Ty's life was largely an open book. Hadn't it been naïve to suppose that Santal would not bother to read through it? On the other hand, perhaps they had anticipated exactly this turn of events yet felt sure that Ty could make his own story appear less dramatic than it was. Until the President had approached him at Camp David, he'd had no connection to the army or any branch of the government since his discharge. Anyone who searched for one would search in vain. Intelligence, moreover, was a large branch and by itself indicated little. Few of its members were operatives, and the special operations in which Ty had participated kept only the most secret of records. All he had to do was maintain his calm, admit what was true, and in doing so make it seem that that was all there was.

"Intelligence," Ian pressed on, "can be a very . . . dangerous place to be. I remember a colleague long ago telling me that the life expectancy of an American second lieutenant in the intelligence corps was fifteen minutes. That was in the days of Vietnam and even then doubtless an exaggeration, but one that nonetheless hinted at a larger truth. That lieutenant, after all, would probably have served as a forward interrogator, wouldn't he? He would have gone out pretty much alone behind enemy lines."

Calmly, Ty nodded in agreement. "Very likely, he would have."

"And in Afghanistan? Or in Iraq?"

"The landscapes were different, the principle the same."

"When you were there?"

"Yes. After all hell broke loose."

"Fighting the so-called War on Terror, a war on a tactic?"

"For better or worse," Ty said, "that's been the world post-9/11, hasn't it?"

"Technology drives history," Ian instructed him. "It's a divine law of nature, not subject to repeal. About certain things and certain trends, at the end of the day one must be a fatalist."

"I hope you're wrong about that," Ty said with a carefully measured sense of irony. "The future's a pretty scary one if you aren't."

"The future is and always has been scary," Ian mused, "but it has always come to pass. Strength creates resistance that in turn creates strength and so on. The world survives because, before it's too late, people inevitably find an equilibrium point from which they can manage to stand each other off, just as we, as individuals, survive by finding a similar point at which our warring instincts cancel out each other."

Ty sipped his champagne, his eye momentarily caught by Ian's splendid parquet gaming table. The older man's proclivity for games was all too apparent in the conversation they were having now. "Clearly this is a subject you've been thinking about for a long time," he conjectured.

"Most of my adult life," Ian assured him. "I know I am thought of, if I'm thought of at all, as a man of action—in the marketplace, of course. In my own mind, however, I'm more of a philosopher. My actions are based on a rigorous logic that I've struggled hard to develop over the years. That logic tempers what I observe, experience and learn in any other way.

"Enough of this. *You* are the man of the moment. Tell me about Ty Hunter."

"You seem to know a lot already. Are you sure you want to hear more?"

"Doesn't everyone? Especially from the horse's mouth? For example, do you miss being a soldier?"

"Not at all," Ty said. "Apart from my accident, I enjoyed it, but not that much. Everything has its day, and I caught a break. I'd be nuts to pine for the past."

"You caught a big break. If you hadn't been wounded, who knows, you might have joined the family business."

"Unlikely. I wasn't cut out to be a detective."

"I meant the CIA."

"Those are old rumors. I thought they'd been extinguished years ago," Ty said, "but I guess the Internet has resurrected a lot of such rubbish."

"Talk about the long half-life of lies," Ian replied gracefully.

"Of course, I'm not entirely blameless in the matter. I mean, I made no effort to set the record straight when the PR types tried to make me out as larger than life. All that stuff about speaking all those languages, for example—it was absolutely crap. Sure, I took courses. And we lived abroad for a while when I was a kid, but I don't have the right kind of mind for that stuff. God knows I wish I did. I wish I hadn't lost whatever I once had. The truth is, maybe I'm a little bit dyslexic. I have enough difficulty remembering my lines when they're in English."

Ian laughed along. "Never discount the value of appearing larger than life," he said. "What makes you so certain your dad was just a detective?"

Ty gave a dismissive laugh. "We lived in a small house. I was the only child. It would not have been an easy place to keep that secret."

"Not to contradict you," Ian said, "but I once knew a woman who as a school leaver was sent to work at Bletchley Park, where the British decoded the Germans' Enigma machine. She was given the job because the people in charge there knew her and had known her family for generations. Basically, it was secretarial work, but it was being done in one of the most secret places in the world, and her superiors told her then that she was never to speak of it to anyone. Well, the Second World War was over in April 1945, and she died in May 2005, having gone on to marry and raise a fine and very happy family. Do you know when her husband and children first heard about her work at Bletchley? When it was mentioned in her obituary notice in the *Telegraph*!"

"Apparently whoever recruited her chose wisely," Ty observed.

"Apparently," Ian repeated, and smiled broadly, as if finally admitting defeat. "Well, you were there. You know your own history far better than anyone else. No doubt you're right about your dad, but the media can't resist a good story, can they? A dollop of espionage goes a long way to luring readers' attention. Never mind, tell me about *your* plans."

"I don't have many at the moment. Right now I'm taking a breather. I'm not even reading scripts."

"I assume you're sent a stack of those every day."

"My agent is. Some have roles for me. Some are meant for my production company. Others are for both. Netty does a great job culling the stacks, but I've just shot four films pretty well consecutively, and I need to clear my head before choosing a fifth. Back when I *was* reading scripts, I didn't come across anything that—"

"Raced your motor?"

"That about says it."

"Comedy or tragedy, though, which way are you inclined for your next project, or are you ambivalent?"

"'Ambivalent' is precisely the right word. It will all depend on the script. It always does."

Ian nodded approval. "If I were casting you, I think I would make you an adventure hero, a figure of action but also judgment that the audience might not expect from a man in possession of your looks."

Ty laughed. "You sound just like my agent. They call those projects 'tent poles.' The suits on the business side all love them."

"Why shouldn't they?" Ian asked. "You would be a very credible Indiana Jones—updated, of course."

"Perhaps," Ty replied, in a tone intended both to deprecate and deflect the very idea, "but I didn't become an actor in order to play a single role, which can be a hazard for action heroes."

"No, of course you didn't," Ian reflected. "A young man with your gifts would be barking mad to put so much promise in such jeopardy."

Chapter Thirty-one

Aboard *Surpass*, breakfast was served on bridge deck. From half an hour after first light until nine-thirty, a buffet was set out and refreshed. On a table nearby could be found whatever newspapers the crew had been able to scour from the nearest port.

Ty was quenching his thirst with a tumbler of the best orange juice he had ever tasted, glancing at a copy of that day's *International Herald Tribune,* when Ajay Prajapti whispered, "Well, sadly, we're off after breakfast."

"We'll miss you," Ty replied. "Off to where?"

"Home, where I am told it's extremely hot at the moment. That was a lovely little party," the elder Prajapti continued, referring to the previous evening.

"Yes, it was," Ty replied, although he had found it neither fun nor in the least useful. As the dancing had worn on, he had continued to worry and later, in a post-midnight e-mail to Oliver, had written, *"Wasting precious time here. Santal suspicious. If I were not Ty Hunter, I might be dead. Escape strategy?"*

"I didn't know anyone, really," Akshar Prajapti offered softly.

"Nor did I," said Ty, who had felt on display among the Arab women and their enigmatic men. Right now he studied the Prajaptis, amused by the confidence required for a father whose name meant "Invincible" to give his own son one that translated to "Imperishable."

Just then Isabella arrived. "Good morning," she said breezily, then turned to approach the buffet.

"My heavens, what's that?" Ajay gasped at the sudden purr of an unfamiliar motor followed by what sounded like a vast wall retracting.

"The tender's being started, that's all," Isabella explained, only minimally distracted from the steaming scrambled eggs. "I've no idea who's going where."

"I thought the plan was that we would be going back to Gib by helicopter."

"Really, I've no idea," Isabella said, and smiled lavishly, taking the seat next to Akshar and across from Ty. "Transport is Ian's department."

"Speaking of whom," Ajay Prajapti said as Ian descended the stairs from his deck, followed by Philip. Both men wore sharply creased trousers and had jackets draped over their wrists.

"Morning, darling," Ian said at once. "Good morning, everyone!"

"Morning," Isabella replied then, when the two men seemed to forgo joining them at table, asked, "What's the form?"

"Philip and I are going into Tangier."

"Just you and Philip?" Isabella inquired plaintively. "Why don't we join you? There's plenty of room in the tender."

"There will be time for that, I promise you. Now, pretty much everyone else said good-bye last night and, I presume, got off early."

Jean-François, standing nearby, nodded.

"The Prajaptis are leaving on the chopper at ten-fifteen. You and Ty will entertain them until then, please," Ian instructed. "Look, I really am sorry, darling, but I simply must concentrate on business on this particular trip. I've no time for sightseeing and cannot be constrained by the movements and whereabouts of others."

"I understand," Isabella said.

"Of course you do."

After they had waved good-bye to the tender, the Prajaptis excused themselves to pack. The cigarette boat's engines could still be heard, its high, white wake still traced when Ty drew Isabella back to the breakfast table, where, on a scrap of found paper, he wrote, *"We have to talk without being overheard. Where is the best place?"*

"Why?" she whispered, but stopped short. Seconds later, on the same paper with the same pen, she wrote, *"Epidendrum."*

After finishing their meal at a pace calculated not to draw attention, they made their way to Isabella's stateroom.

Ty surveyed the walls and ceiling with obvious circumspection, then returned to Isabella.

"No one would dare," she admonished him.

"Even Ian?"

"Especially Ian! Are you mad?"

"I suffer from an excess of caution, with good reason."

Isabella stood still in the center of the lemon yellow sitting room. "It's not who he is. It's not how he sees himself."

"Then why did he place a GPS in your car?" Ty bluffed.

Isabella's answer surprised him. "That was done with my permission. Ian wanted to be sure I would be safe. The roads around Pond House can be treacherous, as I'm sure you've seen. Anyway, why would I mind? I'm not living a secret life."

"No," Ty said, "I'm sure you're not."

"He loves me. In his mind he might as well be my father. What the hell is going on? Who are you? Forgive me. That's a stupid question. Let me rephrase it: *Who* are you?"

"A guy in a corner," Ty told her.

"How uncomfortable!"

"Who finds that the only way out is to uncover the truth."

"Bravo! Well acted."

"I'm not acting. I wish I were." Ty hesitated. He had been ordered never to speak of the matter to anyone outside the small circle who had gathered at Camp David, but circumstances had changed. Time was growing dangerously short. On his own he had come up empty-handed and without Isabella's help was sure to continue to do so until it would be too late. To confide in her now might be fatal, yet not to confide, given the protocols aboard *Surpass* and Ian's suspicion, would almost certainly doom any chance he had of succeeding. He drew a deep breath, then said, "Ian or Philip or both, or maybe neither, may be in the process of transferring nuclear warheads."

"Next joke," Isabella said. "Who told you that? Obviously it's another lie."

"What if it isn't?"

"The only thing either one of them has ever had to do with nuclear weapons is that Philip has practically killed himself trying to rid the world of them."

"Perhaps," Ty said. "No one would be happier if you turned out to be right."

"Are you sure?"

"Warheads *might* be missing from a Russian installation that Philip decertified," Ty said. "If they are, each could be used to launch nuclear attacks on up to thirty targets. That would be the end of the world as we know it."

"You didn't answer my question. Where did you come by this extraordinary information?"

"I can't tell you that."

"Then tell me this: Does anyone else believe this preposterous story?"

"That I *can* tell you," Ty replied. "The President of the United States does, for one. At least he believes that it is more than possible and therefore cannot be ignored. I'm pretty sure the same can be said about your Prime Minister."

"Now I *am* lost," Isabella said. "All this, not from some secret agent but a film star! I'm sure you can understand how it could be too much to take in."

Ty kept silent.

"Or are you both?" she wondered aloud. "It's as though Matt Damon really were Jason Bourne, isn't it?"

With that she retreated to her bedroom. After a few seconds, Ty heard water splashing in her basin, a drawer being opened and closed, after which she returned.

"Look around you," Ty said. "At some time you must have asked yourself where this yacht and Pond House and everything else came from."

"Ian is a genius. I've told you that before."

"And it may well be true, but what if he's even more than that? What if he's so much of a genius he feels himself above the common morality that binds most other men? You read the newspapers. Every few days, there's a new alarm about loose nuclear materials somewhere. Usually it's small amounts of fissile stuff. But what if Ian thought bigger? He would, wouldn't he? What if he laid a plan so simple and audacious and for such momentous stakes that no normal person would think it possible? You have to admit, *that* would be entirely in character."

She shot him a ferocious look but did not speak.

"Tell me," Ty said, "that it has never once occurred to you that someone just like me might knock on your door one day."

"Oh, please!" Isabella exclaimed. "Someone like you with a story like yours—the odds against that must be one in how many gazillions?"

"What I meant was, just a stranger who came suggesting that everything wasn't as it appeared. You have to have wondered."

From her pocket she withdrew a Derringer and pointed it at him. "I'm going to call Jean-François," she said.

"Put that down," Ty insisted.

"No, I will not! I'm afraid of you."

"If you were, you would have called him already. You haven't because you know I might be right and you don't want to be responsible for what will happen if I am. You don't want to live with that."

Isabella glared at him. "What do you want? You're too rich to be a thief."

"First, put that damned thing down."

"Why should I?"

"Because I'm not a thief and whether you know it or not, you and I are on the same side."

"We're not."

"Somewhere buried in that beautiful, stubborn head of yours, you know that we are. Now, for the last time, put it down or I'm going to take it from you. You'll have to shoot me to stop me."

Isabella took a deep breath. "I'm not going to shoot you," she said.

"Good, that's a relief."

"Not because I believe you, but because I don't want to end up in the tabloids and be known for the rest of my life as 'The Woman Who Shot Ty Hunter.'"

Ty smiled. "I imagine that would be very bad for jewelry sales," he said as she reluctantly handed him the gold-plated, ivory-handled Derringer.

Isabella looked down shyly, then up at him again. "Now will you please tell me what it is you want?"

Ty said, "First I have to get into your godfather's quarters."

"Impossible," Isabella told him. "They lock automatically whenever he leaves. I have no way to get into them. No one but Ian does, not even Crispin. What are you looking for in there?"

"I have no idea, but whatever it is, if it's on *Surpass,* it's bound to be there."

"Even if I tried to break in, I'd be stopped before I could. Also, Ian would know immediately, because the alarm would sound on his BlackBerry."

Ty considered their options in light of what she had said. "The Prajaptis are leaving for Gib," he said. "We're going with them."

"We can't."

"We were told *not* to come along to Tangier and *to* entertain the Prajaptis. Ian gave no other instructions."

"Why are we going to Gibraltar?"

"To see the apes," Ty told her.

Chapter Thirty-two

"The bouquet of decay." Ian sighed. "Savor it!"

Philip regarded him silently and with the just-shy-of-disdainful curiosity he was apt to show whenever Ian became overly philosophical.

"Breathe it in, Philip," Ian urged. "Tangier is like a rare orchid. It flowers, as it last did in the fifties and sixties, fades, then, when least expected, blooms once more. And bloom it will!"

They had landed at the yacht-club quay, where *Surpass*'s shore agent from Agence Med had greeted them, along with the British consul and the *commissaire divisionnaire de police*. Now they were in the backseat of a hired car commencing its ascent along the rue Portugal with the Grand Mosque and the wall of the medina, the Old City, at their right. The white city, dappled by soft morning sunlight, rose with the hills upon which it had been settled by Carthaginian colonists in the fifth century B.C.

Just beyond the Légation Américaine, Ian instructed the driver to stop. He and Philip exited quickly. Drifting on the tide of tourists they proceeded on foot to a narrow iron gate. The gate opened onto a courtyard garden in full flower, at the center of which stood a fountain in whose colorfully tiled mosaic basin water burbled softly. They crossed the garden rapidly, proceeding through the shadowy rooms of an Arabesque mansion until they came into an arbor of astounding luxury, so peaceful and fragrant it might have been hours from any city.

Wazir and Fateen Al-Dosari were waiting for them, along with Sheik al-Awad and three other of their middlemen colleagues from the Arabian Peninsula and the Persian Gulf.

Ian greeted them as though it were they rather than he who had just arrived. "Our adventure is about to have a happy ending," he declared.

"I am very glad to hear this," said Wazir Al-Dosari.

Ian's quick nod betrayed a trace of impatience. "First I want to thank each of you for your good work so far. I also want to let you know that, as agreed, we are, as of this moment, issuing the required seventy-two-hour notice for the transfer of the first tranche of funds. Philip will now review those details."

"You have each subdivided your own accounts into units that should be able to fly below the regulatory radar," Philip said. "Moreover, you have wire-transfer instructions relating to our accounts, which will be capable of receiving funds on the same basis. Clearly it will be in the best interest of everyone involved if such transfers are sequenced between now and the close of business three days from now. Are there any questions?"

When no one spoke, Philip continued. "The final half of your payment will be expected at the moment our merchandise is delivered to you on behalf of your clients. In both instances, let me assure you, the money will orbit the earth far faster than any satellite. Where it originated and where it is destined will be undeterminable."

"I wish you all good luck," Ian said. *"Salaam."*

"Salaam."

"If I might have a word," Sheik al-Awad said, taking Ian aside as the brief meeting dispersed. "I shall, of course, deduct the funds I've laid out on gems and jewelry from my share."

"Exactly as we agreed," Ian said without slowing.

"Short and sweet," Ian said when they had come back into the rue Salah Eddine el-Ayoubi. "It's better that way."

"I think so," Philip said.

"No one can claim there was a misunderstanding. The participants know both what's expected of them and when to expect their own reward. The truly beautiful part with this cast of characters and three separate pieces of merchandise is that, as you once suggested and I've long believed, we should be able to create our own private standoff in the region, paradoxically making conflict amongst the various parties less likely than it already is."

Philip smiled. "While reaping tens of billions doing so," he added.

Ian laughed. "Yes, there is that."

Ian's disinclination to accept the reality and consequences of his actions and his need to justify them on elaborate theoretical grounds alternately amused and perplexed Philip, whose approach to life had always been to face it directly. Like so many men, Ian could not bear to conceive of himself as acting other than out of some essentially good motive toward some essentially good end. But how could such a canny operator go to such lengths to blinker himself from the truth? Philip had no illusions about the transaction they were concluding or the people with whom they were dealing. The al-Awads and Al-Dosaris of this world were syndicators, go-betweens. Behind them lay a constantly changing cast of shifty principals, dictators and desert princes wielding absolute power, usurpers and warlords, drug lords, nihilistic fanatics and terrorists. So what? That was neither of Philip's making nor his responsibility. He lived in the world he found and planned on neither heaven nor hell. If anything, beyond the fortune he would reap, absolved him of a last vestige of guilt, it was his conviction that the time had come for the cat to be let out of the bag. Where it would scramble was not for him to say. All he could do at this unstoppable historical moment was to seize it and profit from the weapons he now controlled, as other men would surely soon profit from the sale of other weapons to other dubious and dangerous parties. And he had to keep his ear to the ground, to stay a step ahead of trouble and as far away as possible from any theater in which such weapons seemed likely to be exploded. Life was replete with dangers. What were nuclear warheads but one more on a very long list?

"Let's walk, shall we?" Ian suggested. "It feels rather good to stretch one's legs when one's been at sea. Have a word with our driver, would you? Tell him to meet us at the Petit Socco in . . . what do you think? Half an hour?"

"He'll know where that is?"

"He'll know, all right."

The street was sun-drenched, with an eclectic crowd already gathering by Popeye's Restaurant. At the next major intersection they turned right, past the City Wall into the medina on the rue Siaghine. Here in the souk, the doors and shutters of almost all the shop fronts had been opened, and vendors selling local melons, apples, bananas and dates worked adjacent to those in whose chaotic premises fresh chickens hung from clothesline while live roosters patrolled a sawdust floor below. Still other shops offered various Moroccan arts and crafts; desert clothing such as white dishdashahs and hijabs, pashmina scarves in vivid hues and of complicated design and caftans sewn with elaborate beadwork. Every few yards another emporium offered an array of last season's electronic gadgetry. Ian and Philip climbed the hill in silence until, displayed on a shop's front table, an intricate pyramid of wooden boxes caught Philip's eye.

"Do you mind?" he asked Ian.

"What is it with you and boxes?"

Philip sighed. "It isn't *me* and boxes. Isabella loves them."

"I know she does, but must she have one from everywhere."

"I won't be long. I'll catch you up."

These particular boxes featured parquetry inlays in the repeated geometric patterns typical of much Islamic art. Tiny squares of blond and darker woods, inscribed by contrasting circles, had been fancifully arranged to produce an illusion of depth and movement in their handsome lids. Philip understood that each square represented the four elements of nature—earth, water, fire and air—and that each circle represented the physical world that those elements made possible. He had long appreciated the mathematics of such art, and as he studied several such boxes now, he tried to locate the imperfection in their patterns that their creators would have deliberately introduced as an expression of their own humility and faith that only Allah could achieve perfection.

The shop was narrow, deep and dark. A merchant soon came forth, a man of perhaps forty with sun-cured skin and an angular smile that revealed a missing bicuspid. For several seconds, he watched Philip. Finally, in a hoarse voice, he proclaimed, "They are beautiful."

"Yes," Philip said. "They are very nice."

"This one has a secret compartment," the merchant said. "Turn this knob once, nothing happens, but twice, *voilà!*"

Philip smiled. "How much?" he asked.

"For this, fifty euros."

"For the simpler one? I don't require a secret compartment. Besides, the simpler one is more elegant."

"It is," the merchant said. "For the one you prefer, thirty-five euros."

"Rubbish," Philip said. It was not his nature to bargain, but he knew he would sacrifice the Arab's respect if he did not. "I'll give you half that, no more, but for the first one."

"You have come a long way," the merchant said. "Where from? Germany?"

"Spain," Philip replied.

"Take that one with you, back to Spain, for forty, I beg you."

"Twenty-five," Philip countered.

The merchant shook his head.

"Twenty-five," Philip repeated.

Toward the rear of the shop, a boy of twelve or so made careful note of Philip's insolence. Already a skilled bargainer himself, he understood that it was a game decent people played with a smile rather than as a matter of life and death.

"Twenty-five is not enough," the merchant said.

"Twenty-five is my final offer."

The merchant shook his head.

"Twenty-five or I am gone and the box will still be yours."

"Please!" the merchant said. "I have a shop to run, a son to bring up."

"None of that is my concern," Philip said coolly, scanning the room, taking only the briefest notice of a boy clutching a balsa-wood ukulele. "I don't bother you with my concerns. Don't bother me with yours."

"It's not right," the merchant said.

"Here is twenty-five," Philip said, producing two crisp notes. "Take it or leave it."

The merchant hesitated. He had been prepared to accept thirty-five, and in a better year would not have accepted less. It would hurt to be humiliated before his son, but that would be on the European's conscience, not his own. He needed the twenty-five euros. Reflexively, he fetched a sheet of printed tissue paper from below the counter and began to wrap Philip's purchase. It took him less than a minute to complete the familiar task, write out a receipt, then place both in a green plastic carrier bag.

Philip had to work quickly. The explosive he intended to use was a binary one that Andrej had purchased for him on the black market in Sevastopol. It would require half an hour from the addition of the sensitizer for the white solid and red liquid to set. He'd had no opportunity to do a proper reconnaissance of the area but wasn't worried. Acting quickly meant that potential witnesses were less likely to recall, in meaningful detail, someone they had seen only once and fleetingly.

A third of the way to the Grand Socco, a shadowy passageway of lesser shops and stalls flowed south from the rue Siaghine. One of dozens of such tributaries, its opening was marked by a sign whose vertical orange letters, faded by years of exposure and neglect, read HOTEL BELGIQUE. Philip turned into it. Soon a rivulet of melting ice washed over the soles of his loafers and he realized that by happenstance he had come in at the rear of a large *poissonnerie*. To his left, row after row of ice-covered tables were laden with the catch of local fishermen: mullet, mackerel and sea bass, salt cod and Saint-Pierre, langostinos, squid and shrimps. Crabs squirmed in wooden baskets. Lobsters struggled to swim in large barrels. In the distance, beyond a ribbon of daylight at the far end of the market, stood what he assumed to be either the Grand or the Petit Socco. To Philip's surprise, the fishmongers paid him no attention as they went about their business, folding fish in old newspapers or placing them in the ready buckets of their customers. Then a door opened and from it a single weather-beaten seaman emerged. Surmising that the raised, scuffed *H* on the door stood for *Hommes,* Philip entered the small lavatory, then immediately locked it from within. Overhead, a solitary incandescent bulb threw down ample light for his work. When the explosive had been created and attached to a tiny mobile-phone-activated detonator, he carefully rubber-taped both to the bottom of the secret drawer of his new box, making sure they would be held in place there. Then he snapped the drawer closed and slid the box back into its tissue wrapper, resealing the expertly folded end from which he had withdrawn it.

As he had expected, he found Ian at an outdoor table in front of a café in the square. Even in the midst of urgent business, Ian could seldom resist such places and the chances they afforded to observe people without being closely observed in turn.

"Un citron pressé?" Ian asked, beckoning Philip to a chair.

"Pourquoi pas?" Philip replied, and, flagging a waiter, ordered the lemonade. "You look very relaxed."

Ian smiled. "The moment calls for it."

"I understand," said Philip.

"At a moment like this, in a deal like this one, one wants to relax, to put oneself in fifth gear rather than first. Otherwise it may be difficult to deal with uncertainty should it arise."

Philip nodded. They talked again about Tangier as Ian had first known it, about its successive histories as a Berber, a Roman, a Christian and, since A.D. 702, a Muslim city; about everything but the subject on both of their minds. Between Ian's paragraphs, silence occasionally fell, and when it did, Philip wondered what he was thinking.

Philip was glad for the delay, which played into his hands, and for a few minutes found his thoughts adrift.

When his iPhone rang, it appeared to startle him. He looked at the screen, then at Ian. "Fateen," he explained quietly.

"I wonder why," Ian replied.

"Hello," Philip said, then pretended to listen for a moment. "Is there a particular reason, may I ask?"

To Ian, Philip quickly mouthed the words, *He wants to meet.*

"But everything's all right, then?" Philip asked. "Good, I'm glad. Where are you? We'll stop by on our way back to the tender."

Philip hesitated. "No, we'll be gone long before lunch."

Ian nodded.

"Just a moment, I'll ask," Philip said, muting the telephone.

"Fateen wants me to have lunch with him. He assures me there is no problem. I think he wants his hand held."

"Many people are like that," Ian said. "I would not have expected Fateen to be one of them, but pressure does strange things to people. Go, steady his nerves. You can call for the tender when you're ready."

"I'm sure you would be more than welcome."

"Not in a million years. When a deal is in play, it's in play. Agree to nothing we have not already agreed to."

"That," Philip said, "goes without saying." With the iPhone once again switched on, he said, "One o'clock. I'll find it, don't worry. I'll meet you there."

On the drive back to the yacht-club quay, Ian seemed resigned. "Just be careful," he told Philip as he prepared to step out of the car.

"I'm sure it amounts to little more than that he simply doesn't like to eat alone," Philip suggested with a piteous laugh. "I could almost tell that from his voice."

"Good," Ian said.

"You could do me one favor," Philip said, seemingly on impulse. "If you wouldn't mind taking this box with you? Then I won't have to worry about leaving it behind in a restaurant."

"Pleasure," Ian said. "Where is he taking you, by the way? The Minzah?"

"No. Someplace called the Tom Yam."

"That's too bad," Ian said. "The Minzah's very salubrious. I'm afraid I don't know Tom Yam."

"Number five avenue Youssoufia," Philip said as offhandedly as he could manage, for the depth of Ian's curiosity had unnerved him. "The best Thai food in Tangier, he said."

"Well, that's the world today, isn't it? I'm sure there's wonderful couscous in Bangkok."

As *Surpass*'s tender motored slowly toward the breakwater gulls circled overhead. Philip glanced at his watch. It was 11:59. He quickly found Fateen Al-Dosari's mobile number in his iPhone's address book and rang it. When Fateen answered, Philip said, "Any chance you're free for lunch?"

"This is a surprise," Fateen told him.

"Ian asked me to stay behind to do a business errand for him. Nothing very important," Philip explained, "but you know Ian. When he gets something on his mind, no matter how small, there's no getting it off, is there?"

"All too true. Still, I admire a man who clears his in-box every day," Fateen replied. "As a matter of fact, I *am* free for lunch."

"How would the Tom Yam at one o'clock suit?"

"Perfectly," Fateen replied.

Relieved that their conversation had not been interrupted by a query directly from Ian to Fateen, Philip drew a momentary breath. He would not have put such a call beyond Ian in normal circumstances. For it was Ian's nature to either confirm or erase his suspicions. So Philip had erred on the safe side. His alibi was intact.

On sudden impulse Philip instructed his driver to take him to the Hotel El Minzah. Once there, he would walk in the fabled hotel's gardens, perhaps have a drink, then go on to the restaurant. As the Mercedes crossed the railway track that ran along the shore, Philip reached into his jacket pocket and switched off his iPhone. It was important he be incommunicado. From the opposite pocket, he removed a small pay-as-you-go Nokia he'd bought the previous December with a false ID. Careful to hold it low and forward on his lap, thus out of the driver's view, with obsessive care he punched in, then confirmed on the telephone's screen the number of the detonator in the box he had left with Ian. On the near side of the place de la Tannerie, once he judged that they were finally far enough away from the waterfront not to hear an explosion at sea, he pressed the green CALL button. With the phone now on speaker, he waited out six unanswered rings. Then, displaying only normal frustration, he pressed the red STOP key and immediately wiped the call from the telephone's logs.

At the Hotel El Minzah, having time to spare, he told the driver to meet him exactly where he had before, in the Petit Socco. In the meantime he would walk, both because his body craved the exercise and because it was easier to get to know a city on foot. In the Minzah's lush garden, the sun felt warm against his face. As he paused before a stand of cedar and bay trees, his thoughts suddenly wafted back to school holidays on which his father had sometimes taken him when he was a boy. In those days, immediately following his post at the United Nations, his father had been based in London as a partner of a travel agency that specialized in high-end excursions, often through the byways of more libertine cultures. He had received large discounts, sometimes even complimentary rooms at luxurious hotels on every coast of the Mediterranean, and it had been on their holidays together that Philip had first tasted the seductive North African climate in which desert and sea air merged. How long ago that was, Philip thought now! His father had been shot, accidentally, on safari in Kenya when Philip was just shy of fourteen. He could not help but wonder if the seed of a man who could kill with such impressive ease had been within him from birth or planted later in the course of his life. At Le Rosey, like many of his schoolmates, he had become accustomed to a measure of parental neglect, to being loved from a distance, but this had left him not so much desperate as on his own. In those days, although he had charged exuberantly onto playing fields and ski slopes and shown a precocious flair for mathematics, he had been invariably more careful than the children of rich and powerful men who surrounded him, many of whom had seemed to float above the world, buoyed by a charm so instinctive they could neither recognize nor repress it. Unlike Luke Claussen, Philip had recognized even then that he was bound for a different, more serious fate. Thoughts of murder had not yet surfaced as he studied beside the shores of Lake Leman, fifty kilometers north of Geneva, and on the school's alpine winter campus in Gstaad.

No, he reflected, he had developed the capacity if not the instinct to kill incrementally. It was the logical extension of the first lesson he'd imbibed from Ian. Nothing mattered more than success, and success was achieved by capitalizing upon every moment, every person and every opportunity. Over his years in the City of London, under his mentor's tutelage, step by step he had abandoned whatever morality he'd once had—first, innocently enough, by canceling obligations to friends in favor of clients; then by assisting raiders and their hedge-fund backers as they stripped bare the assets of firms that had required decades to build and saddled the resulting corporate skeletons with plainly unsustainable levels of debt; by profiting, always surreptitiously, from confidential information that should not have been acted upon; eventually by early-stage algo trading against his own customers, excusing his actions as if the very nature of markets required it. It had been a short enough journey from destroying a person's livelihood to destroying his life. He was not bloodthirsty, merely pragmatic. Philip did not enjoy killing any more than he recoiled from it and, with a certain wistfulness, appreciated the irony of his having just had to eliminate the very man who had set him on his way.

The Minzah's bar had not yet opened for the day, but, a distant memory having been triggered by Ian's mere mention of the hotel, Philip entered it and stood alone before Lavery's legendary portrait of Caid Sir Harry MacLean, the early-twentieth-century British army officer and adviser to the Sultan of Morocco, who had been kidnapped and ransomed.

From the hotel he headed on foot toward the place de France. Once he had made a circuit of it, he retreated in the direction of the Medina, where several minutes later he happened upon a courtyard textile market in one upstairs room of which men of several generations had gathered for prayer. Their shoes and sandals had been left, carefully arranged, at the entrance, and Philip made note of both its location and the time.

He walked the streets of the bazaar spontaneously but before long began to feel himself on familiar ground. A moment later he was approached by a young boy with a balsa ukulele for sale.

"Sir," the boy said. "You buy for your son?"

Philip shook his head. After a few seconds, he recognized the boy from the shop in which he had purchased his box.

"I give you good price."

"Not interested."

"Eight euros."

"No. I told you."

"Your son will like very much this gift. It is beautiful instrument."

"For Christ's sake," Philip said. "I don't have a son."

"One day very soon," the boy said, "you wait. Until then, six euros."

The remark disturbed Philip. "I'll say this," he said. "You are a better bargainer than your father."

"No," the boy told him. "Come on, six euros is cheap."

"It's not, and you know it's not, but I don't want your damned ukulele at any price. Understand?"

"Five euros?"

"Get lost."

"You give me two euros?" the boy asked. He seemed to be dancing around Philip suddenly, with the speed and directional improbability of a fly.

"For what?" Philip asked over his shoulder. "Why should I give you two euros?"

"I can be your guide."

"I've no need of a guide."

"Please, sir, just two. What's two?"

Philip gestured with the back of his hand. "I'll give you nothing but trouble if you don't stop bothering me. You get the hell away from me this instant! Go on!"

"Sorry," the boy said, retreating at last, "but you make a big mistake, sir. What I offer is very fine."

"Somehow I doubt it."

"Trust me, you will be sorry you did not buy it for your son. Just wait."

Chapter Thirty-three

Isabella studied her watch. "I'd better ring Ian," she said.

"What time is it?" Ty asked.

"Not quite a quarter past eleven."

"Go ahead. He'll know we've gone ashore. Why should he object? Actually, I think the Prajaptis were flattered we came along."

"People like to be seen in the company of film stars. Anyway, to be honest, it isn't Ian's reaction that worries me."

"I can handle Philip," Ty assured her, "when the time comes."

"What if you're wrong?" Isabella asked. "About that and about this whole damned business?"

"I'll apologize," Ty said. "Here comes Oliver now."

Isabella looked across the natural rockery, in which the last of the candytuft flowers were still in bloom, and focused on the rugged figure approaching them. They had taken the cable car to Top Station and begun their partial descent from there along the steep Mediterranean Steps. High above Europa Point, these afforded spectacular views but had to be navigated with care and complete concentration. A few steps down, pausing to steady herself, Isabella grabbed hold of a large iron ring that had been embedded in a rock and awaited Oliver Molyneux. "Sorry not to meet you halfway," she told him as he drew near, "but this comes in handy."

"I can see that," Oliver said. "You know, in another time they would thread chains through those rings and use them to manhandle cannon."

"How reassuring!"

"This is Commander Oliver Molyneux," Ty said, "a very old friend of mine."

"How do you do?" Isabella said. After a second's hesitation, as she shook his hand and regarded him carefully, she added, "I know you. You're Laura Moly-neux's cousin?"

"Is she a friend of yours?" Oliver inquired.

"She was a year ahead of me at school."

"I'll be damned."

"We were great mates then, but we seem to have lost track of each other over the years. How is she?"

"She's very well, married with two children, an impish little boy and a very pretty girl, so no complaints!"

Isabella smiled. "Tell her I asked after her, please, and send her my love."

"I will," Oliver said. "So, Ty, where do things stand?"

"It feels like a kettle is about to boil, but that's purely intuition. All sorts of people come and go, but it's hard to pin down who's who. Ian has many more than one ball in the air at any given moment."

"That's an understatement," Isabella added.

"I'm glad you two have found a connection," Ty said. "Maybe that will make it easier."

"Make what easier?" Isabella asked. "I haven't agreed to anything as yet, only to you hear you out."

"That's all I meant," Ty said. "If you know who Oliver is, that should make things easier."

"Oh, I know who he is, all right. He was already in the navy, the Special Boat Service, I think. He came to Founders' Day at our school in his uniform the year Laura was head girl. We all just about died."

"Back to the matter at hand," Oliver said. "If I need further vouching for, you can ring Admiral Cotton. I believe you know him."

"I've met him. That won't be necessary. Let's get on with it, then, shall we?"

"All right," Oliver said. "Straight to the point: If there are warheads, we've lost track of them."

"You think they may have been offloaded in Naples?" Ty asked, for Isabella's benefit.

"It's a distinct possibility."

"Do you know anything about Ian's connections in Naples?"

Isabella squinted. "Nothing at all," she said.

"Never mind," Oliver said. "You can see where this is headed. We are going to have to figure out their destination and work back from there, and the only clues to that will be aboard *Surpass.*"

"As I've told Ty," Isabella said, "I don't have any idea what those might be. If they exist, they will doubtless be somewhere on Ian's deck, which is effectively— and I do mean *effectively*—off-limits to anyone but him, including Philip. Beyond that, I wouldn't know where to start. Who is involved and who isn't? It's all smoke and mirrors, isn't it?"

"Your words, not mine," Oliver said.

"No, but it *is* smoke and mirrors," Isabella explained, "and that's the wonderful thing about Ian. He creates this air of mystery, and that mystery then empowers him. It gives him all sorts of leverage he wouldn't otherwise have."

"You wouldn't hazard a guess as to his customer?" Ty asked.

"Mine would be no better than yours. It could be anyone, or none of the people you've met since you've been here. It could a king or group of kings. What it could not be is a terrorist. Ian wouldn't have a hand in that."

"A group of kings is an interesting concept," Ty said.

"Isn't it?" Oliver agreed.

"Maybe not just a group of *kings* but a syndicate of sorts," Ty continued, "that would allow Ian to justify his action to himself. It would also conform to his widely espoused theory that safety results from standoff. If such a syndicate does exist, who would its members be and who would be in charge?"

Ty did not lift his stare from Isabella.

"If, and only if it did," she said, "Philip would have to be someplace very near the head. He's the only one Ian trusts enough. And much as it pains me to say it, Sheik al-Awad would probably be involved, too."

"Why al-Awad particularly?" Oliver wondered.

"Well, for one thing, he's spending a fortune on gems he doesn't appreciate. He doesn't know a ruby from a piece of stained glass."

"So," Oliver said, "either the man's mad as a hatter or the gems are simply a way of funneling money, a device for Santal to skim, perhaps."

Isabella frowned. "That's not exactly his style."

"Assuming your guess is a good one," Ty said, "who are the natural bedfellows for Sheik al-Awad?"

Isabella laughed. "You're asking the wrong person. I'm not in that loop."

"Tim and Celia Foo?"

"Definitely not! She's a gossip. That bores Ian. He's a prude—about business. I've heard Ian say as much. That bores him even more. I think they are only still on Ian's list for old times' sake."

"All right then, what about Harry Kosmopoulos?"

"It's a possibility, but despite the hail-fellow-well-met façade, he's timid by nature. He's one of those a-little-here, a-little-there, don't-bet-the-estate types."

"Okay, we'll put him to the side for a moment. What about Rahim Kakar and Aurelien Strigoi?"

"Both candidates, I suppose. I don't really know them. I only met them when you did."

"But not the Prajaptis?"

"Absolutely not. The Prajaptis are . . . well, they're the Prajaptis. They have every reason to be more than satisfied with the status quo."

"Finally," Ty said, "the Al-Dosari twins?"

Isabella laughed out loud. "They present the biggest question marks, don't they? I mean, if one accepts your narrative, Wazir and Fateen have to be implicated in whatever conspiracy might exist. They have hired Philip. They run an enormous fund. They move money all over the world every day. Or at least that's what I'm told. On the other hand, the raison d'être of their fund is to bring civilizations together, not force them apart."

"Allegedly. Do you trust them?"

"I've never thought about it one way or the other."

"Is it your impression that they are especially greedy or just good, clever businessmen? In other words, would they risk their legitimacy in honest markets in order to operate and score a big win in the most dishonest one there is?"

"You'd have to ask Philip," Isabella replied.

"That's the problem," Ty told her. "I can't do that until I know the answer. Oliver, have the SIGINT guys spotted anything?"

"Not even a flurry of innocent wire transfers."

"Who's looking?"

"The best geeks we've got."

"I'll take your word for it."

"They'd better be. You know how much they're paid, don't you?" Oliver asked.

"No idea," Ty said.

"A lot more than any of us."

"Not possible."

"We'll, maybe not more than *you* are. Excuse me. I'd forgot for a moment just what a dish of cream you'd fallen into, but more than the President or Prime Minister. Geeks of their sort are the highest-paid employees of either of our governments. Of course, they're not formally employees. I believe the correct term is 'contractors.'"

As this thread of conversation hung in the air, Isabella's mobile rang. She glanced at it, then at Ty and Oliver. Both men grew silent.

"Hello," Isabella answered.

"Hello, darling," Ian said with characteristic enthusiasm, yet against a background of engine roar. "Where are you?"

"On Gib," Isabella said. "We brought Ajay and Akshar over in the chopper. Ty had never seen the place, so . . . well, naturally . . ."

For an instant, Ian did not respond. Then he said only, "Yes indeed, that's nice."

"I can barely hear you," Isabella said.

"I'm on the tender. What time will you be returning?"

"Soon, I should think. What time do you want us?"

"I don't know. Whenever you wish, really. What time is it now?"

"Just past noon," Isabella told him.

"So it is," Ian said. "I didn't realize it was that late already."

Before Isabella could respond, the unanticipated thunder of an explosion tore at her ear, with such volcanic ferocity that she dropped her phone. Ty caught it in midair and handed it back to her. "Ian!" she cried out, frightened but at last raising the speaker to her lips. "Ian! Ian . . . what's happened? Talk to me!"

Chapter Thirty-four

"Who profits?" Ty whispered.

Oliver nodded toward Isabella, who was on the phone with *Surpass*'s captain, asking one insistent question after another, desperately clinging to hope. It was clear from her fraught yet self-disciplined tone that her emotions had not yet accepted the fact of Ian's death. She had yet to shed a tear.

"What do you mean, he was alone?" Isabella demanded. "He and Philip went in together."

Ty and Oliver listened intently.

"Then where is Philip now?" Isabella asked. "Have you tried his mobile?"

As she digested the captain's answer, Ty caught Oliver's eye. "It doesn't have the feeling of a coincidence," he said, still quietly. "And if it's not, then it's much more likely there *are* loose warheads, that Philip was the instigator of Ian's murder, and that this transaction is now so far along that Philip feels confident he can handle it on his own."

"Of course, it's a big leap to that conclusion, but not an unreasonable one," Oliver replied.

"Can you come up with a more likely hypothesis?" Ty asked.

"Don't I wish I could," Oliver admitted.

"That's impossible," Isabella told the captain then. "Philip's phone is always on. He would answer any call from you, unless there's a problem with the reception. Let *me* try."

As soon as she had disconnected from the captain, she found Philip's number on her speed dial. While she waited for the call to go through, she looked at Ty and explained, "Ian spoke to the captain from the tender. He must have rung him just before he did me. He wanted the captain to know that they would not be pulling up anchor until Philip returned sometime after lunch. The captain doesn't know why he stayed behind."

"Is it ringing yet?" Ty asked.

"It's just begun to," Isabella said, and frowned as she waited in silence. When Philip's voice mail finally picked up, she said, "Philip, where in God's name are you? Call me right away. It really is urgent."

"Let's go," Ty said. "You ought to get back to the boat."

"I'll make my way down in the next car," Oliver said.

"Bye, Ollie. I'll be in touch," Ty said

"Do. Let me know what you find," Oliver said as one of the celebrated apes that inhabited the Upper Rock dashed toward him on four legs and then with the front two snatched his canvas bag.

By the time they reached the base of the mountain, Isabella was finally crying. Ty put his arm around her, and she sobbed against his shoulder. The EC130 was on the tarmac at Gib Airport, its pilot already in communication with the control tower. Ty saw Isabella into the front passenger seat, then slid into the one behind. As the chopper rose and arced and her nightmare solidified into reality, she felt irretrievably lost, as if not only had the man who might as well have been her father died but in doing so had displaced her from the landscape of her life. To Ty the formidable young woman in front of him all at once seemed a vulnerable young girl.

High above the Med now, he studied the coastlines of Spain and Morocco, the intricate roadways, sea lanes, mountains and caves, particularly those of Gibraltar into and from which the sea ebbed and flowed. Everywhere there was movement—cars and aircraft, tankers, barges, pleasure boats. There were more pieces to this puzzle than any man could comprehend, yet this was the battle-field upon which he must triumph or fail.

Philip had just begun his main course of red curry with beef when his driver unexpectedly entered the Tom Yam and began to make his way to Philip's table. Across the cool room with its Zen decor, the emaciated man appeared distraught. Without bothering to introduce the chauffeur to Fateen Al-Dosari, Philip said, "What's the matter, Martin?"

"The office has called," the driver said.

"Whose office?"

"The livery, head office."

"And?"

"There has been a . . . a bad explosion in the harbor," the driver stammered.

"Go on."

"They told me it was the boat from your ship."

Philip immediately froze his gestures, then regarded Fateen with manifest concern. He said, "*How* bad?"

"Very bad, Mr. Frost."

Philip reached into the pocket of his jacket, feeling for his iPhone, but where it had been he found only a dented tin cigarette case. He clutched the mystifying case and studied it, then set it to the side on the tablecloth. He was sure he had not seen it before. He checked his jacket's other pockets, patted the side pockets of his trousers, stood up and checked his chair and the floor beneath it. "Goddamn it!" he exclaimed.

"Perhaps it slid out in the car," Fateen suggested.

"No, I always check the car each time a client leaves," the chauffeur said.

"Check again, will you?" Philip asked. "Never mind, I'll come with you."

The search of the Mercedes came up empty, as Philip knew it would. Whoever had stolen his iPhone had substituted the cigarette case, which was of nearly the same shape and size, so that Philip would not feel the absence of the phone's weight for as long as possible. He tried to think back to when he had last used or even seen the iPhone and remembered clearly that he had turned it off in the car almost immediately after delivering Ian to the harbor and then, by instinct, checked again to be sure it was off in the textile market, outside the makeshift mosque in which men had gathered for prayer. He had done so less out of respect than to provide an excuse for being unreachable in the immediate aftermath of the explosion, but it had been before then that he had disposed of the Nokia in three well-separated rubbish bins—first its shell, then its battery, finally its SIM card. So he had not tossed it by accident or allowed it to slip from his pocket then. He had passed so many people in the streets since. To whom had he spoken? Apart from his driver and the Tom Yam staff, Philip could recall only the obnoxious boy who had attempted to sell him a wooden ukulele, then begged for money. But the boy hadn't come close enough to steal his iPhone, had he?

Even if he had, there was nothing that could be done about it now. The iPhone was password-protected, which gave him some comfort. It would take an expert to retrieve from it any meaningful clues to Philip's activities, and such an expert was unlikely to be found in the boy's orbit. Indeed, if the boy had lifted it, he might well have sold it already, perhaps to someone who would soon sell it again. But no function of the phone would perform without the password, and its SIM card would be useless the moment Philip notified his carrier. Philip drew a deep breath. As vexing as the loss of his iPhone was, he had to maintain his focus, demonstrate the composure that Isabella would find fitting and a calm that would reassure others he remained firmly in control of the pending arms deal.

"May I borrow your phone, please?" he asked the driver.

"Of course, but it will not make international calls."

"Here, use mine," Fateen interjected.

"Thank you," Philip said, and tapped in Isabella's number.

"Oh, thank God, Philip, it's you," Isabella said when she heard his voice. "We've been trying to find you everywhere."

"I just heard," he told her.

"It's too awful," Isabella said.

"I'm sorry you couldn't get hold of me, darling. It seems I've lost my phone. Don't worry, I'm on my way."

"Be careful," she told him.

"Careful and quick," Philip promised.

It was well after two o'clock when Philip arrived on a dilapidating tender he'd managed to charter at dockside. Let off at the stern, he hurried through the yacht's passages until he found Isabella and Ty on bridge deck. Isabella had a handkerchief in her right hand, and a reddish residue of tears lingered in her eyes. She stood at once and stepped into Philip's arms. Philip held still. He could feel her heartbeat. "I'm so sorry," he whispered.

"It can't be true," she said.

Philip said nothing in reply. His palm traced her trembling spine.

"What happened?" Isabella asked, doing her best to disguise her new wariness of him.

"It's way too early for that. No one at the harbor seems to have any idea at this point," Philip said. "They've not even begun to piece things together."

"That boat was faultlessly maintained, and it was better protected than the Crown Jewels. An engine like that doesn't just blow up, does it?"

"I wouldn't have thought so," agreed Philip in a restrained tone of voice. "We'll need to wait to hear what the authorities have to say."

"Can they reconstruct it?" Ty asked.

"At the moment no one seems to think so, but it's early days."

"Time isn't usually a friend of the truth in accidents of this sort," Ty said. "If it were a bomb rather than an engine, what sort of explosive could do so much damage without Ian's realizing he'd taken it on board?"

"I've no idea," Philip said. "If—"

"I don't want to hear any of this," Isabella interrupted. "I'll see you both upstairs."

When she had fled, Ty said, "But I thought you were a physicist."

"I studied physics at university. You're asking a question more properly asked of a chemist."

"Yet you disarmed nuclear bombs."

"I decertified them. There's a whopping big difference."

"Have they recovered his body?" Ty asked.

"No, and they won't. According to what I hear, Ian and the boat were essentially vaporized. Naturally, I didn't want to say that in front of Isabella."

"Naturally," Ty agreed. "She's going to need to lean on you."

Philip nodded. "I'll be there."

"No doubt you'll need to lean on her as well. You and Ian were very close."

"We were. He was my mentor, my senior partner, so to speak, and, most of all, my friend."

"He liked young people, didn't he?" Ty asked. "That much was obvious, even to me, and I barely knew him."

"In many ways he stayed a kid. That's true."

"Who would have wanted to hurt him?"

"Oh, there are lots of people, I suppose. Jealous people, people he got the better of in one deal or another. He was always honest but often tough."

"What were you doing in Tangier?"

Philip stopped short. "Is that any of your business?"

"You're right, it's not. I'm sorry. All I meant was, could any of the people you saw there have—"

"Wanted to hurt him? Absolutely not! Leave it to the police. They're the ones most likely to figure it out."

"Of course," Ty said. "I was just thinking out loud."

"Perhaps you should take up screenwriting," Philip suggested, a momentary twinkle in his eye.

"One day, maybe," Ty said. "In view of the circumstances, I can't help feeling I'm intruding."

Philip let the assertion dangle in the air before replying, "Nonsense. Isabella likes you. You're—please don't take this the wrong way—a useful diversion at this point."

"I'll add that to my credits," Ty said. "I've never played that role before."

"Why not continue to play it for a little longer, then?" Philip suggested. "I'm going to have to go ashore in the morning to deal with various and sundry officials. It's not anything Isabella should be put through. Soon after that, no doubt, I'll have to do the same in Gib and Spain and who knows where else. It will be good for her to have company, a friend she can talk to. If it becomes too much for you, of course . . ."

"It won't," Ty said.

Philip offered a cool smile, sketched with irony. "How could it, right?"

"Oh, it could easily," Ty said. "After all, it's not as much fun to play a supporting role as it is the lead."

"I love her," Philip said. "Do you love her, too?"

Ty shook his head. "No," he said, but even as he spoke, he wondered if that was really true.

"I'm sure you have the widest possible field to choose from," Philip said, glancing reflexively at his watch. "Oh, my, the day's getting away from me. If you'll excuse me, there are a few calls I really must make, people who should hear the news from me rather than the media."

"I understand," Ty said.

Chapter Thirty-five

"Do you mind if I take the chopper?" Philip asked Isabella early the next morning, over their first coffee of the day.

"Do *I* mind? Of course I don't. Take it," she replied.

Philip smiled. Her seeming indifference to certain realities had long astonished and intrigued him. Ian's intentions, if not his actual last will and testament, were an open secret. Surely Isabella must know that all that had been his was now suddenly on its way to being hers.

"It will make it much easier," Philip continued.

"What will it make much easier?"

"Sorry," Philip said. "Sometimes my thoughts get ahead of my words. I'll have to go Tangier, first of all, just to make sure the authorities are on their way to more than putting their paperwork in order. They have a mystery to solve. In Gib there's Ian's entire office. The staff there will want to hear something from someone they know; the same in Spain and at the house. In Geneva and Zurich . . . hell, there are all sorts of people whose interests were entwined with Ian's. They'll have to be dealt with."

"I could go with you," Isabella said, but there was no energy in her voice.

"As Ian didn't have a next of kin and you are as close to that as there is, it may come down to that. But we're not there yet, darling."

Isabella smiled. "Well, whenever we are."

"Ty," Philip said, having noted Ty's arrival on deck, "I hope you don't mind."

Ty shook his head. "If there's anything I can do."

"I'll try to be back tonight," Philip said, "if I can put Switzerland off for another day. Otherwise tomorrow, but not late."

"Do what Ian would want done," Isabella said. "That's all that matters."

Philip kissed her, deeply. "I've borrowed Crispin's mobile," he said. "He'll know the number."

"I'm sure he will," Isabella said, "but ring me just in case, so that I'll have it."

"Promise," Philip said.

"What now?" Isabella asked Ty as the chopper ascended.

"That's up to you," he told her.

"We've missed an opportunity, I'm afraid."

"To jigger Crispin's phone? I don't think so. Philip will go where he said he would go and for the reasons he gave. He's right about what has to be done. If the phone is GPS-enabled, Oliver's boys can track it. It's not where he'll go that concerns me right now, but what he'll say and to whom. And he won't say that on Crispin's phone."

"Okay, I'll play, Mr. Movie Star. How do you know he wouldn't lead you to the warheads?"

"That's the last place he would go. There are too many eyes on him, and he knows it."

"Then why exactly is it up to me?" Isabella demanded.

"Because we must get into Ian's quarters," Ty explained.

"I've already told you: That's impossible."

Ty rolled his eyes. "There's been a change of circumstances."

"Assert myself? Is that what you're telling me?"

"You'll be good at it."

"And if anyone objects?"

"Say that there are things you need for the authorities, never mind what. That's none of their business. Smile that smile of yours, Isabella, and push forward like the dreadnought you'll have to become to keep control of your new empire. Trust me: No one will stand in your way. Not the captain, not Jean-François, not Crispin or any other member of the crew. They work for you now. You may not have absorbed that fact yet, but I assure you they have."

Ty followed Isabella upstairs to the door flanked by Venetian theatrical masks. The smiling mask of comedy, at the starboard side of the entrance to Ian's quarters, seemed almost sacrilegious now, its chalk-white lips and lifted cheeks an affront to both Isabella's grief and Ian's memory. To their astonishment the door had been left open, so they descended into the study, then across its enormous Turkish carpet cautiously, fearful that they might not be alone. Ty examined the papers still resting on Ian's desktop and others in a green leather tray on the credenza behind it. All had to do with his collections. None appeared relevant to the warheads. They opened each drawer of the Chippendale desk and examined every bookshelf, unlocking the stays that held the expensive volumes in place when the ship was at sea in order to be sure that nothing had been secreted behind them.

"Is there a safe? Behind a picture perhaps?" Ty asked.

"There's a safe in the floor," Isabella said, "just below Ian's desk chair. I don't know its combination, but I saw him go into it once to take out a birthday present he'd bought for me."

Ty pushed the chair away and rolled back the carpet from the wall. "It's been opened," he said.

"I don't understand," Isabella said.

"No doubt it happened while you were sleeping."

"Philip ought to have told me."

"Yes," Ty said. "He should have."

"There's no point looking much further, I suppose. Whatever was here is gone."

"I'd say that's a good guess," Ty agreed.

"Oh, what a shame!" Isabella exclaimed suddenly. "I wonder what happened."

"What is it?"

"Ian's gaming table," Isabella said. "He loved it. It's just about the most valuable one in the world. Louis XVI. Notice the gold-embossed leather writing surface. You turn it over and it's felt, for playing cards. Beneath it there's the most beautiful backgammon board inlaid with ivory and ebony. But just look at the red's thirteen point! I can't imagine how that could happen, can you?"

"I think you should ring for Crispin," Ty said.

"There's a call button on the desk."

"Good. When he comes, ask him the obvious questions—diplomatically, of course, but firmly and as though I weren't here."

Crispin Pleasant appeared a moment later.

"I didn't know anyone else had access to this room," Isabella said.

"Didn't you?" replied the old retainer, in familiar tartan even at this hour. "No, I suppose not, because no one did. Mr. Santal, however, did give instructions, on more than one occasion and to both the captain and me, that in the event of his death, and only then, the ordinary system should be bypassed—with this electronic key he kept hidden in a crystal box that was alarmed by lasers, its whereabouts known only to us. Mr. Frost, he told us, was then to be allowed to enter in order to complete whatever business might be going forward. I am sure Mr. Frost will explain that to you."

"I'm sure he will," she said, bathing Crispin in her scrutiny. "I'm sure his explanation will be very correct and that whatever he's doing is what's best for me. Tell me, am I permitted to be here?"

Crispin smiled indulgently. "Why, this is the *owner's* deck, isn't it, Miss Cavill?"

"Thank you, Crispin," Isabella said. "It's a sad time for both of us."

"A melancholy time indeed," he said.

Ty and Isabella remained in Ian's quarters for several minutes after Crispin's departure. There were more papers to review, crevices to be searched, thoughts to be gathered and territorial rights to be established. When they finished, Ty said, "We're looking in the wrong place."

"I was thinking the same thing."

"Let's go," he said.

"To Vanda?"

"Where else?"

They entered Epidendrum, Isabella's suite, then used the pair of interior connecting doors, already ajar, to gain access to Philip's stateroom. "Amazing, isn't it?" Isabella sighed. "A place for everything and everything in its place. Philip leaves practically nothing for the staff to do but make his bed and change his towels."

"He seems very neat," Ty agreed.

"You don't know the half of it: cuff links in his links box, shirts piled or hung according to the colors of the spectrum, trousers folded cuff over cuff on a hanger the way tailors in Savile Row do it, shoes in trees and facing the same direction, toiletries lined up just so. It's not that easy to live with if you're not that way yourself."

"It's completely anal," Ty said before he thought better of it.

"Speak English, please, not American. I don't really know what 'anal' means. In fact, I'm not certain I want to."

"It's something like obsessive-compulsive disorder."

"I'm sure you intend that to be reassuring," Isabella replied with undisguised sarcasm. "Do you see anything?"

"Not yet. At least with an obsessive-compulsive there's no need to look on the floor in case something has dropped," Ty pressed on. He had gingerly searched the drawers of the bedroom's large campaign chest and was checking the pockets of Philip's jackets and trousers. "Matches," he said after a moment.

"From where?"

"The Four Seasons, Prague."

"No surprise there."

"What's surprising is that he didn't empty his pockets before he hung up his clothes. That seems out of character with the man you've just described. He must have been thrown by events. Wait! Here's a receipt of some sort."

"What kind of receipt?"

"It's in Arabic."

"That's too bad. I don't read or speak Arabic. There must be someone aboard who does."

"Let me take a stab at it."

Isabella looked incredulous.

"It's from a shop in the rue Siaghine. Apparently he bought a box there."

"That makes sense. He's always bringing me boxes. He was wearing those trousers yesterday, wasn't he? I remember him coming down the stairs behind Ian."

"Give him an hour, then call him," Ty said. "You're lonely and sad, that's natural. Find out where he is."

"Better if I text him on Crispin's phone, I think," Isabella said. "It's more what he'd expect, and it will make it harder for him to change his plan—or mine, for that matter."

After confirming his number with Crispin, Isabella pressed a message into her own phone: *"P., miss you! Hope things under control in Tangier, if you're still there. Love, I."*

"It's ready to send," she explained, "whenever you give the word."

"Will he respond?"

"I'd think so."

"He bought a box he never gave you, never even mentioned. He would have sent it home with Ian, most likely. It could explain a lot."

"Or not. It's a theory."

"But I'm right that he hasn't brought up the subject?"

"Would you have done? What would be the point? He might well have reasoned that it would only make me sadder."

"That would have been tender of him," Ty said as they returned together to bridge deck.

"I've never been very good at killing time," Isabella said after a few minutes of dismissing the contents of the day's newspapers, then staring into space.

"I've never had much time on my hands to kill," Ty said. "Do you play gin?"

"I did once, poorly," she replied as he broke open a pack of cards he'd discovered on a shelf nearby, "but I'm a fast learner."

Less than an hour and several unimpressive hands later, she was far behind Ty and it was her turn to deal again. As she peeled off ten cards for each of them, plus a last one to start the discard pile, she looked at him, then at her phone. "Do you think it's time yet?"

"I do," Ty said. "It feels right."

Isabella sent her message. A few minutes later, as she knocked, laying down a run of the king, queen, jack, ten and nine of hearts, her phone flashed. She read the short text, first in silence, then aloud: "'I., all pretty well under control here. Leave for Gib next quarter hour. Love, P.'"

"Let's go," Ty said.

Chapter Thirty-six

After *Surpass*'s chopper had flown overhead, Ty followed Isabella to the interior dry dock in which the small tender was now cradled alone.

The berth was already filling with seawater, the craft rising nearly to the level of the steel mesh treadway upon which they stood. No sooner had the tender escaped the yacht's open stern than Isabella floored its throttle, steering it toward shore. After the breakwater she slowed the craft, maneuvering it along the frenzied waterfront to the yacht-club quay from which Ian had departed the day before. This unnerved her, but she understood there was no other choice, as that was where their shore agent would see them through immigration and the *douane*.

They hailed the first taxi that swerved toward them and directed the driver to 111 rue Siaghine, the shop address shown on Philip's receipt. The late-morning traffic was halting, and Isabella felt her impatience rise as so many motorists jockeyed for starting position at each red light, only to bunch up in every-man-for-himself congestion. It was hot and the taxi's air-conditioning was in desperate need of coolant. Isabella looked anxiously at Ty, then rolled her eyes. At the corner of rue de la Poste, stranded in another jam, they paid the driver and got out, deciding that it would be quicker to walk. The shop they were looking for was not far along on the southern side of the street. A short green awning had been lowered over its windows in an effort to protect its wooden merchandise from sunlight.

Once inside, they were at first left alone to examine the various boxes, frames, knickknacks and utensils on display. The cool, shadowy interior was pungent with the scent of shaved cedar and beeswax. No sooner had Ty begun to investigate the enormous pyramid of boxes than the merchant with the slanted smile and missing bicuspid approached him. "Aren't they beautiful?" he said.

Ty nodded. "There are so many different ones," he replied.

"Here, let me show you my favorite," the merchant said. "This one has a secret compartment. You turn this knob once, nothing happens, but twice, voilà!"

"How fiendishly clever," Isabella remarked as Ty examined it and the merchant withdrew for a few seconds to greet other customers. "It could hardly hold a bomb, could it?" she whispered.

"Don't be so sure," Ty said. "There are binary explosives that wouldn't require any more space. Of course, they'd be hard to come by."

"But not impossible to come by?"

"Not for a certain sort of person."

"Try it yourself," the merchant said upon returning.

"That's exactly what I was doing," Ty said. "How much do you want for it?"

"Fifty euros."

Ty understood he was expected to bargain, although something about the process had always felt indecent to him. "Is that your best price?"

The merchant raised his palms as if to say, *Why would you even ask a question like that?*

"Do you like it?" Ty asked Isabella. "Or is there another one you prefer?"

"I think it's sweet," Isabella said.

Ty regarded the merchant, still awaiting his answer.

"For the American"—the merchant smiled—"forty euros. Do we have a deal?"

"We have a deal," Ty said with relief.

"I am so glad for your wife."

Isabella smiled.

"You could do worse," Ty told her.

As the merchant withdrew a sheet of printed tissue wrapping paper and set about his ritual, a group of tourists suddenly appeared on the shop's threshold, chattering among themselves as they debated whether or not to enter. They were a traveling party of American retirees, several women and only three men, and as they drew closer Ty recognized the soft Virginia dialect of his youth.

The shopkeeper was about to hand Ty his purchase when one of the American women said, "Excuse me, but aren't you Ty Hunter?"

Ty put out his hand. "That's the name my parents gave me," he said.

"I know your mother," the woman said.

This stopped Ty in his tracks, for he would not, he knew at once, be able to negotiate his usual gracious exit from such an encounter. "You do?" he asked.

"So do I," said another woman.

"Well, I can't claim to," added a man in an extra-large golf shirt that did its best to contain his paunch, "but I can tell you that I've heard so much about her I feel I do."

"I know what you mean," said one of the other men, a taller, gaunt gentleman in a Hawaiian shirt.

Ty laughed. "My mother gets around," he said. "How do you all know her?"

"Yoga . . . aerobics . . . and gym. We're all part of the same senior center."

"That's great," Ty said. "What brings you to Tangier?"

"It was cheaper than staying home," one of the women suggested, laughing at her witticism.

"What my wife means is that the tour was offered at an awfully good price. We wanted Dorothy to come."

"I wish she had," Ty said.

"Oh, but you know her! She's always got so much going on," said the first woman. "She's *so* proud of you. She talks about you all the time."

"We should have a photo," one of the others implored.

"Would you be kind enough?" inquired the gaunt man of the shopkeeper.

"It would be my pleasure," the latter said, with a measure of trepidation.

As he spoke, his son came in off the street, wiping his brow from exertion. The shopkeeper immediately handed him the American's Cyber-shot. "He's a very much better photographer than I am—a real technologist!"

They formed a close arc, with Ty and Isabella at the center. The boy, with a steady grip, aimed the camera at them. "I count to three," he commanded. "You say, 'Big movie star.'"

They laughed. The boy snapped two successive exposures, then handed the camera to Ty for his approval of each. As Ty returned the camera to its owner, the boy, without warning, darted out of the shop but within seconds had returned from the newsagent directly across the street, bearing a furled copy of ¡Hola!, a Spanish celebrity magazine that featured Ty on its cover. The boy placed the oversize magazine directly in front of his father and then, when his father had had time to absorb the identity of his famous customer, opened it to a two-page spread devoted to Ty's recent appearance at the Film Festival in Cannes.

Eventually, having been rewarded with their photograph, the Virginians began to drift way.

"Thank you," Ty said as the merchant finally handed him his package. "Oh, and one more quick thing, if I may." He directed his remarks not only to the shopkeeper but to his son, who seemed caught in the spell of Ty's fame, taking in every word.

"Of course," the merchant said. "Whatever I can do for you, Mr. Hunter, will bring me joy."

"Have you ever seen this man?" Ty inquired, producing a flattering, wallet-size photograph of Philip Frost that Isabella had lent him.

"Yes," the merchant said, "I have. And it was only yesterday, I believe."

Ty exhaled a deep breath. "That's right, it would have been yesterday. Did he buy anything from you?"

The man's eyes grew curious. "He did. He bought a box."

"Like the one I've just bought."

"Very, very similar it was. Of course, no two boxes are ever exactly alike."

"I understand," Ty said. "Apparently he was a better bargainer than I."

"I'm not sure I understand," the merchant replied.

"He paid twenty-five euros," Ty said, but when this appeared to distress the man, tempered his remark with a laugh. "Not that I mind about that. I think you gave me more than a fair deal at forty."

"I am so glad."

"He wasn't nice," the boy interjected.

"What do you mean?" Ty asked him.

"Nothing," the boy said.

"No, tell me, please," Ty said.

"You're his friend."

"Not exactly."

"He wasn't fair," the boy explained nervously. "He took advantage. He wasn't nice like you and the lady."

Ty studied Isabella's face.

The boy continued. "I did not know who he was or where to find him. I did not know he was the friend of Ty Hunter, the movie star."

"Never mind all that," Ty said. "Why would you have wanted to find him? I thought you didn't like him very much."

The boy hesitated. "To give him *this*," he replied at last, withdrawing Philip's iPhone from a pocket of his cargo shorts.

"Where did you get that?" the merchant demanded of his son.

"He dropped it."

"You should have given it to me in case he came back for it."

The boy kept eyes on the floor. "I know," he said. "I am sorry. I did wrong."

"Thank God you did," Ty said. "May I have it please?"

The boy appeared relieved to place the phone in Ty's hand.

"It is pass-code-protected, isn't it?" Ty asked.

The boy nodded. "It's too bad," he said, cracking a momentary smile.

"Well, thank you for looking after it so well," Ty said. "I'm sure the owner will be glad to have it back." Reaching into his wallet, he found a ten-euro note and pressed it into the boy's quivering hand.

Bewildered, the merchant said, "I don't understand why he deserves a reward."

Ty smiled. "Oh, but you'll have to trust me that he does. Your son did a very important and good thing, even if it was by accident."

In the street again, Ty said, "It makes you sad, doesn't it, a kid like that? You'd like to take him away, but of course you can't, because this is his home and it doesn't matter that the opportunities are so much greater just fourteen miles across the sea."

"It would break his father's heart," Isabella said, "and his mother's, and doubtless his, too."

"That's the problem," Ty said. "The world's just not fair." He paused, struck by and now reflecting upon how much more thoughtful Isabella was than most of the women he had encountered recently. Then, returning to the task at hand, he asked, "Do you know Philip's pass code?"

"I did. Try F1D1C and see if it works."

Ty did as she suggested, and the iPhone sprang to life. "The second big break of the case," he said with a laugh. "We're on a streak. What's F1D1C?"

"Pi, alternately in letters and numerals, backwards. Philip's an engineer, never forget that."

"It's cute, I suppose, but it's not a very strong pass code, which makes me think there isn't much on the phone he cares about protecting."

"He was upset when he discovered he'd lost it," Isabella said. "Do you have any idea what you're looking for?"

"A way in," Ty said.

"Obviously, but will you know it when you see it?"

"Chances of that are slim to none," he said, "but I won't be the one doing the looking."

They walked downhill for several minutes until Ty paused in front of a small shop whose crowded window featured all manner of gray-market electronics products. Inside, he purchased and quickly pocketed a four-gigabyte SanDisk memory stick and a USB connecter cable for the iPhone. At the next intersection, they came upon a taxi discharging its fare and immediately jumped into the old white Citroën. Ty directed its driver to the place de France, where the electronics dealer had told him they would find an Internet café.

"Café" was hardly the word for the bustling, casino-like room that reminded Ty of the Japanese pachinko parlors he had encountered during his tours to promote his films and endorse watches and men's cosmetics. Rows of solitary, transfixed individuals in red-and-yellow carrels sat before flat computer screens with wide, blank stares and, in most cases, no more than a half-consumed, forgotten latte or espresso or decaf perched on one of the identical black Formica tables before them.

The laptop Ty rented had been fitted into a steel frame that in turn had been bolted to the table on which it rested. He paid in advance for an hour's use of the computer. From the start menu, he pressed RUN, then IPCONFIG. When the computer's Internet protocol address appeared in the display box, he entered that number in his BlackBerry. From the same phone, employing it in its encryption mode, he called Oliver. "I have a Christmas present for you," he said.

"I hope it's female."

"No, but it rhymes with female."

"Here it is, and lovely it is, too: an IP address. What the fuck, if I may ask, am I supposed to do with it?"

"Call in the geeks. Have them send me a program into which I can download the contents of Philip Frost's iPhone."

"Bloody hell!" Oliver exclaimed.

"It's a long story," Ty said.

"I'll bet it is."

"Once I've done that I'll download the same contents onto a memory stick. Better safe than sorry is what I'm saying, and if there are any large files, I don't want to take the chance of their being corrupted in transmission. How will I get it to you?"

"Where are you now?"

"Tangier."

"So you said in your e-mail this morning, but where in Tangier?"

"L'Homme Sage Café d'Internet, just off the place de France."

Oliver paused. "There is a fellow at the American Legation," he said, thinking out loud.

"Not far, really, but not exactly the right building to be spotted going into or out of," Ty said.

"Nor was I suggesting that you do so," Oliver replied. "I take it you plan to go from where you are back to the tender and then to *Surpass*."

"Where else? I'm used to the good life, you know."

"Only too well," Oliver said. "So when you leave there, stroll for a minute or two. You're tourists, right—why not? Then, on impulse, decide to have a drink or a croque-monsieur or whatever you fancy at the Café de Paris. Do you know where that is?"

"I'll find it."

"If it looks familiar, that's because it was the backdrop for that explosion in *The Bourne Ultimatum*. So you won't be the first fellow in your line of business to find his way there."

"Life imitates art," Ty replied.

"Take a table outside, on the Terrasse des Paresseux side. When you see a young Moroccan in his early twenties selling flowers on the street corner opposite, that's your signal. He'll be wearing a loose white shirt and a green baseball cap. Don't rush. He'll wait for you. He'll keep you in his sight even when he isn't in yours. When you approach him, give in to one more impulse. Buy the lovely Miss Cavill some flowers. What could be more natural? Ask the young man if he has any white roses available. If he seems not to recognize you, then says, 'As in the famous painting by van Gogh? I fear not, but if you have three minutes, I can find you some lovely yellow ones or perhaps others the color of a peach,' you can take what he has on offer and hand off the memory stick with your money."

"And if he doesn't?"

"Then you've got the wrong vendor. Thank him, move on, and keep your eye out for the next bloke selling flowers. But, Ty . . ."

"Yes, Oliver."

"That won't happen. He's ours. He'll find you, and no one would ever know that, watching him work."

Chapter Thirty-seven

Philip Frost collected the papers from his desk. There weren't many. The Gibraltar outpost of the de Novo Fund had opened only recently and would close as soon as it had succeeded in coordinating and masking payments for the nuclear warheads. The offices were cramped but well located in Irishtown, an appropriately discreet outpost.

Philip looked at his watch, a Patek Philippe Sky Moon Tourbillon. Ian had given it to him after the decertification of the installation near the Strait of Kerch because, he'd said, "I couldn't resist. It is both exquisitely beautiful and the first two-faced watch the illustrious firm has ever made." Philip smiled to himself, thinking how odd it was that he seldom consulted it. These days, on most occasions when he needed to know the time, he found it on his iPhone, the loss of which now bothered him anew. Having misplaced or lost or allowed it to be stolen had been careless and out of character, but as he reviewed its contents in his mind for the hundredth time, he remained all but certain that they contained nothing incriminating. Meticulously, he separated the papers before him into stacks. Those for which he had no immediate use he locked away in the cabinet behind his desk; those he wished to have to hand he placed in his black cowhide attaché case. When he had finished, he closed and locked the case and left the office. "I shall work out of Mr. Santal's office for the time being," he told the only recently recruited secretaries as he exited through the fund's reception room. "There's a lot to be done, and it will be easier to do it from there."

"Again, we're very sorry," one of the secretaries told him. She was a hefty local girl with closely cropped dyed-blond hair and celebrated word-processing skills.

Leaving the office and coming into the street, Philip experienced unexpected elation. Events were on schedule despite Ian's death. Although he had prepared the option, he had not actually decided to eliminate Ian until their dispute at Pond House. Granted, that had been restrained, but it had clearly revealed an incipient fissure in Ian's faith. Had he been precipitous? Philip did not think so. What if, for example, Ian had discovered the account in Vienna through which Philip had all along intended to skim funds for his own benefit? What if one of the warheads was used, forcing Ian out of denial about the devastating consequences of his actions? That might prompt a confrontation that could bring them both down. Even without such an argument, Philip could imagine Ian discarding him once he was no longer essential to the great man's plan. As close as he had grown to his mentor, Philip did not feel the familial bond he pretended to. How could he be sure that Ian felt it? Would a man like Ian truly rejoice at the prospect of his beloved Isabella's marrying a man like Philip? Perhaps, Philip reckoned, but only if it were Ian's amorality and not his ambition that defined him. By culture if not blood, Santal was English and highly sensitive to the slightest gradations of status. What if, in the endless procession of the great and the good to Ian's altar, a better catch were to come along? A scion or a future duke, even a prince of the realm or of Hollywood? The last thought sickened him. He did not like or trust Ty Hunter, although for the moment, unwittingly, Hunter was performing the very useful role of keeping Isabella out of Philip's way while he concentrated on bringing his deal to fruition. Without Isabella between them, he and Hunter might have got along passably, but Isabella *was* between them. Never mind! One way or another, he would soon bid farewell to Ty Hunter.

Ridding himself of inconvenient people was a talent at which he excelled and which over time had given him a profound competitive advantage. When Billy Claussen had threatened the warhead deal by withdrawing from the Russian resort project, Philip had found that poor, pathetic loser, frocked him as a priest, and turned him into an assassin. No sooner had Ian betrayed his uncertainty about him, threatening not only his future security but his claim to Isabella, than he had done the job himself. After those efforts—not to mention Andrej's dispatching of Colonel Zhugov, which Philip had choreographed—the untimely demise of an overconfident film star would not be difficult to arrange.

Ian's office, like *Surpass,* was an assertion of megalomania. Constructed within the interior of a cave that had once served as the wing of a war museum, it featured a massive desk, an oval slab of malachite mounted on intersecting stainless-steel hyperbolas, behind which stretched a long row of ancient gun emplacements. Through these the Class A runway of Gibraltar Airport could be seen in the foreground, intersected by Winston Churchill Avenue, which was the broad main road connecting the Rock to the Spanish mainland. Both the new civilian terminal and the old Royal Air Force headquarters were in plain sight. In the distance the frontier, with its usual bustling queue of cars, motorcycles and pedestrians, was also clearly visible. Beyond it spread the inner harbor and the crescent of the coast, where on an isthmus of honey-colored sand, beneath vast striped tents, a boat show was under way in the seaside town of La Línea de la Concepción.

Philip looked across the desk at Andrej. "What's the matter?" he inquired.

"Nothing," Andrej replied.

"Then why are you so whey-faced?"

"I didn't know I was. It must be the mephitic atmosphere. I've never cared for caves. Or perhaps it's the light."

Philip let Andrej's complaint and latest big word go without comment. He knew that "mephitic" meant noxious, but had no time for small talk. "Andrej," he said, "this is no time to let one's nerves become unsteady."

"Mine aren't," Andrej insisted.

"Good," Philip said. "Can I assume that all three teams are ready to be deployed?"

"You can, absolutely."

"The first squad will remain here. The second will accompany me to *Surpass*. The third will remain on standby until just before the moment of transfer. That's understood?"

"Yes, fully understood," Andrej said. "Thus far it's gone like clockwork, hasn't it?"

Philip smiled. "Remember our rule: no questions. Simply because you are on the point of becoming a very rich man is no reason to forget it."

Andrej let out a single laugh, played along as though Philip had asked no more than to be humored a bit longer. "I have to hand it to you," he said.

"Better to save the compliments, too, I think, until the final phase of our project has been successfully completed," Philip admonished him, his smile disappearing.

"Perhaps, but that ruse in Naples—only you, Philip, could have conceived it, much less pulled it off. Somewhere between Istanbul and Naples, a few labels or perhaps the cartons themselves are changed and the warheads go ashore as teas and textiles. Brilliant in itself, but what I truly love is that once the ship has been searched and cleared, they come right back on, fully vetted, as something else entirely. It's the perfect double bluff."

Philip relented before Andrej's flattery. "It *was* worthy of Ian, wasn't it?"

Andrej nodded. "Should anyone have caught on to us by then, which I very much doubt they had, it would have sent them off on more wild-goose chases than an army could follow."

"What makes you so sure no one is circling us?"

Andrej appeared puzzled. "The fact that we have come this far. I mean, so far, so good."

"Those questions that were being asked in Moscow," Philip said, "are bound to intensify in the wake of Ian's death."

"Possibly so," Andrej replied. "Or they might vanish into the night with him."

"Just so," Philip said, "but I think it only prudent to deflect them before we know the answer to that for sure."

"Of course, if you can."

"Well, leave that to me. And, Andrej, don't go too far afield. Things will begin to move quickly very soon."

When Andrej had left, Philip returned to the stacks of papers on Ian's desk he had been sorting before his comrade's arrival. It was mostly routine correspondence but included the *Times* of London, in which the explosion of the tender was described by witnesses as an "inferno." Apparently the bomb had done its damage too swiftly to be captured on film. Among the financial statements, requests for interviews or advice and personal letters, there was only one that had, on first reading, disturbed Philip, and he now turned to it again:

Dear Mr. Santal,

I wonder if you would be kind enough to intercede on our behalf and help us ascertain why, almost six months after our previous chief executive withdrew Claussen Incorporated from participation in the redevelopment of a disused Russian military base into the Mineral Bay resort complex on the Sea of Azov near Kerch, elements of our involvement appear to continue. At the urging of our majority shareholder, Mr. Luke Claussen, whom I believe you know, I have consulted all the agreements relevant to this matter, and although I well understand the need to have phased out our participation according to an agreed schedule, it would seem that more than enough time has now passed for that to have been accomplished.

I am writing to you as I have been unable to gain satisfactory answers from those nominally in charge and because I know that, as a close friend of the late Mr. Wilhelm Claussen, you were instrumental in brokering our original involvement at Mineral Bay.

As you will understand, Claussen Incorporated is engaged in projects on every one of the world's seven continents, many of them extensive and involving both governments and other major corporations. We jealously guard our reputation and, frankly, have lately been concerned that European and particularly Italian authorities appear to suspect our ships of complicity in illicit traffic, of which we do not have and have never had any knowledge. Naturally, we—my fellow officers and board—are eager to clear up any misunderstanding as expeditiously and comprehensively as possible.

I would therefore be grateful to you if you would investigate this matter and so help us to disentangle ourselves from any lingering connection with the Mineral Bay project.

Sincerely yours,

Simon Stonesiefer

PRESIDENT AND C.E.O.,

Claussen Incorporated

Copies: *Mr. Luke Claussen*

Hon. Blaine Burr,

Secretary of State of the United States

When he had finished rereading the letter, Philip stood and, focusing the telescope mounted on a nearby tripod, surveyed the land- and seascape stretching away from Gibraltar. He was not searching for anything in particular. Rather he was employing his hands, his eyes and the scenery before him to spur his imagination, to locate, isolate and neutralize, if it existed, any remaining threat to his plan. After a few minutes, he smiled to himself and, returning to Ian's desk, picked up the telephone. "Please, would you get me George Kenneth, the President's National Security Advisor, at the White House?" he said.

"Will that number be public?" inquired Ian's principal secretary.

"Yes," Philip replied. "I'm positive there is a number listed for it."

While he waited for his call to be put through, Philip thought again of Isabella alone with Ty. Ian had been suspicious of Ty, but, as he had related it to Philip, that suspicion had had more to do with Ty's nature than any mission in which he might be involved. Ty's history was colorful. Philip had to admit that. Still, his adventures in the military were those of a young man with an uncertain future. Now Ty Hunter was a phenomenon, and it was too fanciful, even for Philip, to suppose that the most famous film star in the world had come into Ian's orbit other than by accident. Were there more to it than that, Ty would not have come alone.

Just then the telephone buzzed. "I have Dr. Kenneth for you."

"Thank you," Philip said. "George, this is Philip Frost."

"It's been a long time," George Kenneth said.

"Hasn't it?" Philip parried. "I trust you're well."

"As well as can be expected of anyone in this eighteen-hour-a-day-plus job."

"I know you're a busy man in a demanding job, so I shall come straight to the point. You may have heard the news about Ian Santal."

"Who hasn't?"

"You may remember that he was a mentor of mine and a great friend. His goddaughter is my girlfriend. So you will appreciate that what I am about to say is in the strictest confidence."

"Of course."

"Ian was a brilliant and, in many ways, a wonderful man. He could not have been more devoted to Isabella, for example, or more helpful to any number of worthy causes."

"But?"

"He had a penchant for shenanigans, shall we say. Nothing serious, mind you, but occasionally he liked to dance at the edge of civilized behavior—not over the edge, but just within it."

"Do you have a particular instance in mind?" George Kenneth inquired.

Philip deliberately hesitated. "That's the thing," he said. "I don't know if I do or I don't. Right now I'm helping Isabella, who is Ian's heir and as close to kin as he had, to begin to get an idea of his affairs, which are madly complicated. And I've come across a letter to Ian from someone called Simon Stonesiefer. Does that name mean anything to you?"

"It rings a bell."

"He's the new CEO of Claussen Incorporated."

"That's it."

"Mr. Stonesiefer is concerned that Claussen is being tarred by the brush of some deal into which Ian inveigled his predecessor, the famous Wilhelm Claussen. As it happens, I know a little about that deal. It involved the conversion of a base by the Black Sea that I had a hand in decertifying. Just after I'd finished there, Ian rang to ask my opinion of the site as a possible resort. I told him that my opinion wasn't a very high one—quite the opposite. The weather there had been god-awful. I was sure its season would be too short. Never mind all that now. What I'd like to do, for Isabella's sake, is get to the bottom of whatever might have been going on, as diplomatically and quickly as possible. I'd like to see Claussen right, if that really does need doing, and spare my old friend as well as my intended fiancée any sort of embarrassment. Any transgression is bound to be very minor. He can no longer be punished for it and she shouldn't be."

George Kenneth said, "'Intended fiancée.' It's the first time I've heard that expression. Congratulations, I suppose, are *almost* in order. In the meantime, how can I help?"

"What I would really appreciate is a little hitchhike through the bureaucracy," Philip said. "Mr. Stonesiefer not only wrote Ian, he copied Secretary of State Burr, heaven knows why."

"To protect Claussen's licenses, almost surely," George Kenneth replied. "I understand your situation, Philip. And I both empathize with and envy it. I've recently seen a photograph of your future wife."

"Have you? Don't tell me it was that one at Cannes."

"It must have been. Otherwise why would the *Post* have printed it? Anyway, don't worry too much about this other business. I'll give it some thought and have a word with the appropriate people. I can't make any promises, but off-hand it sounds like something that should be able to be sorted out pretty easily and quietly."

"Thank you very much indeed, George," Philip said, then cradled the receiver, sanguine that he had deftly deflected unwanted attention from himself.

A moment later the mobile he had borrowed from Crispin rang in his pocket.

"Hello," Philip said.

"It's Jean-François, sir."

"Yes, Jean-François, what can I do for you?"

"It's probably nothing, but even so I thought you should know. I tried to ring you earlier, but the call went through to voice mail."

Philip glanced at the telephone's screen. Jean-François was correct. There was a message waiting. "Damn it," he said, "I must have been in the street and not heard it. Go on!"

"First things first: Miss Cavill went to Mr. Santal's quarters this morning. You said to let you know if and when that happened."

"What did she want there? Do you know?"

"No, not exactly," answered Jean-François. "According to Crispin they were looking for something. He didn't say what. I don't think he knew."

"They?" inquired Philip.

"Mr. Hunter was with her."

"Where are they now?"

"I don't know."

"Well, are they on bridge deck or the owner's deck or—"

"They've gone ashore."

Philip swallowed hard. "How did that happen?"

"They took the small tender."

"Before you realized it, I presume."

"Yes."

"Did they go into Tangier?"

"They did. I have already checked with the dock agent there."

"I wish they hadn't. It could be dangerous for them. I wish they'd just stayed put until we are sure what happened to Ian, that whatever threat there was had been confined to him and passed."

Jean-François listened. "I'm sorry, sir," he said at last.

"It's not your fault," Philip said. "It's mine."

"I'm not sure I understand," Jean-François said.

"I'm not sure you need to," Philip replied. "I should have planned for this contingency."

"When they return, what shall I say? What would you like me to do?"

"Assuming they return, *say* nothing. And *do* nothing out of the ordinary, unless of course you must to keep them there. That's your goal, J-F, to keep them there without them realizing what you're doing."

Chapter Thirty-eight

"Isabella is right beside me," Ty told Oliver.

"I'm glad to hear it," Oliver said. "Where are you now?"

"Almost at the yacht club," Ty replied. "Naturally, she's very concerned."

"As well she should be," Oliver said, "but what other choice is there?"

"The Witness Protection Program," Ty suggested.

"That would be more difficult for you than most."

"Very funny! Here, she'll tell you herself," Ty said, about to hand his Black-Berry to Isabella. "She didn't ask for this, Ollie. That's what you have to remember."

"Hi, Oliver," Isabella said calmly.

"Hello, Isabella," Oliver said.

"Let me get this straight," she said. "You're asking me to go back to a man you believe—and I'm not saying I agree with you—killed my godfather and may be instrumental in killing how many more people? Why?"

"Because he'll expect you," Oliver answered. "*Surpass* is yours now. Where else would you be? We can't afford to have Frost panic and change his plans at the last minute. At this point he's our only lead and you our only means of keeping him in sight. Ask Ty if you don't believe me."

"Oh, I believe you," Isabella said.

Intuiting Oliver's end of the conversation, Ty said, "The man has a point. Philip may be willing to see a large part of the world go up in flames, but I doubt he sees himself burning with it. We'll be safe for the time being."

"I'm not so sure," Isabella told him.

"You don't have to do this," Ty said.

"Yes I do, and you both know it. I slipped on a banana peel, and fate caught me."

"Happens all the time," he said.

"In your minds this really *is* Waterloo, isn't it?"

"It is," Ty told her, "and we had better be cast as Wellington."

In a windowless anteroom off Admiral Cotton's office in the NATO command post, Oliver regarded Bingo Chen with approval. Chen's uniform of jeans, sandals and baggy palm-leaf cotton shirt worn with its tail exposed was typical of his profession. He was a hacker. With his aviators nesting in his gelled hair, an open can of Coke Zero on the coaster beside him, Bingo studied the Asus computer screen in front of him. "Say hi to the guys," he told Oliver as images of three young people around twenty years of age appeared side by side. "Left to right, Delilah Mirador, alpha geek from Shaker Heights, Ohio, now at Hebrew University by way of Caltech; Jonty Patel, first from Mumbai and now the University of Maryland, ostensibly; and Nevada Smith, from Laguna Beach, Harvard and Berkeley."

Oliver smiled quickly into the webcam, then studied the hackers. The first two, especially the fetchingly zaftig Delilah, seemed to fit the intense and untidy profile he expected, but Nevada Smith would have settled more naturally into a Ralph Lauren advert.

Observing Oliver's surprise, Bingo said, "Nevada's our outlier. He's a descendant of Isaac Newton, or that's his story anyway, and he's sticking to it. No question he has the best abs, the best style on a surfboard and by far the prettiest face in geekdom."

"Can you tell us what you're looking for, Commander?" Delilah Mirador asked. "It would save us time if you could."

"I wish I knew," Oliver said. "Our man is way too neat to leave traces of much on his iPhone. My guess is we're looking at tangents, where one thing touches another, maybe all very innocently, and that thing touches something else, and so on and so on until the contact becomes less innocent and more interesting. But it's only a guess."

"You used the word 'neat,'" Bingo said. "Are you aware what that means in our world?"

"I'm not," Oliver said.

"'Neats' design programs to resemble human reasoning and logic. 'Scruffies' take a less theoretical, more empirical approach. In this case, guys, I think we go at it both ways at once."

"Sounds right to me," said Jonty Patel.

"I can't help but wish we had the phone itself," Delilah said.

"Too risky," Oliver said.

"I don't know why," she said. "We might have found something under electron microscopy."

"The odds are slim," Bingo said. "I *might* win the lottery next Friday. The beautiful creature behind the counter in the café down the road *might* slip into my bed at three o'clock in the morning. It's nice to dream, but we go with what we have."

"Fair enough," said Nevada. "If for some reason you ever want him to think he's got his phone back, there's no way you'd fool him with a substitute. It could be the same model, but the scratch marks would be different. It wouldn't feel the same, like a dog of the same breed that wasn't your pet. I'd know in a second and be on my guard from then on. Also, you'd have to jigger the SIM card and the whole e-mail setup. The very idea is pathological."

Oliver listened with amusement. "How much time do you think we're talking about?"

"Impossible to say," replied Bingo. "We don't know our destination. How can we give you an estimated time of arrival?"

"Commander," implored Delilah, "you're telling us we don't have much time, aren't you?"

"We're in a race against the clock."

"And if the clock wins?"

"It won't be pretty."

"But *we'll* still be alive?" Jonty inquired, cued by Oliver's somberness into a newly solemn tone of his own.

Oliver shook his head. "What makes you so sure?"

Chapter Thirty-nine

Shortly before four, by the pool on bridge deck, with the midsummer sun angled in the western sky, Isabella looked at Ty and asked, "Oliver isn't married, is he?"

"Why do you ask? Are you interested?"

"I just wondered."

"He wouldn't be easy to be married to," Ty reflected.

"What man would be?"

"On the other hand, he'd be away a lot of the time. And for a girl seeking thrills . . ."

"Sorry I asked," Isabella said.

"He's not dead yet," Ty said. "He still has lots of time."

"Because you two are about the same age?"

"Sounds like a good enough reason to me."

"My parents got married when my father was twenty-one and my mother twenty."

"Mine were both twenty-two, I think."

"What happened to us, our generation? Spoilt for choice?"

"Speak for yourself," Ty said.

"Now you *are* being disingenuous."

"Ah, but you flatter me," Ty said as Jean-François appeared from the dining room.

"Excuse me, Miss Cavill," Jean-François said, "but the Tangier police have been in touch with the captain. And he wanted you to know that the *commissaire divisionnaire de police* is on his way here."

Isabella kept a blank face. "I wonder what he expects to learn."

"Nothing," Ty said. "I'm sure it's routine."

"They could have questioned us at dockside."

"True, but it's his big chance to come aboard."

Jean-François could not conceal his smile.

"Even more likely, it's you he wants to see," Isabella suggested.

"I hope not," Ty said. "I'm not inclined in that direction."

"Do you always think the worst of people?"

"I never did, but lately it's seemed like the way to bet."

By the time the *commissaire* arrived, they had accidentally changed into almost-matching casual clothes: tan linen slacks and pale blue polo shirts, Ty's knit, Isabella's piqué. The *commissaire,* a lean and elegant Moroccan man of extraordinary height, was accompanied by his adjutant, a more solidly built, much shorter and younger man with pudgy features and a one-step-behind deferential bearing that Isabella thought made him appear almost as though he were his superior's pet.

"It's very kind of you to see me on such short notice," the *commissaire* told them.

"Of course, we're happy to see you. As you might well imagine, we're eager to do anything we can. . . ."

"Mostly it's a matter of tying up loose ends. We wanted to see for ourselves where Mr. Santal began his day and where he was bound at the time of his tragic accident."

Isabella nodded. "You use the word 'accident.' Do you believe that's what it was?"

The *commissaire* hesitated. "At this point it is difficult to say."

"I suppose what I'm really asking is, will we ever have an answer to that question?"

"May I?" asked the *commissaire*, gesturing to a chair.

"Please, do sit down," Isabella said. "I'm sorry. Forgive my manners. I've been rather overwhelmed by all that's happened."

"Thank you. My long legs tire more and more easily these days," the *commissaire* mused, lowering his frame into a leather chair. "Can you think of anyone who might have wished to harm your uncle?"

"No, and I've tried. Ian, by the way, wasn't my uncle. He was my godfather."

"Sorry," the *commissaire* told her. "Correct that, will you?" he instructed his adjutant, who had assumed a similar chair and was taking notes.

"Ian Santal, as I am sure you know, was a very successful and, in certain circles, even famous man."

"'Legendary' would not be too strong a word," the police chief added.

Isabella thanked him with a gracious smile. "There are always people who begrudge others those particular qualities, but in his case I honestly have no idea who they could be. He knew an enormous number of people, from every walk of life, high and low and in between. Not all his friends were rich or celebrated, although many of course were. All through his life, he thrived on people. That's one reason he became a writer—"

"Ah, yes, I read *Train Travel*," the *commissaire* interrupted. "Did he write other things as well?"

"Mostly science fiction," Isabella explained. "Writing was his first ambition, but it didn't take him long to find that the work was too solitary. Ironically, it was science fiction that led him into science. The academy, finance in the City, his fantastic career as an entrepreneur—all that came later, as he found his medium, which wasn't words on a page or numbers, but people. Ian put them together, endlessly recombining them and their interests until out of nothing something great and usually unexpected had been created."

"This is very interesting to me," said the *commissaire.*

"Who would have wished to harm him, I cannot imagine. Perhaps it was someone he won out over. He was a competitor at heart and not above winning." Isabella laughed.

"He would seem to have done it very well."

"Yes, that's true," she said, then, noticing Crispin's quiet approach, added, "Would you like something to drink?"

"Would an iced coffee be possible?" the *commissaire* inquired.

"Very possible, sir," Crispin replied.

"I'll have the same, please," said the adjutant.

"I had the pleasure of greeting your godfather upon his arrival in Tangier yesterday. A Mr. Frost was with him."

"Yes, I know."

"And Mr. Frost is . . . ?"

"A very close friend of mine," Isabella replied.

"Then you may know that he came to see me earlier today."

"I knew he was going to meet with the authorities."

"He was very helpful."

"I'm sure he was."

"If I may ask, what was the relationship between Philip Frost and Ian Santal?"

"I'm not sure I understand your question."

"Forgive me. What I meant was, was it a business relationship or a social one? Was it that of a mentor and his protégé, for example, or more similar to that of a father and son?"

"Somewhere between the two," Isabella conjectured after a few seconds' thought.

"When they disembarked at the yacht club, I happened to notice that neither was carrying anything. They both had jackets on, but neither had anything in his hands. For instance, neither was carrying a briefcase."

"Why should that have surprised you?"

"They are businessmen." The *commissaire* chuckled at the simplicity of his own analysis.

"Yes, but what business they were involved in yesterday is beyond me. You'll have to ask Philip about that. They left in a hurry, I remember, and you're right: They didn't take anything with them."

"The tender was watched by the dock agent, by the mate running it, presumably, and by the yacht-club staff. Anyone coming aboard or going ashore from it would surely have been spotted by one or more of them. The police and officials of both Moroccan immigration and customs were also nearby the whole time the tender was berthed. Is it too much to assume they would have witnessed if not actually deterred anything untoward? I think not."

"Then you believe that it was an accident," Ty said.

"I have reached no conclusion. The boat could well have had a fault in one of its systems. Cigarette boats of that type carry massive stores of fuel, which, if sparked . . . Alas, the point is, we may never know with certainty whether there was indeed such a fault. There is no black box, so to speak. If we're to do our jobs properly, therefore, we must eliminate, as best we can, every other possibility, including, regretfully, that of sabotage."

"In the tried-and-true manner of Sherlock Holmes," Ty interjected lightly.

The *commissaire* smiled. "Are you a fan, Mr. Hunter? Or perhaps you've played Holmes. If so, it must have been onstage, or else in a film I don't know. I thought I'd seen all of yours."

Isabella glanced at Ty and smiled.

"You're safe. I've never played him," Ty told the police chief, "but my dad was a great fan, and that was contagious. I read all the stories growing up."

"Naturally, I'd like to talk to the crew, have a look at the tender's berth, where it would have been *before* Messrs. Santal and Frost took it in to Tangier. Also, it would be useful, I think, to see Mr. Santal's quarters as well as Mr. Frost's."

"We'll give you the grand tour," Isabella told him.

"Thank you. By the way, did Mr. Frost mention anything about a box to you?"

"No," she answered, and in a flicker caught Ty's eye.

"What sort of box?" Ty asked.

"How to describe it?" the *commissaire* said. "A jewelry box or a box for odds and ends, lightweight and made of wood. Mr. Frost said he had bought it in the souk for Miss Cavill and then, when Mr. Santal suddenly asked him to stay behind in Tangier through lunch, that he had asked Mr. Santal in turn to take it with him back to this yacht. That would account for the carrier bag."

"What carrier bag would that be?" Ty inquired.

"A bright green plastic one, I believe, with yellow, or maybe it was gold, printing. Several witnesses noticed it swinging from Mr. Santal's right wrist as he departed."

"Surely," Ty said, "if it were some sort of improvised explosive device, he wouldn't have been able to swing it."

"That is my assumption, too," said the police chief, "although I don't know."

"Did Philip say anything about the business they were conducting?" Isabella asked.

"Only that it had to do with a fund. Doesn't everything these days? Businesses, it seems, no longer make products, only money."

"Even so, that would appear to me the logical place to start. Whoever he was dealing with would have known both when and exactly where he would be in Tangier. Find out who was there, then find a motive amongst them and you'll be well on your way to an answer, if there is one."

"Would you like a job with the Tangier police, Miss Cavill?"

"Thank you very much, but I am already employed. Anyway, you have to admit that my theory is rather less far-fetched than yours."

"You misunderstood me. I have no theory. The notion of a bomb in a carrier bag is not a theory, merely a possibility, albeit a remote one. One is forced to deal with facts, and the bag is a fact of this case, but apparently it bore a gift for you, and as far as we can tell Mr. Frost bore no malice toward Mr. Santal. Why should he have, when it was Mr. Santal who had enabled his rapid rise? No, he had everything to lose and nothing to gain by Mr. Santal's death. In fact, the only person who stood to gain was you, but one does not have to look for very long into your eyes to see that as profound a gain as that may be, your loss is incalculably greater."

After a comprehensive tour of the yacht, including a prolonged and fruitless search of the large tender's bay, the *commissaire* and his aide departed. Isabella and Ty were still waving good-bye as the police skiff veered toward shore. Then Isabella turned to Ty. "Why did you look at me the way you did when he asked about the box?"

"I could ask you the same question," Ty said.

"I wasn't sure what you wanted me to do."

"You handled it perfectly."

"Well, I didn't lie. He asked if Philip had mentioned the box, and he hadn't. I kept waiting for him to tell us not to leave Tangier without permission. I've seen too many television programs, I suppose."

"You were right not to say any more. For the time being, the police don't need to know what we know."

"You think Ian's death is connected to those warheads, don't you?"

Ty nodded. "I do. They rearrange the incentives."

"Then maybe we should set sail. I'd hate to find myself holed up in some Moroccan prison."

"There's nowhere to go. We have to see this through. Watch Philip! Let him play his cards until we can get a glimpse of his hand!"

"I'm not sure," Isabella said. "The *commissaire* practically told me I was a suspect, though he was as cryptic as he was solicitous."

"He was probing," Ty said. "That's his job. If we suddenly pull up anchor and move on, he'll see it as reason to probe harder. Then, even if you aren't charged, you may never be able to clear yourself of suspicion in the public mind. You know how people are. The conclusion would be too delicious to abandon. And who knows how leaving would affect what happens with the warheads?"

"It's like driving a golf ball down a fairway in the fog," Isabella reflected, leaning gently into Ty's side. "A few days ago, for the first time in I don't know how long, I had begun to have a very clear idea of my future. It was rather pretty. Then you turned up, and now I have no idea what's out there."

Ty knew she was ready to be kissed but dared not chance it in view of the crew. He took a single step away.

"What's the matter?" Isabella whispered. "And don't say I'm too much to hope for. I'm sure you're an expert at letting a girl down easily."

He smiled. "Never confuse luck with aptitude," he said. "I have no desire to let you down, but to break cover now would be to put all that in jeopardy."

"I'm not as strong as you are," she said. "I need to hold on to something, someone, Ty—to *you* right now. . . ."

Ty paused reflectively. "Where?" he asked.

Isabella led him along the corridor through which he had first entered *Surpass*. "It's your move."

"I'm still absorbing the fact."

"Quickly, I hope. Don't worry. You're not taking advantage of the moment, Ty. If anything, the moment's taking advantage of you."

"I can't tell you how much better that makes me feel."

"Let me make it easier still. This isn't just in reaction to all that's happened. It isn't even quite as sudden as it seems, at least for me. It's something that's been in the back of my mind, then the front of my mind, then all over my mind ever since I collected you that evening in Cap d'Antibes."

"Since you're telling me all this, I'll return the favor. That Ty Hunter, the one you sped in all by yourself to pick up on that quay, had gone up on a screen twenty feet tall and forty feet wide a long time ago. This one's real."

"I wouldn't have him any other way."

"That's good, because he wouldn't want you to be disappointed."

"Somehow that hadn't crossed my mind."

Ty studied her. "A moment ago you said it was my move. Now it's yours. Where do we go?"

"The screening room," Isabella said. "No one will look for us there, and if they do, so what? We can screen a film and the door can be locked from the inside. What can I say? Ian was a rake. It was part of his charm."

"It sounds very daring," Ty said. "You're a naughty girl."

"You haven't seen anything yet," she told him. In the screening room's library, Isabella found a digital copy of *The Boy Who Understood Women* and, relishing the irony, brought it up on the enormous LED screen that filled the far wall. "You look so young there," she told him, "almost callow."

Ty slid his arm around her and drew her to him on the plush double-depth sofa that occupied the center of the luxurious theater's first row. "You're great at it," he said, "but no more chat, okay?"

"Okay."

After they had made love twice and fallen into and awoken from a nap, Ty looked at Isabella. His palm cupped her shoulder, then slowly descended, his fingertips tracing the smooth swell of her breast. He knew his own hands well. There were times when it had seemed to him that only his hands and his mind, the long memory that had made and kept him who he was, had survived his accident intact. Feeling Isabella's touch at his shoulder, then gently over the blades of his back, urging him toward her, he told himself it was possible she had seen past his mask and image to the simple Virginia boy he'd once been.

"You look worried," she said.

"I am," he told her.

"Are you worried about how this changes things?"

His senses continued to drink in her presence. "What worries me," he said, "is that it doesn't change what we're up against."

An hour before sunset, from bridge deck, Ty spotted *Surpass*'s EC130 approaching in the northern sky.

"I was sure he would call first," Isabella said.

"Never mind," Ty told her.

"I can't do this," she said.

"Yes you can."

"'Close your eyes and think of England'? Is what you're telling me?"

"No woman needs advice from any man on how to fool another."

"Is that supposed to be funny?"

"Yes," Ty said. "Just relax."

"Now you *are* asking too much," Isabella said, almost breaking into a laugh. The chopper put down on the bow helipad, but it was several minutes before its door opened and Philip emerged. By that time Isabella, alone, was descending the steps that led from bridge deck to *Surpass*'s bow. At the sight of Philip, she raced toward him—altogether a natural actress, thought Ty, who watched from the wheelhouse.

"Sorry," Philip said, taking her into his arms almost perfunctorily, as if his mind were occupied elsewhere, "last-minute phone call, and I had to wait for the blades to stop in order to hear what the damned idiot was saying."

"Not to worry," Isabella said. "I'm so glad you're back." She could feel the agitation within him.

"As am I," he said, while other men, one by one, emerged from the helicopter.

Isabella, registering them, looked at Philip. "I thought you would be coming alone. You didn't say anything about bringing anyone else with you."

On first impression the men, who were uniformly fit and dressed in matching dark trousers, shirts and shoes, resembled a combat unit. Carrying themselves more in the manner of staff than guests, they made Isabella immediately uncomfortable.

"Calm down, Isabella," Philip said. "It's a long story. As you know, I met with the authorities this morning."

"Yes, I do know that. The *commissaire* was here afterwards," she said.

"I didn't know that," Philip said. "In that case you probably already know some of what I'm about to say."

"Which is?"

"That it is likely Ian was assassinated."

"The *commissaire* didn't seem convinced."

"He's a functionary. Such men do not commit themselves until they have to. Nor is it they who must live with the consequences of their indecision."

"Get to the point. Who are these men?" Isabella demanded, raising her gaze to the silent posse behind Philip.

He placed his hand on her shoulder, stared into her eyes and, summoning his most empathetic smile, said. "They are here to see that no harm comes to you."

"I should have thought we have enough crew for that."

"Humor me," Philip said.

Isabella drew a deep breath. "I appreciate your concern, Philip. I really do, but I feel quite safe here with Jean-François and Crispin and everyone else. And with you, of course. Even if it wasn't an accident, why would the people responsible want to harm me? I have nothing to do with his business."

"You're asking me to read the minds of madmen," Philip said.

"Or are you worried about yourself?"

"That's entirely unfair. I can take care of myself. You know that."

"You're right. I'm sorry," Isabella retreated.

"It's just a precaution and just for a few days. They won't be in your way. You won't even know they're here."

"Where did they come from?"

"They're from one of the security services associated with my former job. This is a bit of spare change for them."

"Do they speak English?"

"They do, all of them."

"And do they understand that I'm their boss, that they're at all times to do as I say and not the reverse?"

"The reverse wouldn't occur to them. Believe me."

"You must be even more confident than I'd thought," Isabella said as notes of laughter rose into her voice, "to be willing to leave your girlfriend alone with six gorgeous Slavic men."

Philip regarded her with an intensity that was unfamiliar to her, determination and hurt balanced in his eyes. "I trust you, darling," he reminded her. "I left you with the number-one box-office star in the world, didn't I?"

"Who's turned out to be a milquetoast," Isabella bluffed.

Philip's countenance came alight. "Has he? I'm surprised. But that's not important. What's important is that you please, right now, trust me."

Chapter Forty

Bingo Chen said, "Ask me a question." It was almost midnight, and the young man had just roller-skated into Oliver Molyneux's makeshift office and seated himself, with his legs crossed, in order to tighten the loose striped lace of his right red-and-yellow plastic skate.

"I'll bite," Oliver said. "Do you have a particular question you'd like me to ask you?"

Bingo nodded. "'When was the last time you earned your name?'" he suggested.

"Consider it asked. We're short on time."

"Not more than ninety seconds ago," Bingo answered.

"What did you find, exactly?"

"An open back door in the source code."

"The source code of what? Frost's iPhone?"

"The iPhone?" Bingo asked with manifest incredulity. "We're in deep hack mode. That phone was just the starting gate."

"That much I get," Oliver said, "but not having been born digital, I'd appreciate a clear and concise explanation in English."

"What can't happen can," Bingo said.

"Nor am I in any mood for the I Ching," Oliver objected.

"Delilah ran all the computers with which the iPhone had been in contact. Of course, there was nothing. Your man's a prick. At the same time, Jonty ran the phone numbers. Nothing obvious there either—well, except that one was to a bank. Big deal, right? Right! You know Finagle's law?"

"I must have missed it," Oliver said.

"'Never attribute to malice what can be adequately explained by stupidity,'"

Bingo said. "The asshole calls a bank. Don't know who he talked to, don't know what he said. But it's a bank in Vienna, and he doesn't live in Vienna, and Jonty, who loves films, is immediately thinking *The Third Man,* Orson Welles, and all kinds of intrigue and shit—that nothing's quite what it seems. So he zooms in to take a closer look, a much, much closer look indeed."

"Are you telling me he went in through a back door in the source code of the bank's computer?"

"Faster than John Dillinger or Bonnie and Clyde could have robbed it," Bingo said, "and a lot more quietly, of course. It's an old trick. Someone inserts a back door—"

"Who would do that?" Oliver interrupted.

"*We* might," Bingo said stoically. "Or it could have been some black hat. Anyhow, as I said, it's an old trick. Whoever's computer it is hires some IT security boys to take it out, which they do, but when they recompile the compiler, they have to use the computer, so there it is back in again, but this time not apparently so. I tell you, Jonty Patel is, no effing question about it, a Knight of the Lambda Calculus."

"What in hell is a Knight of the Lambda Calculus?"

"Your numero uno hacker fraternity. Some say it's imaginary, others that it's real, but it's always the same, isn't it? 'Those who talk don't know and those who know don't talk.' What the Knights Templar were to the old church, the Knights of the Lambda Calculus are, pretty much, to the new. But that's beside the point. It turns out that there are no accounts in this particular bank under Frost's name or any conceivable variation of it, but—and it's a whopping-big 'but'—the bank's computer has been in touch with computers using the very same encryption key that Frost used in his previous line of business, as well as with computers that employ the very same key he does now."

"And that surprised you?"

"It surprised me, but Nevada even more so, probably because the first of those keys is fairly esoteric, which, considering they were dealing with nuclear arms and all, it effing well should have been, and the second . . . damned, I shouldn't say this, but I will: Nevada, on behalf of our employer, is one of the guys who designed and inserted that back door precisely so that fellows like you, with your insatiable curiosity and incomparable knowledge of and instinct for what's in the best interest of our country and its allies, could, when circum-stances necessitated, drop in and . . . how should one put it, snoop."

"Can you give me an executive summary?" Oliver asked. "My head's spin-ning."

"But of course," Bingo replied. "Come over to my workstation."

Bingo, on skates, was already before the semicircular panel of terminals when Oliver arrived in the room next door. On the central screen were the split images of Delilah, Jonty, and Nevada. "Delilah first," Bingo said.

"Good evening, Commander," she said.

"Good evening," Oliver replied.

"From my perspective it's important to remember that we're talking about many degrees of separation, which makes some things more probable and oth-ers less. You're familiar with disambiguation?"

"The butterfly effect," Oliver asked, "the idea that just a slight change in the initial condition of a dynamic system can effect a very large change in that sys-tem's behavior over the long term? Yes, I'm familiar with it."

"In a very real sense," Delilah said, "that is what we're dealing with here. But we have to be careful when retracing the steps back from the ultimate variations to the initial variation. It's an epistemic question, isn't it?"

"Are you trying to tell me that you can make a good guess but not be certain of it?"

"More or less," Delilah replied. "The Viennese bank's computers talk to thousands of other computers all over the world all the time. It's a constant conversation, almost no element of which is of concern to us. But this much may be: Sometime yesterday funds began to flow into and out of a few of that bank's newer accounts at a vastly accelerated velocity."

"Were these large transactions?"

"No, and that's the point. Individually they were small, always under ten thousand U.S. dollars, even when denominated in euros. But they were rapid—seconds apart, in some instances even less—and there were a great many of them. In aggregate we're talking about plus or minus, probably plus, one hun-dred million euros."

"Where is that money now?"

"Alchemized," Delilah Mirador said. "Most of it was wired to gold brokers.

Where that gold has gone could be anybody's guess, gold bars being much harder to trace than currency."

Oliver shot a pensive look into the webcam. "Something's missing, isn't it?" he said.

"How did you know?"

"It's a matter of scale."

"You're correct," Delilah said. "Almost all the moneys that were moved into those Viennese accounts had recently passed through, although not come directly from, a larger list of accounts, based in Geneva, Zurich, Liechtenstein, Singapore and elsewhere, which have also experienced a spectacular rise in both inflow and immediate outflow since yesterday."

"Can you estimate how spectacular a rise?" Oliver inquired.

"It would be a rough estimate: in the tens of billions of U.S. dollars."

"Now we're cooking with gas," Bingo said. "Over to you, Jonty."

Jonty Patel nodded, wiped his brow with a bandanna, then said, "It's late for you guys, isn't it? I'll come straight to the point. From the phone's logs, we took away nada."

"That's too bad, although not unexpected. Frost's cautious to a fault."

"But from the provider's logs," Jonty resumed, "we picked up a number for one Andrej Melinkov in Moscow. Apparently Melinkov was Frost's Russian number two during his last days in the disarmament game, so no surprise there. What is surprising is that on further investigation this Melinkov, a former soldier and still nominally a civil servant, has apparently been looking at properties, mostly in the South of France, he ought not to be able to afford. And one of those Viennese accounts Delilah mentioned spit money into an account whose number, at least, was on his laptop."

"How the hell did you get into that already?" Oliver asked.

"I would like to be able to say that I'd planted a little daemon, but the damned laptop wasn't switched on. I took a chance that a man with so much at stake would back up his files in the clouds somewhere. The fortunate thing is, I found him in the second service I tried. I almost had a geekgasm!"

"Those things are meant to be encrypted, aren't they?" Oliver said. "That was fast work."

"Thank you. The best ones use the same encryption standards banks do."

Oliver smiled. "While you're at it," he said, "you couldn't just add some zeroes to the left of the decimal point in my bank account, could you? And maybe some offsetting entries, **the way the** Bank of England does, so that there won't ever be anything there to cry foul?"

"Don't kid yourself. That sort of thing's been done," said Jonty Patel matter-of-factly.

"More than once," Bingo embellished.

"And more often than anyone would like you to know, but that's a conversation for another day," Jonty said. "Right now Nevada's got one more juicy little tidbit for you."

The hyperphotogenic Nevada Smith smiled. "Just this," he said. "In that cloud of storage, we found a photograph album, snaps of family, I'm supposing, and/or friends, harmless stuff, but lots of it. Also some photographs of the properties in Saint-Tropez that Jonty just mentioned. I have no idea why, but for some reason it all just seemed too pat, too neat. So I drifted back a little and then, for the sheer hell of it, took the scruffy approach and subjected it to steganalysis."

"No need to pause," Oliver said. "I'm familiar with steganalysis."

"Then you know that it's nothing more than a format for hiding data within images or within other files that don't appear to be encrypted, often files of enormous size."

"Which is how it differs from cryptanalysis?"

"Yes, essentially, for the purpose at hand," Nevada continued. "I applied various steganography algorithms to the various photos and, to my astonishment and annoyance, came up blank. That's when it struck me. All of a sudden, I had this crazy thought: What if I'm right? What if Melinkov had more information to store than he could trust to his memory? Where would he hide it? If he's in league with Frost, who as far as I can tell is a fastidious son of a bitch and never colors outside the lines, he would be used to taking the cautious approach. Nor would he slip up by disguising a document as a photograph. He would know that either he would escape scrutiny entirely or that, if he were scrutinized, it would be by people like us, on whichever side, people who would run the same algorithms I did until one or another cracked the code or they all came up empty. So I asked myself that question and immediately answered it with another question of my own: What if steganographically encoded data were buried not in a picture or even text but within variations of white background or black keystrokes that would be imperceptible to the eye?"

"And what did you come up with?"

"On Melinkov's computer, zilch," Nevada said in a voice absent of regret, "nothing but the idea itself. It was when I applied that same idea to some mundane-appearing documents in one of Frost's computers that my cock stood straight up."

"I'm sure that must have been a reassuring sight," Bingo told him.

"There've been women who've thought so," Nevada parried. "You'll be a better judge of what they mean than I, Commander, but what I found appear to be tracking numbers."

"Let me guess," Oliver said. "Those numbers are for parcels on a Claussen ship."

"That's right, the Claussen *Wayfarer.*"

"That ship's route began at the top of the Black Sea, did it not?"

"Correct, in the Strait of Kerch, to be exact."

"And the parcels would have remained on board through a stopover in Istanbul, during which other parcels were unloaded and still others taken on."

Nevada said, "I can't speak definitively about other parcels. If you want me to go in that direction . . ."

"Hold your horses," Oliver said. "Just tell me that those parcels remained on board at Istanbul."

"That's what the record shows."

"The next port of call was Naples, wasn't it?"

"The parcels remained on the ship there, too."

"That's where you're wrong," Oliver said. "The labels and crates remained there, but the merchandise they contained came ashore, disguised as something else entirely. That's where it vanished and the trail went cold."

"With all due apologies," Nevada said, "I think you may be only half right."

"What makes you think that?"

"Let me put it somewhat differently," Nevada continued. "If whatever it was he was shipping *was* permanently offloaded in Naples, why would he have been following or have kept, at any rate, the tracking numbers of three new parcels that came aboard there?"

Stunned, Oliver stared into the webcam as he considered the implications of Nevada Smith's revelation. From a recess of his memory, a line from his school days' reading surfaced: *"Absence of evidence is not evidence of absence."* The astronomer Carl Sagan had penned it in regard to the possibility that there might be life in outer space—but oh my, how perfectly it described Philip Frost's deception. "What were those parcels?" Oliver asked after a moment.

"All I know is that they went by the same basic code: 'engines and turbines,'" Nevada said.

"Do you know where they are now?"

"Not precisely, but they can't be very far. The ship arrived in Gibraltar early this morning. It's only just been offloaded."

"Did it put in to any ports between Naples and here?"

Nevada's smile filled the screen. "Apparently not," he told Oliver.

"Do we know who if anyone has taken delivery of these 'engines and turbines' here?"

Nevada nodded. "It would seem that the freight service to which their bill of lading was addressed did so several hours ago, but the fixed address we have for that—Cardigan & Sons Transport—appears to be an office suite rather than an actual depot of any sort. I can try to drill deeper."

"As quickly as you can," Oliver told him. "In the meantime I'll get our people over there."

"Won't they be closed at this hour?" Bingo asked.

"They can open."

Chapter Forty-one

Entering Admiral Cotton's office a minute later, Oliver said, "Frost's even cleverer than I gave him credit for. I mean, a man has to be very clever indeed to be this unpredictable." After explaining Frost's ruse to the senior officer, he added, "I'm sure he chose Naples not in spite of but because of its well-polished rep for corruption. He could accomplish what he had to there. Anyone watching him, meanwhile, would be left to draw the inevitable conclusion we did."

Cotton shook his head in disbelief. "It's a lot to reckon with. And, of course, it remains a surmise, doesn't it?"

"Technically I suppose it does, but the geeks have gathered an awful lot of facts to support it."

"Those kids!" Cotton exclaimed. "They never cease to amaze. When I was a boy, there was a run of films about aliens arriving on earth from outer space and taking control of all the levers of power. Some of them were so realistic they gave you nightmares for weeks. Who could have imagined that those aliens would turn out to be our own children?"

"You don't hack, yourself?" Oliver inquired with a smile.

"I'm afraid not."

"I'm surprised."

The admiral laughed. "I've fat fingers, as the young would say. I did try following the keystrokes of one of them once as he worked his magic at War College, but when it came my turn to input the data, the program simply 'jumped off into never-never land'—at least that's how he put it."

Oliver's phone rang as the admiral finished. The fleeting blue light showed that it was in secure mode, with a randomly generated encryption key. "Yes," he answered.

"Commander Molyneux, this is George Kenneth," said the cordial if businesslike voice on the other end of the connection.

"Dr. Kenneth," Oliver replied, laughing suddenly to himself when he recalled that that had also been the name of his mother's gynecologist.

"Where are we?" Kenneth inquired.

When Oliver had brought him up to speed, he added, "I don't know where we'd be without Ty or the computer jocks. It's been a good team."

"That was the intention," George Kenneth said. "Look, Oliver, I appreciate how far you guys have come."

"But we're coming down to the wire—"

"Very rapidly," interrupted the President's National Security Advisor, "and we're placing all our bets on one possibility. What if we've guessed wrong?"

"You don't doubt that Frost's our man?" Oliver asked edgily.

Kenneth hesitated. "No, not really, but I wouldn't rule out the possibility that he isn't."

"You wouldn't? Come on, if there really are loose warheads—which, granted, no one's seen—and if Santal was involved in capturing and brokering them, Frost has to be involved, too. Otherwise what in hell is he doing on both sides of the equation? Facilitating Santal's plan, whatever it was, whatever it *is*. That's what! Any other premise flies in the face of reason."

"Are you that sure you've considered them all?"

"Don't be gormless," Oliver said.

"Watch it, Commander," Kenneth snapped.

"Sorry," Oliver replied, "but there's absolutely no evidence that points elsewhere and lots that points to Frost."

"No one suggested abandoning surveillance of him, but we have only so many eyes and ears, human or electronic, and we have to keep a certain number of them free for and alert to other scenarios. We can't be caught flat-footed."

"By what? Phantoms? If we were bound for a court of law, I might be inclined to agree with you. Right now, though, it isn't proof we need, but information. Our goal is to prevent a transaction, not convict anyone for it later on."

"Frost called me," Kenneth said.

"Is he in the habit of doing that?"

"No, but it's not without precedent. We *have* known each other for a long time. I recollect telling you that."

"I'm all ears."

"The CEO of Claussen Inc. had written to Ian Santal, worried that his company's whiter-than-white reputation was being tarred by its involvement in a deal Santal had put them into."

"That deal wouldn't happen to be the redevelopment of a missile installation into a resort near the Strait of Kerch?"

"Of course it would. Against that incriminating fact, one must question why Frost would contact me. He said it was because Claussen's CEO had copied the Secretary of State on his letter to Ian Santal, no doubt to register his purity and protect the company's many international licenses. But I think Frost called me because he was trying to protect Ian Santal. He as much as admitted that Santal had cut it close on occasion. Afterward I began to wonder if we might not have been a bit cynical about Philip. He *is* planning to marry Santal's goddaughter, after all."

"I didn't know that," Oliver said.

"Why would you? Mind you, I am only suggesting, not positing, that what appear to be the actions of a very guilty man might be explained as no more than those of a young man in love."

"There's another possibility," Oliver said.

"That Frost is playing me?" George Kenneth replied.

"Spot on."

"I would have heard it in his voice."

"Have you spoken to the President about this?"

"Of course, and he's put the ball in my court."

"The flow of funds would seem pretty conclusive," Oliver suggested.

"It's a complicated world of complicated people doing complicated things. More than one interpretation could be valid."

Oliver drew a deep breath. "Cards on the table?" he said. "I believe that from very early on in their deal Philip Frost intended to skim, using an account in Vienna to do so. I further believe that the de Novo Fund, suddenly flush with other money, was actually purpose-built as a conduit for the sale of the missing warheads. Santal must have become suspicious of Frost and made that obvious, catalyzing Frost's own suspicion of Santal, an apprehension that grew into a fear that led to murder. If that's what happened, he will wind up his business as quickly as he can. So we have no time to lose painting in pictures of the conspiracy, or trying to plumb or game it further. We have to act else, before we know it, the warheads will have vanished from our grasp once and for all."

"Slower, please," George Kenneth insisted. "Supposing he did manage to wind up his business, what would he do then?"

"I don't know. My guess is that he would tie up any loose ends, perhaps first by marrying Isabella Cavill, as apparently he told you he planned on doing. Then, for the time being, he would probably go dark."

"Finished?"

"Not quite, but it's your turn."

"These warheads have been around a long time," George Kenneth said, his tone of voice suddenly remote and professorial. "In fact, the International Atomic Energy Authority recorded 1,562 incidents where nuclear material was lost or stolen between 1993 and 2008, mostly in the former Soviet Union, and sixty-five percent of those losses were never recovered. What haven't been around until recently are people who would use them. Which raises the question: How do sane men deter madness?"

"You're only proving my point."

"What I'm proving is that we have to be like a Cyclops, with an eye in all directions."

"This is not the time to dilute the strength of our effort," Oliver said.

"Is that your decision or mine?"

"I can tell you what you ought to do," Oliver said. "You ought to hoover those funds right out from under them as quickly as you can. Don't tell me that that's impossible! I've been with a few of your players lately, as you well know. I have a pretty damned good idea what's possible."

George Kenneth snickered. "There is a larger view to be taken," he said, with a calm Oliver found distressing.

"Not in this instance."

"Again, who is to decide that?"

"The man you work for, I would have thought," replied Oliver. "How could the stakes be greater? If you were to seize their funds, they would be bound to panic and almost certainly make mistakes. Their plan would grind to at least a temporary halt. What else could it do? So we'd buy time as well as very likely gain the opening we need."

"Take a deep breath and think about it, Commander. Even if we do have genies on a leash, we can't just let them slip. To do so would be to confirm that we possess capabilities best left unconfirmed, but that's the least of it. Stealing that money could well destroy the fragile faith that underlies the whole modern economy. No transfer would ever again be deemed secure, no bank anywhere sound, no deal final. That strikes some people as far too high a price to pay, most especially in today's delicate financial climate."

Oliver shook his head. "Does it really?" he asked.

"You mentioned Secretary Burr a moment ago. He is of that view, as are the Secretary of the Treasury, the Chairman of the Federal Reserve, your Chancellor of the Exchequer and the Governor of the Bank of England."

"Where, if I may ask, do the Joint Chiefs and the Secretary of Defense stand?"

"Conflicted, I think that's the apposite term. The point is that the President has already come down against having the geeks fiddle the world's financial system."

"Which means you've thought this through?"

"Eight ways from Sunday," George Kenneth insisted. "It isn't just yours truly flying by the seat of his pants."

"I wish I could say I am relieved to hear that."

"Don't lose your focus, Oliver. You're too valuable. Keep Philip Frost in your sights, but not so tightly that you miss whatever else might turn up."

"In other words, do what I can with what I've got?"

"If you *are* as close as you believe, you'll have more than enough. Adding to it now could be counterproductive—in fact, a distraction."

"That's an interesting way of looking at it," Oliver observed.

Kenneth left a thoughtful pause. "But you take my point?"

"Oh, yes, indeed, sir. I take it completely," Oliver said before switching off his phone.

Reading Oliver's face a few seconds later, Giles Cotton said, "When I put a man in the field, I don't second-guess him."

Oliver smiled. "The way the great Dr. Kenneth sees it, it is *I* who am second-guessing the President and most of his cabinet."

"In my experience it often comes down to a tribal thing with politicians and civil servants," Cotton reflected. "Sooner or later a line of demarcation develops between those who believe the world is abstract and those who know it's real."

"It's real, all right," Oliver said.

"What are you going to do?"

"My job," Oliver answered, "with one hand tied behind my back. What the hell, that's the way they play the game. Because that's what it is to men like Kenneth: a game. Life and death, sure, but by remote control."

"Don't be too harsh," Giles Cotton implored.

"Is that possible?" Oliver asked. "Considering that this is the same clique that sends kids to war without body armor?"

Chapter Forty-two

Across the carefully laid, candlelit dinner table, Ty regarded Philip with intensified wariness. Since Philip had returned later than expected from Gibraltar, the meal before them was actually more of a supper, scallops Mornay and a Caesar salad with a chilled bottle of Ian's favorite Corton-Charlemagne, Remoissenet. They had barely begun it when Philip, in a puzzled tone, asked, "What do people in the States make of your President?"

Ty shook his head. "That's difficult to say. I suppose it's pretty much the same as with most of his predecessors. Any president is lucky if his popularity ends up a bit over fifty percent. Why do you ask?"

"No reason in particular. I happened to catch a glimpse of him on television while I was waiting for the pilot to finish signing the necessary departure forms at Gibraltar Airport, and it struck me not for the first time that I couldn't make up my own mind."

"I wish I could help you," Ty said diffidently.

"Have you met him?"

"I have, but 'met' is the operative word. I would never claim to know him."

"Of course," Philip said, then added, "I gather he has an interesting background."

"He does. Not long after they got out of college, Garland White and a friend started a restaurant—the Skillful Skillet, if I remember correctly—that was on its way to becoming one of those very successful chains when, who knows why—probably too much optimism spiraling into too much debt—it suddenly went belly-up, which left him a rising star at twenty-seven and a burned-out one by thirty. Then a strange thing happened. In the early days of his restaurant, he had done a television promotion in which he'd been featured on-screen."

"Shades of you and the American army," Philip observed.

"I suppose," Ty said, deflecting the analogy. He assumed Philip had come by this information from Ian, though he might have read it elsewhere. "Anyway, I think his line was something like, 'There's no VIP room at the Skillful Skillet, because here everyone's a VIP.' At the time the publicity not only made him a local celebrity but aroused the interest of pooh-bahs in his state's politics. When the congressman from his district died jogging a few months before an election, they urged Garland White, who was then a buck short of bankrupt, to put his name on the ballot. He did. Those ads were replayed a million times during his campaign. He won, and the rest is history."

"More precisely, 'an accident of history,'" Philip corrected. "Do you think he's a ditherer?"

"How would I know?"

Philip laughed. "When it comes to politics, lots of people have firm opinions on subjects they know precious little about."

"I'm not one of them," Ty said.

"I wonder why."

Half an hour later, forgoing coffee, Philip wiped his brow with his handkerchief and said, "I'm afraid, for me, the time has come to turn in. It's been a busy day, and tomorrow promises to be another."

"Not tomorrow, too," Isabella reacted plaintively.

"I'm sorry, darling. There's no choice."

Isabella shot a friendly glance toward Ty, then a more amorous version to Philip. "How much longer must we stay here?" she asked.

Philip said, "God willing, I should be able to wrap things up tomorrow."

"Wouldn't that be wonderful?" she exclaimed. "Including with the Tangier authorities?"

"I don't see why not. Barring something unforeseen we ought to be able to lift anchor and be under way well before dark. That's not a promise, though."

"Just an educated prediction?" Isabella teased.

"Yes," Philip said. "That's exactly what it is."

"It's meant to be lovely tomorrow," Isabella told him.

"It was lovely today," Ty said.

"Yes, but tonight's gone filthy. I hate it when the levanter comes up and forces us inside. It's so muggy. Just listen to that drumroll of rain against the deck."

"It's only a storm," Philip told her as he stood. "It will pass. Coming, darling?"

"I'm right behind you," Isabella said. "'Night, Ty."

Back in Vanilla, Ty stretched himself across the comfortable bed. He had to contact Oliver. Deciding that a conversation would be more effective and easily camouflaged than an e-mail, yet afraid even of his end of it being overheard, he fumbled for his BlackBerry and, when he found it, pressed first the MENU key, then the appropriate encryption code followed by the speed-dial number for his friend's mobile.

"Hello," Oliver answered.

"Hi, Netty," Ty said, employing their familiar code. "How are things in California?"

"Heating up," Oliver said, "even more than usual for this time of year."

"I'm still on vacation," Ty said.

"Well and good," Oliver replied, "but I have to tell you, interesting things are happening on this end. I wouldn't stay away too long, or they'll go to others less deserving than you."

"You can't swing at every pitch."

"But when they come at you straight over the plate . . . well, never mind, we've had this conversation before. One thing I should tell you is that I've been meeting some resistance where your new rider is concerned."

Ty smiled at Oliver's ingenuity and the facility with which he had acquired and adapted the language of Hollywood. A "rider" was appended to a star's contract for a particular film. It spelled out, often in embarrassing detail, that star's requirements while on the set, the studio lot and location during a shoot. "What kind of resistance?" Ty asked. "And from whom?"

"To staff levels, mostly. No one gives a rat's ass about the color or thread count of your sheets, the brand of your water, or that you happen to prefer Lapsang souchong tea and cannot stand the smell of ammonia. They gave up long ago on the square footage of your trailers, but the boys in the front office—and I mean just about as high up the corporate ladder as you can climb—would prefer to pay for less in the way of backup."

"I'm sure they would, but will they?"

"Not today."

"That's too bad, but not all that important, really, until I choose my next script."

"Agreed, but I've always found it's handy to have certain things in boiler-plate. What if you wake up tomorrow and not that script itself but the idea for it smacks you in the face?"

"Can't we deal with that then?"

"Depends on who we're dealing with," replied Oliver, "and when. In this business the generosity of the fellow across the table depends on the moment. And moments pass."

"You're a pessimist, Netty."

"I've heard that before. Oh, I almost forgot. Your contractor called my number two. He's pretty sure he'll be getting things under way in your kitchen tomorrow."

"Does he have everything he needs?"

"He has the keys and he has your money. What else does he need?"

"The appliances he's going to install."

"I believe he expects them tomorrow as well," Oliver said. "I'll be in touch if it's otherwise,"

"Bye for now then," Ty told him.

Despite the humidity outside, the atmosphere in Vanilla was perfect, Ty thought, as he stripped and entered the shower. As the tension in his muscles eased, he felt first aroused, then a simmering rage that Isabella should have to be with Philip for another night or longer. As he rinsed off, he regarded his own physique, a scar unknown to his public on his right side, a second arthroscopic puncture wound hidden closer to his waist. He was still youthful, but only because of the discipline he brought to his diet and workouts. He had left behind that magical time of life that forgave recklessness. Without self-control he could all too easily begin to show signs of age. He had seen it happen to other film stars and had no intention of succumbing to such weakness himself. He had not exercised in several days, and his body craved what it was used to. He would do a hundred push-ups and a hundred crunches, a sequence of isometrics before he gave himself over to sleep. Dried off and with the plush towel around his neck, he entered his sitting room in search of a jockstrap and shorts.

Caught off guard by the unexpected presence of a small Slavic man dressed in black and carrying a miniature nylon duffel, Ty felt his temper flare. He was an instant away from raising his knee and twisting his body to deliver a side kick, a *yoko geri,* to the Slav's solar plexus when reason got the better of him. Obviously one of the crew Philip had brought on board, the man was, Ty recognized at once, a breacher, an op who specialized in silence; who came in like the wind, usually to lay an explosive charge on a high-value target, then retreated.

Quickly wrapping his bath towel around his waist, Ty stood the expressionless breacher down. "What the fuck do you think you're doing?" he demanded.

The intruder, who was at least eight inches shorter than Ty, replied in a calm but fearless voice. "Security check, that's all."

"I feel very secure," Ty told him. "So that won't be necessary."

"Yeah, but I must go by my orders," insisted the Slav.

"*I* must go to bed," Ty said, showing his uninvited guest the door. "Good night."

Without resistance, the intruder departed, then waited until Ty had slammed and double-locked the door to Vanilla before reaching into his duffel and switching off the electromagnet it contained.

Ten minutes later the telephone on Ty's night table rang.

"Mr. Hunter, this is Jean-François."

"Hello, Jean-François, what's up?"

"I must apologize for the intrusion," Jean-François began.

"Never mind, everything's all right now."

"Yes, I am happy about that. The man was merely following procedure, perhaps too eagerly."

Ty processed this information as well as the ambiguity in Jean-François's voice. "What procedure is that?"

"It has been decided to crash the ship."

"What the hell? Are you crazy?"

"Not a literal crash," Jean-François explained, nearly laughing, "merely a security one."

"I see," Ty said. "A strange choice of verb, but I take it that it refers to a kind of lockdown."

"Exactly so," replied Jean-François.

"On whose order is this being done?"

"It is the captain's order, of course."

"And it meets with the approval of Miss Cavill, does it?"

"Implicitly, the answer to your question has to be yes. Mr. Frost approved the order, and Mr. Frost and Miss Cavill are, as you are aware, together."

"So they are," Ty replied, "so they are."

Jean-François cleared his throat. "If you need anything, please ring the steward's office, but until first light please do not leave your suite. You will be safe there, I assure you."

"Now that you put it that way," Ty said, "I'm sure I will."

No sooner had Jean-François hung up than Ty returned to his sitting room and picked up his BlackBerry. Philip, he reasoned, would not be able to get away with crashing *Surpass* for very long. The authorities might return at any time. Isabella might ultimately object. And it would be difficult to explain the imprisonment of Ty Hunter indefinitely, especially once the excuse that it was merely as a safety precaution had worn thin. The fact that Philip had taken such a drastic step gave strong evidence that there were indeed warheads missing and that he was on the brink of transferring them. Oliver had been right. Now a way had to be devised for Ty to escape *Surpass* and get to shore, where Oliver would need his help.

He once more pressed the speed-dial number for Oliver, but although the screen lit up, no number appeared, nor could a ring be heard. He made a second attempt, with the same result. He tried another number and another after that. Finally he held the red END/POWER key until the phone, with an unfamiliar shudder, seemed to shut down. When it had, he removed its back and battery, checked to be sure its SIM card was in place, counted to five, and replaced both the battery and the back. Again he pressed the red key until the screen brightened, but it was clear that his smart phone no longer possessed a brain. His logs and contact lists were blank. The instrument he held was the same device. He was sure of that. He'd found it where he'd left it. And it had worked only a short while before. There was no doubting what had happened. The breacher had exposed it to an electromagnet powerful enough to wipe clean its circuitry.

Ty settled into bed and turned off the light. Now there was nothing to do but wait and plan for every possibility. *Let yourself go,* he told himself. He felt a heavy weight on his chest. His nerves were frayed. The tips of his fingers and even his face where his skin had been cut and stretched in surgery began to tingle. *Put that out of your mind. Don't be distracted,* he commanded his brain. Imagination was his enemy at a time like this. He had been taught that in the army. He had been taught as well how to neutralize his imagination, but before he could do so, his mind snagged on that old acronym, SERE: *S*urvival, *E*vasion, *R*esistance, *E*scape. Those were the skills he would need in the coming conflict. And summoning those skills required rest.

Chapter Forty-three

By morning the levanter had stilled. The new wind, from the southwest, was dry and sweet and the weather clear.

Ty was surprised to find breakfast being served, as usual, outside on bridge deck, although he observed that even there they remained under a discreet yet heavy guard. Six men, including the breacher, had disembarked with Philip from the chopper the night before. Ty identified four of them, hiding in nearby shadows.

"I'm sorry for that misunderstanding last night," Philip said over a single poached egg.

"What misunderstanding?" Isabella asked.

"Actually, I was speaking to Ty," Philip said. "One of the security men entered his room without knocking and caught him—"

"Buck naked," Ty interrupted.

"I hope you didn't get him too excited," Isabella teased.

"No chance of that," Philip sniffed. "They're not that sort."

"Well, I hope he didn't have a camera," Isabella continued. "People post pictures of naked movie stars on the Internet, you know. Or so I've been told."

"They do more than that," Ty said. "They'll attach your face to entirely different bodies."

"What an elegant subject of conversation," Philip said. "It's too bad I have to run."

"Before you go, would you mind putting us in the picture a little bit more?" Isabella asked resolutely. "How long is our leash?"

Philip stopped in his tracks, hesitated, gave a thin smile, and said, "You are not on a leash, darling. You're free to go anywhere and do anything you like. The men are here for your safety. In my judgment it would be imprudent to expose yourself to unnecessary danger, certainly before we leave port. Perhaps your own assumption is correct and there's none lurking. But it would be rash to discount the possibility that there is. If Ian *was* murdered, then as I said last night, there is at least one murderer on the loose."

"Do the men know all this?"

"Yes," Philip snapped, but at once recovered himself. "Isabella, please, I beg you, I love you, please indulge my paranoia for one more day."

She gave a solitary laugh. "As long as you realize that's what it is," she replied.

"I do, and that's all I ask. Ty's free to go, if that's what he really wants to do."

"I wouldn't dream of abandoning Isabella," Ty shot back immediately, "at least until things here are on their way back to normal. She needs someone around, if only to make the time go by."

Isabella smiled.

"You're too good to be true, Ty Hunter," Philip said, barely concealing his sarcasm.

As the EC130 prepared to lift off, Isabella turned toward Ty and asked, "Why didn't you go?"

"It was a bluff."

"Are you certain?"

"Certain enough not to have risked it," Ty told her. "If I'd forced him to play his hand, he would have done so. It would have been six armed men plus Jean-François and whomever else he's co-opted against a single unarmed one, very likely with you as a hostage."

"He said he'd told the men—"

"I heard that. If it's true, why do they look so ready to use their weapons should we get out of line?"

Isabella frowned. "I'm going to test one of them."

"Don't! That's the last thing you want to do. Right now let's go back to the deck just as we would after breakfast on any other day. I meant what I said seriously. I'm going to bore you senseless with my stories and want you to do the same to me until—"

"Until . . . ?"

"Until I've figured out who is where," Ty said, "and how to eliminate them."

"You're full of surprises," she told him.

"Try not to show your fear."

"That shouldn't be difficult. I'm so frightened I'm numb."

"Never mind," he told her as the chopper rose and its shield of noise slowly dissolved into the deceptively innocuous quiet of a high summer morning.

After an hour Ty thought he had a good idea of the four guards' mission and routine, which was clearly to corral the couple on bridge deck even as they appeared to keep their distance.

"I think I'll go for a walk," he said.

"You'll have followers," Isabella whispered.

"Care to join me?"

"In fact, I think I would," she replied, without conviction. "A walk sounds nice."

"Let's keep to the starboard deck," Ty said, slowing his speech and focusing on Isabella just enough to emphasize that this was an essential part of his plan.

They had advanced only a short distance when they spied one of the Slavs at the entrance to the wheelhouse, feigning nonchalance but nonetheless, Ty noticed, poised to spring into whatever action might be required.

Stopping amidships, Ty quickly put his arm around Isabella, resting his left palm on her bare shoulder, turning her toward shore as if in the distance, perhaps hidden in a valley of the Atlas Mountains, there was something that demanded her attention. "I'm going to kiss you," he said.

"Do I have a choice?"

"You could fight me off, but after what happened in Marbella, Ty Hunter breaking up in public is a stale story. Don't you want me to kiss you?"

She didn't reply immediately. "What woman wouldn't? Is that what you're thinking?"

Ty drew her toward him, lowered his hands to the center of her back and, feeling the fullness of her breasts against his chest, brushed her lips with his. "Now, once more with feeling," he said, then kissed her deeply. It was his best screen kiss and had about it the air of something he'd done many times before, which bothered Isabella.

"Very nice," she said, as though she were his director.

Ty permitted himself a grin, but before he could respond saw Jean-François approach with the Slav who had been stationed by the wheelhouse door. "I'm sorry to disturb you," said Jean-François, making no effort to disguise the disapproval in his voice, "but we've had word—"

"Word?" Isabella demanded. "About what, from whom?"

"Our sources," Jean-François explained, with a twinkle in his eye that suggested this was as far as he was willing to go. "Until we can be absolutely certain that there is no threat to you, it would be better if you remained belowdecks."

"Thank you for your opinion," Isabella said, "but it's a sunny day and I would prefer not to spend it inside."

"It would be better if you did, Miss Cavill," Jean-François insisted, glancing at the Slav, whose right hand had by now settled into the side pocket of his tight black trousers.

"Philip made it clear that I was free to do as I wished."

"Mr. Frost may have been operating under a different, now false, set of assumptions," Jean-François replied.

"Last time I checked, the lines of authority around here ran from me to the captain to you, not the other way around."

"These are special circumstances," Jean-François declared, shaking his head in disgust, as though the embrace he'd happened upon had not only confirmed his expectations but provided him serendipitous leverage.

"Get out of our way," Ty demanded.

But Jean-François stood his ground.

"If there *is* danger, call the police," Ty insisted.

"We are better equipped to face down whatever threat exists than they are. Police are the same, all over the world. They do their job only after the fact. Now, for your own good, please follow my friend."

"We're not going anywhere," Ty said.

"Only to your staterooms," pressed Jean-François, "for your own safety."

"No," Isabella said flatly, as adamant in her refusal as Ty.

Jean-François's use of the plural had at once rung in both their ears. Clearly his intention was to separate them, hold each incommunicado for however long it took Philip to execute his plan. Later, Ty supposed, Philip could make a show of blaming Jean-François, perhaps encourage Isabella to discharge him, but by then it would be too late. The warheads would have been transferred. They knew that their strength, probably their only hope, lay in remaining together.

Again Jean-François gestured to the compact Slav, then showed them a smile ripe with confidence.

"Are you going to shoot us?" Ty inquired.

Jean-François made no reply.

"Right here, in front of so many paparazzi?" Ty continued.

Jean-François smirked. It was his most natural expression, Ty thought. "I don't see any paparazzi," Jean-François said.

"That's because they're doing their job. They're good at it. You have to give them that much credit. They lurk. They wait. Only when they've snapped their shutters do you sometimes see the telephoto lenses."

"It is a very nice bluff," Jean François countered, "but I have my instructions."

"Yes, I forgot. You're to keep us safe."

"That's right, if possible."

"Suppose we jump."

"There's a man in the water to assist you."

"He's not bothered by the sharks?"

"There are no sharks in these waters."

"You're not handing us that old canard," Isabella said, "about sharks being functionally extinct in the Med? What if a stray bull's lost his way from the Atlantic?"

Jean-François considered the question as the Slav drew closer.

Ty moved farther away from Jean-François and his enforcer. "Man overboard!" he called out suddenly.

Reflexively, Jean-François turned. He had no sooner begun to turn back than Ty was coming at him. Ty delivered a thrusting front kick to the steward's stomach, knocking him onto the deck. "Grab his gun," Ty ordered Isabella before the Slav could reach it. But for an instant, shocked by the abrupt violence, she froze. Then, trembling, remaining as far back as she could from Jean-François, she bent to collect the weapon. It was centimeters from her fingertips when she felt the pressure of the Slav's coarse hand on the back of her neck.

"Drop it," he commanded. His voice was guttural, his English uncertain.

Isabella hesitated, then slowly stood in compliance. The Slav motioned her toward the stern. His SIG Sauer withdrawn and unlocked but held out of view, he stepped with caution around Jean-François, then marched them in single file, with Ty in front and his own pistol in Isabella's back.

In the distance, along the cabin wall, Isabella espied one of the chrome emergency buttons that were spaced at crucial intervals about *Surpass*. This morning's brilliant sunlight danced upon its surface, which was etched with a stylized silhouette of a human figure adrift upon the sea. As the Slav forced their retreat at a steady, cautious pace, Isabella prayed her abductor had not spotted it as well. Only a few steps more, she told herself, edging closer to the cabin wall. As she came alongside the button, she let her right ankle twist suddenly, then broke her fall with her hand, allowing her an instant to depress the OVERBOARD button. At once a siren wailed and was quickly followed by the dash of several members of the crew toward the starboard side of bridge deck. Behind them three Slavs kept watch.

The sudden alarm and frantic maneuvers disoriented their captor, as did the approach of small boat traffic. But his hand retained a firm grip on his pistol. To stall for time, Isabella drew a deep, exaggerated breath as she recovered herself, then struggled to stand. Perhaps Ty had been right about the paparazzi lurking over the horizon, she thought. He was used to them. She wasn't. Regardless, theirs were not the only craft now closing in on *Surpass*. The enlarging flotilla included pleasure boats of curiosity seekers, local fishing rigs and a few commercial transports, all lured by the enticing siren with its intimation of trouble aboard the magical yacht that for days had dominated the harbor and transfixed them. In the distance a shriller siren intensified. Soon Ty could make out a police boat racing toward them.

The Slav was growing frantic, Ty thought, as he helped Isabella resume her stride and then, with lightning speed, pressed her against the cabin wall and turned to face the Slav directly. He quickly assumed the *juchum seogi,* the Horse Riding Stance he had learned from tae kwon do, drew in his feet and bottom, let his knees drift sideways until they were over his toes, and tightened his core muscles. In the next instant he raised his hands, crossing them before his face. Then, as the Slav raised his pistol, Ty delivered a percussive hand strike to the man's wrist, dislodging his weapon. Before the Slav could retrieve it, Ty managed a dynamic front kick, a *mae geri,* to the man's groin, followed by a *harai goshi,* a sweeping hip throw, that landed the Slav squarely on the deck. After the Slav rebounded but before he was fully upright, Ty seized his upper arms and managed a *morote seoi nage,* a two-arm shoulder throw that landed him, with a splash, in the Mediterranean.

"As I said, you're a man of surprises," Isabella told Ty as he gathered her to him. "Let's go," he said.

"Go where?"

"Ashore."

"Follow me," Isabella said, leading him urgently up the stairs to the owner's deck before the conquered Slav's comrades could reach them.

Crispin was there, standing to starboard and looking, with a mystified expression, toward the sea. "What's going on?" he asked. "How many men are overboard?"

"Only one," Ty answered, revealing the silenced SIG Sauer he had appropriated from the Slav.

"How did it happen? He couldn't have slipped and gone over the guardrail."

"I threw him," Ty said.

Crispin did not immediately reply. Instead he regarded the pistol in Ty's right hand. Eventually, in a soft, wary voice, he said, "There'll be no need for that."

"That's good, because I like you," Ty told him, after a few seconds allowing himself the hint of a smile.

The black man in the kilt said, "My loyalty was always to Mr. Santal. Now it is to you, Miss Cavill—if you wish it, that is."

"I do very much, Crispin," Isabella told him. "Now that that's settled, we need to get into Ian's cabin."

Crispin nodded. "In due course," he said, "we'll change the iris and palm-print scans to yours."

"When we have a bit more time," Ty suggested.

"Certainly," Crispin said, then, employing the electronic key Ian had bequeathed to him, unlocked the door.

"They'll figure out where we are soon enough. Let's hurry," Ty said.

They were standing on a marble mosaic floor before an expanse of mahogany paneling. "Crispin?" Isabella asked, her voice conveying urgency.

He handed her the electronic key.

Flanking a small landscape by Matisse were two identical niches, each of which held one of a pair of jade owls. Isabella brought the electronic key to within an inch of the left eye of the owl on the right, and in immediate response the wall opened toward them.

"I did not know you knew," Crispin said.

Isabella winked. "Little girls can be more observant than you might think."

The pie-shaped section that had spun forward was the size of the compartment of a revolving door. Ty followed Isabella, squeezing into what, on closer inspection, appeared to be a lift. The air inside was cool, almost frigid.

"I'll be back," Isabella told Crispin.

"Of that I've no doubt," Crispin said, and smiled. No sooner had he spoken than he felt pressure in the small of his back. The man holding the pistol was as close as a dancing partner, and across the cabin now stood yet another Slav, also with his weapon withdrawn. Between them a weakened Jean-François hovered in the entrance to Ian's quarters.

"It would be a pity to have to kill him," Jean-François said directly to Ty, then let his gaze wander quickly to Crispin and back.

"Yes," Ty said, "I wonder how you would justify that as being for our own good."

Jean-François snickered. "You think you are very clever, don't you?"

"I take a dim view of being kidnapped, as does your mistress."

"What are you up to? Why are you here?"

"Let me ask you the very same question."

"The man with the gun asks the questions. Isn't that the way it is in every film?"

"Some of us like to break the mold," Ty said.

Jean-François nodded. In a more ominous tone, he said, "Step out of that lift, please."

Ty raised his arm to block Isabella. "This boat will be crawling with police and with the press right behind them any minute now. Surely you understand the futility of trying to hold us."

"Not at all," replied Jean-François. "I have my orders."

"Which, if I remember correctly, were to keep us safe?" Isabella said.

"To keep you *here*," Jean-François corrected.

"Whatever's happened up to now could be written off as miscommunication," Ty told him. "Think about it! Beyond this point it's piracy."

"'Beyond this point,'" Jean-François repeated with a dismissive laugh, "will lie only oblivion if I allow you off this ship. I would far prefer to take my chances in court, especially a Moroccan one, than with . . . well, never mind all that. I don't know what you are planning or how much you know, but I think it must be a great deal more than you've let on."

"Philip will kill you when he hears what you've done," Isabella bluffed.

"There is always that possibility, but look who's talking. When he sees the two of you in tomorrow's tabloids, somehow I don't think it will be me he'll want to kill." The commotion on deck was growing louder. Jean-François cocked an ear toward it. "Now, I am only going to ask you this one more time," he warned.

Ty hesitated, still restraining Isabella.

"Go!" Crispin cried out suddenly. As he did so, he placed his right leg behind the Slav who held him at gunpoint, lowered himself into a squat, grabbed his assailant's knees, then rotated his body before throwing him onto the cabin floor.

"Down!" Ty commanded in a booming voice. It was the voice of a younger man, ready to kill, unready to die. Shoving Isabella to the floor of the tiny lift, he fell into prone position, withdrawing the loaded SIG Sauer and taking aim.

Crispin had pinioned the Slav with his left knee and was now planting his right knee to the other side of the man's head in order to pinch and squeeze it, then draw out the man's arm and crack his elbow.

As the second Slav was preparing his shot, Ty fired at him but narrowly missed when his target suddenly shifted position. Immediately, the second Slav got off a single shot that grazed Crispin's left shoulder. Ty took aim a second time, counting down, in silence: one . . . two . . . three. His bullet entered between the intruder's eyes.

Jean-François moved toward the gunman's pistol.

"Forget it," Ty advised him.

But Jean-François pressed on.

"I told you to forget it."

Defiant, Jean-François grabbed for the silenced SIG Sauer P220. When he had it in his grip and had begun to pivot but before he could take aim, Ty fired two fatal rounds into his chest.

"How badly were you hit?" Ty called out to Crispin.

"I've been hit worse," Crispin answered, instinctively disparaging the sharp puncture, deeper than expected, from which blood had now begun to pulse.

"They'll get you to a doctor," Ty said, hearing the approach of others on the stairs.

"More of a nurse's job, really," Crispin replied, the lilt of his voice reassuring. "Wherever you're going, I'd go now if I were you."

Ty stepped into the elevator, dragging Isabella with him. "Do you still have that key?"

She opened her palm.

"Then let's get this show on the road."

Isabella nodded, presented the key, and at once the door swiveled closed.

"Whew," Ty said, exhaling as the lift descended. "Now that we've saved ourselves, let's go save the world. What do you say?"

"Do you think we have a chance?"

"There's always a chance," Ty said.

Chapter Forty-four

"This is—was—Ian's private lift," Isabella explained to Ty. "It operates in a high-security, fireproof shaft on its own power source. On every level its exterior door is disguised. As you might imagine, Ian liked to appear and disappear by surprise."

"That would seem to have been entirely in character. What did Crispin mean when he said he'd 'been hit worse'?"

"He fought in the Gulf War, with the British army. Ian met him just after that." Isabella studied Ty. "It's pretty obvious that you've also seen combat."

"Once a soldier, always a soldier?"

"Once a spy, always a spy?"

So smoothly and quietly did they land on LEVEL ONE—SUB that they were both taken by surprise when the lift stopped and a door slid rapidly upward on the opposite side of the compartment from the one by which they had entered. Beyond, in an eerily silent high-tech crypt, stretched the same woven-steel tread-way Ty had encountered upon first coming aboard *Surpass* in Cap d'Antibes. At the end of it, low in her berth, sat an elliptical submarine whose pontoonlike hull had been painted in the variegated blues and greens of sea camouflage. Using touch-screen controls mounted in a nearby wall, Isabella opened the clear-domed passenger compartment at the craft's center, then followed Ty aboard. Inside were seats for six passengers, in three rows of two, and a tortoiseshell dashboard that made the interior redolent of a sports car.

"Have you done this before?" Ty asked.

"Never," Isabella said.

"Would you like me to have a go at it?"

"I don't think that will be necessary, do you?" she replied, pointing to an LED screen on which appeared a list of commands: PREPARE DEPARTURE, DEPARTURE, GPS WAYPOINT ORIGIN, GPS WAYPOINT DESTINATION, DEPTH, SPEED, OVERRIDE. "This thing could be run by a child in a bath."

"If you say so," Ty said.

"I do. Ian wasn't mechanical. He appreciated machines but saw their role as freeing human beings like him to think about bigger things. Beyond that and the predictable masculine taste for gadgets, particularly the latest ones that no one else had or could get hold of, he wasn't interested."

In no time the transparent roof snapped tightly back into place atop the submersible and the shadowy berth filled with enough seawater for the magnificent toy to float. When the twin hatches beneath it opened, it descended like a diving bell into the Mediterranean.

Outside, caught in the strong, conical beams of the submarine's searchlights, dolphins frolicked among a hundred other colorful varieties of fish while coral formations, anchored to the rocky seabed, flowered in bursts of vivid peach and perfect white. Algae lined the undulating floor of the ancient sea, coming ever more sharply into focus as they descended.

"Is there a phone on board?" Ty asked. "There must be."

"I reckon," Isabella said, and pushed the icon for a telephone in an upper corner of the touch screen. "It's got to be the same as on the tenders. When you hear a tone, just speak the number you want."

Ty did as she instructed and a few seconds later heard Oliver's voice boom from the speaker.

"Bloody hell!" Oliver exclaimed. "What the fuck happened? Where are you?"

"Twenty thousand leagues under the sea," Ty said, "on our way to you. What do you mean, what happened?"

"You're all over Sky News, you *and* Isabella."

Ty smiled. "Pitch me the story line."

"No need to, really. Use your imagination."

"Was there anything about Frost's boys?"

"They're calling them suspected pirates for the time being. Never mind. It's that kiss they're giving airtime to. Frost's thugs, *Surpass*'s crew, the Moroccan police—they're not even bit players at this point, they're extras."

The beginnings of laughter spread across Isabella's face.

"Those paparazzi saved your bacon," Oliver continued. "I'll say that for them. You really owe them one."

"And how would you propose I discharge that debt?" Ty asked. "I mean, let's not give them too much credit, Ollie, when they're so easy to manipulate."

"Anyway, the question the press is asking, and I'm sure the authorities, too, is what's become of the two of you."

"And they can go on asking it," Ty said. "From now on we're playing by Hollywood rules. They'll have to stay till the climax to find out what happens."

Oliver sighed. "In the meantime I can think of one person who won't have enjoyed that kiss."

"I'm sure he's got bigger things on his mind," Isabella offered.

"I suppose it depends on how he weights things, darling," Ty told her.

She started. It was the first time either of them had used that word.

"Putting myself in his position," replied Oliver, "I'd say it's a game changer. Before it he could have had everything. Now he must make do with whatever's left, whatever's still under his control. But let's get to the point, shall we? How far out are you? I presume you're in some sort of submarine—only you would have found one of those handy—and that you're headed for Gib."

"Correct on each count," Ty replied. "I'll need a waypoint for surfacing. Once I have that, I'll be able to give you an ETA. We'll require relatively deep water, obviously, but that shouldn't pose much of a problem around here. And, Ollie, the less exposure the better right now. We'll both need a change of clothes."

"I'll ring Prada."

"And phones," Ty added. "The goons neutralized ours. Most important, we'll need ordnance."

"Got you," Oliver replied. "Now, take this down. It's the waypoint for a spot just within the entrance to a cave not far beyond Europa Point. Don't worry, it's safe. Legend has it that it's depthless. Stay submerged until I give you the signal. It shouldn't be long. There will be two fishermen, SBS blokes, in a blue skiff. Don't hit them on your way up. They'll change places with you, and we'll collect you shortly thereafter."

"What else do I need to know?" Ty asked.

"That we're in countdown mode," Oliver replied.

"Oh, that's just great," Ty said. "I'm breathing easier already."

In the Range Rover that ferried them from a landing site not far from the shadowy, stalactite-filled cavern where they had transferred from *Surpass*'s submarine to the nondescript skiff, Oliver brought Ty and Isabella up to date. "Cardigan & Sons Transport," he said, "turned out to be not so much a front as a holding company. As a result, we lost a bit of time there."

Ty furrowed his brow. "How much time?" he inquired.

"Enough to have made the situation more difficult but not irretrievable, which is to say that we have—one—identified each of that firm's subsidiaries, and—two—sequestered all the lorries and barges, whether Cardigan's or anyone else's, into which cargo from the Claussen *Wayfarer* was offloaded. As for vetting the lot by hand and eye and other sensors, we are rather short of manpower."

"Why?" Ty asked.

"Principally because a threat of this sort is not information one wants to share widely, but also because of—and you won't believe this, Ty—one George Kenneth."

"The old school tie?"

"No doubt that's part of it. Another part is the tendency of men like Kenneth to overintellectualize every goddamned thing."

"Is there any way around him?"

"None through London," Oliver said. "I've made stabs. So has Giles. But it's a NATO op, and our boys aren't going to contravene the PM, who's not going to contravene Washington."

"The Prime Minister could call the President," Ty suggested.

"But who is going to call, much less persuade, the PM? You seem to think everyone at every level in government is on a first-name basis with and has the same priorities as everyone else. The truth is that the higher one goes, the less likely it becomes that that's the case. Too many people have too many contrary reasons and too much turf to protect."

"*You* could call the President," Isabella told Ty.

Ty smiled. "What do you think?" he asked Oliver.

"Off the top of my head, I'd say that the odds are rather slim. Ten to one the call would be redirected to George Kenneth."

"In which case," Ty said, "we'd be back where we started."

"Pretty much, but with Kenneth pissed at us," Oliver countered, "and on a much higher state of alert."

Ty paused. "Why would that matter? Surely at the end of the day we have the same objectives."

"Up to a point," agreed Oliver, his voice all at once contemplative. "We want to find the warheads; so does he. But suppose that somewhere in his heart of hearts George Kenneth really believes that that's a lost cause. And suppose he's further concluded that no amount of extra resources, given the people and material available, could possibly affect that outcome. Drift down from the firmament for a minute and think like a courtier, Ty, like a bureaucrat! Mightn't he prefer us to fail on our own without ever bringing his boss or, God forbid, *him* into it?"

Oliver paused as Ty absorbed what his friend had said.

"Hear me out," Oliver resumed. "They could cut us loose. We wouldn't be the first. After that they could start over. For all we know, they may already be doing that."

Ty laughed. "This, in a nutshell," he told Isabella, "explains my change of career. Come to think of it, I'll bet you miss the jewelry business, don't you?"

"Not really," she said. "How many women get the chance to stand in the very spot where the Fates forced Hercules to hold up the world only to have to do the same thing all over again?"

Ty reached for her hand and held it. "You're the first one I've heard of," he told her softly. Then, returning his attention to Oliver, he asked, "Where is Philip at this moment?"

"In Ian's office—*his* office now—as best we know."

"How can you not be sure of something like that?"

"You've never been to Ian's office, or to Giles Cotton's, have you? If you had, you'd understand. Have you ever wondered what kind of rock the famous Rock of Gibraltar really is? It's limestone, completely unlike any of the landscape that surrounds it. Do you know why? Because limestone is formed from sea creatures that have died, dried and solidified. The peak of the Rock was once a seabed. Think about that. And from there to the base, as far under the surface of the Med as you can go, it is shot through with caves and tunnels. Well, not all of the tunnels are natural, mind you. Over the last two centuries, ever since the Great Siege in 1782 when Spain and France sought to recapture the Rock from us whilst we were otherwise distracted by the Rebellion of the Colonies, men have excavated ever more elaborate ones, not only for HQs but for barracks and hospitals and simple warehousing. Most of all, especially in the upper reaches and outcroppings, these galleries were the sites of gun emplacements. What strategic positions they commanded! There are extensive maps of them in the Garrison Library and elsewhere, but there are also an infinite number of passages that are not recorded on any plan. Like one of those ghostly castles in horror films, Gib is riddled with dark and secret corridors. So when a man, in this case Frost, enters the mountain at one point, then stops at another within it, to anyone on the outside it remains far from certain he's still there, or from which point he will eventually emerge."

"Another reason we're stretched thin?" Ty suggested.

"Sure," Oliver agreed. "There aren't enough forces in the army, navy and police to plug every hole and monitor every crevice in the Rock of Gibraltar. But we have to operate on the assumption that Frost will conduct himself in the manner of a man who is above suspicion, come and go naturally, do as little as possible to draw attention to himself. That's the impression he will wish to give. Where we *are* stretched thin is, first of all, in our capacity to carry out the necessary searches of cargoes received from the *Wayfarer,* although by now it may be too late to mobilize any more support we might receive in time to make a difference. Secondly, and far more distressingly, we are hampered by your government's unwillingness to employ the sort of financial sorcery it is more than capable of doing."

"I take it you're talking about diverting funds," Ty interjected.

"Yes, and in very complicated ways, such as making them disappear from those accounts where they ought to be and appear in those where they ought not to be," Oliver said. "What worries me is that if Washington should, in even the slightest way, loosen the noose we've begun to tighten around Philip Frost's neck, he'll sense that and slip through it."

"I have an idea," Ty said.

"Let's hear it," Oliver told him.

"Not quite yet. Let's get to where we're going first, think things through calmly. Then, maybe, I'll give it a try."

Chapter Forty-five

Philip Frost regarded the attaché cases arranged upon Ian's malachite desk.

Sitting across from him, Andrej Melinkov returned Philip's expression with a puzzled look. "Forgive me," he said, "but I expected you would be—"

"Somewhat more upset? I know. Strange, isn't it, but what I feel at this moment is virtually nothing. Not emptiness, not possibility—nothing. Perhaps this is freedom, Andrej."

The Russian nodded uneasily. "I am certain freedom takes many forms," he said.

"Go ahead, Andrej, ask the question that's on your mind. It's acceptable under the circumstances, especially our having come so far."

Andrej hesitated.

"Fine," Philip snapped. "I'll ask it for you. Did I expect it? Yes and no, no and yes. But I am not an adolescent. My heart doesn't break."

"That's good, then."

"As far as it goes," Philip conjectured. "For a man's heart to break, he has to believe in love, and I do not. I do believe in desire, but desire is, almost by definition, transient. It exists within time while love, supposedly, does not. Will I crave and covet tomorrow that which I do today? As I ordinarily do not hunger today for what I might well have killed for yesterday, 'Absolutely not' would be my answer, or rather only those aspects of today that are fungible."

Andrej's black eyes glistened. "Such as the gems and jewels in those cases," he suggested, "whose beauty will not fade."

"Whose *value* will not fade," Philip corrected. "Mr. Santal concerned himself with aesthetics. I am less bothered where material possessions are concerned. Beyond an easily obtainable level of comfort, my tastes, in fact, are spartan."

Andrej laughed.

"Well, in comparison to Ian's," Philip acquiesced.

"You appreciate a beautiful woman."

"The most natural thing in the world, isn't it? I appreciate them, and I *have* them. I command them in the marketplace. Such women are perverse and cannot resist what's unobtainable. They relish nothing more than being fucked by a hard body and a stiff prick who they know is bedding them entirely for *his* satisfaction. I had Isabella Cavill at her peak, Andrej. The novelty wore off long ago, though plainly there were other compensations. Had our liaison gone on very much longer, would these have been enough to endure the inevitable slippage, the eventually monotonous and mundane quality of our lives as husband and wife? I very much doubt that. I would have tired of her before she'd tired of me. Besides, when a man is fool enough to make that sort of commitment and then live by it, he has imprisoned himself within not only his own horizons but hers."

Andrej hesitated. "Well, then," he said.

"This is not self-justification," Philip pressed on, less temperately. "It's simply the truth, as well as an unfortunate turn of events I had already provided for, with the utmost care, in my plans."

"I understand."

"Not entirely," Philip assured him, for Andrej could not possibly know that Philip had induced Isabella to draw up and sign her will in his favor.

"As you wish," Andrej relented.

"Which has nothing to do with my right to feel betrayed, does it, or to revenge that filthy, sickeningly public betrayal?"

"You are asking a highly personal question," Andrej said.

"So? Answer it."

"It is well known that there exists such a thing as a crime of passion," Andrej replied.

"Indeed," Philip concurred, "there have been many celebrated *crimes passionelles*. Books and plays, even operas have been written about them. Paintings have portrayed them. But I can tell just from your expression that you would find it difficult to imagine me as the perpetrator of one."

"It's not your style."

"That's very useful to know," Philip said. "Thank you. I take it we are ready."

"Correct," Andrej answered.

"And Hans and Franz understand what they are to do?"

"They do. Hans is just outside. You can judge for yourself."

"In a moment," Philip said. "We have a great deal to accomplish over a shorter period of time than I'd hoped for, but if we don't permit ourselves the luxury of any further mistakes, at the end of the day that might well prove to our advantage."

"I can't imagine what happened on Santal's yacht," Andrej said.

"That's because you don't know Jean-François. Whatever triggered their unease I am sure had to do with him, not your men, who barely speak English and surely looked the part of the guards they were meant to be. No, I misjudged Jean-François. I thought all along there was a chance he might overplay his hand, but who else was there? Still, it was out of that concern that I devised the contingency plan we are now following."

"I assume the men are ready to take their positions in the upper galleries."

"Yes, within fifteen minutes' notice," Andrej replied. "They have been fed. They are resting now, waiting for my call."

Philip glanced at his watch, then said, "The last wire transfers will have been completed in less than twenty-four hours. Tomorrow night, if not tonight, you should sleep like a baby, Andrej."

"I will welcome that."

"Okay," Philip said, as much to himself as to Andrej. "Hans is to leave here in exactly one quarter hour. I will follow by my own route no more than ten minutes after that. Your men should be in their positions, with weapons locked and loaded, by the time I leave. Please confirm this before I do. Isabella and Ty Hunter will be arriving sometime within the following hour."

"You seem very certain of that."

"They will have made their way here somehow. I don't know how, but they will have concluded that Gibraltar, not Tangier, is the new playing field. Of course, there is always the possibility that they won't. In that case perhaps they will flee to a love nest in Marrakesh. Or perhaps the whole scene was staged for the press, to evade pirates who had betrayed not merely them but me. Then they'll call at any minute to let me know that they are safe and not really together, to ease my concern. We'll soon see. If they *have* flown off to Marrakesh, they can be dealt with later. If they call, I'll listen to what they have to say, but it is my strong suspicion I won't have to. They will come in person, because while the search parties search, they will want to have a look around, hoping to find a clue everyone else has overlooked. Ian Santal's inner sanctum, after all, should contain a mother lode of information, and as his heir, Isabella will expect to have the run of it. She'll be given that, too, at least to start.

"Why not ask Hans to come in now?"

"I'll do that," Andrej replied as he set off toward Ian's reception room.

A moment later he returned with a young man of almost exactly Philip's age, height and weight, with hair of the same color, cut in the same meticulous style, but combed, for the moment, differently. The young man was wearing jeans, a T-shirt and sandals.

"Good afternoon," Philip said.

"Good afternoon," replied his doppelgänger in overprecise yet halting English.

Reaching into the well of his desk, Philip removed a blue canvas garment bag and handed it to the man. "I would like you to put on these clothes."

The man nodded.

"You will find shoes that fit you in the dressing room just over there. Study my hair, then go into the loo and rebrush yours in the same style. Once you have done that, come back here. It should not take you long."

When the man returned, he could have been mistaken for Philip's twin, particularly in profile and at the distance from which he was likely to be observed. Philip studied him. "Take off that tie," he said. "I will show you how to tie a half Windsor, which is the knot I use. Where, I wonder, did Andrej find you?"

"Through my agency in Berlin," the German replied.

"You are an actor or a model."

"Sometimes one thing, sometimes the other, sometimes something else entirely."

"I see," Philip said. "Play this role well and you will be handsomely compensated."

"Instruct me and I will do my best."

"Now I want you to put on the panama trilby you see on the seat of that chair by the door through which you came in. I'll adjust the angle for you and the brim. Once that's done, you will take it off, hold it in your left hand and not put it on again until the very instant you leave this building. When you do put it on, arrange it exactly as I have shown you. My car will be waiting for you. It is a dark blue Mercedes S600 with Gib number plates and tinted windows. Assume the owner's seat, rear right, as though you've never sat anywhere else. Breathe deeply, pause, then collect the newspaper you will find folded in the seat-back pocket in front of you and begin to read it. The driver knows what to do. He will take you on a circuit of the harbor and airfield. Whenever the car stops and it seems appropriate to do so, retract the window, but before you do, be certain you are wearing these," Philip said, handing his impersonator a leather case bearing a pair of custom-made Italian sunglasses. "Choose a ship or an aircraft, look at it intensely for a moment, as if you are trying to discern what is going on aboard it, then raise the window as if you've satisfied yourself. That's all there is to it. It should not be a difficult assignment."

"No," agreed the young man, "it won't be."

"One more thing," Philip added, with a transient smile, "say as little as possible."

"Understood," said the German.

"I'll just be a minute," Philip told him, and with that retreated to the reception room where two secretaries were seated at opposing desks.

"I shall be going out shortly for a few hours to see to some business," Philip instructed them. "Should Miss Cavill come by in the meantime, please ring me at once. Ask her to make herself at home in the office. It is, after all, hers. She may be alone, or she may have Mr. Hunter with her." Philip watched the secretaries carefully, wondering if they, too, had already seen the video of Ty and Isabella's embrace. "One more thing," he said. "I wonder if you could round up the files relating to Mr. Santal's last venture with Sir Timothy Fan Dang Foo."

"That would have been a while ago," replied the buxom woman whose desk faced Ian Santal's office. "They'd be upstairs in the records room."

"Not to worry." Philip smiled. He had expected that she, the office's unofficial archivist, would be the first to answer. "If you could have them on my desk when I return, I'd be grateful."

"I'll just go and have a look," she told him.

"Thank you," Philip said.

Back in his office, he addressed the young man. "We're almost ready. If you would excuse us for a moment," he said, indicating the dressing room in which the man had recently changed.

The man withdrew immediately.

When he had, Philip beckoned Andrej toward his desk. "Ready?" he inquired.

"The men are in place," Andrej told him.

"What about the incendiary device?"

"All neatly tucked away in the bottom drawer of that campaign chest," Andrej said, pointing to the brass-trimmed walnut cube at the center of an interior wall.

"And you've changed the office access codes?"

"Not yet, but they've been prepared. When you call the number you have for the device, you will not only trigger a twelve-second countdown to detonation but effect the change of access codes and thus enforce a barrier in both directions. No one will be able to enter or leave this room without them."

"That's good. The fire will purge any record of the change, of course."

"Exactly and there will be no record anywhere else. It will also devour any clue as to its origin."

"The fire is a necessary piece of business, Andrej. Certain things must be erased, and it will erase them. In the process it should also serve to confuse the curious, which is to our advantage. One thing it most definitely is not, however, is a crime of passion."

"Of course not," Andrej dissembled. "For it to be that, you would have to be overcome by a passion you don't feel."

"Just so," Philip said. "In any event, I shall miss you, Andrej. It *has* been fun, hasn't it?"

Andrej nodded. "You will always be welcome at my villa."

"Yes, well, when you've finally bought it, let me know, and I may take you up on that. There are some lovely women in the South of France. In the meantime, I've downloaded everything I need off site," explained Philip, walking slowly toward then rapping gently on the door to the dressing room. "So, all that remains is for you to escort our young friend out.

"Take this iPhone," Philip told the young man when he emerged.

"It's brand-new, isn't it?" remarked the young man.

"I bought it and one just like it this morning. Don't talk into it. Rather hold it intently, as though you are listening to something important and can't be distracted. Give a quick and friendly wave to the secretary in the next room as you pass her, but don't stop. She will see only the back of your head if you move quickly. The woman who ordinarily faces her has gone on a fool's errand, so you'll have no trouble standing in for me once you hit the street."

When the young man and Andrej had left, Philip returned to the dressing room, where he carefully removed all his clothing except for his shorts and folded it into a duffel. From a second duffel, he removed a pair of peacock blue Bermuda shorts, a pair of swim trunks to substitute for undershorts, a white tennis shirt, a rope belt and a pair of Top-Sider deck shoes, which he put on without socks. At Ian's desk he proceeded to load the second duffel with the three slim attaché cases bearing the gems that Sheik al-Awad had purchased from Guardi, the same ones that had been delivered to Isabella both at Pond House and shipboard and that Philip had taken from *Surpass* that morning. Then, balancing one bag in either hand, he beat his retreat through the cavernous gallery that led to a spiral of old stone stairs that eventually emerged at the base of the Rock.

Chapter Forty-six

Ty Hunter looked in the mirror, then at Isabella and laughed. The wardrobe available at NATO HQ on a moment's notice had been limited and, emerging from the ladies' and gentlemen's cloakrooms almost simultaneously, they found themselves dressed identically, in blue sneakers, white socks, pressed khakis, web belts with brass buckles and navy blue, short-sleeved madras shirts that constituted the post's unofficial summer civilian dress.

"Fancy a G&T?" inquired Ty.

"I think I'd rather a Pimm's," replied Isabella.

"Next joke," said Oliver. "You wasted a lot of precious time in those showers."

"Three minutes," Ty said, "tops."

"I took no more than two," Isabella countered.

"Easy, Ollie," Ty said. "If we're going to play these roles, we have to look the part. I don't know about Isabella, but that shower is in *my* rider."

Oliver shook his head. "I beg your pardon. For a moment I forgot. It's not what you do that matters, but how you look doing it."

"You've got it," Ty said. "When this is all over, if we're still alive, you should come back to L.A. with me. I'm pretty sure Netty would take you on."

Amused but not distracted by Ty's suggestion, Oliver pressed, "On the way over here, you said you had an idea."

"It's a long shot," Ty said, "but Isabella's right. There might be a way I could get through to President White without going through George Kenneth."

"And what would that be?"

"What time is it there?"

"Washington's six hours behind us, so it must be almost eight-thirty in the morning."

"A lot's happened while they were sleeping," Ty mused. "Do you have a number for the White House?"

"I have Kenneth's direct number and his mobile, but not a number for the switchboard."

"Never mind, it shouldn't be that difficult to find," Ty said, already maneuvering the touch pad of the new BlackBerry Oliver had given him. When he had found it, he tapped in the number and waited. As the recording played, he looked up and repeated it out loud. "'If you know your party's extension, you may enter it now. Otherwise please remain on the line.' If I knew it," he said with a wry smile, "would I—Oh, hello, yes, good afternoon, or good morning rather. This is Ty Hunter. I wonder if you could connect me with Daphne White."

"Did you say your name was Ty Hunter?"

"Yes."

"Does Miss White know you?"

"She does. I recently visited the family at Camp David."

"I'm afraid Miss White is unavailable at the moment," replied the White House operator.

"Most teenagers are unavailable at this hour once school's let out for the summer," Ty said. "It is very important I speak with her."

"You said you were a guest at Camp David. Let me see if we have a number for you, then. Yes, here it is. You're John Tyler Hunter, is that right?"

'Yes."

"And is your number still the same?"

"Actually, it's not," Ty said. "That phone was damaged. What's my new number?" he asked, gesturing to Oliver, then fumbling until his friend had written it out for him.

The operator said, "Could you tell me, please, what your old number was?"

"Of course, but it doesn't work any longer."

"I'm sure you understand that we have to confirm that you really are Ty Hunter. Sorry for the trouble."

"Of course," Ty said, drawing a breath as he gave her his old, unpublished number.

"I'll leave word for Miss White with the Ushers' Office," the operator said. "Can she reach you at your new number?"

"Yes," Ty replied, "she can. And please tell her that it's urgent."

"I already have. And, Mr. Hunter, my husband and I both loved *The Boy Who Understood Women*."

"Thank you," Ty said as he hung up.

"Nothing beats a try but a failure," Oliver said.

"It's too soon to call it that," Ty told him. "While we wait for a teenager to wake up, we should do something useful."

"The boys who know what to look for are looking for it," Oliver said, "and so far the geeks are in chains. I feel helpless, and I don't like feeling helpless."

"Where's your on-site geek?" Ty asked.

"Bingo? He's just down the hall. Why?"

"I'd like to borrow him for a while."

"Are you going to let me in on your plan?" asked Oliver.

"Or me?" added Isabella.

"You and I," Ty told her, "are going to a pay our dear friend Philip a visit."

"Do you think that's wise?"

"More than that, it's necessary. The clue we need, if there is one, is most likely in Ian's office."

Isabella frowned. "What's Bingo's role?" she asked.

"Bloodhound," Ty said.

At which moment Oliver's mobile rang. He listened with concern, said only "Thank you" to the caller, then, after he had disconnected, said, "Frost's been spotted."

"Goody," Ty said, "where?"

"By the western edge of the harbor," Oliver said. "He's keeping an eye on one of the barges."

"Where are your men?" Isabella asked.

"Searching it," Oliver told her.

"That sounds promising."

Oliver's phone rang again. This conversation was even briefer than the first. The instant it concluded, he said, "Frost's moved on."

"Have they lost him?"

"No, he's checking out another barge—at least that's what they think." He paused. "Three warheads, three vessels," Oliver said. "It makes sense in a way."

"Or does it?" Ty countered.

"We'll miss Philip if we go to the office," Isabella said.

"So much the better," Ty said.

Oliver said, "We're missing something. I don't know what it is, but I can't shake this feeling that it's important."

"Or maybe we're taking too much on board," Ty said. "It's not like Philip to expose himself."

"Isabella?" Oliver asked.

"The Philip I know would gloat in private," she replied.

"Exactly," Ty agreed.

"You two and Bingo go to the office," Oliver said, "find out what you can there. I'll shadow Frost."

"We'll need a protocol," Ty said.

"Keep the GPS on your BlackBerrys on," Oliver said. "We'll text each other every fifteen minutes. *GHU* will mean no change. *D,* for 'delta,' will mean change, to be elaborated by e-mail or voice."

"What does *GHU* stand for?" Isabella asked.

"'God help us,'" Oliver said. "I'll chase up Bingo for you, then we're off."

"Right," Ty said. "Let's cover ground before it covers us!"

They were still in their navy car a few minutes away from Ian's office when Ty's phone rang. "White House operator," said a male voice. "Is this Mr. Ty Hunter?"

Ty held up a finger to silence Isabella and Bingo, who were chatting about computer-aided design software. "This is he," Ty said.

"I have Miss Daphne White calling for you. Please hold."

Ty heard a quick beep, after which the operator said, "Miss White," and Daphne's high, adolescent voice came immediately on the line. "Hi, Ty," she said. "This is a surprise. I mean, when the ushers told me you'd called, I was like, 'Get out of here, I can't believe it!' How are you? Are you well?"

"I'm fine," Ty said. "I hope you are."

"I'm good," Daphne said. "Are you coming to Washington? I hope that's why you're calling."

"One day," Ty said. "I'm not exactly sure when."

Daphne paused. "That's too bad," she said finally.

"Look, Daphne. I hate to bother you with this, but it is very important that I talk to your father and that *no one* on his staff knows I'm talking to him."

"Why?" Daphne asked, her tone abruptly suspicious.

"I can't tell you that," Ty said. "I wish I could."

"That sounds strange."

"Can you get a message to him?"

"Of course I can. He's my father. Anyway, he's off campus at the moment, giving a speech at a breakfast somewhere."

"In D.C.?"

"Yes."

"When he comes back, would you ask him to phone me on this number?"

"I have a question I want to ask you first, though, okay?"

"Sure," Ty told her.

"I mean, like, is this very important because he's the President, or is it more a personal thing?"

"The former," Ty said. "It's not personal at all."

"Okay, then," Daphne said, "why not?"

"Remember," Ty said, "only *he* should know about this, and he should not get anyone else involved until we've spoken."

"I heard you the first time," Daphne said. "Where are you anyway? Those sirens in the background sound foreign."

"Gibraltar," Ty said.

"That's awesome," Daphne said. "I've never been there."

In the courtyard outside the front entrance to Ian Santal's office, in the shade of an umbrella raised above an empty café table, Ty huddled with Bingo and Isabella. "What would you like to do that you haven't been able to?" he asked Bingo.

"The simplest thing, as I explained to Oliver, would be to jigger the accounts."

"To which Washington has responded that you could bring down the world's financial system in the process?"

"They're politicians," Bingo said with unmasked exasperation. "Which is another way of saying that they're natural-born critics. Most of them can barely navigate Windows or OS X. They have no idea how elegantly what I want to do can be done. At the same time you hoover the funds, you make it look like a simple computer error. All that your victim, if he's legitimate, would have to do in that case would be to spot the error and ask for it to be corrected. *Pas de problème!* Now, if he's not legitimate and it's going to raise a lot of eyebrows when he asks for his missing tens of billions that he can't account for having had in the first place, then damn straight it's going to cause his ulcer to bleed."

"I'll do my best," Ty said, and followed Isabella into the discreet entrance.

In Ian's outer office, both secretaries welcomed the impromptu trio. The more slender and severe of the two, whose desk was just outside Ian's door, said, "Mr. Frost had to step out for a moment, but before he did, he especially asked that I make you comfortable."

"That's very kind," Isabella said, glancing warily at Ty.

"Did he say how long he would be?" Ty asked.

"I'm afraid he didn't, but he's not long usually. Gibraltar's a small place. He did ask me to ring him on his mobile when you arrived. Or, if you'd like, you could ring him."

Isabella smiled. "Let's wait a few minutes," she suggested. "It would be much nicer to surprise him."

"I wouldn't want to get crossways with him," the secretary said. "He seemed to be expecting you. Are you sure you'll be able to surprise him?"

"Fifteen minutes," Isabella said, her inflection suddenly proprietary. "Let's give it that long, if you don't mind."

The secretary nodded reluctantly, then, reaching beneath the central drawer of her desk, pressed a remote that unlocked the first of two heavy, sequenced doors that led to Ian's private lair. Only once it had closed behind them was the second door released.

"Another of your godfather's vaults," Ty remarked. "It reminds me of his quarters on *Surpass.*"

"Same man, same concerns, same standards," Isabella said.

"Shall we have a look around?" Ty asked.

"Are you asking my permission?"

"I was taught to."

She laughed. "Well, of course you have it. It would help to know what we're looking for."

"We'll only know that when we find it," he said.

Bingo was already at the laptop that rested on a console table behind Ian's desk. "Straight out of the box, this is funny," he said. "Funny as in peculiar. It's warm, so presumably Frost was just using it, but it doesn't seem to be password-protected. Don't you find that odd for a man with a lock fetish?"

"Is it Ian's or Philip's?" Isabella asked.

"Who's to say, really?" Bingo told her. "No icons. No programs. Not even an ISP number. It's been wiped."

"The whole room's been wiped, it looks like," Ty said.

Isabella swiveled to take in the room from every angle. "I'm not sure," she concluded. "Philip is manically tidy. That could be what gives it this feeling of . . . What am I trying to say? This feeling of having been vacated.

"If the computer is Ian's, why would Philip wipe it clean when he's meant to be getting Ian's affairs in order?" Isabella continued. "If it's his, why would he *want* to lose *all* the information that was on it? Even if he did want to get rid of something, why wouldn't he expunge only that and nothing else? I presume that's possible."

"It would depend on what it was," Bingo said. "If it were a document or file, he could manage that. But if it involved something he'd done on some network or where he'd been on the Internet, there would be traces of it elsewhere, on servers and routers to which he would have no access."

"All the more reason not to wipe it, then," Isabella said.

"Not really. Think about it. He'd be betting against anyone's finding a needle in a haystack, as well as depriving whoever might be looking of a vital clue to its location."

Bingo removed a flash drive from the pocket of his fisherman's vest and inserted it into the laptop's USB.

"What are you doing?" Ty asked.

"Interrogating the machine," Bingo said. "I want it to run a little operating system and in the process tell me its MAC address."

"It's what?" Ty asked.

"Its Media Access Control address," explained Bingo. "It's a unique identifier, a forty-eight-bit number given to every network adapter or NIC—sorry, network-interface card—by the manufacturer. It's used in the Media Access Control protocol sublayer. Want to know more?"

"What will it tell you?"

"Maybe nothing, maybe a lot," Bingo said. "Once I've got it, the team can hack into the various servers of service providers around here, and if Frost has been anywhere interesting, we'll know pretty quickly when and where, if not perhaps why. Shall I include or exclude porn sites?"

"They're not one of his vices," Isabella replied with a dismissive yawn. "All Philip requires in that regard is a mirror."

"Just joking," Bingo told her.

"It really is the end of privacy, isn't it?" Ty mused.

"What's privacy?" Bingo said. "Only people above a certain age remember or expect it. Wait! The fish is nibbling. Yes! Just look at that screen! And here comes that MAC address now, in six beautiful groups of two hexadecimal digits."

A few seconds after Bingo had transferred the MAC address to his phone and e-mailed it from there to Delilah Mirador in Jerusalem, Jonty Patel in College Park, Maryland, and Nevada Smith in Berkeley, California, a landline rang. Isabella picked it up to hear the secretary in Ian's outer office calling on the intercom. "I wanted you to know that it has now been fifteen minutes," she said.

"I don't mind waiting a bit longer," Isabella said.

"How long do you think?"

"Let me ask the others." Isabella put the phone on hold, then inquired of Bingo, "How long will this take?"

"Longer than we can stall, probably," he said. "One thing we already know is that this isn't one of the computers we've been tracking."

"That's interesting," Ty said. "Look, Bingo, why don't you return to your office and coordinate your end of the search from there. Whatever information comes back is going to come to you, and you may be the only one who'll understand it. It's pretty plain from looking through the few papers that are still here that we're unlikely to find anything else of much use. We'll wait until Philip appears, *if* he appears."

"And if he doesn't?"

"Ollie and his mates have got him covered."

"I don't know. I'd feel better if you came with me."

Ty shook his head. "No, we're too close. At this point it's much better to have some of us on the inside trying to figure a way out than all of us on the outside trying to figure a way in."

"I hope you're right," said Bingo.

"Has there been any word from Mr. Frost?" Isabella asked both secretaries as she saw Bingo out.

"Not as yet," the more severe of them replied. "I really should let him know you're here, don't you think?"

"I suppose you're right," Isabella said. "Go ahead, why don't you?"

Chapter Forty-seven

Back in Ian's office, Isabella asked, "What do you think, Ty?"

"I don't really know what to think," he told her. "I'm an actor in this mystery, not its author."

"That secretary is certainly frightened of getting on Philip's wrong side, but I don't think she has much to worry about, do you?"

"Because you don't think he'll be coming back?"

"Why would he?"

"To explain himself to you," Ty replied. "To blame others, conveniently dead, for what happened aboard *Surpass.* To persuade you to choose him over me and thus keep control of everything."

Isabella shook her head. "I think he'd be afraid I wouldn't believe him, and he'd be right. He'd know I'd dig very deeply before I did, and I think he would fear what I might find out. No, knowing Philip, I'd say it would suit him far better to go off as the jilted man, sell his weapons and enjoy his money."

"Just because he'd vanished from your life wouldn't mean you could no longer dig."

"The only thing I really yearn to know is why and by whose hand Ian died. And, sadly, Philip is probably the only one who can tell me that."

Softly, Ty touched Isabella's shoulder. "How much do you know about your godfather's will?" he asked.

"He told me, more than once, that I was his sole heir. Just that, really. How I'll deal with all that, I've no idea. I'd supposed Philip would see to it for me."

Ty smiled. "Do you have a will?" he asked.

She nodded. "Until very recently I had nothing much to leave—the little bit my parents left me, a few quid I'd saved—but yes, I do have a will."

"Who is *your* heir, if I may ask?"

"Philip," Isabella whispered.

"How did that happen?" Ty asked. "Isn't it the sort of thing people ordinarily do *after* they get married, not before?"

"We were headed that way."

"Did you suggest it, or did Philip?"

"I did."

Ty hesitated. "Why?"

"It was in response to his generosity, or at least that's how it seemed to me at the time," she said. "We were in Cambridge. We'd driven out for the day from London. Philip had wanted to attend a lecture on disarmament at Trinity, and we had dinner at the Midsummer House. Between those two events, we walked past the house where I'd grown up. Naturally, that stirred memories of childhood, which led to the fact that neither of us had parents who were still living. We were relatively young to say that. And, of course, neither of us had children of our own yet. Anyway, a few days later Philip told me he'd named me in his will. Apart from bequests to a charity or two, I was to be his only heir. It wasn't a fortune, he said, but he'd done well enough in the City as a young man. It hardly mattered, because Philip Frost was nowhere near dying. He'd never been ill a day in his life and had the stamina of a draft horse. What touched me, though, was when he said he'd done it because I was the only person in the world he loved. At the moment I felt the same way about him. And why shouldn't I have done? He seemed a kind, thoughtful and, God knows, a very beautiful man. Even now I'm not ashamed of having fallen for him. Eventually I went to a solicitor and responded in kind. Perhaps it was slightly premature, but it seemed preferable to dying intestate and forfeiting whatever little I had to the government. If it was a setup, it was very elegantly done, a masterpiece."

"Let's hope it wasn't," Ty said, then felt his BlackBerry vibrate.

The red light was still blinking. On the screen were two texts from Oliver, the first reading GHU and the second, sent less than a half a minute later, DELTA.

Ty pressed the encryption key, followed by Oliver's speed-dial number.

"He's on the move again," Oliver said.

"He's probably on his way here," Ty replied. "He'd instructed the secretary to call him when we arrived. How he knew we'd be arriving, when we didn't, I have no idea. He played a hunch, I guess. Anyway, Isabella stalled her as long as she could, but the secretary will have called him by now."

"Not to insult you, but I don't think he's exactly headed your way."

"Why is that?"

"He started on the western side of the basin, as I told you. From there he moved gradually east. Now he's suddenly turned south."

"I wonder what he's looking for," Ty said.

"It's difficult to tell. He retracts the window, stares out at this vessel or that, sometimes with a pair of mini binoculars, then stays there and waits until, when you least expect it and can't figure out why, he goes on."

"He hasn't boarded any of them?"

"He hasn't even got out of his car," Oliver said.

Ty looked at Isabella. "Come on," he said. "We've been had!"

"What are you talking about?" she asked.

"Come, quickly," he demanded.

At the door Ty pressed the panel that should have opened it, but there was no response. He tried it again, but the inner door would not move. He pulled frantically on its enormous brass knob, but the door was sealed fast.

"Hurry!" he shouted. Isabella fled across the massive, encapsulating office toward the long, dim gallery. Ty threw his frame on top of hers as the office exploded behind them, as the intensifying heat and fumes raced toward them, as the flames devoured everything within the cold stone walls.

Finally he managed to raise his phone to his ear. "Oliver," he gasped.

"I could tell you were beginning to get bored," Oliver said, "but were you really that starved for excitement?"

"This is a bad time for jokes," Ty said. "There's a fire. It's got us trapped. We're going to have to come out through one of the gun-emplacement openings."

"You can't go forward? At the far ends of those galleries, more often than not, there are stairs."

"There's no way," Ty said. "The flames have shot through the tunnel. We're pinned into a little recess on pure rock beyond the wooden floor. If we weren't, we'd be dead by now." The ceiling was low and jagged, and he had to stoop as he maneuvered himself around a nineteenth-century cannon to assess the position of the opening. "It's a sheer drop," he said at last, "certainly more than five hundred feet."

"What do you see from there?"

"A runway," Ty said.

"Hold on. We're coming now."

"What about Frost?"

"We'll mind him. The Royal Navy can still do two things at the same time."

The old cannon wagon was fixed to the gallery walls on either side with decorative ropes of black chain. Ty leaned forward and tried to undo the last link of the chain from the large iron hoop on the left side of the wagon, but it was welded in. The chain on the right, which coiled out into the path of the fire, was inaccessible and would be too hot to touch even if it weren't. So he retreated to the emplacement opening and, using only his butterfly knife, began to dislodge its fitted double-glazed window. When he had finished, the new air that suddenly flooded inward brought them a moment of relief from the acrid fumes and thickening smoke but, even as it did, added fuel to the rampaging inferno. Hanging as a curtain before the emplacement were a series of ropes, two of which Ty now spared while cutting the others, then tying them into strands long enough to reach through and several feet below the opening. With bowlines he tied one strand onto each of the ropes he had left dangling.

"Were you a Boy Scout?" Isabella asked as she scrutinized the one Ty gave her, then, with a mixture of gratitude and reluctance, gripped it.

"Yes, and worse," Ty said. "Go on," he urged her. "Wrap it around your wrist a couple of times, like this"—he demonstrated—"to make sure you've got hold of it."

Isabella was quiet and attentive. When she had the rope firmly in her grip, she said, "After you, Captain."

Ty started. "What did you say?" he asked, urging her forward.

"That's your rank, isn't it?"

"Who told you that?"

"No one told me anything, but I've read about you. Who hasn't?"

"Never believe what you read. I don't hold any rank anymore."

"Maybe not officially," she said as she lowered herself against the mountain's flank, "but you're still a soldier."

"Stop talking and concentrate," he said, settling beside her a few feet away.

"I can't," Isabella said. "If I do, I might look down."

Chapter Forty-eight

When Philip Frost, feeling unnatural in the ill-fitting outfit of a middle-class tourist, exited the Great Siege Tunnels, the sunlight startled him. He had been within the mountain for hours, traversing long galleries, navigating the uneven rises of hundreds and hundreds of stone steps in darkness. Near the old *cementerio,* exactly where Andrej had promised it, Philip found the four-year-old Subaru Outback that Andrej had bought secondhand under an assumed name in Cádiz. The car was covered with just enough of summer's dust to render it invisible, a nuance Philip appreciated. He loaded his twin duffel bags into the car's hatch, stretched and got in behind the wheel. Careful to maintain a moderate speed, he drove west on the Devils Tower Road, but at its intersection with Winston Churchill Avenue found himself blocked by traffic. Once the traffic cleared, he proceeded across Winston Churchill Avenue to Ocean Village and the Gibraltar Marina, where he had no difficulty locating the thirty-one-foot *Contender* in its assigned slip. Parking in the public lot as near to the quay as he could, he unloaded the two duffels. Only after he had ensconced himself in the forward cabin, however, did he remove the three gem-laden attaché cases and, with tremendous care, place their contents into a small red chest that had been designed both to float and to accommodate containers of cold drinks. Atop the jewelry he spread a white kitchen towel and atop that a folded plastic bag. He placed a few bottles of water on top of the plastic bag, then returned to the cockpit. The *Contender*'s twin F350 outboards started at the first turn of his key in the ignition. Confirming that his tank was full, Philip set off, without a wake until he'd cleared the marina harbor, across the Bay of Algeciras.

By the time he reached Gibraltar Canyon, he had opened the throttles and was doing thirty knots. Dolphins followed him to port, and closer to shore water-skiers and Jet Skiers sped in high, wide, graceful arcs whose wakes rocked the *Contender* and demanded his attention. Once he reached his destination, he slowed, turned off his boat's engines and quickly dropped anchor. Nearby, a cobalt blue hulled *barco* with butterscotch decks sat easily in the sea, almost dissolving in his sight as he observed it. None of the expensive and cumbersome fiberglass and steel toys that surrounded it could do that, Philip thought, although the *barco* seemed less a fully independent craft than an elaborate skiff. For almost twenty minutes, he stretched himself across the *Contender*'s rear bench seat, remaining still as he absorbed the June sun's perfect warmth and kept watch on the nearby craft.

Still, he was caught unawares when its sole occupant suddenly dove from it into the sea. He heard the loud splash first. Seconds later he spotted the powerful young swimmer surface, then begin an impressive Australian crawl. Philip waited several minutes, until the swimmer had given up doing laps and begun to tread water, before diving into the beckoning Med. Keeping his distance, he commenced several laps of his own. When he had completed the last of these, the other man greeted him, as if on impulse. "Isn't it a glorious day?" he said.

"More glorious than I could have imagined," Philip replied. Gradually they moved closer in the clear blue water, in the manner of strangers who had just met.

When it was obvious that no one was near enough to overhear them, Philip said, "You are Franz?"

"Of course," the young man replied. In the sea, with their wet hair, they might have appeared twins; out of the sea, even more so as, by design, they were wearing identical swim trunks.

Philip smiled. "Are you younger or older than your brother?"

"If you mean Hans, he is my cousin. We are the same age."

"You do look remarkably alike. I'm sure you've been told that before."

"Our mothers are sisters. Their side of our families has particularly strong genes," replied Franz.

Philip nodded. "And you and Hans work together, I gather."

"On occasion," Franz said. "We are employed by the same agency."

"I understand," Philip said. "Are you clear as to your instructions?"

"Completely," Franz told him.

"And you understand both the rewards and, should it come to that, the penalties involved?"

Franz put the tips of his right forefinger and thumb together to signal that, like his cousin, he was okay with Philip's terms. "To tell you the truth, there is not much either of us hasn't seen," he said. "We may look younger than we are, as do you, but we have both been around the block."

"Good," Philip said. "I'm partial to realists."

"Where money is concerned, what other choice is there?"

Philip smiled. "The number I have for you, it remains the same?"

"It does."

"And where is that mobile now?"

"Aboard the *barco*," Franz answered.

"And are you certain that it is waterproof, as was specified?"

"Yes, to a depth of one hundred meters. *Your* man gave it to me."

"I know. I would like, Franz, to offer you a drink."

"Thank you."

"We will have that drink aboard your boat, facing to sea as we do. As you do not have any drink aboard, I will fetch my cooler. It will be a quick drink. When it is over, you will swim back to the *Contender* with your mobile, but the cooler will remain with me."

"It's your cooler," Franz said.

"Indeed it is, and I shall fetch it now," Philip said, taking a first stroke toward the *Contender*.

When he returned, he handed Franz a bottle of Badoit and took one for himself, then closed the lid of the cooler and settled it low and safely in the *barco*'s cockpit.

"Tell me about the life of a model in Berlin," Philip said as they drank. "Is it fun? Or less so as one ages?"

"Less so," Franz said, "as one contemplates the future."

"Aren't most things?" Philip sighed. Men who lived life day to day without a plan to accumulate wealth or power had always struck him as inexplicable, all the more so when they bore such a sharp resemblance to himself. "This particular assignment should buy you and your cousin some time."

"It will buy us both a great deal of time," Franz replied. "You are a very generous man."

"It's kind of you to say so," Philip said, "and it also reminds me of something I forgot."

"Which is?"

"In a duffel in the *Contender*'s cockpit, you will find a very good suit that will fit you. Hans now has one just like it. Keep it."

"Are you sure?"

"I would not have said so otherwise. Now, off you go!"

His face still to the open Med and sunlit, Franz smiled. Then, as he lowered himself from the stern and began his short swim to the *Contender*, Philip assumed the *barco*'s helm. Three minutes later both boats had pulled up anchor and, once more oblivious of each other, were heading for the open sea on widely divergent courses.

Chapter Forty-nine

Ty was not sure how much longer he could hold on as the rope burned the skin at the bases of his fingers and on his palms, tearing the flesh as it filed toward his metacarpal bones. His shoulder, too, felt the strain, so with a sudden surge he released his grip and regained one an inch or so higher, just above one of the hasty bowlines he had tied. When he had succeeded in this maneuver and caught his breath, he looked at Isabella, who was clinging desperately to her rope. "If nothing else," he assured her, "this gives new meaning to the phrase 'hanging by a thread.'"

"Shut up, Ty," she said. "I know you auditioned for the part, but you are *not* James Bond."

"They wanted someone grittier."

"How little they knew!"

"And you're wrong. I didn't audition. I don't anymore."

"A fine point," Isabella told him.

"Agreed," he replied. "It might help if you changed hands."

"Thanks for the advice. I'm sure it would also end the pain if I fell."

"Not now, stop it," Ty said. "Those kinds of thoughts are verboten."

"Are they?" Isabella asked. "Verboten to whom?"

"People who are literally holding on for dear life."

"Only literally?" Isabella replied. "Not metaphorically?"

Ty shook his head. "They're exempt."

At that moment the BlackBerry in his pocket rang.

"Aren't you going to take that?" she asked. "It might be your president."

"He'll call back," Ty said. "They always do."

Above them smoke billowed from the open emplacement. Flames, too, were more visible, approaching the wall with accelerating speed. They both understood that it was only a matter of time before those flames would burn through the ropes upon which their lives depended.

"And why shouldn't he?" Isabella bantered. "I mean, it's never wise to be seen to be *too* available."

Ty hesitated. Soon enough he made out the loudening grind of an industrial motor. Isabella heard it as well but dared not look down. When Ty did, he saw a giraffelike piece of equipment with an unfamiliar Japanese name painted on its torso lumbering across the *cementerio* and up the rough incline.

"What is it?" Isabella asked.

"The cavalry," Ty told her.

"In a chopper?"

He shook his head. "They couldn't get in close enough in a chopper to do anything but get a better view of our demise. Hold on, it's almost over."

"*What* is almost over? This nightmare or our lives?"

"This nightmare, with any luck," Ty said. "Oliver's a good director. He's going to save us in the nick of time."

"With what?" Isabella asked. "A hook and ladder?"

"Hardly," Ty said.

"Some sort of cherry-picker?"

"You've been spoiled. Here it comes right now. He's going to let it down between us. Nice and easy, that's the way. Sweet, Ollie!"

"It is a hook," Isabella said.

"First class was booked. Grab onto it tightly with both hands, one fist above the other, just as if you were on a merry-go-round. Seat yourself on the hook as though it were a horse, and definitely *not* sidesaddle. I'll come behind you."

Without replying, Isabella moved as Ty had instructed, her posture stiff as they were lowered. His hands next to hers on the cool iron hook, his chest against her back, his shoulders wrapping hers, he could feel her rapid heartbeat at last begin to slow as fear subsided.

Once they were safe beside the old *cementerio,* Oliver gave them each a towel and water. There was no time for a change of clothes or rest.

"The Royal Navy just happened to have a piece of equipment like that on hand?" Ty asked incredulously. "That was convenient."

Oliver smiled. "It doesn't exactly belong to the Royal Navy," he admitted.

"Then whose is it?"

"I don't know."

"You stole it?"

"I think 'borrowed' is a much nicer word. I do intend to give it back. Anyway, it was the nearest salvation available."

"You can count on us as character witnesses, Ollie," Isabella promised. She leaned toward him and kissed him on the cheek, then put both hands on Ty's shoulders and kissed his lips.

"Thanks. I'm sure you'll be very convincing," Oliver told her.

"We will be," Isabella said. "I'm a damsel in distress, and Ty's an action hero, after all."

"What have we missed?" Ty asked.

"You mean, apart from a call from the President of the United States?"

"So it really was him," Ty said, reaching for his BlackBerry. "Good for Daphne. I should return his call."

Oliver raised his hand in caution. "I'd give it another minute or two."

"Why?" Ty protested. "I'm all right."

"I know you are," Oliver said, "but Bingo should be calling in any second now, and I think you might want to know what he's come up with—"

"Or hasn't."

"Or hasn't—before you go all the way to the top. A bloke can only ascend Everest so many times."

Ty smiled. "That's good advice," he said. "I'll take it. Where's Philip, incidentally?"

"Still keeping an eagle eye on whatever he's keeping an eagle eye on, still under surveillance."

"Which gives him a nice alibi," Ty concluded. "No doubt he'll say that whoever killed Ian torched his office. He'll probably claim to feel more threatened than anyone. There's a pretty good chance he'll be believed."

Oliver's BlackBerry rang. "Bingo," he said, raising his hand in mini triumph, "I'm going to put you on speaker, is that okay?"

"Where are you?" Bingo asked.

"With Ty and Isabella," Oliver explained.

"But *where* are you with Ty and Isabella?" Bingo pressed. "There seems to be a lot of noise in the background."

"Sorry about that," Oliver said. "We decided to go for a picnic. We can hear you fine. Can you hear us?"

"Well enough, if there's no other choice," Bingo admitted petulantly.

"That's good, because I want them to hear what you have to say. Start where we left off."

"Well, there's good news and bad news," Bingo began.

"Let's have the bad news first," Ty said.

"No," Bingo told him, "because there's so much more of it. The good news boils down to this: That laptop does not appear to have been involved in any wire transfers of the kind we've been looking at. And it's not otherwise connected in any way to anything on our radar. It is registered to a company with an alphabet name, doubtless one of Santal's, rather than to any individual. Who may have had use of it, I can't possibly say. In fact, what we've come up with, in a short time but with a shitload of our resources deployed, suggests that it was used primarily, if not entirely, for personal expenses and records and the like. These weren't always small, but none was sufficiently large to set anyone's jaw dropping."

"Define 'large,'" Oliver said.

Bingo laughed. "That's difficult to say when we're talking about a man like Santal. I don't know, perhaps one million euros?"

"If there were no transfers," Ty inquired, "were there any charges that were otherwise worth noting?"

"Give me an example," Bingo said.

"Whores," Ty said.

Isabella's expression maddened.

"None," Bingo replied, "excepting a transfer to a numbered account in Liechtenstein two days ago."

"Don't jerk me around, Bingo—those firewalls are your field of dreams, and you know it. You already have a name to go with the account. The time's come to pull it out of the hat."

"The bank is called Höchsmann. Where places like it are concerned, I possess no magical powers."

"And why is that?" asked Ty.

Bingo chuckled. "Very little is known about it other than that it exists. It's one of a very high-end and discreet breed we are beginning to encounter more and more often, especially in upmarket financial institutions, which conduct and record their business entirely offline. They've fled the perils of the twenty-first century by retreating to the early twentieth, in some cases the nineteenth."

"How much are we talking about?" Oliver inquired.

"One million, eight hundred sixty-seven thousand, three hundred fifty-seven euros," Bingo replied.

Ty mulled over the number in his mind. "So we have no idea who received the money or what it was being paid for. For all we know, in fact, Santal could have been sending it to himself or to Frost, or vice versa."

"All things are possible. It is not an account that has previously shown up in our surveillance of Philip Frost, however. There *was* one notation next to it in the ledger."

"Keep us in suspense," Ty said. "We've got all the time in the world."

"PDP," Bingo said. "That was the notation."

"Oh, splendid," Ty said. "That's really helpful."

"It sounds like a designer drug," Oliver said.

"Or, more likely, they're someone's initials."

"That's probably right," Isabella said, "*or the PD* could stand for '*puerto deportivo.*'"

Both men studied her. "What makes you say that?"

"Only that it was the abbreviation Ian always used in his itineraries. A *puerto deportivo* is a Spanish port."

"Or a marina," Ty added, "of which there must be hundreds in Spain alone, not to mention in former Spanish colonies."

"I'd bet on Spain," Oliver suggested.

"So would I, but I wonder what the final *P* stands for. There's probably only one way to find out for sure."

"And that would be?"

"Hold on. Let's hear the rest of what Bingo has to say."

"There's not much," Bingo replied. "That particular trail ends there. The other transfers we've been following are still proceeding, including the skimming operation in Vienna. That one, in fact, seems particularly efficient. Moneys park there for a few hours and then, abracadabra, they disappear offline, not necessarily to another bank. Wherever they go, the effect is the same as at Höchsmann. These firms are a hacker's worst nightmare. I mean, in today's world if something's not virtual, it's not real."

"You said two days ago," Ty repeated, then looked at Oliver. "You have Luke Claussen's number on your phone, don't you?"

"I should," Oliver said. "Yeah, here it is."

"Call him," Ty said. "Just in case, Bingo, can you or one of your team also check every port authority between Naples and here to see if the *Wayfarer* may have made an unscheduled stop two days ago?"

"Do you want to give me odds?" Oliver asked.

"I can't count that high," said Ty.

"I've got Luke Claussen on the phone," Oliver said a few seconds later.

"Good. Ask him."

Oliver nodded. Into his phone he said, "Is it possible that the *Wayfarer* made an unscheduled stop in the past week?"

"*Un*scheduled?" Luke Claussen repeated. "The *Wayfarer* is the one ship whose itinerary I do know pretty well by heart, but as for an unscheduled stop, honestly, I don't know the answer offhand. I can certainly find it out. Do you want to hold on, or should I call you back?"

"Happy to hold on," Oliver told him.

While they waited for confirmation from Luke or Bingo, Ty said, "We know the warheads went off, then back on again in Naples. We also know that the financial arrangements for their sale are going ahead. Philip appears to be awaiting them on Gib, but why would he be so obvious about it? What if they *aren't* here and that *isn't* Philip your guys have been watching? If there does turn out to have been an unscheduled stop, the warheads will almost surely have gone ashore there, been placed on other transport, then been brought to somewhere not too far away from here until the transfer is ready to be made."

"The Med's a big place," Isabella said. "What makes you so sure they are near here?"

"When was the last time anyone had a good, unmistakable look at Philip?" Ty asked. "Not in his car but up close."

Oliver considered the question. "When he went into Santal's office this morning, I suppose."

"That would have been shortly after he left us on *Surpass*," Ty said. "The man we had breakfast with was definitely Philip. So was the man who entered his office. But the man who exited it, then got into his car and has since been touring the harbor staring hither and yon, has to be a ringer."

"We could run facial recognition," Oliver suggested.

"Too late for that," Ty said. "Better to have the local authorities pick him up on some pretext."

"You still haven't answered my question," Isabella said.

"Why are the warheads nearby? Because Philip's nearby," Ty replied, "and he wouldn't risk crossing any border with the gems he stole from *Surpass.*"

"There you go with another leap. How do you know he took them? If you remember, we escaped with our lives on the submarine. We didn't go back to Vanilla, much less to the vault."

Ty smiled. "Do you really believe he would have left them behind?"

"Well, it's certainly possible," Isabella said. "Don't forget, he hadn't seen those pictures of us yet."

"But Philip harbored suspicions—about me, at any rate. If he hadn't, he wouldn't have sent in those unconvincing goons. And because he harbored them, he would have taken precautions. You can't tell me he's not a man who believes, first and foremost, in precautions."

"Touché," Isabella said.

"If you have any lingering doubts, call him. His phone won't be on. Probably it hasn't been since before he skulked out of Ian's office. Your instincts told you the truth. We know that now. Philip had already made his decision, packed up, and gone invisible."

"Quiet," Oliver said suddenly, then, "Yes, hello, Luke. I'm still here."

Ty and Isabella studied Oliver as he listened. After less than a minute, he looked back up at them and said, "It wasn't on the published schedule, of course, but you're right, *Wayfarer* did encounter a propeller problem en route from Naples to Gib—"

"A propeller problem," Ty repeated, inflecting the phrase as if the very notion were preposterous.

"It has been known to happen," Oliver said, "although rarely so conveniently. Anyway, as you suggested, the ship did put into port two days ago."

"Which port?" Ty asked.

"Palma, Majorca," Oliver said.

"And what's Palma known for?"

"It's the marine servicing center of the Med," Oliver said. "It's full of dry docks and moorings, shipbuilders and repairers, chandleries and brokers. Everyone and his uncle is a broker. Any sort of boat or ship you're looking for you can buy or sell or charter in Majorca."

"That's right," Ty said, "and do you know what else it is? It's a *puerto deportivo*."

Oliver smiled. "Luke says there is no record of cargo being loaded or offloaded there."

"Oh, I'm sure of that!" Ty exclaimed. "There never was and never will be. Whatever ship or ships, boat or boats those funds bought will be as invisible as the money that bought them."

"Thanks, Luke," Oliver said.

"From all of us!" Ty called out, in a voice loud enough to reach the mouthpiece of Oliver's open phone.

"We're going to need aerial surveillance and all kinds of support in one hell of a hurry," Oliver said as soon as he had disconnected.

"Indeed we are," Ty agreed, "but we're also going to need a better idea of what we're looking for before we institute a search. You've seen how many boats there are on the water, just around here?"

"And there are even more than usual at the moment," Oliver said.

"Why do you say that?" Isabella asked.

Oliver pointed to the enormous green-and-white marquees flapping in the strong breeze on the mainland shore.

"Ah, the La Línea Boat Show," Isabella observed, in a tone that suggested she had been there more than once.

"Everyone at HQ's been chattering about it," Oliver told her. "We need to zoom in, but we don't have a lens or even a target. What do you suggest, Ty?"

"Even if we're lucky and even though we can eliminate any that are under a certain size, it will require days to track down the vessel or vessels we're looking for. That's too long. And we can't initiate a ship-by-ship search unless we want to bet the fate of the world on our coming up with an ace-high straight flush on the first inspection. If we don't, we'll succeed only in alerting Philip so that he can then slip quietly away. I suppose we could quarantine Gib Harbor, but how can we be sure the vessels are really in Gib Harbor rather than Algeria or Tunisia or you name it? And if we did that and they weren't there, they'd soon find their way to wherever they *are* going."

"Maybe they're not going anywhere right now. Maybe Philip's planning to hold on to them for a while," Isabella suggested.

"Not likely," Oliver told her. "They're far too hot to handle, and there's too much money moving for that to be the case."

"You're right," Ty said. "It's Philip's show now, but Ian wrote the original script, and Ian was a broker, not a long-term investor."

"I don't want to ruin your day," Oliver said, "but there is another possibility."

"It's already been ruined," Ty told him. "Go ahead. What is it?"

"Just because Majorca is famous for boating, that doesn't mean they bought a boat. It could have been a plane or planes."

"That *is* reassuring," Ty said.

"Maybe not, but it's true."

"Look on the bright side," Isabella said. "Majorca's an island. So we can rule out cars, lorries and trains."

"As I see it," Ty said, "if Philip Frost has a weakness, it's that he's a perfectionist who can't abide loose ends. Whenever one appears, his instinct is to tie it up. We're going to have to tear at the fabric of his deal in a way that will force him into actions he hadn't expected or planned. And we're going to have to be alert to them."

"So *that's* all there is to it," Oliver said.

"Not quite," Ty said. "We have to do it all in the next few hours."

"Not a problem," Oliver replied, "but we'd better get rolling, and you'd better call the President."

"I'll do that on the way," Ty told him. "We Americans can also multitask."

Chapter Fifty

"The President," **announced the** White House operator as she put through Ty's call.

It took almost no time for Garland White to come onto the line. "Hello, Ty," he said. "What can I do for you? Whatever it is, my daughter sensed it must be urgent."

"Daphne was right," Ty replied. "It couldn't be more so, Mr. President." He drew a deep breath. They were in a Royal Navy Land Rover racing toward the dockyard at the waterfront. "Forgive me," he said. "It's been a long day."

"And it isn't over? Is that what you are trying to tell me," the President replied.

"Yes, sir," Ty said. "In a way it's just begun."

"Welcome to politics."

"I'm not suited to politics," Ty said.

"Really?" said Garland White. "I would have thought you'd be a natural. If I was mistaken, count yourself fortunate. Go ahead, Ty, shoot!"

"As I'm sure you've heard, your suppositions do appear to have been correct, but it's not going to be easy to find the warheads. Even with the combined force of the British and Spanish navies, the Sixth Fleet and every radiation sensor in Europe, it will be almost impossible to locate them without giving ourselves away. You heard that the senior partner was murdered?"

"I did," said the President.

"Dr. Kenneth told us you had rejected the idea of letting the geeks loose on Santal's and Frost's bank transfers."

"That's true. Not only would it be unconstitutional and a clear violation of the Fourth Amendment, but I've been convinced that such action could well—indeed *would*—undermine faith in the sanctity of the international banking system and thus risk putting an already fragile world economy on life support."

"Not if it's done correctly," Ty said.

"You're very accomplished in many fields," the President replied. "I didn't realize economics and cyber-warfare were among them."

"They are not, but you know what Albert Einstein said: 'Imagination is more important than knowledge.'"

Garland White laughed. "What do you propose? How can I help you when no one else can?"

Ty exhaled. "I don't want to put you in the position of having to balance a flutter in the world's economy against the survival of its cities or the millions of people who live in them, even though to me it's not a close call."

"Don't worry. You're doing nothing of the kind. And I agree with you. It wouldn't be a close decision *if* there were a guarantee that whatever stunts the geeks pulled off would work, but there isn't. In fact, it's the remotest of long shots."

"As I understand it, the geeks are contractors."

"They are contractors with one client," said Garland White.

"I would like you to release them from that exclusivity. Temporarily, of course."

"Who else would they be working for?"

"Me," Ty said. "At the same time, I would like you to instruct the various NATO commanders in the area that they are to give Oliver Molyneux whatever other more conventional resources he feels he needs. He may have to move quickly."

"You've got that," said the President.

"What about loosening the reins on the geeks?"

"That depends upon what you plan to do with them."

"Mr. President," Ty asked, "do you really want to know?"

Garland White hesitated. "I'll have hell to pay with George Kenneth, not to mention others in my administration and elsewhere, especially on Wall Street. But I'm damned if I do and damned if I don't."

"It's the right thing to do," Ty said.

"What you mean is that if it *works* it will be seen as having been the right thing to do."

"Mr. President, contrary to the impression my military record may have given you, I have always hated fighting. But if there is one thing I hate more, it's fighting with one hand tied behind my back. We've done too much of that. If we don't use everything we have in our arsenal, sir, and do it now, those warheads are going to escape."

"I'm betting more on you than any studio ever has," Garland White observed.

"We both know what an understatement that is."

"Are you going to pay them?"

"In some currency," Ty said.

"Well, it's your money, I suppose."

"Easy come, easy go," Ty said.

At the dockyard Oliver vaunted jauntily out of the Land Rover, almost like Peter O'Toole in *Lawrence of Arabia,* Ty thought. "I'll catch you up at HQ," he said. "I want to check on things here first. We're going to require every high-speed patrol boat and flat-bottomed inflatable we can get our hands on. You'll check in with the airfield?"

"Better than that," Ty said, "I'll get the admiral to do it. I'm going to need him to put some drones in the air and to download in real time from the satellites."

"It was a short conversation," Oliver said. "Do you think White meant to authorize all that?"

Once he had shifted into the driver's seat, Ty gave an affirmative nod. "Implicitly," he answered.

"What more can a man ask for?"

"We've got to get this right," Ty said. "My dad always said, 'There are many wrong ways to do the right thing—'"

"'But no right way to do the wrong thing,'" Oliver chimed in, completing the maxim.

"The last part's Frost's problem," Ty said.

Giles Cotton was on the telephone when Ty arrived. "We meet again," he said, "under rather different circumstances."

"Yes, I'm sorry for that part of it," Ty said, "and I am sorry about the loss of your friend Ian."

Giles Cotton issued a faint smile. "He was probably the most intriguing man I've ever met, but I always thought better of him than this."

"He paid the price," Ty said.

"Sadly," said Admiral Cotton. "The person I was speaking to when you arrived just now was the Supreme Commander of NATO."

"That was fast," Ty said.

"Apparently you and Molyneux are to have the run of things. As far as this whole business is concerned, the two of you are in charge."

"Whatever must be done will be done through you," Ty demurred. "We will not disturb the chain of command."

"I appreciate that. Molyneux's involvement doesn't surprise me. Yours, I must admit, does."

"It surprises me, too."

Ty followed the admiral down the hall to the cool, interior room in which Bingo sat before two levels of LED screens arranged in a crescent. On the three upper central of these were the faces of Delilah Mirador, Jonty Patel and Nevada Smith.

"Don't worry," Bingo said. "They can't see you, and as long as you stay out of the cone whose borders you see painted on the floor in bright yellow, they won't. Nor will they be able to hear you until I turn the audio back on. Of course, I realize that your voice is almost as famous as your face. But as long as you speak into *this* microphone, it will be unrecognizable."

"Thanks," Ty said. "I'm sure it would be safe even if they knew."

"It would," Bingo said, "but they have no need to know."

"Shall we start?"

"Counting down," Bingo said. "Five, four, three, two, one . . . Lights, camera, action!

"Good morning, evening, afternoon, boys and girl," he continued as the images of his colleagues unfroze. "As I suggested, we've got a variation of the proverbial needle-in-a-haystack problem. We have to find, and effing quickly, a moving object in this area of the Med—an object, not a person. It is very likely to be a boat or a barge, though it could be a plane or both. It is probably bound south, but not necessarily so. It might reveal itself to radiation sensors, but depending upon how its storage hold has been constructed and its cargo packed, it might not. Come on, children, you're paid for your bright ideas!"

"Is there a minimum size?" inquired Nevada Smith.

"My omission, sorry," Bingo said. "It would have to be large enough to carry a crate at least four by two by two meters. It might help to visualize a crate that could accommodate a grand piano."

"Or a nuclear warhead?" speculated Delilah Mirador.

"That would be of about the same size, yes," Bingo agreed.

"We don't know from what direction it has come?" asked Jonty Patel.

"Not with a high degree of certainty. Two days ago it would have been in Majorca—in Palma, to be exact."

"We could rewind the satellite coverage, see what the drones saw if any were doing practice runs off the fleet."

"Let's do that," Bingo said. "Nevada, will you take care of it?"

"Done," Nevada said.

"Great, but we'll still be swamped," Delilah said, "and a lot of the recognition won't be exact. Sure, we'll narrow down the field, but we won't find it, not in time."

"Precisely my thought," Bingo said. "We need to lure it our way, or at least out of its routine."

"But how?" inquired Ty.

"Whose voice is that?"

"The brass," Bingo explained. "Again, I'm forgetting my manners."

"Well, hello there," said Delilah.

"Yes, hello there," Jonty and Nevada echoed, almost in unison.

"Is he camera shy?" asked Delilah.

"Just insecure," Bingo replied. "He doesn't think he's photogenic."

"You can't fool us that easily," she said. "A spook's a spook."

Bingo paused until the matter dropped. "Can we answer his question?"

"What do we know not about the cargo but about the personality involved?"

"We're talking about the same personality we have been all along," Bingo said.

"Philip Frost or Ian Santal?" asked Jonty.

"Santal's dead," Bingo said.

"Did you see the body?"

"It burned."

"Are you certain?"

"No, but it is a safe assumption. It's Philip Frost we want to provoke."

"How hard can that be?" Jonty asked.

"Extremely," Delilah said. "We have gloves on, remember?"

"They've been taken off," Bingo said.

"Really?" asked Delilah. "By whom?"

"They've been taken off," Bingo repeated evasively.

"Use your imagination! They were put on by Kenneth. Only one person could remove them," Nevada Smith said.

"Let's keep the ideas rolling," Ty said.

"Here's the protocol," Jonty said. "We rewind the satellite and download all drone data. What we're left with, just as Delilah suggested, will be our field, except that we'll add to it everything we pick up from port and airport logs. Once that's been done—"

"How long will it take?" Ty asked.

"Longer than you'd like, but less time than you think," Bingo said, "with help from Fort Meade and GCHQ Cheltenham."

Jonty resumed. "As I was saying, once that's been done, we'll begin to send out stimuli. Do I have a free hand with the lords of finance?"

"You do," Ty said. "Don't anyone ask again. Just do what you have to."

"This is great," Jonty said, with an incandescent smile. "All the thrill of bank robbery with none of the consequences."

Ty laughed. "Maybe for you," he said.

"Like, am I free to park money in my account? Think how great that would be for my street cred—well, at least with my bank manager."

"Calm down, Jonty," Delilah said. "The trick is going to be to make our friends suspect each other. Most of all we want to engender suspicion in Frost, but to the extent that we can make the others just as wary, they'll be bound to act in ways that will trigger the desired reactions from him. Desired from our point of view, that is—dangerous from his. As soon as we can, we take a snapshot. Then, once we're positive our boundaries are actually wide enough, we put it into motion. Slow motion at first, then gradually work up to real time. Bingo, you have access to the beta CVP we were playing with a while ago, right?"

"How could I not?" Bingo demanded. "I wrote it."

"Like most authors, you love your own writing, don't you?" Nevada said.

"No, not always, but in this instance yes, damn it, I do. I love my beta CVP. Tell me there's better wanking material anywhere out there! If anyone would know, it would be you."

Ty chuckled to himself. The longer he listened to these geeks, the more they reminded him of certain players in the movie business. "What exactly is a beta CVP?" he inquired.

"It's a hybrid derivative of both facial-recognition software and aggressive-driver imaging. It finds not an image or a form but a pattern of movement. Once it has established that pattern, it begins to look for deviations from it, especially inexplicable deviations. Say you're walking down a street that runs north by northwest for two blocks and then suddenly you turn east. The CVP, which stands for 'characteristic variation program,' will pick that up."

"And apparently," said Delilah, "impart a thrill the likes of which you may never before have experienced."

"Can we let that go?" Bingo said.

"Before it sticks?" asked Nevada.

"That would be nice," replied Bingo, turning at once back to Ty. "Now, if it's just you who is walking, maybe it's not such a big effing deal, right? But if we're looking for the one man or woman in a large crowd whose behavior is out of character, then it's often a different story. Say you're in Shanghai and you're headed from the Bund to Pudong. You might want to watch the screen on the lower left. That's what's on it. There must be a hundred ways to make that trip, many of them zigzags. The program knows them all, and it won't target you for choosing one or another or even changing between two different routes, but if you've been traveling to wherever long enough for the CVP to assume that's where you're going and then out of nowhere you decide to turn around or go somewhere else or you change your rate of advance appreciably, that's when it lights you up. You're supposed to be right-handed, but you pick up a pen with your left—the same story."

Ty considered the plan. "So you propose to prod him with one program and do surveillance of him with another?"

"Simultaneously," Delilah said. "It's simply a matter of superimposing one lens upon another, then determining what we've trapped in the intersection of both sets of data."

"How much have we learned about the people on the other end of Frost's transactions?" Ty asked.

"Alphabet soup again," Bingo explained. "By and large their real names never make it online, and even when they do, that's seldom all there is to the story. There's a whole sorry cast of in-betweens out there, from the A-list to the penny-ante. From time to time, we have our suspicions, which are eventually confirmed or contradicted, but whoever they are, they're just one more set of hands through which bad things pass on their way to the really dangerous fellows, most of whose names are household words. Not even Santal would have dealt directly with them. It would have been far too dangerous for both parties. No, Frost's clients will be mere cutouts, über-hedgies, in-and-out types. Only instead of some broad, it's the world they fuck."

"We haven't talked about one thing," Ty said.

"The odds," Nevada shot back.

"You read my mind," Ty said. "Do we have any idea of the odds of a cyber-search like this actually working?"

"How could we? We're playing on a far frontier," Jonty said. "And on far frontiers there is never enough history to draw that kind of conclusion."

"That's what I thought you would say."

"It's still our best shot," Bingo said.

"We're long past the point of being able to reconsider that question," Ty said, "but you know the old military maxim, don't you? 'No battle plan ever survives contact with the enemy.' So right now it's up to you and Lady Luck."

Bingo smiled. "Luck's where you come in," he said.

Chapter Fifty-one

Philip steeled himself. For a man of his age, he had been required to make many fateful decisions, yet never before so many in one day. Had he made them with admirable resolve, or had impetuousness gotten the better of him at any stage? It was still too soon to tell, but as the summer afternoon lengthened, he felt not only the thrill of the impending moment but an apprehension he could not identify. Before him in the pilot house of one of the two trawlers that he, with Ian's sanction, had had fitted in Majorca sat a Sony VAIO laptop, its seventeen-inch screen alight and subdivided into graphs, much like the home screen of a Bloomberg machine. Unlike those on a Bloomberg machine, however, the functions expressed on these graphs reflected highly privileged information. These were, in fact, functions Philip had designed himself to express not merely the times and amounts of the myriad wire transfers that were now under way but the orderliness with which they were being completed. Suspicious by nature, he was especially afraid of shenanigans now that his own life and future were on the line and so had conceived an imaginative list of variables that, when put into equations elaborated from the basic $y = f(x)$ structure of calculus, would alert him to trouble in time to adjust his plans and resolve it.

So far no such alert had been raised, but forty-seven minutes ago there'd been a thirty-second hiccup when one of the subdivided screens had frozen. Doubtless it had had to do with transmission or reception, he'd told himself. They were at sea, after all. Still, the fear that it might, just possibly, have been more than either of those had begun to torment him.

For the moment the Mediterranean was still, although a front was predicted to bring unsettled weather overnight. Because of this, Philip was tempted to advance his schedule, set sail sooner. The schedule had been carefully worked out, taking into account all imaginable contingencies. The trawlers were seaworthy. To alter such an intricate plan at this stage would risk the introduction of unknown factors. To find himself closer to Arabia than Europe even a moment before the funds were where they should be would be to chance fate and human nature with an abandon only a fool would summon.

So long as the functions reported on the laptop were satisfactory, with money flowing toward him in millions of small, innocent-seeming increments, he decided he would not deviate from his course. The arrangement, of his devising, still struck him as ingenious. A deposit of one-third of the total was his already. A second third would be held by his various banks in various lockboxes, either to be transferred to his accounts when the warheads had crossed over the halfway mark, defined as the north latitude of 35.575242 degrees, or returned to their originators if for any reason the warheads had not done so by a time certain. The final third of his new fortune would be released to his accounts from the same or similar lockboxes at the very instant the warheads had passed inspection and changed hands. An encrypted code to authorize such releases had already been provided to the purchasers.

The ever more brilliant western sky drew his attention, turning his thoughts to the Atlantic and, across it, to Washington. He wondered how the government there would react—indeed, *if* it would. It might be a long time, or no time, before the American security services found out. Even then it would take them longer to trace the weapons back through Europe to the Strait of Kerch, at which point suspicion might begin to settle on him or, more likely, the authorities would ironically seek his help. Confident that he possessed the wit, charm and reputation to placate—and would by then possess the resources to fend off—anyone, Philip was prepared for either eventuality.

Would he miss *Surpass*? In a way, as one mourned the loss of any luxury, he expected he would, but he was not meant to live on the sea or against a canvas of incessant hospitality. His psyche was more private, more selfish and, in its cool insistence upon logic, perhaps even more rational than Ian's. Where would he live? In Switzerland, probably, for Switzerland was the most orderly state in the world. And perhaps he would have an estate somewhere in eastern Germany, where the wild forests only appeared to have been tamed.

His mobile rang. It was a new and, as usual, temporary telephone. He knew that it was Andrej, for Andrej was the only one who had its number. "Yes," Philip said.

"I don't know if you've heard. Tragically, there was a fire at Mr. Santal's former office," Andrej said.

"No," Philip said, his voice aghast. "I hadn't. When?"

"Not very long ago," Andrej said softly. "I just heard about it from someone who had seen the smoke. My first thought was, what a run of bad luck. My second was that someone really was out to get him."

"It would certainly appear that way," Philip said. "I hope no one was hurt."

"I don't know about any of the staff," Andrej replied, "but you will be much relieved to know that your friend Miss Cavill and that actor—what's his name?"

"Ty Hunter," Philip said, struggling to disguise the rising irritation in his voice.

"Yes. In any event, fortunately, they did manage to escape. I don't know what they were doing there, but according to the person I spoke to, theirs was a feat of real derring-do. Apparently they were hanging by ropes from one of those old gun emplacements until they were rescued. I am sure it will be on television."

"They had probably come to see me," Philip said. "I'd been trying to help Isabella."

"I know you are close to her. That's why I thought you'd want to know."

"I *was* very close to her," Philip said, with feigned melancholy. "I'm not sure if I am anymore. That's her call. But thank you for telling me. I'm sorry, but much relieved."

"You are most welcome."

"And how are you, by the way?" Philip inquired as an afterthought.

"One has a plan and one sticks to it." Andrej sighed. "That's how I am: on course to die, like everyone else, but hoping for a modicum of fun in the meantime."

"Oh, yes indeed, concentrate on the fun," Philip advised, then switched off his phone. This was a complication he had not expected but was nevertheless prepared for. If, eventually, he were to be confronted by Isabella, he would shatter her with a simple narrative. He had not received her call nor contacted her because he himself had been kidnapped by the same Slavs who had attempted to sequester her and Ty. He had no idea for whom they were working, but it was no secret that a man in Ian's position would have enemies, not all of them known to him. As for Ty, Philip would dismiss him and his theories, if there were any, with flattery. What was an actor but a fabulist, weaving imaginary tales? The more he thought about it, the more convinced he became that the ploy could work. At the end of the day, Isabella was a European. So was Philip. Ty was something else, dazzling but as transient and unstable as a comet. He might have a face and a form ripe for infatuation, the careless investment of young girls' idle dreams, but surely not for commitment.

Philip relished his newly hopeful thoughts, discerning not only danger now but opportunity in the still sea through which the trawler slowly sailed. Only when, from the corner of his eye, he registered unfamiliar motion did he return his full attention to the transaction at hand.

One of the functions displayed on his laptop had frozen. He stared at it as if his gaze might correct a false image, but instead of unfreezing, the function began to reverse itself. Did this mean that money was being taken from him or simply put into escrow until the second and final payments were made? Uncertain, he watched attentively. Again the function froze. Again it reversed itself. In the right angle where the x and y axes intersected, when he right-clicked on the touch pad, a small green neon wheel cycled rapidly backward, signaling, he feared, the unraveling of his expectations. Then it stopped, jerked forward as if to park, and that square of the screen went momentarily dark. When, with a jolt, it subsequently restored itself, it was back to where it both had and should have been, and Philip breathed a sigh of relief.

It was not to be a long sigh, however, for another screen, displaying yet another function, suddenly began to tremble, showing a rate of transfer at first accelerating far beyond what was prudent, then halting entirely.

For ten minutes that status quo prevailed.

Disciplining his agitation, Philip stood. "I'm going for a breath of fresh air," he informed the captain, a sullen veteran of North Sea rigs and also one of the Slav mercenaries who had remained with him.

When he returned to the pilot house, he was relieved to discover absolutely no changes on his computer's display, but shortly thereafter, one by one, not in sequence but randomly, all the functions began to misbehave, to shiver, or fast-forward, or rewind at intemperate, unsteady speeds. He lowered the special program, called up Google, which was at once steady as a rock. So was the *Financial Times*. No, Philip concluded, the problem resided in neither his software nor his device. Someone—perhaps one or both of the Al-Dosari twins, or al-Awad, or a rogue banker, or perhaps, God forbid, a government—was toying with his accounts. He had to resign himself to that probability quickly, and he had to act in light of it.

He immediately picked up his mobile and telephoned Andrej. "I think it's time to let the dog out," he instructed.

"He hasn't been asking to go. Are you certain?"

"Trust me. He's bound to give you problems later if you don't."

No sooner had Philip disconnected than Andrej pressed in a number that activated a small motor that only partially retracted the lid of a lead box he had the day before managed to place in the hold of an Airbus 330 cargo plane on the tarmac of Gibraltar Airport. He then telephoned the leader of the team of Slavs who had taken up position in the galleries above Ian Santal's office. "Is Mrs. Potyomkin there?" he inquired, according to a preestablished code.

"I'm afraid she's not here at the moment," answered the gravel-voiced mercenary, "but she is expected."

"Suppose I call back in a quarter of an hour, then?"

"Please. That should be fine."

Chapter Fifty-two

"**The bastard's got titanium** nerves, I'll give him that," Jonty Patel said. "We've been pulling his chain for over an hour, and he's still steady as you go. I wouldn't be."

"Or he isn't and the CVP's missed it," Ty said.

"I'm not sure what he's seeing," Delilah said.

"They have to be functions of some sort," said Nevada Smith. "I'm assuming he doesn't possess our capabilities, because, as far as we know, no one else does. So there's no way he'd be able to penetrate and then deencrypt data from so many different financial institutions. No, what he'd have to do would be to rely on his access to his own accounts, meaning de Novo's and those of whatever other nominees he has, and to be watching not only their balances but— somehow, according to some algorithm—the habits of those who are depositing into them. I say we go for broke. If we can't arouse his suspicions to the point where he'll act on them, let's make him *sure* he's being played."

"You mean, steal everything?" asked Jonty gleefully. "I agree. That ought to do it."

"Actually, more now you see it, now you don't," Nevada said. "We can't keep it, of course. We'd be thieves if we did. Eventually they'd have to prosecute us, and they would, somewhere. And, what's just as important, our cover story wouldn't hold up."

"Regrettable but true," replied Jonty. "Where shall we park it?"

"In Bingo's current account," suggested Delilah.

"Hardly fair," said Jonty, "when it could do so much more good in mine."

"The problem is, I doubt that Frost's afraid of either of you," Delilah ventured. "He *will* be afraid of the people who gave it to him, though."

"Let's go, then," Jonty acceded grudgingly.

But before Bingo could reply, Admiral Cotton appeared at the side door of the geeks' office. Stepping forward, he beckoned both Bingo and Ty toward him. "We have a lead," he said quietly. "One of the radiation sensors at Gib Airport has picked up something from one of the cargo planes."

"I'm on my way," Ty said.

"Not yet," said Giles Cotton. "Let the hazmat crew go in first. In the meantime there are both police and military cordons around the plane and all air traffic's been grounded."

"Do you want us to hold off?" Bingo queried.

Giles Cotton looked at Ty.

"I don't really see any reason for you to," Ty said. "Do you, Admiral?"

"No," the admiral told Bingo. "Keep doing what you're doing."

When Bingo stepped back into the camera's line of sight, Ty followed Giles Cotton into the corridor. "Was it about to take off?"

"No," the admiral replied. "Which is surprising, isn't it?"

"Unless Frost was following a hide-in-plain-sight strategy," Ty said. "Does Oliver know?"

"He does. I spoke with him just before I came to find you. Until we hear back from the hazmat team, he's staying put organizing the task force."

"How long will it take for us to hear back?"

"I shouldn't think very long. In fact, this may be the word we're waiting for," Giles Cotton replied, directing Ty's attention to the rapid approach of a young naval aide.

The plane in question had been parked as far from the new civilian terminal as was possible without trespassing on the domain of the Royal Air Force. Surrounding it now were members of that air force's police detail, as well as of the local constabulary, their vehicles arranged like the points of a compass at a safe distance from the aircraft. Only the van bearing the hazmat crew was permitted through the perimeter. It halted forward of the plane's wing assembly. Four men emerged from it, anonymous in camouflage Type 1 Nuclear Biological Chemical suits. The last of these proceeded swiftly to a set of portable stairs that had recently been abandoned by a departing flight, then drove the stairs across fifty meters of restricted tarmac to the forward cabin door of the Airbus. When it was in place, the others followed him up it. He had just withdrawn the door's recessed handle and begun to turn it counterclockwise when a sharp backfire resounded in the distance. The men on the lower steps turned at once, unsure what it was or where it had come from. A second backfire followed, then a third, a fourth and a fifth. The first round from the Heckler & Koch PSG1 struck the hazmat worker at the door in the right shoulder. He stumbled against the stair rail before crumpling onto the top landing. The third entered the man one step from the bottom on the ladder at the base of his neck as they fled for cover. Within a minute he was dead.

"What in God's name is going on?" Admiral Cotton raged when informed of the sniper's shots by his lieutenant. "Do they have any idea where the gunfire originated?"

"It's too soon for forensics," the lieutenant said.

"I know, I know."

The wail of sirens rose outside, piercing even NATO's mountain fortress.

"I expect this answers our question," Admiral Cotton declared. "Someone had better get hold of Molyneux."

"Of course," Ty said, "but I'm not so sure it answers anything. Why would you store warheads, if you had them, on a high-security tarmac where access would be difficult at the best of times and where, if you aroused the least curiosity coming and going, you'd be outnumbered by a whole garrison?"

"Because it's the only airfield in the area. Because air is how you brought them in, and air's how you mean to take them out. It's hardly long-term storage we're talking about."

"That could be," Ty said. "I'm just not convinced."

"Let me ask you this," Giles Cotton said. "Presuming you had imported them by air, why would you take the risk of transferring them first to ground, then to sea transport?"

Ty paused. "I wouldn't."

"Is the sniper still firing?" Cotton asked his aide, who detached his mobile from his belt and repeated the question into it.

"No," the lieutenant replied finally, "and the airport's locked down."

"As it damn well should be!" exclaimed the admiral. "How many shots were fired in total? Does anyone know?"

"Yes, five," the lieutenant answered.

"So far," said Giles Cotton.

"Why would he stop at five?" Ty wondered aloud.

"You're asking me?"

"If he meant to head off a search, even temporarily, he—or they—would need to fire many more rounds than that."

"Temporarily is the best they could achieve," Admiral Cotton mulled, his expression signaling a sudden appreciation of Ty's perspective. "You'd need an army to take the airfield."

"That's correct, sir. And some help from a navy and an air force, too."

"You think it's a diversion."

"It's possible. What isn't possible is for a plane without a pilot to get off the ground. So we've got some time."

"Unless there are more shots," the admiral said. "It's difficult to imagine where the bastard's hidden himself."

"Not that difficult," Ty said. "You've been to Ian Santal's office."

"Indeed I have."

"I was there earlier today, as you know." Ty smiled. "I looked out the window behind his desk smack at the airport. There are galleries all through that mountain, many of them left over from the Great Siege, I'm told. I realize they're closed to the public, but you and I both know that that's only in theory. From Ian's office, and no doubt from other points of entry as well, a sniper could make his way up or down the Rock to just the vantage point he required. He wouldn't be seen. He couldn't be hit. It wouldn't matter how far his shell casings flew. And he could almost certainly get away before attention turned to those galleries and that emplacement. He'd have multiple routes of escape, *if* he didn't linger."

Giles Cotton nodded. "All too true," he said, "but if the objective is merely diversion, what about those positive readings from the radiation sensors?"

Ty shrugged. "Your guess is as good as mine," he said. "We'll find out eventually, but not until they secure the whole site, throw a tent over it and send in an armored crew, which could take . . . what? At least an hour, probably a hell of a lot longer."

"I'm sorry to interrupt, Admiral," Isabella said, coming into the corridor from Bingo's office. "Bingo's looking for Ty. He says it's urgent."

"I'll come with you," Giles Cotton said.

"Here's news you can use in a nutshell," Bingo said. "Bingo Chen wins the Nobel Prize."

"There is no Nobel Prize for computer science," Nevada Smith interjected.

"Or even for mathematics," added Delilah Mirador.

"And it's not *really* physics," commiserated Jonty Patel.

"Peace, then," Bingo said. "They can give me the Nobel Peace Prize. Watch this! On the lower central screen, which is formatted to 1080p, is a real-time satellite picture of the seas around Gibraltar, extending six miles out from the coast of Spain as far north as Málaga, as far west as Tarifa and the straits and including the Bay of Algeciras. Over it I have dropped the soon-to-be-prizewinning, fortune-making CVP filter. One feature of the CVP is its ability to display timelines. The one you're looking at records the stimuli we've put out there since we began this operation. Remember, the image beneath the timeline will in all cases correspond to that timeline. Let me put it into motion."

Ty studied the scene, which reminded him of the focus groups that studios sometimes did after sneak previews of their movies.

"Heavy traffic at sea," Bingo continued, "and why not, on a beautiful day at the peak of summer? So here's the way our little corner of the Med looked when we set off on our adventure. We teased. No change. Correction, one boat did suddenly change course, but on inspection it was below our minimum capacity constraint and had turned around because it was running out of petrol."

"You followed it?" Isabella asked.

"The satellite is naturally nosy," Bingo said. "Moving forward, we raised our tease to a tickle. In the aftermath of that, we waited and kept waiting for a reaction, but once again none came. Obviously we hadn't catalyzed any second thoughts. Next we advanced to titillation. At this we were both more clever and insistent, but not sufficiently. In hindsight I suppose we should have done more. Remember that old question 'How do you titillate an ocelot?' Answer: 'Oscillate its tit a lot.'"

Isabella rolled her eyes. "You're too much, Bingo," she said.

"One hour ago here we are. But as of fifty minutes ago, we were still stuck with the same result. Either Frost wasn't paying attention, which I don't believe is possible under the circumstances, or the man has the most stifled emotions on the planet."

"You guessed it," Ty said.

"Look carefully at what you are about to see. It's just minutes old. We sent a signal we were pretty sure would wake him up, as you know. The signal goes out. Now his money's gone, except for what he's skimmed and taken offline. All the funds de Novo's been accumulating have been wiped. He can't be sure what's happened. Sometimes, when you play with rogues, the rogues get the better of you. Has one or have the lot of them taken it back? Or has someone else? In either case or any other that comes to his mind, how? He's got to wonder. Fixed as he is to his plan, he can't go forward until he gets to the bottom of what's happened and why. As you can see, the Med's a bathtub full of toys, many of them tracing circles or ellipses anyway as they cruise or troll for fish or pull water-skiers. That makes things more difficult for the CVP, but, alas, not impossible."

"Cut to the chase, will you, Bingo?" Ty asked.

"That's just where I was heading," Bingo said. "Five minutes after that signal, out of literally thousands of vessels in our field, only fifty-four make discernible changes to their patterns of speed and direction. Of these, fifty-two can be eliminated because they would not have the capacity to carry cargo the size of warheads. The two we are left with are both trawlers. You can see them toward the right edge of the screen, lit in lovely phosphorescent green. Pinning them and then rewinding the satellite feeds, we can trace them back to where they came from, which of course was Majorca, the day before yesterday."

"Where are they now?" Ty asked.

"Less than a third of the way from Gibraltar to Ceuta, but they're standing still or drifting back rather than going forward."

Ty smiled. He had to admire not only the ingenuity but also the deviousness of Bingo's program. That deviousness more closely resembled Ian's or Philip's nature than Ty's. Only the end served, not a habit of mind, separated Bingo Chen from them. Ty was savoring the irony of this fact when his BlackBerry vibrated. He looked down at the bright letters on its dark screen then, to the surprise of the others, immediately took the call.

"Hello," he said

"Mr. Ty Hunter?"

"This is he."

"White House operator, please hold for the President."

"Apparently I didn't know or you didn't understand what I'd signed off on!" barked Garland White.

"I'm sorry, sir."

"There is a rumor out there, fast gaining currency, that the systems technology that underlies our international banking system has been penetrated and corrupted."

"Really?" Ty said in a theatrically deadpan voice. "I hadn't heard that. I've had other things on my mind in the last few hours."

"Well, the Secretary of the Treasury hasn't, and neither have his counterparts in other capitals. They are not yet certain of what's going on, but at first glance it appears that while invading a small Swiss bank, technothieves instructed not only that bank's computer but the computers of *all* Swiss banks to forward all funds on deposit to a checking account in Mumbai. I kid you not!"

Ty laughed. "It sounds like a short circuit," he said.

"It had better be something like that," Garland White said. "Are you having any luck with your search?"

"Yes, but it's a long story," Ty said, "which I don't have time to go into right now if we're hoping for a happy ending."

"Understood," said Garland White. "And, Ty, make sure there is one. And call me the moment it happens."

When he had hung up, Ty at once turned to Bingo. "You're going to have to press the reset button," he said.

"If I do, if I *can*, it will turn the clock back on, you understand that. Frost will assume it was a systemwide error of some sort, in which case he will be bound to revert to his previous schedule."

"He'll assume that anyway," Ty said, "before very long."

"Why do you say that?"

"Because the entire international banking system is in crisis, as will no doubt be reported in the news momentarily. Apparently Jonty lifted not only Frost's funds but those in all accounts in all Swiss banks."

"Oops!" said Bingo. "How much time do you think you'll need?"

"How can I possibly answer that?" Ty asked.

"Good point," Bingo said. "Suppose I hold off for two more hours."

"Can you restore everyone's funds but Frost's in the meantime?"

"Can we? Of course we can. We can make Peru rich and bankrupt

Switzerland, as we've just shown. But if we do that, Frost may well get wind of it, assume his will be the next account to recover, and go on about his business."

Ty considered this. "Two hours," he said. "I don't know how long it will take him to find out, but once he discovers where his money has landed, he'll know that what happened wasn't due to his partner's treachery. Of course, he'll probably also kill Jonty."

"We'll have to find a way to keep him in the dark, then."

"More likely we'll have to *put* him there," Ty said. "Bye, Bingo, gotta go."

Bingo shook Ty's hand. "Jonty," he said a few seconds later, "you got a bit overzealous, didn't you?"

"Sure, it was a mistake," Jonty demurred. "But not just mine. How was anyone supposed to know that the Swiss had recoded their damned prefixes the night before? I meant all accounts with de Novo's prefix, not Switzerland's."

"Whatever, the result's *not* great," Bingo scolded him sharply.

"Don't talk to me in that tone of voice, please," Jonty protested. "I am a very, very, *very* rich man, you know."

Chapter Fifty-three

"Are you sure you want to do this?" Admiral Cotton asked as Ty stepped aboard a high-speed patrol boat at the dockyard. Oliver, nearby, had assumed command of an identical vessel, and there were four more, each containing twenty petty officers, a machine gun and one M79 grenade launcher. Additionally, six flat-bottomed inflatables, carrying six petty officers each, were in the process of shoving off from the harborside.

"I've done it before," Ty told him.

"I don't mean on film."

"Neither do I, and those were darker waters than these."

"What's he talking about?" Giles Cotton asked Isabella, who was standing beside him.

"I have no idea," she said.

On the telephone Oliver said, "Once the trawlers are in sight, we lie back in our respective positions, then advance at once together. The attacks have got to be simultaneous."

"They appear to be about the same size. Which do you want?"

"It doesn't matter," Oliver said. "We'll take the first. The important thing is to bracket them, leave them no choice, but not to fire a shot if we don't have to. We can't be sure where the cargo is."

"Surely it must take more than a single shot to detonate that sort of weapon," Ty said.

"You would think so, but I've never tried it."

The eastern sky was filling with clouds that turned the sea behind them to dark topaz. Ahead, beyond the straits, where the Phoenicians had imagined the Unknown to begin, the sun still sparkled on waves and ripples, on the casual motorboats and sailing craft, the determined tankers, fishing rigs, barges and ferries that defined the life of the basin at high summer.

On Oliver's order the vessels of the task force had left port one by one then assembled a few miles out to sea. There they had formed a loose collection, soon dividing into two discrete but equal groups. The forward task force, which was Ty's, required an extra eighteen minutes to be in place behind the second trawler, and while it advanced, the three patrol boats and three inflatables under Oliver's command did their best to feign idle exercises. Both trawlers had blue hulls and white decks, but the farther of them was several meters longer, and the roof of its pilot house, while not quite a gargoyle, was a peaked rusty red cone.

As Ty began to advance from Oliver's position and the craft with Oliver gathered into a lethal fighting force, Philip stood in the center of that pilot house, his eyes fastened to his laptop. When the Slav mercenary who was captaining the trawler approached him, Philip initially waved the man away, but the captain was insistent. "What is it?" Philip asked.

"Intelligence," the captain explained.

"Go on."

"You asked me to see to it that we enjoyed eyes on the ground."

"I did, just yesterday. Did you think I wouldn't remember?" Philip asked.

"No, of course not."

"You told me you had made a friend of the chandler."

"That is true. He has just telephoned."

"Saying?" inquired Philip.

"That the navy has gone to sea."

"The navy is *always* at sea. That's precisely its point."

"But this time, the chandler said, they put out in a manner that reminds him of task forces."

"I see. One can never be too cautious, I suppose," Philip said. "It does seem the least of our problems at present, but here is what I want you to do: Launch the *barco*. Make sure it is equipped with a GPS transponder. Whoever goes with it should be a strong swimmer."

"They are all strong swimmers," the captain replied.

"He should also be prudent, because in my experience," Philip told him, "it's always the strong swimmers who drown. They are simply too confident and leave too much to chance."

"I understand."

"If necessary, *I'll* find *him,* which means he can go far afield, but not *too* far."

"As we discussed," the captain said.

"As we discussed," Philip confirmed. "I will inform Andrej."

The chandler's recognizance, Philip understood at once, was what he had most feared and labored so assiduously to avoid. As he struggled to stave off the sense of defeat and depression that now enveloped him, that he knew would destroy him if he yielded to it, he began to conjure ways to loosen and escape from the net in which he was suddenly trapped. Even now he was a realist. He would no longer be able to take for granted those profound benefits upon which he had come to rely. Rather than a model son of the establishment, he would be a hunted man, a high-value target of both intelligence agencies and their adversaries—the despots and middlemen whose funds he had skimmed—all over the world. How this had happened concerned him less than the fact that it had. He had no time for regrets or retrospection. He had to play offense. Other men in other times and other places had been hunted, he reassured himself, yet with cunning had eluded fate and survived to reinvent themselves in triumph.

Eight minutes later, over Channel 16 VHF, the emergency channel all vessels were supposed to monitor, the lieutenant who was in nominal command of the task force carrying Oliver delivered an ultimatum. "Attention, *Paradise,*" he declared, slowly and in the lustrous voice of his native Wales. "This is Royal Navy vessel *Stalwart,* off your starboard. Stop your engines! We are coming aboard."

Ignoring this command, Andrej stared at the small book he had been reading. *Riviera,* it was called, *The Rise and Rise of the Côte d'Azur.* "Full speed ahead," he instructed the captain.

The captain regarded him with incredulity. In the distance, uninvolved in the navy's present attempt to capture them but near enough to be co-opted if necessary, an American destroyer, doubtless on its way to rejoin its battle group, formed an ominous and moving silhouette against the southern sky and the North African coast.

"*Paradise,* stop your engines," repeated the lieutenant.

Meanwhile a second voice, higher in octave, came over Channel 16. "*Jezebel,* this is Royal Navy vessel *Fortitude.* Stop your engines! We are coming aboard."

Within moments both trawlers were surrounded by high-speed patrol boats and inflatables, most of which were closing in on them as inexorably as though a knot were being tightened.

Andrej remained in the pilot house.

"Paradise, repeat: Stop your engines!" the Welsh lieutenant commanded, and when there was no response, he ordered that a shot be fired into the air.

The trawler *Paradise* moved forward, under way upon Andrej's irrational faith that the British navy and the forces allied to it could be outrun. Only when the task force had bracketed the trawler, firing just before its bow and aft of its stern, did the captain relent and, ignoring the silent disapproval of his master, extinguish the ship's engines. Gradually the mercenary sailors, including the captain, came onto the wide deck, their opened hands raised just above their shoulders.

Oliver led a crew into the hold, where he soon found one of the three warheads, still in the same inner casing it had been in upon its theft from the installation near the Strait of Kerch. Only when he returned to the pilot house did he encounter Andrej, alone with less than half a liter of Stolichnaya on the table in front of him. Next to the bottle rested his book as well as a heavily thumbed copy of *Le Petit Larousse,* which he had been studying in an effort to improve his French, and the latest glossy brochure from a property agent in Saint-Tropez. In his left hand, firmly in his grip, was his Makarov pistol. Pointing the handgun at Oliver, he said, "Drop your weapon to the floor." He had been coughing since sometime in the night before, and his voice had grown hoarse.

Oliver evaluated him across the cabin. He was a man with a plain view of his end, the most dangerous kind. Oliver placed his own gun carefully on the floor.

"Now kick it away."

Oliver did as instructed, then said, "You are in an impossible situation. Don't make it more painful for yourself than it needs to be."

"You talk as if you were holding this gun."

"If you think the men out there will allow you to leave, even with me as your hostage, you are badly mistaken. There are many of us and one of you. If we have to wait you out, we will. If we have to endure casualties, we will do that, too, but those casualties will only make things worse for you. They will not result in your freedom. Where is Philip Frost?"

Andrej replied as though Oliver's question had not been asked. "I would prefer to be in a British rather than an American prison."

"That is not for me to decide. Is he aboard the other trawler?"

"He might be," Andrej said. "What does it matter? Will I be taken to Guantánamo?"

Oliver continued to study the plaintive Russian. "I do not see why you would be, but again it's a question I can't answer."

"I fear Guantánamo," Andrej said, as though his thoughts were becoming dissociated. "I fear all secret prisons."

"Then put down your gun and cooperate with us, help us understand—"

"Understand?" Andrej echoed. "What? That we almost made it?"

Oliver offered him the start of a smile. He said, "I will do what I can to help you. I promise you that if—"

Outside the pilot house, sailors had taken up protected positions. Andrej wondered how many sharpshooters' firearms were trained upon him. "This is no way to die," he told Oliver.

"No," Oliver said, "it isn't."

"Would you like some vodka?" Andrej asked.

"Thank you," Oliver replied, playing along as his training had taught him to do, striving, most of all, for time. "That would be very nice right now."

"Here, help yourself," Andrej told him, nudging the Stolichnaya toward Oliver with his right palm. "I've never enjoyed drinking alone." With his left hand, as he spoke, Andrej turned the Makarov abruptly toward himself, inserting its barrel between his chapped lips until he could feel the chill and pressure of gunmetal against the parched roof of his mouth. It was the smile of a man who could salvage only irony from failure that exploded across his face.

Aboard *Fortitude* as it approached the trawler *Jezebel,* Ty Hunter donned a muslin hangman's mask the color of flesh. In an effort to further confuse identities, several of the petty officers joined him, deploying the same effective cloak of anonymity.

Unlike the captain of the *Paradise,* however, the *Jezebel*'s was not inclined to surrender. He had halted the ship's engines and immediately led his crew to quarters below. The forsaken stillness the boarding party encountered upon seizing *Jezebel* not only surprised but disoriented them. That the crew would retreat into the bowels of the ship suggested to Ty that they believed it was the strongest corner from which they could fight, but why? What was there?

Commando style, he advanced in silence with his squad, rounding each corner with his back arched against the steel walls. In the shadows of intersecting corridors, they stopped short of every door, testing each handle and lock with the delicate touches of safecrackers before kicking them in from the side, then resuming safe positions. The galley was empty. The next cabin, an expanded cupboard with two shallow bunks on each side, had been deserted, as had the one beyond that. The head, too, was uninhabited.

He raised his hand, motioned the men behind him toward the entry that led, via an exposed spiral staircase, to the hold below. Just before it Ty noticed, flush with the wall, a panel too small for a man to fit through. Although securable by a dual key and combination lock and fitted with an alarm, these had been left undone. Inside the recess he found an armory, fitted for twenty rifles and as many pistols, for knives of various lengths and grenades and masks. All were missing.

At once he stopped his men. "It's a trap," he said, mouthing rather than speaking his words. He gestured to one of his team that he required a pencil and paper. The petty officer scurried, and both were quickly found in the pilot house, then handed down to him, whereupon he sketched his plan.

To start with he had to answer the question upon which all else depended: Was Philip Frost still aboard or had he somehow managed to flee *Jezebel*? If he was aboard and cornered, who knew what he might do? If not, could the crew be lured into thinking he had returned? An invasion of the hold could not even be considered. His men would be picked off on the stairs. The other obvious possibility, of using gas to subdue their adversaries, posed too many complications. Would the missing masks defeat any such attempt? Would the tactic even work if the hatches of the hold were opened and the resulting ventilation proved sufficient to disperse the fumes? Ty had no idea, but he was less worried about these constraints than about the possibility of a gunfight with explosives going off or, even worse, a direct assault on the warheads. Caged men faced with futility would resort to anything, and though he did not believe that nuclear warheads could be so nimbly detonated, like Oliver he did not wish to put his supposition to a test.

He touched his forefinger to his lips, signaling utter silence. On his pad he drew instructions for the deployment of the other sailors in the force. How odd life was, he thought, that it might be his acting talent he would have to rely upon in this most real of adventures. Closing his eyes, Ty let his mind drift back to the challenging and exhausting classes in dialect he'd taken before shooting his second film, then to the glissando-like conversation of Ian's guests, settling finally, he was not sure why, on the mysterious Al-Dosari twins.

When he spoke, it was in Arabic, then in English tinged with the accent of Arabia, the accent he had acquired as a boy. "Philip!" he called sharply, more as a command than a request, for at the bullfight in Seville he had noted Philip's deference to both Al-Dosaris. "Philip!"

Ty waited. When no response came from below, he said, in rapid Arabic, as if one twin were addressing the other, "Where could he be?"

"I've absolutely no idea," he replied to himself, in the same language and yet a slightly differentiated voice.

"Philip!" he called again. "Show yourself, please! You don't understand what's transpired. We've reached an accommodation."

Again Ty hesitated, his eye on the stairs, his Glock aimed at the entry leading to them. "They are being entirely reasonable," he said, resuming his original Arabian-English diction. "We've been granted safe passage in return for our cooperation."

The instant he concluded, the silence returned. On the pad, hurriedly, he wrote, *"Captain's name?"* then tore the page at once from its binding and handed it off to a nearby sailor. The sailor moved stealthily, first backward through the cabins, then to the pilothouse above.

"He must be on the other trawler. Pity," Ty said with resignation, still in character.

When the sailor returned, he handed Ty a wrinkled receipt from a chandlery in Palma. Although the last name had been smudged, the first, Roman, was plainly legible. Ty shot the sailor a smile. The time had come, he realized, to go for broke. He entwined the fingers of both hands, at which point a sailor opposite him crossed himself.

"Ah, there you are, Philip!" Ty exclaimed, still an Arab at home in English. "Where on earth were you?"

Summoning his best impersonation of a caustic Philip, Ty replied, "Where did you think I'd gone? For a swim?" He hoped it would suffice for the Slavs who were his audience.

"It's not as big a problem as you think," the imaginary Arab continued.

"I am glad to hear it."

"As a matter of fact, the hounds have been called off."

"Interesting," said Ty's Philip.

"Isn't it just?" intoned the Arab, whose voice was of deeper register. "Where are your captain and his crew? We should be under way."

"I don't know, probably hiding. Wouldn't you be?"

"What's the captain's name?"

"Roman."

"Call him, then, won't you? The sooner this business is done, the better."

"Roman!" Philip shouted into the hold.

"Roman!" echoed one of the Arabs.

But the uneasy quiet immediately returned. Ty listened. Hearing only his heartbeat, he began to count, in his head, slowly down from ten. On three he thought he could hear shuffling; on a long-delayed two, the response that rose from the hold was unambiguous.

"Mr. Frost," the captain inquired, in a deep voice rendered tentative by fear.

"Get up here, will you?" Philip said. "We're losing valuable time."

"Mr. Frost," repeated the captain.

"Roman," Ty's Philip snapped, with pitch-perfect admonishment. "I will explain everything you need to know when you get up here. But I can't keep shouting."

Then, hearing footsteps strain the iron staircase, Ty settled beside the entry. The steps grew louder. As the captain emerged into the corridor, Ty forced him back with a fierce and sudden choke hold, then pressed his Glock 23 into the man's thick, sunburned neck. Before the captain's eyes, Ty now held a sheet of paper. *"Tell them to come up,"* it read. *"Tell them that everything is all right. No tricks. Мы говорим на русском языке."* The last, which translated as "We speak Russian," constituted, along with the words for "hello," "good-bye," and "thank you," all the Russian Ty knew. He prayed the captain would not see through his bluff.

The captain attempted to nod. Ty tightened his grip then loosened it sufficiently for the captain to breathe more easily. Even as he did so, Ty ground the gun deeper against the Slav's skin. Once the captain had spoken, Ty gagged him with a wet bandanna. Withdrawing his pistol and stepping slightly back, Ty shot out his hand to deliver a swift knife edge blow, or *shuto uchi,* to the side of the man's neck, a blow not often as disabling as it appeared to be on the screen, yet in this instance sufficient to disable the captain long enough for him to be taken into custody.

Now, one by one, the Slavs ventured forth from the hold, and one by one, off balance after their climb and afraid to arrive with a weapon pointed at Philip Frost himself, they were seized from behind, subdued, disarmed and bound.

In the hold the two at-large warheads, like the one aboard *Paradise* still disguised as turbines, were immediately surrounded by sailors, Special Boat Service boys who had trained for such work. These sailors would guard the weapons until they'd been safely returned to their makers, after which they would be disarmed and decommissioned.

Ty exhaled a deep breath. Exhausted, he let his frame collapse against the wall, his legs stretch prone across the corridor as the trawler's engines started and the old ship turned back from what had once been the edge of the world.

Lost in the view from the trawler's stern as it gained speed and distance, painted out by the shadows of gathering clouds, was the ascent of a solitary diver on the far side of one of hundreds of local fishing boats. Clutching the *barco*'s wooden hull with relief, the diver handed up the underwater jet that had brought him so far so rapidly. The man in the *barco* accepted it willingly. Searching the horizon before removing his mask, the diver drew himself up and flung his legs over the narrow washboard. As soon as he removed his mask, Philip wiped his face with a proffered towel, keeping himself close to the boat's floor, too low to be spotted from shore or other craft. From within his wet suit, he removed a soft waterproof kit and from that a telephone. When he had scrolled to the number he sought, he immediately pressed CALL. "Hello, is this Franz?" he asked.

"I hadn't expected to hear from you so soon."

"No, well, it's because I've had a sudden change of plan," Philip told him, with almost ethereal calm. "I would like you to meet me at the eastern extreme of Tarifa Harbor in one hour. Would that be possible?"

Franz hesitated. "With the same boat?" he inquired.

"You haven't sold it yet, have you?"

"No," Franz assured him, "of course not."

"I will also be in the same boat," Philip said. "When you spot us, keep a distance of fifty yards. *I* will swim to *you*."

"As you wish," Franz conceded.

In fact, it was exactly one hour later when Philip spotted Franz slowing the *Contender* far from the bustling ferry lanes of Tarifa. "We'll anchor here," he told the mate who was now captaining the *barco,* then checked his tanks and underwater jet. "You'll want to lose yourself for a time. That will be something more easily accomplished in Morocco or elsewhere in the Middle East than in Spain right now."

The mate returned his unforgiving scrutiny.

"This should both erase your memory and help," Philip said, unfolding his left hand to reveal two Golconda D-Flawless Type IIa brilliant-cut diamonds he had removed from the waterproof kit along with his mobile and a single silicon chip. He could not be sure of the diamonds' exact worth but guessed that even in a distressed market where no questions would be asked they would be likely to fetch a quarter of a million euros. "I may require your services in the future," he told the mate. "Have you an e-mail address that will not change?"

The mate grinned, then slowly spoke his address, repeating it a second time, just in case. "Are you certain you'll remember it?" he asked.

"Yes," Philip said. "I don't forget." For a few seconds, he hesitated, studying the shiny microchip that contained the algorithmic codes to the suddenly and forever lost warheads.

"What's that?" asked the mate.

"Nothing," Philip replied, his voice wistful and resigned as he let the chip go in the evening wind to skim, settle upon and drown in the unforgiving Mediterranean. "Absolutely nothing but useless information, the curse of the world we live in."

All at once he lowered himself over the *barco*'s side and, without a splash, descended beneath the surface of the ancient indigo sea.

Chapter Fifty-four

"What are we are doing on this plane?" Isabella asked.

"I told you," Ty said. "We're going for a ride." Ever since they had arrived back at the Gibraltar dockyard, Oliver had shepherded Ty, first to a clandestine rendezvous with Isabella in an overcooled holding room at the Royal Air Force terminal, then, almost immediately and with her once more in tow, aloft.

"I've had enough adventure for one day, thank you very much" Isabella shot back, glancing about the burled-wood and glove-leather cabin. "What kind of plane is this? I'm not sure I've ever seen one quite like it."

"Very few people have," explained Oliver. "Actually, it's a prototype for the new QSST."

"QSST?" inquired Ty.

"Quiet Supersonic Transport," Oliver said.

"Of course," Ty said, "how dim of me!"

"I thought you might have guessed as much from its sleek beak and aft wings."

"Whose is it?" Isabella asked.

"It belongs to a friend of a friend," Oliver said.

"Where exactly are we going?" Ty asked.

"What a good question," Isabella added.

"*You* are going home," Oliver said, "in time, in fact, for dinner out."

Ty looked at Isabella in a way he hoped would project his own astonishment. "And Isabella, where is she going?"

"That's entirely up to her."

Isabella immediately grimaced—in a way, Ty now realized, of which he had become more than fond. "But I can't go anywhere," she said. "I don't even have my passport."

"You won't need it tonight, and you'll have it by tomorrow," Oliver said, "along with whatever else you want from *Surpass*. Have you been to La-La Land before?"

"No," Isabella admitted, "never."

"Everyone should see it," Ty assured her.

"We'll be traveling at Mach 1.6. Flying over the pole, we should be there in a bit more than four hours," Oliver continued. "Given that it is nine hours earlier in California, we'll arrive five hours before we left. By that time, should reports of Ty's involvement with our mission here surface, they can be as quickly dismissed as fanciful by his presence at home."

"If Frost's still alive, he'll know otherwise," Ty said.

"Who will believe him?"

"That's just the sort of thing you never know, isn't it?"

Isabella, her moist eyes wide open, looked up at Ty as though she had suddenly found her way through a bewildering thicket. "You really do believe that Philip murdered Ian, don't you?" she beseeched him.

Ty glanced at Oliver.

"Philip had the most to gain," Oliver said, "and perhaps the most to lose if he didn't."

"Ian was a player, not a killer," Ty told Isabella. "His blood ran warm, not cold. I can't prove it yet, but I strongly suspect that every killing that took place as this plot unwound was expedient, above all, for Philip. Ian's death, as Oliver's just said, fits that description. So do the deaths of many others, including Colonel Zhugov and, when you think about it, Luke Claussen's father."

Isabella breathed heavily, her fury at the completeness of her betrayal by a man she had once thought she loved rising as her head shook in disbelief. "It's awful."

"It's *over*," Ty told her.

"Only for the moment," Oliver said quietly, then looked out from the oversize window as the QSST completed its ascent to fifty-five thousand feet. With the setting sun rising before it and the sky above permanently dark, it burst through the sound barrier.

"I didn't hear *anything*," Isabella remarked when the digital airspeed indicator flashed this fact.

"Nor did anyone on the ground," Oliver said. "This plane's equipped with sonic-boom-suppression technology."

Ty regarded his friend circumspectly. "Is that a joke?"

Oliver shook his head. "The speed of light's next."

Now, as the plane banked, through the window that framed Isabella's profile Ty observed the gentle curvature of the earth.

"What do you mean by 'only for the moment'?" Isabella asked Oliver a few seconds later.

"That out of sight isn't necessarily out of mind," Ty interjected. "I think that's what Commander Molyneux was trying to say."

"Don't mistake me," Oliver elaborated. "I'm thrilled we recovered the warheads. That was the most important thing. But I hate it that Frost got away, just as I hate it that events forced us to act as quickly as they did. I'd like to have tracked down the entire conspiracy for intelligence purposes, to have neutralized, and I mean for good, every bloody one of those bastards. It tears my guts out that that diabolical murderer eluded us—and with money and, no doubt, those jewels! Nevertheless, he escaped for today, not forever. He'll pop back into sight sooner or later. He won't be able to help himself."

"I hope you're right," Ty said, "but if you are telling me to expect another call, much less another unannounced visit and summons from you, I am going to change my number and beef up the security at La Encantada."

"You won't do that," Oliver said.

"I will." Ty's forceful insistence dissolved into a smile.

"Tell me it doesn't piss you off every bit as much as it does me. Tell me you wouldn't relish another—this time final—crack at Philip Frost."

Ty paused in reflection. "You know I can't tell you that," he said. "You know *exactly* how I feel."

Oliver drew a long breath. "That's all I wanted to hear," he said. "Look, I don't know about you, but I'm knackered. There are two cabins at the rear of the plane. You two take the one to starboard. It's the owner's."

"That sounds like a good idea," Ty relented. "You *are* staying on with us in Los Angeles, Ollie, aren't you? I hope so."

Oliver shook his head. "Someone's got to return this toy."

Ty winked at his friend.

In their cabin Isabella suddenly shuddered. "I don't know what to think," she whispered.

"Don't think anything," Ty told her.

"How is that possible?"

"With experience," he promised. "This never happened."

Isabella considered this, disbelief and hurt suddenly swimming in her jade green eyes. "None of it?" she asked softly. "What about the parts worth remembering?"

Ty drew her to him and kissed her. "Those, darling, are between us."

ACKNOWLEDGMENTS

Although the character of Ty Hunter appeared almost fully formed in my mind, his history and personality grew—and, I hope, became deeper and more intriguing—over time. So, too, did the particular nature of this, his first recorded adventure, not only alter but elaborate itself, often in unexpected ways (even by me), as I set it down.

In the process, many friends and experts gave advice and encouragement of inestimable value. First among these is my longtime agent, Peter Lampack, without whose faith, patience and keen editorial insight this book would surely not have found its way to readers. Peter was consistently supported in his efforts by his amiable and astute son, Andrew, as well as by the high standards of his unfailingly good-humored associates Rema Dilanyan and Christie Russell.

At Viking I have benefited beyond measure from Kathryn Court's innate, penetrating, uniquely subtle sense of story and human behavior and from Allison Lorentzen's invariably fresh, intelligent and rigorous attention to every line of the manuscript. They have made the editorial process a pleasure, as has their colleague Tara Singh.

Beyond a professional context, I am, of course, inexpressibly grateful to President Clinton—not only for reading the novel in an early draft and the skill with which he wielded a literary scalpel that decidedly sharpened the story's narrative, dialogue, focus and tension, but for his gracious and evocative introduction.

For reading and commenting upon *The Spy Who Jumped Off the Screen* at various stages of its development or for particular knowledge that they were generous enough to share and that has enriched the text, I am indebted to: Philip Bobbitt, Tom Campbell, Bill Cassidy, Susan Eisenhower, James and Arabella Gaggero, Robert Gottlieb, Geordie Greig, Giuseppe Guillot, David Hutcheon, Jamie Kerr,

Riccardo Lanza, William and Sandra Lobkowicz, Ileen Maisel, Jim Moore, Flavio Murarotto, Diana Patterson, George Porchester, Marykay Powell, John and Jane Prenn, Giovanni Revedin, Sean Routt, John Saumarez Smith, Michael Scaldini, Steve Scheffer, Alex Schemmer, Michael Sheehan, Andrew Solomon, Michael Sudmeier, David Walton, Alice West and Hope Winthrop.

As every lucky writer knows, particularly during a sustained period of work, the confidence and support of friends—even, sometimes, of acquaintances—can be crucial buoys in a sea of vicissitudes. A list of all those who kindly offered such to me, often at pivotal moments, would be far too long to publish here. But they know who they are and so do I. My appreciation to them is boundless and will be felt as long as I feel anything.

Thomas Caplan
British Embassy
Paris
September 5, 2011